/IN THE SHADE OF THE SUN

BEN E. LEWIS

DEDICATION

To MRT.
You know why.

CONTENTS

1-12	Palmer	3
13-20	Jon	67
21-27	Stuart	106
28	Matilde Marujo	137
29	Palmer	142
30	Stuart	147
31	Jon	152
32	Palmer	156
33	Stuart	161
34	Jon	166
35	Palmer	171
36	Stuart	176
37	Jon	181
38	Salvador Marujo	186
39-46	Jon	190
47-53	Stuart	230
54-65	Palmer	271
	Epilogue	329

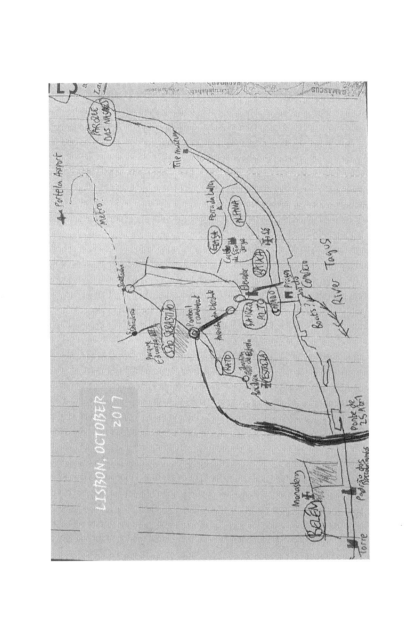

ACKNOWLEDGMENTS

Friends, family, teachers, students and all those I've ever known and loved, thank you.

Immeasurable thanks and apologies also to Patricia Highsmith and the Portuguese tourist board.

i

1.

Palmer stumbled down the ramp and clutched at the rail helplessly to right himself. The cool evening air had done little to revive him and had only confused him further, with expectations of waves of Iberian heat imagined on the flight.

"You ok mate?" asked the portly Mancunian who Palmer had had to suffer for company during the three hours cooped up on the plane.

Palmer had deliberately booked two seats in order to avoid having unwanted company and to be able to stretch out his aching limbs a little more, but after nodding off during one of the flight's many delays at the airport, he'd awoken to find a talkative, overweight man with a jowly, sweaty face and a baseball cap which barely fit his enormous head, now installed next to him. Palmer, being thoroughly English in the worst possible way, had been too polite to comment directly to the man and was hoping for a scenario in which the man went to the bathroom and an air hostess passed so that he could grass on him with slightly less guilt and an enormous amount less direct conflict. But the man didn't budge once, content to stuff his face with a gigantic bag of cheesy puffs which he continually offered to Palmer despite his first polite refusal.

All Palmer wanted to do was to sleep, rest his legs and get the flight over and done with, but no matter how many times he closed his eyes, sleep would not come to him and his new-found travelling companion had filled the hours with much inane chatter about his trip, his home life and his windfall (a combination of P.P.I. reimbursements and shrewd investing). When the air hostess brought a snack of a small overly-herby chicken sandwich and the

3

offer of a free glass of wine, Palmer keenly accepted both and prayed that the strong painkillers he'd taken pre-flight, along with a half-tab of diazepam for his anxiety would combine with the crisp red dispensed into a plastic cup to allow him to rest, but sleep still proved elusive. Palmer became annoyed when his neighbour began to summon the curt but smiling air hostess for a number of refills of his own wine cup and so finally closed his eyes and began to make faint, fake snoring noises as they passed over Brest.

The remainder of the flight passed without event although Palmer spied out of his scrunched-up eyes a tasty-looking biscuit being offered and regretted his false slumber. He was meant to be cutting back on sweet treats but had read a recent article on sugar being far more addictive than even cocaine and had meant to forward the piece on to his mother, who nagged him incessantly on the topic. Palmer noted angrily that his neighbour took the biscuit and even a second, on the pretence of offering it to him once he awoke and yet only moments after greedily devouring the first biscuit, the second was unwrapped and consumed without even checking on his sleeping status. Once he'd pretended to wake up, just as the final announcements before landing began, he pointedly looked at the double helping of wrappers his biscuit thief of a travelling companion had passed to the air hostess, but the man had no shame about his gluttony whatsoever. Thankfully, the man was nervous about the landing and made no further attempts to converse until the plane had touched down.

"Yes, I'm fine thank you," said Palmer brusquely, shrugging off the offer of a helping hand from the man in front. He then paused on the steps, knowing he had a few moments before the group of hobbling Portuguese ladies caught up behind him, which was enough to let the man move off ahead. He couldn't bear the idea of having to walk to the terminal alongside him, but as he reached the ground, he was appalled to see an idling bus ahead and the man grinning like an idiot, waiting for him.

"So, where are you stayin' in Lisbon?" asked the man and Palmer tried to recall if he'd even been listening when he said what his name was. He certainly hadn't told him his.

"Oh, with friends," lied Palmer. "Out of town."

He was as economical with words as he was with the truth and his light-headedness was worsening, probably the wine he thought.

"Oh yeah, you did say," said the man, confusing Palmer further. "I'm at the Sana," he continued, pronouncing it like 'sauna'."

Palmer merely nodded, not even sure what the man was talking about any more. The bus driver was clearly late for something and whipped the long vehicle fiercely around some sharp bends, taking them into what looked like a giant multi-storey car park before pulling up sharply by an entrance into the airport. The man continued to make small talk about the weather, the Euro and a restaurant he'd heard of that had been on an episode of MasterChef or something and was looking forward to sampling, but all Palmer could think about was how to ditch him. That and the obvious further awkward encounter he was to have soon.

The man stayed with him through passport control but Palmer was thrilled when he realised the man had luggage to reclaim whilst he himself had travelled with only his hand luggage, carefully weighing in at 7.9kg to avoid a further charge. This gave him the perfect chance to say a hurried and disingenuous goodbye and wishes of a pleasant holiday whilst the man cheerfully waddled off to find the correct baggage carousel. Palmer breathed a sigh of relief and even remembered that his small case had an extendable handle so treated himself to a rest from its burden by pulling it along on its wheels through the 'Nothing to Declare' channel and into the main concourse.

He always found airports troubling places, but at night, their bustling clamour and dazzling lights and welcoming doorways were often replaced by shadowy corners, unfriendly shuttered shopfronts and sad-looking airport refugees, sitting alone with mountains of baggage awaiting some broken promise or endless delay. Humberto Delgado airport was no different and even though it was barely 10pm, the place was desolate. A few taxi drivers and airport transfer agents were holding placards and Palmer gave them a cursory glance as he passed, but he was under no illusions that he would be welcomed or indeed *welcome* in the city tonight. Ignoring an insistent man with dark, unkempt hair and untucked shirt who promised him the cheapest rates to the city, Palmer exited the main building and looked around. He'd done his research and knew that the airport was not far from the city itself and easily reachable by the metro system although he hadn't banked on it being quite so late or so dark and cool. In London, the underground system held no fears for him after night fell, but there was something about making the same sort of journey in a foreign city with different customs and signage, alone and unable to call on anyone for help.

As he reached the stairs descending into the metro station, he replaced the extended handle in his case and gripped it with both hands as he struggled down. His left knee was throbbing and swollen and the stabbing pain in his shin had resumed once more after giving him a few hours of peace. There had been a lift, but the last thing Palmer wanted was to be trapped in another enclosed space quite so soon after the flight. He chuckled slightly to himself as he realised that not only was he definitely getting into another enclosed space by riding on the metro, but that he was beginning to buy into his mother's own morbid fears for his life and her own, with her constant sharing of articles she'd read about one such transport disaster or another. He reached a mezzanine sort of level which opened up cavernously into a white-tiled airy hall and spied some automated ticket machines. Thank goodness the days of having to speak to someone in your own faltering attempt at their language or their own marginally better English were long gone, he thought. The machines even had an English language option. He bought a single fare ride for €1.40 and carefully returned his change to his money belt, hidden beneath the waistband of his jeans.

As he turned to look for the correct direction to the platform, he spotted the man. There were only a few other people in the station at this hour, quite a few he recognised from the flight, but this man stood out mainly because of just how out of place he looked. Amongst the garish garb of a dozen tourists, this man was wearing bright salmon-pink shorts which were on the wrong side of short, white socks which came up to above his ankles and that greatest fashion crime – sandals over them. His shirt was tailored but a lurid yellowy-green, almost like a hi-vis jacket and even though it was dark outside of the station, he wore large aviator-style sunglasses which did not suit his face. On his head was a straw hat, too rough-looking for a panama, smaller than a sombrero, but entirely incongruous with the rest of the man's appearance, like it was a last-minute acquisition as part of a disguise. The man had pale skin, too pale to be a native and his white-pink skin was clean-shaven. The hat being pulled low meant that little of his hair was visible, aside from a few tufts of red-orange hair at the ears.

Even as Palmer stared at him, he knew the man was staring back from behind the sunglasses. They were to hide his eyes, not protect them from the non-existent sun. Was this who he was here to meet, an agent acting on their behalf, or simply a bizarrely dressed tourist hypocritically passing judgement on Palmer's own fashion sense? His legs demanding that he either sit or stand and stop moving, he ignored them and moved as rapidly as he could towards the strange man. It took a few moments for the man to react, but when he did, it was decisively and he turned and fled up the main steps to street level. Palmer cursed him out loud and gave chase as best he could, huffing and puffing through the atrium, swinging his bag furiously as he went so that it repeatedly bashed into his own thigh. There was no way he'd ever catch him like this, and no guarantee the man was anything more than a stranger, despite him fleeing. Reaching the top of the steps and seeing the bright lights of the airport terminal in front of him, Palmer was hit with a huge wave of regret. This wasn't what he'd come for, to be chasing around after mysterious men within minutes of his arrival. Worse still, he could see his seat-stealing, biscuit-thief of a plane buddy coming through the main doors hauling a large suitcase on wheels.

He turned to go back down the stairs to the metro station and suddenly felt his legs go weak, as if they'd entirely given up working. A dizzying kaleidoscope of colours and sensations followed as he tumbled down the stairs, landing painfully at the bottom, his hand luggage bust open and scattered on the ground around him. Instinctively he felt the back of his head but despite the sharp pain, there was no blood on his fingertips. His back and his bottom felt bruised but it was his leg that was screaming out with a searing pain that said whatever recovery he'd made over the last few days was now cruelly and horribly undone. Feeling stupid, he craned his neck to see if there was something he'd tripped over on the steps but all he could see was the outlandish man he'd pursued. He'd removed the hat, or else it had fallen off during the chase, revealing a shock of ginger hair, but it was the huge, satisfied grin on the man's face which offended Palmer the most. It widened into a huge, toothy laugh which Palmer imagined he could somehow hear despite the ringing in his ears and the babbling which he now realised was the concerned voices of a group of people who'd gathered around him to see if he was okay.

Painfully getting up and begrudgingly accepting the help of a young couple who were mortifyingly gathering his personal possessions and underwear back into his bag, he reassured a worried looking Portuguese woman that he was fine, in the best 'loud English' that he could muster. His head was still spinning but now at least the pain in his leg had company. He took his bag back, shooed away the remainder of the concerned people and was about to try his best to reclimb the steps once more when a large, sweaty hand landed on his shoulder. The man from the plane had caught up with him and was now also fussing over him.

"You alright mate?" he asked, his nasal voice grating on Palmer. "What 'appened to you up there? Too much wine on the plane, eh?"

Palmer snarled inwardly, hating the man for his own excessiveness but also repulsed at his touch and newly-revived association.

"Thought you were being picked up, pal?" continued the man, referencing another of Palmer's earlier lies about his plans once at the airport.

"Plans changed," muttered Palmer, still massively disoriented.

"Let me 'elp you then, pal," said the man, grabbing Palmer's bag and balancing it on top of his own wheeled luggage. "As far as the platform at least any rate."

Palmer couldn't hide his embarrassment and he couldn't get rid of this annoying man but more than anything else, he couldn't shake the very strong feeling that the red-headed man he'd chased up the stairs had in fact pushed him back down them and then watched and laughed.

2.

It was late when Palmer finally reached his hotel, drenched and limbs both stiff and aching from an avoidable detour caused by his anxiety. The incident on the stairs still playing on his mind and the insufferable company of his plane buddy, he had suddenly and almost without warning got up and made to disembark the train a full station earlier than he intended, nearly abandoning his bag in the process. Still somewhat rather dazed and relying on his newfound friend's navigation, he had slowly realised that they were both heading for the same station, the end of the line at *Sao Sebastiao* which would mean further conversation, offers of help to his destination and the potential for yet more interaction. Fixing on the route map on the wall next to him, Palmer decided that he could still alight at the earlier station of Saldanha and make it to his hotel and avoid more contact. The Mancunian was startled at Palmer's urgent attempts to disembark, but dutifully called him back to hand him his bag before the train doors closed. Palmer tried not to look as the carriage departed the platform, thinking that the man may even be watching which exit he headed for, intent on learning more about his plans.

Of course, the man wouldn't have been watching and his interest in Palmer's final destination were through the strange friendliness caused by travellers sharing a method of transport, the camaraderie of foreigners abroad together and perhaps some genuine interest in his health and well-being following his stumble exiting the plane and further tumble at the metro station. Palmer was simply becoming paranoid as per usual and was dreading some of the decisions he had made back at home without putting much thought into them. Not arranging an airport transfer was now top of this list of regrets as he tried to remember the street address of his hotel. He moved to the left exit at the station and cursed to find only steps, a sign indicating lifts were available at the right-hand exit.

Finally reaching street level again, he found that it was now drizzling interminably and pitch black. The streets he had pored over on Google Earth now looked nothing like the shadowy cobbled avenues glistening precariously around him and were strangely deserted. He took his phone out of his pocket and saw that it was after 10pm, with no time alterations necessary, Lisbon being in the same time zone as Manchester. A text informed him that he could use his contracted minutes, texts and internet without incurring further charges, but he eyed the message with suspicion and replaced the phone, ever aware of muggers and street thieves keen to prey on a confused-looking tourist on a dark avenue. A group of teenagers were gathered at the outdoor seating of a kiosk from which lively music was playing and had he been in England, he might have considered the benefits of approaching them and asking for directions. Even in English, he would have reservations; in Portuguese, not a chance.

He squinted up in to the rain looking for a street sign and was annoyed to find he couldn't quite read the words from this side of the street. He crossed over, remembering to look the opposite way for traffic and paused under the awning of a jeweller's. The sign read '*Avenida Defensores de Chaves*' which rang a bell as being somewhere near to where he was headed, though in which direction he could not recall. He set off purposefully in what he hoped was the right way, wincing at his leg and trying not to look around too much, lest he make eye contact with a potential hoodlum or appear too much to be a lost tourist. After a few minutes he reached an intersecting road and realised not only had he not been walking down the street he'd thought, but that it was definitely in the wrong direction. The rain was starting to soak through his clothes and annoyingly, he had had a weatherproof jacket available to him the entire time which he had forgotten was in the side compartment of his bag. It seemed too late to put it on now and the breezy chill at the airport was now a muggy, sweaty feeling, totally unsuitable for extra layers.

Retracing his steps back to the metro station exit, he passed the teenagers at the kiosk again who were animatedly and raucously entertaining themselves. It was closer to 11pm now and they showed no signs of letting up. Palmer had to remind himself that it was only a Monday evening in mid-October and that this was clearly a local tradition. The street opened up into a vast intersecting highway, wide and busier with traffic, but still very few pedestrians. Traffic hurtled along at an alarming speed on this larger road which Palmer found was '*Avenida da Republica*', a name he definitely as being close to his hotel. In the dark and without a map, he was wasting time chancing things, so he waited until he found a wide canopy outside what appeared to be a swish office building with a drowsy-looking concierge at his desk to nestle under and set down his bag and got out his phone. At least here, if he were accosted, he could bang on the glass and alert the concierge, or worst-case scenario, the building's CCTV would pick up his attacker.

He accessed the map app on his phone and was pleasantly surprised to see the location crash zoom out from his last location of Manchester before hurtling back in to the district of Lisbon he was navigating. Using two fingers to manipulate the map, he found the wrong turn he'd made earlier and the metro terminal of *Sao Sebastiao* not far ahead. Another reason he'd kept quiet when being cheerfully interviewed by his travelling companion was the mention of the hotel chain he was staying in. As far as Palmer knew, there were many Sana hotels around Lisbon and indeed Portugal, but didn't want to contemplate the possibility that they were both booked into the same one. He needed a base to rest, recuperate and begin his search of the city without question or inconvenience. He had almost booked an apartment in the city centre but had found the footnote on the booking website that he would need to contact the owner prior to arrival to negotiate collecting keys to be a social encounter outside of his comfort zone. Also now thinking about his much-delayed arrival, he dreaded to think of having to either contact a grumpy key holder to meet him at this late hour, or having to find somewhere else to stay for this first night simply to avoid the awkwardness.

The Sana Reno hotel was 4 minutes ahead according to the app and other warm, desirable hotels now started to spring up around him. The street he was on was much quieter than the wider Avenida and had a green tarmacked cycle path which he absent-mindedly found himself following. There was no one at all out at this hour, in this weather, in this part of town and all at once Palmer was filled with waves of regret for making this idiotic journey at all. Even if he found who he was looking for, how on earth could he convince them of what had truly happened, let alone persuade them to return to England? He wasn't even sure they were still alive. He stepped into the road, spotting a hotel sign on the other side of the street and was almost run over by a speeding taxi which swerved to avoid him and continued down the street blaring its horn angrily. Palmer couldn't even think what the Portuguese was for sorry, thinking only of *por favor* and *obrigado*, neither of which seemed suitable to yell.

He reached the other side of the road and took a moment, putting his phone away and catching sight of his reflection in the window of the neighbouring building to the hotel. He looked dreadful and even excusing the recent trials he'd been through, a shadow of his former self. His eyes were barely slits in the dark sunken hollows of his eye sockets, their boyish gleam entirely gone. His hair was sodden and where once its thick locks would have absorbed a good deal of the rain, it was thinning now and water was trickling down his forehead and collecting at the tip of his nose before dribbling on its downward trajectory. His cheekbones which had once caught the eye of many an admirer and indeed once a man claiming to be a talent scout for a modelling agency, although Palmer assumed it was a scam, looked painfully sore beneath the small amount of foundation he'd applied that morning and he seemed to have acquired new bruises to his mouth and chin. He'd seen many a bored officer at passport control or an airport check-in desk give a casual glance to him, then his passport and do a visible double-take at how handsome he had once looked in the photograph but on this journey, the look had been more one of concern, noting the bloodshot eye, the swollen lip and his generally shaky demeanour.

Preparing himself for the social expectations of greeting the hotel receptionist and making some sort of small-talk, he was pleased to step into the spacious marble foyer to see a smiling man, probably a little light on duties at this hour and grateful of a task, greet him with a "*Boa noite!*" before quickly switching to "Good evening, sir!". Palmer loved how perceptive service staff were abroad, spotting an English tourist a mile off, even after a clumsy attempt at the native tongue, politely stepping into a language both parties had a mutual grasp of. Palmer smiled a weak smile, all he could muster and to save additional words, handed the receptionist the printed booking reservation from his pocket.

"Palmer," he said, as the man tapped away at the computer, taking information from his crumpled handout.

"Of course, Mr. Palmer," said the receptionist with a decent accent. "You are staying with us for six nights, yes?"

Palmer nodded as the man continued tapping and preparing a room key.

"Breakfast is already paid for," began the man and Palmer drifted off, barely interested in the location or hours of service as it was, but more intrigued by something he saw in the lobby.

"Excuse me one moment," said Palmer, leaving his bag dripping at the desk as he staggered across the plush lobby to the generous leather armchairs around a low, mahogany coffee table.

Scattered across it were the usual array of magazines and tourist-targeted shopping guides, but on top of these, most bizarrely and sticking out like a sore thumb, was a copy of the Manchester Evening News, the local paper in Palmer's hometown. It had almost been placed there to stand out, to draw the eye of anyone paying attention as they passed through the foyer and yet Palmer had only seen it as his eyes wandered, having already missed it as he entered. He looked around. The foyer was deserted and the only sounds he could hear were the trickling of a large ornamental waterfall which ran from the upper level of the room down into the main area and the clacking of keys as the receptionist continued his work.

Palmer moved to pick up the newspaper gingerly between thumb and forefinger, never keen on the idea of sharing second-hand papers or magazines in dentists' waiting rooms or on public transport. He unfolded it and deliberately looked at the date before letting his eyes roam further. It was today's edition, the late edition no less. Someone must have brought it this very evening, most likely on the same flight as him. It was the main image that next grabbed his attention – a dapper looking young man in a photo most likely taken for an I.D. badge or official pass of some sort, his hair swept neatly to one side and a warm, but professional smile on his lips. The photo cut off at the shoulders, but he was wearing a powder blue suit and a neat, red tie. The headline read 'MAN SOUGHT IN CONNECTION WITH WOMAN'S DISAPPEARANCE' and the by-line explained that police were looking for a man in his mid-twenties who had some connection to a missing woman, clearly a continuation from an earlier story.

Palmer didn't need to read any more about the missing woman as he knew the details intimately. The missing woman, one Celia Payne, 42, was just part of the reason he was here in Lisbon to begin with. The part that came as something of a shock, which found him stumbling to the ground for the third time that evening, was that the man in the photograph, the smiling, professional man, was the man he had seen in the metro station. The man who had pushed him downstairs.

3.

Palmer felt queasy and the few pieces of hardly-toasted bread he'd nibbled on in the restaurant did little to change this. He'd gulped down two large cups of very strong coffee and shown mild interest in the array of foods on the breakfast buffet, but only because the smiling employee who had checked his room number upon arrival had seemed very proud of what they had on offer and he didn't want to appear rude by not at least giving it the once over. Omelette, cocktail sausages, mushrooms and baked beans seemed a strangely English convention alongside the more continental options of cold meats, cheeses and pastries and Palmer was surprised to see the dazzling yellow Portuguese egg custards so popular on baking programmes at the moment as a further option. He'd finally settled on a few pieces of yeasty bread which he duly fed into the grilling device which seemed to take an eternity to even give the bread a touch of colour. He'd chosen a table as far away from the breakfast buffet as possible, away from the door and prying eyes, not that there were any at this hour. It was 7am and the room was deserted thankfully, but by sitting so far away from where his bread was toasting, he realised he'd have to hobble back and forth repeatedly to put the bread back through the griller again so gave up and applied a salty pat of butter to the limp yellow results.

He'd slept badly and at one point got up and surveyed the contents of the mini bar, hoping to perhaps drink himself into a light slumber at least. A bottle of Sagres lager and a small bottle of fruity red later and he'd felt wide awake and so resorted to surfing the T.V. channels hoping to find something to lull him to sleep. A British entertainment channel was screening endless repeats of classic sitcoms and so scrunching his eyes up and ignoring the throb in his knee, he wrapped himself up in the weighty duvet and finally drifted off to catchphrases and punchlines he knew off by heart from his childhood. His phone alarm woke him at 6.30am and he found himself drenched in sweat but also shivering. The air con had reduced the room temperature to an unbearably chilly level but it had the fortunate side effect of making him plunge into a hot shower as quickly as he could and gather his belongings into a smaller shoulder bag, getting dressed and ready to leave the hotel.

It was only because he'd mistakenly pressed the wrong button in the lift that he'd even arrived at the restaurant and the wafting smells made his stomach gurgle eagerly, despite him having no appetite previously. He'd gone to investigate the source of the aroma and encountered the beaming employee who ushered him to eat his fill. A few other hotel guests began to drift in now as he ate the last bit of toast he could stomach and he was glad to be leaving. Listening keenly, he detected some French exchanged between a stressed looking young couple with a drooling, bouncing tot and some English from a group of female backpackers but heavily accented and it frustrated him that he couldn't place the accent. Keeping his eyes on the floor, he slipped out of the room and was happy that the woman in charge of the breakfast room was occupied with mopping up a spilled bowl of cereal gleefully hurled by the French tot. He moved as quickly as he could down the curved staircase into the main lobby, making extra sure he didn't lose his footing, following the ornamental waterfall down which was now a more insistent torrent playing a psychological trick on his bladder.

The plan for today was to head straight into town on foot, however painful that might have been, as the odds of missing someone whilst on the metro or a bus seemed too high to risk. On reception this morning was a bearded man who smiled lazily as he passed and Palmer noticed a display of tourism leaflets stocked by the door. Rather than ask the receptionist for directions or a map and run the language embarrassment gauntlet again, he chanced on one of the leaflets containing a map. Thankfully, the third one he selected was for a tour bus operator and a huge, fold-out map showed him exactly what he needed to know. Just a few turns, as long as he kept his eye on the street names and set off in the right direction to begin with, and he could reach the centre. It looked more than manageable on the extensive map which seemed to cover the wider Lisbon areas of Belem to the west and *Parque das Nacoes* to the east, and easily walkable in no more than an hour or so. He wanted to reach the centre before shops opened and things got too busy, so that he could find a decent vantage point and begin his search properly.

Leaving the hotel, he noticed to his annoyance that the *Sao Sebastiao* metro station had an exit directly across from the hotel and that his late-night rain-soaked wanderings had been entirely unnecessary. Still, if it meant avoiding the man from the plane, it had been almost worth it. The street was as quiet as it had been last night, but today had a freshness about it, the cobbled pavement gleaming but thankfully not slippery and the buildings all light, pleasing colours. He headed to the left and found a junction where traffic was much busier and a grey turreted wall with a large iron gate lay across the road. Behind it were tall verdant trees and further signs of medieval or mock-medieval architecture. Possibly the famed Gulbenkian museum, he mused, trying to remember the map. It was now tucked away in his pocket, but he loathed the idea of drawing attention to himself and unfolding it again, giving away that he was either a tourist, or lost, or both.

Crossing the road away from this wall, he found another high-walled official looking building and at the rear, an armed guard, standing solitary and sober with some sort of machine gun looking weapon at his reach. It always chilled Palmer to see heavily-armed police or soldiers on the streets of a city and whilst he had got used to the idea of seeing them at major European monuments over the years, he still found something distressing about seeing them on the streets of London, or here, unexpectedly in what he assumed were the outer suburbs. It was perhaps a government building of some sort, as a flag was flying above it, but Palmer turned his attention away before the guard took notice of him and headed up a steep hill to another bustling road.

Ah yes, the hills. He'd forgotten about those, or else blocked out the knowledge to spare the worry over his knee. It was said Lisbon was built on seven hills like all the best European cities and the fold-out map gave nothing away about the terrain of the city, showing deceptively flat *avenidas* and *ruas* on the journey south to the waterfront. At the top of the rise, he found a huge dual carriageway with plenty of morning commuting going on. People hurried along on foot and by car and Palmer wondered if there was a quieter street available to him. The noise and colour were all too much for him and he had to take a moment to lean against the wall by a bank entrance before continuing.

Across the dual carriageway was a huge mall, *El Corte Ingles* so the sign said, which seemed to run for the entire length of the other side of the road. On this side were cafes, office windows and lots of banks in various states of opening and so Palmer hesitantly crossed to what seemed like the quieter side.

If Celia knew he was here, but didn't want to be found, it was game over. If the mysterious man on both the front cover of a British newspaper and on the concourse at the airport metro station was also in touch with her, then it was possible she already knew of his arrival. Except that the newspaper was bizarrely vague about this man's involvement in the disappearance, not hinting at anything sinister or suggestive, merely asking him to come forward. There wasn't even a name given which Palmer found most odd as the image was clearly professionally taken in some capacity and not the grainy CCTV grab or e-fit which could almost have been anyone and invited the public to play a guessing game. Whoever this man was, he had deliberately sought out Palmer, possibly wearing a hasty disguise, then fled at the sight of him, before turning back and pushing him down a staircase, an action which could have severely harmed or even killed him. Palmer was prone to the melodramatic on occasion, as his mother would often criticise, but this was no exaggeration. He had to stay alert for both a sighting of the elusive Celia Payne and his mystery assailant, again possibly hiding his appearance.

Many of the people around him were locals, some bustling on their way to work, some having a delightfully convivial breakfast with friends and colleagues, some were tourists making an early start before the attractions grew too busy and the weather too hot, but Palmer doubted that many of them, if any, were here on such a bizarre pretext as he was.

Three months ago, Celia Payne had disappeared on her way home from a wine bar in the busy Leopold Square area of Sheffield city centre, just an hour or so away from Palmer's current home in Manchester. She had given no indication of where she was going, other than a few strangely worded texts to a work friend, one to her elderly father and a third to Palmer himself, stating that all of this was his fault. Hospitals had been rung, woods searched, canals dredged, appeals made, and then suddenly, out of the blue, a postcard had arrived at his Fallowfield address, a 'Greetings From Lisbon' picture postcard clearly written in Celia's handwriting and dated the day after her disappearance. Why the card had been written a full two months before it was posted and why the tone of the message on it had been so cheerfully at odds with her last words, both spoken and texted to Palmer were just part of a much bigger mystery. The British police had made overtures to their Portuguese cousins but the return address on the postcard was fictional and no sightings had been made. It was totally out of character for Celia to do something like this, but not unheard of for a person with mental health issues, both grieving and coping with a relationship breakdown to simply vanish and then reappear elsewhere with little appreciation of the trouble their disappearance had caused.

Of course, there was no getting over the passport problem. Celia didn't have her passport with her and couldn't have left the country, although Palmer and a few of his friends had more than a few theories about that. No one with her name had left the country by any of the major UK airports or by Eurostar and similarly, no one had arrived in Portugal either. For her to have sent a postcard was near-impossible and it was far more likely that someone had forged her handwriting for some reason of either sabotaging the search for her or causing more distress to her estranged husband and family. Palmer knew for certain that the postcard was written by Celia, not just by reading the words and hearing her particularly snippy tone, but by a particular detail she had included that she alone knew. The police had questioned him on the meaning of it and he had feigned ignorance, and handwriting analysists had found the postcard inconclusive in terms of proving Celia's whereabouts or continued existence. Many people assumed Celia was long dead, most likely by a random violent attack on a quiet street on her drunken journey home. Some, who knew their full history, had laid the blame at Palmer's doorstep although he was never outright accused of foul play, more of being far more responsible for her disappearance than people, or the police, suspected.

Palmer passed estate agents' offices, a Lamborghini showroom and came to another road junction, even busier than the last. Traffic surged along three or four lanes in each direction, passing towering hotels, another Sana hotel, Palmer noted, office blocks and official looking skyscrapers of metal and glass. To his right, at the far end of the road, Palmer could see a huge concentration of traffic around a sprawling roundabout, at the centre of which was an imposing white stone column and impressive looking figure atop. Something about the sheer volume of traffic heading that way made Palmer reel and so he made to cross over away from this bottleneck as soon as he was able. Across the road was another government-type building and the street in the opposite direction was more much inviting, with some interesting graffiti of a grinning Cheshire cat with its arms wide open as if standing on the balcony it was spray-painted above. Cats were always a good sign in Palmer's mind and he allowed himself a brief moment of sadness for his own cat, Barry, wondering if he was coping back home in England.

A maze of quieter but devilishly sloping streets led Palmer down away from the busier road, until he was craning his neck to the see the tops of the buildings he had stood in front of mere minutes ago and he found himself amidst construction workers renovating a building, having gutted the entire block, carting rubble onto the road and sizzling with sweat even at this early hour. A municipal policeman stood, as if guarding the building site, a curious scene Palmer found, but it still put him on edge. He indicated for Palmer to cross the road and use the pavement on the opposite side and so he did, passing a barber's salon and a pharmacy. Adverts for pain relief and some sort of digestive aid were easy to spot, despite the language barrier and Palmer hesitated before stepping into the shop. He had often noted than unlike British chemists where most products were freely available on the shelves with only the stronger stuff protected behind a counter, that in pharmacies he'd visited in places like Barcelona and Genoa, that there'd been precious little for him to browse over in the shop itself and he'd been forced to engage in staccato English and theatrical mugging to get across what his particular ailment and medical needs were.

This pharmacy was no different and the moment he entered, a beaming bald-headed man at the counter greeting him cheerfully in Portuguese. Palmer managed a mumbled '*Hola*' before turning and looking at a display of multivitamins in the window. He would stay the minimum polite amount of time to avoid looking suspicious but then leave, the social interaction of having to rely on a native's better grasp of English all too much for him. He could manage in supermarkets where at least he could select his own produce, manage a 'hello' and 'thank you', hoping that there would be no small talk or questions of bag needs or loyalty cards, read the amount needed from the electronic display on the till and fumble with his Euros, finally giving away his status as a foreigner by his close perusal of unfamiliar silver and golden coins.

Palmer knew he'd gone bright red and could sense without looking that the bald-headed man at the counter was about to make his way over to him in the shop window and was gathering up a burst of energy to get out when he saw something odd on the street outside. Even through the cluttered glass window and across the road, it stood out as odd. One of the construction workers was puzzling over something he'd found in amongst the rubble on the pavement. He had called over a fellow worker to inspect it and both were wildly gesticulating and beckoning to the municipal policeman to check it out. A cold sweat formed at his brow as Palmer prepared himself for what it could be. A body, perhaps. Celia's crumpled remains, shoved cruelly into a boarded-up building, only found now, weeks later during the renovations. But no, it was nothing so macabre.

It was a large, floppy sun hat and now the construction workers were laughing, trying the hat on and finally placing it on the head of the municipal policeman with whom they must have been on friendly terms. One had a phone out, taking a picture of the policeman as he camped it up for a photo, the hat trailing with white and yellow flowers which had once been part of the hatband but had now come loose. Palmer could feel the pharmacist's breath almost at his neck, so he spun around, barked '*obrigado!*' which he knew again was not quite right for the job and dodged out of the shop onto the street. The hat had now been tossed back into the rubble and was already been covered over by more bricks and stone from a wheelbarrow. Palmer couldn't get any closer to it, but he didn't need to. Whilst there might have been many hats produced like that particular sun hat, across the whole wide world, it seemed weirdly, coincidentally fascinating that he himself had once bought a hat like that as a gift and that the recipient of that gift had been Celia Payne, and that she had been wearing it on the night she vanished into the ether.

19

4.

It was well after half past nine when Palmer finally limped into the huge expanse of the square and plonked himself down on a marble bench. His knee felt like it was on fire and he could feel that it was strangely swollen underneath his jeans. The square was busy even at this early hour and the combination of surrounding white buildings, slowly rising sun and gushing fountains spraying jewels of water into the air made him squint as he tried to survey his surroundings. The floor was an intriguing mosaic pattern of black and white curls like endless waves and he found it strangely hypnotic. Traffic circled the square on all sides and busy shops beyond, but here in the centre on his bench, Palmer felt both safe but also strangely exposed. Anyone could approach him from any side without him noticing and he began to view a shambling homeless man who had set down his belongings on the next bench along with suspicion. Another huge white column dominated the square with another dark, majestic figure on top. Forgetting he wasn't just another fascinated tourist, Palmer almost thought about getting out his guidebook to research the history of the square and its famous figure as he would have done on any other jaunt.

The walk down from the busy roundabout area he'd later realised was the Pombal statue due to the number of signs and similarly named businesses had been painful. It seemed that walking downhill was far worse that uphill and the entire *Avenida da Liberdade* had been a deceptively sharp gradient spread out over the length of the pretty tree-lined route. High fashion boutiques with names he recognised from perfume brands but hadn't realised also sold other items like outfits which trod a fine line between uniquely stylish and disturbingly comedic ran the entire length of the *Avenida* and as he neared the end, theatres and strangely, a Hard Rock Café sprang up. By now he was shuffling painfully and getting in the way of faster moving tourists, but could sense that he was near his first destination and soldiered on.

Watching the homeless man move off to beg money from a group of student-looking tourists, Palmer felt less anxious and finally opened his shoulder bag. In it, alongside the guidebook he'd bought impulsively at the airport in Manchester, were sunglasses, a tiny bottle of suntan lotion, although Palmer rarely tanned, his trusty notebook, water and a room key embossed with the Sana hotels logo. This was not Palmer's key to his room back at the Sana Reno, but rather another odd clue which had led him to wind up hobbling around a foreign city by himself on what would have appeared to anyone else to be a complete and utter wild goose chase.

Palmer's birthday was in December, a full two months away, but he had received a birthday card in the post just two weeks ago, addressed to him in a non-descript hand. The card was the cheap variety found in a bargain greetings card shop or supermarket probably costing less than £1 and it featured a sort of oil painting of a middle-aged man fishing in a brook somewhere in the countryside. The printed message on the front was 'To a Lovely Father' and inside, strangely, the message personally written to him was almost gouged in faltering ink into a thick layer of Tippex which obviously obscured a previous message. Palmer had tried to scrape off the layer of correction fluid to unearth the earlier writing, but unsuccessfully. The new message read:

To Palmer,

Always thinking of you.

Always.

C.

X

Without any sort of tone suggested, the message could be read as both heartfelt and endearing but also creepily warning. To make matters worse, the writing was framed around the pre-printed message which read:

'Birthdays are a special time for sharing love and sharing life,

A father who's as great as you deserves the best, that much is true,

21

I hope you have a special day that's wonderful in every way!'

This added a further impenetrably odd layer of meaning to the whole thing. Palmer had never been a father, knew no one to whom this could have been a funny in-joke and definitely wasn't an error, due to the correctly addressed envelope and handwritten message. He couldn't fathom the thought process of someone selecting both a strange inappropriate card but also then either changing their mind and tippexing out their original thoughts, or else actually recycling a card from somewhere else. The 'C' could be a number of people he knew, but the most obvious was Celia, although what it could all mean was a puzzle. Cellotaped to the inside of the card was the hotel room key and a quick internet search had found the Sana hotel chain existed mainly in Portugal, ruling out further branches in Angola and Germany. The postmark on the envelope had been badly smudged and water damaged but the stamp itself was identifiably Portuguese, celebrating the 150th anniversary of the abolition of the death penalty. Palmer found it disconcerting that he could have been hanged for his crimes as recently as fifty years in the United Kingdom but would have dodged a bullet in Portugal.

Palmer hadn't shared the birthday card with the authorities, not after their strange reaction to the earlier postcard and their confiscation of the item, but instead had taken it as evidence that someone, somewhere knew more about what had happened to Celia and if it couldn't be the woman herself sending these cryptic clues, then it was someone close to her and by extension, close to Palmer himself. Someone who wanted to lure him to Portugal, perhaps specifically to Lisbon and a particular hotel.

He hadn't taken the decision lightly to book into one of the ten or so Sana hotels in the city, given the chance to instantly rule one of them out of his investigations, but also fearful of ending them too quickly by chancing upon the correct one instantly. He was terrified of who or what he might encounter should the room key still be active and somehow allow him access to one of the hundreds, if not thousands of rooms in the hotels. If it were a crime scene and he were then immediately implicated, Palmer knew he could never face a foreign interrogation process or period of incarceration. There would simply be too much suspicion of incorrect translation or some cruel and unusual twist of a foreign legal system which could land him rotting in an overseas jail for the rest of his life, whilst everyone back home thought the worst of him. He simply couldn't rule out the possibility that someone was out to frame him or blackmail and extort him for whatever they thought he was worth. But investigate he must, for that birthday card and hotel room key had sat on the sideboard in his cramped kitchen, disappearing under the daily assault of junk mail ready for recycling, for close to two weeks before he'd decided to act upon it.

Now, sitting alone in such a bright and busy square, a thousand miles away from his kitchen, he felt ridiculous. He had travelled all this way to play detective in a country he couldn't speak the language of, in a city he knew very little about, to try a hotel room card in one of several possible venues which may no longer even work and if it did, could leave him to who knew what on the other side of the door. Certainly nothing good. His warped extrapolating of possible scenarios had considered that finding Celia, alive and well with a gorgeous tan and a stonking hangover, possibly with a handsome local chap on her arm, was probably the best fantasy. The worst, her weeks-old decaying body, somehow politely overlooked by a combination of a pre-paid bill, a 'Do Not Disturb' sign and a slack housekeeping service and a whole world of evidence to tie him to the crime.

He hadn't even mustered up the nerve to try the room key in the hotel he was staying in. A combination of anxiety and weariness of his limbs had prevented him going floor-to-floor, room-to-room, testing the card on the contact panels of the hundred or so rooms in the Sana Reno. He'd convinced himself that because the key was significantly different from the one he'd been issued late last night, that he could potentially rule out the venue for now, and so instead was embarking upon his supposed Plan B which was to take advantage of the extensive public transport network and ride around the city for a day or more, noting down possible sightings, checking hotel locations and distances from main roads whilst giving his knee and stabbing shin a chance to rest and heal. He knew that his plan was as weak as it sounded.

Then there was the added complication of this red-headed man who had made the regional newspaper back home, but Palmer knew nothing about. Someone British with a connection to Celia who had also trailed over here in search of what, exactly? Not to mention the metro station shoving incident. He could actually be in very real danger.

No, this was entirely a terrible idea and Palmer should return to his hotel room, pack and go home immediately. Except that his return flight wasn't for five days and he couldn't stomach the encounter or expense of trying to change it. He was being cowardly and foolish. To rally himself, he opened his dog-eared notebook and read the first page of this particular investigation, the writing being his own, large, bold print and reading 'Celia Payne is alive' across the entire page. Nodding to himself, he closed the book, replaced it in his bag and threw it back over his shoulder carefully. He got his bearings again and headed down through the busier part of the square until he reached a narrower street lined with souvenir shops and wholesalers selling beautiful lengths of exotic fabric. Many of the shops stocked postcards just like the one Celia had sent all those months ago and it heartened him to think of her walking aimlessly along this *rua*, stopping on a whim to coo over a particular material she took a shine to, waxing lyrical about making her own curtains or a dress for a summer party.

This road felt more promising, more positive and he knew that the Yellow Bus stand was at the end, by the waterfront, from the leaflet he'd taken from the hotel lobby. There he could purchase a ticket, possibly even on a double decker open top bus, and sit back and focus on his mission and also enjoy the sun and the scenery. He had almost passed the towering *Elevador de Santa Justa* without noticing, the quirky metal construction with observation platform at the top looking like a strange gothic hammer, tucked away up an innocuous side street. Palmer had wanted a vantage point, but looking up at the vertiginous lift, he felt that perhaps it was a little too high for both his acrophobia and to be of any use when searching the crowded streets. Perhaps on a return visit in another lifetime, he mused.

Reaching the end of the street, the landscape once again opened up into a huge sunny space lined with beautiful marble arched yellow-painted buildings and a whole world of transport from darting tuk tuks weaving between bendy buses and modern trams, to the tiny famed vintage trams trundling by and beyond, in the distance waters of the Tagus river, ferries and sightseeing boats drifted idly by. The sun was now so bright, Palmer reached for his sunglasses and once they were on and he could stop squinting, he spotted the bright stand for the Yellow Bus company just across the busy road. A few tourists, all wearing shorts and short sleeves, he noticed, unlike the locals, some of whom had resorted to thicker winter jackets and coats already, were queuing by the stand and it was then that Palmer noticed who one of them was. It was the Mancunian from the plane, the man he'd suffered next to on the flight, who had come to his aid in the metro station. He had been travelling alone, but was now deep in conversation seemingly with another man wearing mint green shorts and a loud Hawaiian style shirt.

Palmer's instinct was to turn away before he was seen, lurk in the long corridor of arches which led away from the stand and wait until he could buy his tickets without being spotted, but at the same time, he wondered who the chatty man's new victim might be. Crossing the road, but keeping well back, hidden behind other groups of people, Palmer drew close enough to see the animated conversation more clearly. The Mancunian was waving his arms around as if to marvel at the sights around him, whilst the other man had his back to Palmer. Keeping at the side of a fancy-looking restaurant, away from the queue, Palmer willed the man to turn around, something eating at his gut, fearing the answer. Finally, as Palmer's heart began to race and he tried to block out the resulting throb in his knee, the man turned. He was wearing another hat, not a straw one this time, and Palmer had only clapped eyes on him twice as far as he knew, but there was no mistaking that this was the man who had pushed him down the stairs, the man on the front cover of the Manchester Evening News.

5.

The insufferable English pensioner once again yelled rudely across the bus deck to his oblivious wife, yet again trying to point out some mundane item of trivia to her which he had ascertained from his guidebook and thought she should instantly be made aware of. They both had their cheap yellow headphones in to listen to the audio guide which narrated the two-hour tour route, but for some reason, the old man found it necessary to holler above their audio guides and indeed those of everyone around them to add his own personal flourishes. It didn't help that his wife was sitting on the other side of the bus, sandwiched in the middle of a group of Spanish tourists who obligingly kept tapping her every time he called, or that she seemed to be ignorant of his outbursts, either deliberately, possibly embarrassed by her husband's behaviour or that she simply had the ability to drift off into another time and place and not hear him.

"Look, Joan, look!" cried the man, insistently and the Spaniard Palmer thought looked like a Marco dutifully tapped the lady gently on the shoulder for what must have been the twelfth time in the last half hour and she turned, as if suddenly aware she was on a bus and that her name was indeed Joan.

Palmer grimaced, then wondered if the man really did look like a Marco, whether that was even a Spanish name or perhaps more Italian and whether his allocation of the name was a little bit racist.

Joan looked across at her animated husband who was waving a mobile phone in his hand and then suddenly pointing at a building the bus was passing on the right. He used two fingers to zoom in on the map displayed on his phone

26

where an icon showed a restaurant he had previously searched for.

"It's where that restaurant is, just...." The man was half-standing now, waiting to point to exactly where this exciting location was. Only a row of office blocks lined the street. "...Well, it must be behind them there somewhere, Joan," he said, suddenly a little flat.

Joan nodded, almost politely, then turned back to her reverie and the husband, Palmer had branded him Wilbur for some reason, returned to his phone, zooming back out and watching as the moving icon showing his own position trundled on beyond his hope-for restaurant's location. Wilbur was sunburned in that way only a British tourist could be and totally oblivious to the racket he was making and the waves of laughter which would ripple throughout the deck following each of his sudden fits of excitement.

Palmer would normally have ignored such accidentally ignorant behaviour but here he was wedged directly behind Wilbur and penned in by Stuart's enormous mass. There was both a feeling of calm and a terrific rush being on the open top upper deck of the Yellow Bus tour bus with the morning sun pleasantly warming the passengers but a delightful breeze coming from both the Tagus and the velocity of the vehicle itself. Palmer almost felt like a tourist again, as if perhaps he and Stuart had come away on holiday together in some strange arrangement given their flight together and now the coincidence of meeting at the bus stand. That would be tempting were it not for his still churning anxieties and the fact he found Stuart vaguely repulsive.

He had waited until the mysterious red-headed man had turned and left the company of his plane buddy and then nonchalantly sidled up to the rotund Mancunian who was having trouble getting his Euros out of his tight short pockets. As he pulled out a rather careless wad of notes, most of them scattered to the shiny cobbles and Palmer found himself picking them up, both finding himself an in-road to their reunion conversation and also saving the larger man from a manoeuvre Palmer felt sure he could not perform.

"Oh my goodness, it's *you*!" Palmer had cried, barely even convincing himself that this was both a surprise meeting and a pleasant one.

"Blimey," said the man, his ruddy face breaking all at once into the biggest grin Palmer had ever seen. "'arry, mate!" he cried, seizing Palmer's wrists in a strangely brotherly greeting. "What are the flamin' odds?!"

Palmer had never been very good at lying and had once heard the easiest lies to tell were those which were closest to the truth. When the man had introduced himself on the plane and left a gap which was growing more and

27

more awkward by the second in which Palmer was supposed to obey etiquette and return the gesture, Palmer had found himself not wanting to do so. It hadn't helped that he had already completely forgotten what the other man had said his own name was, so that if he were to pluck a name out of thin air for himself, he couldn't be sure it wasn't the same as the one just given to him. He'd finally settled on the innocuous, slightly roguish 'Harry' which he'd then realised made his full identity unbelievable, given his surname and the full name's association with Michael Caine's spy character of the 60s and 70s. Thankfully, he'd seen no mileage in giving away anything other than his first name and had allowed the man to assume many other things during their plane conversation.

Mundanities had been exchanged at the bus stand about how lovely the weather was, especially compared to the drizzle last night, how crazy it was to bump into a relative stranger as one of the only other people you knew in such a huge cosmopolitan and touristy city and finally, plans for the day. Palmer had intended on purchasing a 72-hour pass which enabled him to use any of the company's buses, trams and elevators as well as the scenic river boat tour then to head off on either the blue or purple routes which swung in great two-hour arcs around the city and its environs. Now, however, he first needed to find out just what this man's link was to the strange red-haired man from the metro station. As the queue shortened and their stilted conversation dried up, Palmer fixed a forgetful smile on his face and slapped his forehead slightly theatrically.

"Oh," he said suddenly. "I meant to ask you! I first spotted you from across the road back there-" He gestured towards the fancy restaurant over the road. "-but I thought I somehow knew the guy you were just chatting to though I couldn't place where from!"

The man's face screwed up in surprise and recollection.

"Oh, 'im?" he asked, pointing down the street making Palmer swing around and look, quickly realising he was only indicating a vague direction the man had left in rather than a current location. "The ginger bloke? No idea who 'e was," he continued. "'e were a Brit, s'all I know. Askin' about if I knew which bus he could take to get to 'is 'otel. Then about 'ow long I were stayin' and 'ow long I'd been here. Then 'e went." The man's broad grin returned. "I think 'e were a *poofter* if you ask me!" He then began to laugh a loud, throaty laugh which spoke of years of late nights and cigarettes.

Palmer loved the irony of the man's casual bigotry but needed to feel more satisfied that this was yet another strange coincidence.

"He just looked a bit like a guy I knew from Manchester," suggested Palmer, then realising how that sounded after the man's theory, he quickly added. "From a work seminar or something."

"Oh I doubt it," said the man, shuffling forwards and now next to be served. "'e said 'e were from Edinburgh, 'ad that posh Scottish thing goin' on." Then he seized upon the last thing Palmer had said. "What line of work are you in, anyrate, mate?"

"I.T.," said Palmer, hoping it covered an umbrella of possibilities none of which would give him away.

"I know fuck all about that," laughed the man, a little too emphatically. "Builder, as I told you last night. Sorry love, what were that?"

The pretty, dark-skinned lady at the bus stand was greeting the man and asking him which ticket he required. Palmer was grateful of both the interruption in order to collect his thoughts and process this new information but also the man's gregarious, hopelessly flirty nature as he chatted easily with the bus company lady in his broad Mancunian accent with no hesitation or shame. This extended dialogue revealed that the lady was called Maria, but more importantly, that the man's name was Stuart, which didn't even ring a bell with Palmer, meaning he truly had switched off during their first conversation the night before. Thankfully, this avoided any further strangeness as Palmer now no longer needed to pretend he knew the man's name without ever mentioning it. The chat also served to further reassure Palmer as Stuart only bought a day ticket, meaning even if he failed to escape his company today, he could be assured two whole days away from him.

Palmer had been all set to pretend he was interested in taking a different mode of transport to whichever Stuart suggested he wanted to take, but Stuart, once they both had their tickets, had noted Palmer's hobbling and kindly offered to walk him to whichever stop he was heading for. Palmer's curiosity about the mystery Scotsman and whether he trusted what he had told Stuart were too much for him to simply ditch him for the day and he figured that during a two-hour jaunt around town, he could add a light grilling of his travelling companion to his agenda. Palmer was glad when Stuart eagerly plugged in the free headphones given to them by the driver of the purple bus route, headed 'Olisipo', which meant that small talk would be limited although he would still be free to toss in the odd observation and gentle query about the red-haired man.

The audio guide was lively and full of precise, entertaining details and soundtracked throughout, between stops by authentic guitar music which once again added to Palmer's feeling that if things were different, this could have been a holiday rather than a strange mission. The bus whipped along through beautifully colourful bustling streets in the centre, before heading along the breezy waterfront where dazzling white official buildings stood to one side and gigantic cruise liners were moored at the other, looming over the bus, but still dwarfed in the twinkling expanse of water which ran as far as the eye could see in either direction with hazy bridges visible in both directions. Palmer realised that much of this particular route would be unhelpful to his investigations as it took them way out of the centre to the *Parque das Nacoes* area which was outside of the area Palmer was considering, but would later swing back in to take them close to the airport and within spitting distance of his hotel should he choose to abandon today's activities.

Palmer's weary limbs were glad of the rest and he actually found Stuart with his brief, blunt interjections into the tour to be refreshingly different from the incessant bore of the night before. Now Wilbur had given up trying to call to his wife and the group of Spaniards had rung the bell to alight at the enormous *Vasco da Gama* shopping centre, leaving his wife sitting alone deep in thought. Across the busy street was the *Gare do Oriente* train station which lay like a gleaming, exotic, sun-bleached carcass of white spindly bones and membranes. As the bus pulled up, Stuart nodded in the direction of a group of sexy young ladies chattering away with heaps of shopping bags at their feet, clearly reuniting during a busy day of retail therapy. Palmer couldn't work out how old his companion was, but he was definitely too old to be drooling over these attractive specimens. Palmer himself had no interest in the girls, but obligingly looked and returned Stuart's lascivious smile with a thin-lipped nod. He then let his gaze drift, spotting the Spanish tourists spilling out onto the pavement and heading into the shopping centre, but was stunned, frozen rigid in his seat as one final person stepped off the bus before the doors closed and the vehicle moved off. A woman wearing a beige trench coat stopped on the busy pavement before looking around warily and then making for the mall entrance. She was growing smaller by the second as the bus moved away and she disappeared into the crowds, but Palmer knew for certain that the woman was Celia Payne.

6.

There had been no hiding his strange behaviour after that. Palmer had leapt up frantically, pushed the startled Stuart almost to the floor and hurtled down the steps, ringing each bell button that he passed and yelling for the driver to stop, go back or let him off. The driver refused to do any of these things and from what little Palmer could grasp of his furious Portuguese and limited English, the next stop was the only place he was allowed to, or intended to halt. Palmer realised his behaviour was frightening some of the people on the lower deck and he felt certain he heard an anxious "*Terrorista!*" from among the passengers. He felt a solid hand on his shoulder and was about to turn to face whichever authority had caught him and plead his innocence, when he realised it was Stuart, who had lumbered down after him, clearly worried about the mental state of his recently acquired acquaintance.

"C'mon mate, come back up 'ere," said Stuart, somewhat soothingly for a man so big and blunt. His eyes were begging Palmer to obey and not just in fear of the public embarrassment going on as Palmer knew his own eyes would have been, were the roles reversed.

He allowed himself to be led back upstairs, hearing the driver say something which was possibly swearing, but definitely insulting and exasperated before he was guided into the nearest seat by Stuart. He was shaking and breathing erratically but was aware of Stuart's deep voice repeating something about controlling his panic, something about mindfulness. The Mancunian had wedged himself into the seat next to him once more and the flesh of his bare arms was brushing against Palmer's, something Palmer would have felt reviled by in any other circumstance, but again, here the burly man's presence

31

was somehow calming, his touch, cool and reassuring. Suddenly, Palmer snapped out of his fog and was aware that he still had the yellow headphones in his ears, although the cable had snapped when he had leapt up. He removed them and offered his thanks to Stuart, without making eye contact. A receipt on the floor became mesmerising.

"What were all that about, mate?" asked Stuart, clearing judging his companion now capable of being grilled.

It occurred to Palmer that he could create a myriad of lies to trip himself up on later, that he could spin any kind of embarrassing medical yarn which would silence further questions and adequately explain his outburst, but somehow it seemed to make most sense to keep things simple and just tell him the truth. Or at least a small portion of it.

"Celia Payne," he gasped, not realising that it would be so hard to speak.

"Who?" asked Stuart, his thick eyebrows arched in a picture of confusion.

"I saw Celia Payne," reiterated Palmer, still staring at the floor.

He felt Stuart's strong hand on his jaw suddenly and felt the man lifting his head and forcing him to make eye contact. Any other time, such unwanted intimacy would have made him gag. Here it felt oddly thrilling. He stared into the builder's eyes and knew his expression would look insane, possibly also terrifying.

"Who's Celia Payne, 'arry?" asked Stuart, searching his eyes as if he were telepathic.

Palmer took a deep breath, careful not to exhale too strongly, so close to the other man. He could smell his aftershave, something manly and alluring, see the stubble on his jowly pink chin.

"The missing woman, from Manchester," he said. "A few months ago. Remember?"

Stuart's thinking face was not an attractive one. His forehead crinkled like corrugated iron and his nose scrunched up like a pig. Clearly, it worked though as a memory was jogged.

"The schoolteacher?" he ventured. "I think she were in last night's paper again. Summat about her any rate."

Palmer nodded effusively.

"And you just saw 'er?" continued Stuart. "Did you know 'er?"

Palmer nodded again. Stuart looked suddenly doubtful.

"You can't 'ave 'ad a right good view of 'er from up here, could you mate?" he asked. "'ow sure were you?"

Now that Palmer's pulse had slowed again, it seemed as if the blood was flowing properly around his body and not just to his face and brain and he could suddenly think straight again. Of course he couldn't be sure it was Celia. Not from the upper deck of a moving bus and through a busy crowd. And what were the odds of her having been on the same bus he was on and not having noticed her? Slim, for sure.

"I just thought…" he began, unsure where he was going with the sentence. "I thought…I *wanted* it to be her. But you're right. It probably wasn't."

He was losing his mind, clearly. Making paranoid links between the various characters he kept running into at an alarming rate was bad enough, but imagining that Celia herself was now also stalking him was another thing altogether. Stuart had released his hold on his jaw and moved a hand to his shoulder, half-patting reassurance, half-holding him away it seemed.

"I think I read about it in the paper on the plane," said Stuart. "I 'ad one with me and when you nodded off, I flicked through it. There were summat about people thinkin' she might have run off to Portugal." He stopped, his eyes sparkling with realisation. "Is that why you're really 'ere, mate?"

Palmer nodded again, totally broken by the experience of both the phantom sighting and the way in which Stuart had somehow started piecing him back together.

"Mate," said Stuart, bringing Palmer in for the sweatiest hug he'd ever endured.

He could feel the sweat through Stuart's gaudy shirt and wondered why he wasn't as sickened as he would normally be. Thankfully, the hug was over before it began, a quite manly embrace, and when Palmer was released again, he felt moisture on his cheeks. Not the perspiration from his companion's body, but real tears which had sprung from his eyes during the hug. He was so disappointed in himself and he wiped them away, knowing that Stuart had seen them, but hoping he wouldn't comment on them. Thankfully he didn't. A

33

strange silence fell between them which with any other person would have been awkward.

Palmer looked around and was grateful that the upper deck wasn't too busy and so not many people had seen or heard his flight downstairs or the strange moment between him and Stuart. Wilbur had cajoled Joan into sitting next to him further down the bus and they were enjoying the view of the distant *Vasco da Gama* bridge which ran insanely, infinitely across the Tagus in an unstoppable feat of engineering. The bus was whipping along away from the water, having passed another stop by now near the impressive white tower like a ship's bow, which he recognised from his guidebook as the *Vasco da Gama* tower. He remembered that then bus had reached the furthest point of its journey out east and was looping back past the mall and eventually off across the north of the town towards the airport.

"Better?" asked Stuart, smiling kindly.

The bluff builder had seemed nothing more than a fat bore on the plane, but had suddenly become his saviour time after time once they touched down in Lisbon. Palmer felt exposed and strangely exhilarated by it. He felt that he could probably tell Stuart anything and it not feel like the end of the world, or a pair of desperate hands clutching at his throat as it usually felt whenever he contemplated the reality of the situation. But it was not a good idea to confide everything in this near-stranger, certainly not when he still doubted what the red-headed man's angle was and there was still the matter of tracking down the hotel room key's treasures.

The woman on the pavement *could* have been Celia, he mused, veering back towards his initial thought, but there was no way he could have been so certain it was her from up here. If she were playing a cruel and twisted game with him, then she had gambled rather recklessly by trailing him doggedly across the city and coming very close to being apprehended or unmasked. No, it was either a trick of the mind, or else Celia Payne was about to meet a much more terrible fate than she could have ever imagined.

7.

By the time the bus reached the last stop on its two- hour jaunt around the city, Palmer's nerves had settled once more and his stomach was painfully protesting at his lack of breakfast and the need for lunch. The terminal (although the bus began its route again instantly as it was a hop on, hop off affair) was in a sunny square lined by restaurants and cafés with pleasant outdoor seating where all manner of buses and trams seemed to congregate. Stuart had already proposed they should seek out some lunch before getting the other bus route which also began and ended in the same square. Only a few hours earlier, such a proposition of a shared meal and a further couple of hours in the same company would have made Palmer sweat, palpitate and make his excuses. Now, it seemed perfectly reasonable to share a table with his newfound friend and contemplate an afternoon of more sightseeing, or people-spotting.

Palmer had kept his eyes firmly on the spot he had thought he had seen Celia as the bus looped back on itself, this time passing by the skeletal transport hub, and he was well aware of Stuart's eyes on him as he scanned the crowds. If Stuart thought he were crazy or foolish, he said nothing, passing no further comment on the supposed sighting or Palmer's irrational reaction to it. In fact, it seemed rather odd to Palmer that Stuart made no further reference at all to anything he'd discussed with him and instead proffered him one of his earphones so that they could share a set and listen to the remainder of the tour, with the odd amusing response thrown in, all the while an enigmatic smile on his face.

Stuart was probably only in his late 20s or early 30s, but it was his immense mass which made him seem older. Staring at him rather than checking out the weird and wonderful graffitied derelict buildings at the north of the city, Palmer found that most of the mass he'd leapt to assume was fat, was mainly muscle and not just the toned bulk which might naturally occur on a labouring man, but that of a serious weightlifter or bodybuilder. Palmer had no idea what Stuart's business was in the city and felt sure that the man had definitely told him about it on the flight, but right now he seemed to be enjoying the touristic lifestyle and his enjoyment was mildly infectious. For half an hour, Palmer's mind blanked out the multiple paranoid theories drifting around in it and he listened to the audio guide, nodded at Stuart's riffing on the information and occasionally threw in his own observations on a fine-looking church or a pretty building façade.

A café which Palmer would normally have ignored as being too touristy was where Stuart chose for them to dine, its laminated catalogue of photos of slightly unappetising-looking food and badly translated English captions a sure warning sign in his limited experience, and since the builder was in charge, Palmer acquiesced. The embarrassment of finding a waiter to notice them and seat them was nothing to Stuart, who somehow managed to catch a silver-haired and slightly jolly looking man's eye and get them a decent table, shaded from the harshness of the sun but with a cracking view of the square. Palmer had heard on the audio tour that sardines were a speciality of the city and remembered reading something in his guidebook about an entire shop dedicated to them in cans, so felt like he should at least give them a go here. It also lessened the chances of food poisoning from undercooking or an upset stomach from overspicing to pick something so tame. Stuart ordered something which from the catalogue looked like a McDonalds' fish sandwich and was not disappointed when it arrived and that was exactly what it was. He had ordered a Sagres but Palmer didn't trust himself with alcohol so had gone with a ginger ale, which he was glad of, given how salty his dish was.

They spoke very little during the meal, but it was never awkward and occasionally, Stuart would get out his digital camera and take a few photographs of the square. Palmer was impressed that the man had a separate camera and was not of the generation of smartphones and selfies but was still tensed, ready to refuse a photograph should he suggest taking one of him or them both. It was one thing to befriend this man, another to make him complicit in his plans. As Palmer finished with one last forkful of briny olive, pickled carrot, surprisingly bland sardine and toast, Stuart was pointing out that the other bus had arrived at its stand, so they had a few minutes to finish up and make their way to it. Another social awkwardness ducked, Stuart summoned the waiter again, requested the bill and had folded a wad of his Euros into the waiter's hand before Palmer could even access his money belt.

"You can get the next one, 'arry, mate," said Stuart, winking.

Was this how he was to spend the rest of his time in Lisbon? Dining in the company of this man and relying on his confidence and protection? There were worse ways to pass the time, Palmer supposed, but he at least needed to feel in control of their relationship.

"I'd rather give you my share," he replied, counting out coins from his zipped pocket. "In case there isn't a next one."

Stuart begrudgingly took the money, looking slightly hurt and offended by both the gesture and Palmer's words and they stood silently as the queue shuffled forwards to board the next bus. This route would take them to the western end of the city, to the district of Belem after another sweeping loop of the city centre. The route passed by the location of another Sana hotel and Palmer was keen to check out how far off the beaten track it was. After this second two-hour jaunt, he'd already decided to curtail any further adventuring with Stuart by exaggerating his knee pains and returning to his hotel. Truth be told, his pain had rarely crossed his mind since the Celia sighting and he wondered if perhaps the sun, the change of scenery and a little bit of rest were doing the trick.

This tour was nowhere near as eventful as the first, with no other passengers to laugh at, no phantom women disembarking from the bus and no sign of the hotel he was looking out for either. What it was instead, was a beautiful couple of hours drinking in the atmosphere of the hilly, eclectic city as the bus veered around tight corners and up narrow *avenidas*, sweeping past a fine domed basilica, taking in the grandeur of the *25 de Abril* bridge which looked identical to the Golden Gate in San Francisco especially when framed from an angle to take in the steep hills and meandering trams behind it, and the sheer spectacle of what Belem had to offer from its monastery to its ancient tower and its monument to discoveries which was a tremendous white stone sculpture like a huge ship cresting the waves with noted figures from history lining up to make a new venture in the name of the Portuguese empire. Palmer knew he could spend an entire day just wandering around this area and so mentally pencilled in a visit for tomorrow or the next day, depending on the weather whilst Stuart snapped away with his camera, making the most of his one-day-only ticket.

When the bus swung back into the square they had departed from, Palmer leapt to his feet, having taken the aisle seat this time in case of a sudden need to move, but Stuart remained sitting, looking somewhat despondent.

"C'mon, *mate*," said Palmer, begrudgingly using the man's own vocabulary to stir him. "End of the line."

It took Stuart a moment to look up and respond. Palmer wondered if he should have known or sensed this shift in emotion but it wasn't his fault if people were so difficult to read sometimes.

"You get goin', 'arry," said Stuart quietly. "I might ride around a bit more."

Ordinarily, Palmer would have simply accepted such a statement of release and made good his escape, but for some reason, today, he felt indebted to the dour Mancunian and vaguely interested in the reasons for his change of mood.

"I was going to head back to my hotel, the old leg's giving me some gyp," said Palmer hesitantly. "But we could perhaps get a drink before I hobble off?"

It physically pained Palmer to be so conciliatory, so sociable, so not himself and it hurt even more when Stuart simply said, "No, mate. Not right now."

Palmer could hear the last few passengers boarding below and knew if he didn't move now, he'd be stuck on the ride for at least another stop, potentially in the right direction were he heading for the hotel, but given he actually wasn't and didn't want to be stuck with Stuart for another loop of the city, he decided to go.

"Maybe run into you some other time," said Palmer finally, knowing that despite his propensity for random encounters so far this trip, that the odds were definitely in his favour that they'd never see each other again. No numbers had been exchanged and he hadn't even given the man his surname, let alone his real first name. This was it.

Stuart nodded sadly but said no more, so Palmer lumbered downstairs as quickly as he could and got off the bus, yelling "*obrigado!*" at the driver as he cheerily stepped onto the pavement. He crossed over the road in front of the bus whilst the road was clear and reached a shop window which was filled with creepy looking dolls and toys. He chanced a look back over his shoulder as the bus was still parked up and only metres behind him. Stuart was watching him intently from the upper deck and did a strange salute as their eyes met.

"See you around!" called Palmer, half-mouthing the words so his lips could be read rather than his voice be too loud.

"Breakfast?" came the reply and Stuart was not opposed to shouting.

A few people on the street looked around at the sudden noise. It was mid-afternoon and the streets were busier than ever.

"What?" mouthed Palmer, doing a theatrical puzzled frown and placing his hands out like weighing scales in the universal pose of 'I don't get it!'.

"I'll see you for breakfast," yelled Stuart, now half-standing and gripping the upper rail of the bus. "About 7?"

The bus was beginning to move off now and the sudden lurch made Stuart fall back into his seat. He laughed at his mishap and as his face grew smaller and his words more distant, his final sentence drifted through the air and the noise of traffic and tourism and finally reached Palmer's distressed ears.

Stuart had seen him that morning. They were staying in the same hotel.

8.

Palmer's planned solo mission was to make use of the Yellow Bus company's scenic boat tour and this was something he definitely wanted to do without distraction or interruption. The lady who had sold him his ticket had helpfully noted that due to it being off-season, one boat was in for repairs and only the even houred boats were running in one direction and then odd houred in the other. This meant that he could safely take the 4pm boat from its departure point at the waterfront and remain on board the service which then became the 5pm boat as it returned as the last run of the day. He had no need nor intention to disembark at its Belem calling in point since he'd already scoped the location that afternoon and planned to return in the next day or so, but it was the boat itself that he was interested in.

That enigmatic phrase on the first of Celia's mysterious messages – the postcard – which had led Palmer to believe that there was no doubt it was from her, or at least someone with intimate knowledge of them both had made reference to boats. To her love of them and his hatred and had rather bitterly at the time he had thought stung him, with a reference to his 'yellow belly'. Celia was not prone to such florid turns of phrases, preferring a cold economy with words which had led her towards and served her well in a career of teaching Mathematics. The connection of boats, Lisbon and yellow seemed far too strange to be a coincidence and whilst he admitted it was a stretch to jump upon this as a good clue to waste two hours on, there was one further reference which seemed too neat to be random. The full message had read:

"Messing about on the river simply isn't your game is it, Palmer? Your yellow belly could never face it on boats! Certainly not overseas. An Englishman's

40

home is his palace, after all!"

The words themselves weren't so odd but the tone was bizarrely jovial, mocking and hinting at some deeper meaning which no one else had picked up on. The fact she had apparently mangled the final adage, substituting 'palace' for 'castle' stuck out most in Palmer's opinion. When he had consulted the Yellow Bus guide and found that the departure point was the *Terreiro do Paco* or 'Palace Grounds' in his rough translation, he'd been galvanised to at least see the boat terminal if not rally his nerves to take a trip. It was true he had no gut for water-based travel, having thrown up on many an occasion over the rail of a ferry or pleasure boat taken at someone else's insistence and Celia of all people knew this too well. If she had been in Lisbon recently, she may have taken a boat trip and someone might have seen her. She loved the water and often boasted of her many excursions on the noted rivers of the world. If there was a chance she'd been here, then that ship had definitely sailed.

Palmer chuckled at his own wordplay, noting that Celia would not have approved, and looked around at the terminal. A modern concourse of shops, vending machines and at the far end, a bank of ticket turnstiles which led to the docks themselves lay ahead of him, but with no sign of the Yellow Bus signage. He had plenty of time and although his shin was starting to nag again, he limped back along the riverside to the last tour bus stand he had seen, hoping for some direction as to where to go. A French family were testing the language skills of the young man in the stand and Palmer found it interesting that he could understand exactly what they were saying whereas anything said in Portuguese was a complete riddle. They were attempting to secure an O.A.P. discount for the elderly in-laws travelling with them. Palmer chuckled again at the use of the word '*anciens*' which he supposed was apt for the wrinkly white-haired pair ahead of him. Even though he had half an hour still, the family were slow to make their purchase and it irritate Palmer's patience and his knee.

By the time he reached the front, he was ready for a sit down. Not even attempting to try anything in the native tongue, he simply jabbed at the boat part of his leaflet, showed his tickets to indicate he wasn't wanting a purchase and pointed towards the water. The young man smiled politely and directed him to a large advert for the tour company as part of a barrier running along the waterfront. He explained that he should wait there and just before the time, a door would open to the Yellow Bus company's own jetty. There was nowhere to sit remotely near, so he chose to take his chances by hobbling over to a bench near a small wooden pirate ship which seemed to be designed for children to clamber about on and tourists to mug in front of for their photos. Sitting and watching the busy traffic on the river, Palmer's mind began to wander again. It was crazy to think that he had been in the city for less than 24 hours and had already added so many new conspiracy theories to his notebook. He rifled through it as he waited, purposefully avoiding the first three-quarters, and it seemed to make him feel better, going over the familiar, taking a fresh look at the unfamiliar and adding new notes and ideas such as Stuart and his strange mood swing.

He looked up from his notes to see a yellow boat ploughing and surging through the choppy waters, seemingly very close to the landing point but in reality probably a good fifteen minutes away. The air had cooled across the afternoon and on the blustery river front, was practically chilly. Palmer hadn't packed anything remotely wintery or even autumnal he thought and on reflection should have donned his waterproof jacket much earlier to protect himself. If it was worse on the boat, he resolved that he would definitely put it on. He got up and limped back to where the hidden door was located, noting that the French family were also advancing upon the position from the other direction. As he reached it, he heard chains clinking and a pleasant-faced young man with a designer beard and the tightest skinny jeans Palmer had ever seen opened the door and bolted it in place. He said nothing, but Palmer assumed he should now enter and was relieved when other, faster walkers overtook him along the jetty. The boat was just riding the last few waves and boat hands were leaping ashore to tend to ropes and ramps and the man who had opened the door now stood and smoked two cigarettes in quick, efficient succession. Palmer felt a pang for nicotine he hadn't felt in a while but wondered if his craving was in reality for something else.

A woman in a bright yellow jersey checked his ticket and he joined the now considerable sized group waiting to board. They were on what Palmer realised was a sort of pontoon bridge which was rocking and swaying affected by both the breeze and the restless waters. It was instantly nauseating and Palmer wondered how he would cope on the boat if the jetty were this bad. Thankfully, they weren't left to lurch for long as the passengers already on the boat were allowed to disembark before a cordon was removed and the fresh travellers allowed to board. He followed a snake of people who headed from the dimly lit but warm lower cabin up a narrow wooden series of steps to the chilly upper deck which had a quaint tiki bar and commanded great views of the river. There had been a further set of steps to the uppermost deck, but this was chained off from public use. Palmer took a seat on the side of the boat adjacent to the dock, unsure which direction the boat was going to move off in, but there were plenty of vacant seats should he choose to move. He needed a few moments to get use to the rocking of the boat before he began his visual investigations.

The boat was a bit low-rent for Celia, he noted at first. The white paint on the upper deck was peeling in some places and spattered around in others where a slapdash painter had clearly thrown speed before efficiency. The seats were cold and hard and metal with no hint of comfort to them and Palmer remembered his mother's insistence that one could contract piles sitting on such surfaces. A young man in a yellow fleece popped up behind the bar, hardly the bow-tie wearing waiters of fine travel, and proceeded to boredly check his phone. A customer approached him and it seemed a massive inconvenience for the young man to put it aside and tend to the woman's requests for a drink. There were all manner of alcoholic drinks on display and the woman left with a bottle of rosé and what Palmer assumed to be plastic cups. It was far too cold to think of a boozy drink and definitely not what he needed, but Palmer would have killed for a hot chocolate to nurse between his numb hands.

A crackly P.A. system gave some muffled announcement, firstly in long, complicated sounding Portuguese, then in much simpler English which always made Palmer assume either a bad translation or that English-speakers were not being told the full story. He heard no mention of security or safety announcements and looked worriedly around, seeing no life jackets or escape routes. If the boat went down, he would surely drown. No, the crackly voice seemed to be another variation on the audio tour guide from the buses, but with no earphone jacks to channel the sound, the words were lost to the freezing air. The boat set off after a few more minutes – Palmer checked his watch to see if it was on time - and did a large circle before presenting him with the other side of the Tagus as his main view for the journey west along the river. A few passengers moved across to the other rail to enjoy the view of Lisbon itself from the water, but Palmer figured his side would enjoy that particular view on the return leg and he stayed where he was.

No, he couldn't imagine Celia enjoying such a blustery journey as this on the upper deck, but perhaps with a cocktail in her hand, cloistered away in the warmer lower deck, she might just about have managed the trip with one of her wan smiles or withering looks. The barman being young and attractive might have tipped the balance for her too. He was now leaning over the bar flirting outrageously with a dark-haired girl Palmer hoped he had previous form with or else he or she were fast movers, and Palmer could definitely see Celia enjoying some graceless innuendo with him and his charming ways. Palmer felt like getting up and ordering a drink just to break up their little love-in, but he decided instead to ignore them and take in his surroundings.

The other side of the Tagus looked not to have the geographical fortune of Lisbon, with some rundown looking warehouses, abandoned shop fronts and a fragile block of flats looming over all, before the dark forested mountains swept in and finally the ever-watching statue of Jesus which seemed to be at the top of a dizzying plinth on the hilltop. The deafening sound of traffic roaring over the *25 de Abril* bridge made Palmer feel tiny as they passed under the gigantic construction and one of the humongous cruise ships he'd seen earlier that day loomed ahead, further dwarfing both the tour boat and its occupants.

Everyone around the upper deck was now standing, taking photographs of the bridge, the cruise liner and the statue of Jesus and Palmer felt no one was looking his way, so he got out his mobile phone and quickly flicked through his texts until he reached the one from an unknown number which had landed in his inbox just as he was composing himself for the flight in the Manchester departure lounge. It was a selfie of Celia, although there was something off about the image, as if it were not really taken by her, only made to look like it was, or as if someone else was cropped out that was actually holding the phone. There was no way of knowing when the photograph was even taken, but whoever had sent it to him had wanted him to ponder over it, as there was no accompanying message and the number it was sent from wouldn't connect. The reason he had consulted the image now was based on a suspicion he'd had after zooming in on the image to maximum magnification and pondering over the strange ruddy brown struts behind Celia's craning head. From the earlier tour bus, he'd felt it was possible it was the underside of the bridge, but he hadn't dared check his phone as they passed, with Stuart so close at hand. Now, with no one to look over his shoulder, he could directly compare. The background matched. The shadow that had fallen over Celia's face in the image was the same as the stripes of darkness now falling over Palmer. He felt he could even make out tiny vehicles in the background of the photo, barely visible through the meshed underside of the road bridge, now that he knew what he was looking at. Celia had definitely been on a boat, if not this very one.

Feeling a strange sense of accomplishment which actually meant very little in the scheme of things – he was no nearer to finding who was sending him these strange clues, nor any closer to proving what had become of Celia – he pocketed his phone, sat back and enjoyed the rest of the cruise, marvelling over the riverside view of the *Torre de Belem* and the *Padrao dos Descobrimentos*, wondering what those who disembarked at the Belem stop were going to do and if they knew this was the last return journey and finally, as the boat turned around, enjoying the majestic view of the city as the sun began to dip, igniting it with a furious golden glow.

He had become lost in his pleasure and barely noticed the boat nearing the original jetty and looked around to see that the barman and his girl had disappeared, possibly together and that other passengers were gathering their bags and coats and moving towards the stairs down. The boat was making some wild motions as the crew tried to moor her in and the water seemed rougher than ever. Palmer got up in a leisurely fashion, partly due to the sickening movement again, but mainly because no matter how much he rushed, he would be one of the last, if not the last to disembark anyway and began to distract his lurching stomach with thoughts of his plans for the evening. Whilst he couldn't truly focus on food, he thought of his lovely hotel room and of possibly ordering some room service before retiring for the evening after a long and tiring day. As he reached the steps down, he noticed that the upward steps which had previously been chained off were now open. Perhaps the barman had snook his girl up there to better enjoy the view, Palmer mused and his curiosity got the better of him. He climbed up just the first few steep steps, figuring he'd either be chastised unintelligibly and returned to the public part of the boat, or else he'd catch a glimpse of what was up there and not need to progress further.

His head poked out above the upper level and he saw no sign of the suave barman, but instead saw the bright pink ankles of someone standing right at the edge of the steps. The feet were pointing away so Palmer knew he hadn't been seen, that the person was looking out across the river and he edge up another step to see. Above the legs were lemon pastel shorts and a flowery shirt. Above that, a bright pink neck which had caught too much sun. The freckled arms were tipping the contents of a rucksack over the side, into the river, now unseen by anyone on the boat who was either down two flights of steps waiting to get off, or heading across the rocking pontoon bridge to solid land. In the rucksack were clothes mainly it seemed and they drifted down in the breeze, out of sight. What a strange way to dispose of unwanted garments Palmer thought, noting that they were all female items and that the man was furiously emptying the sack as quickly as he could. The man glanced around and Palmer, in his haste not to be seen, slipped down three steps at a time, landing hard on his knees. He quickly dragged himself back to his feet and lumbered down the flight to the lower deck, his heart pounding as it would burst. The boat crew were ushering the last few passengers off and he took in two things as he hobbled towards their bemused faces: firstly, that as he spied a pink skirt flutter past the window, that no one had been looking in that direction at all, everyone must have had their eyes on the gangplank and a swift exit; secondly, that the man on the top deck was not a member of staff as all the crew had yellow fleece-like jerseys on.

Palmer knew that man and he knew those clothes. Even though he hadn't seen his face, he felt certain that yet again, it was the red-headed man from the metro and that the clothes he'd been dumping overboard belonged to Celia Payne.

9.

But what on earth could Palmer do about any of this? A man haplessly throwing clothes off the top of a tour boat sounded as silly now, hours later in the quiet of the street the hotel was on as it had done when he'd first pondered what action to take. He had simply stepped off the boat somewhat robotically and marched as best he could over the pontoon bridge without once daring to look back. The red-haired man definitely hadn't seen him, nor could be seen from this side of the boat. Whatever his plan was, it wasn't to disembark immediately although Palmer couldn't see how he could hope to remain on board. Surely the crew would check the boat before taking it back to whichever dock or boathouse it was stored overnight in? Perhaps the man was known to the crew after all, but why then would he have sneaked up onto that upper deck, looking suspicious as hell, hurriedly disposing of the contents of that rucksack at the one point on the journey that no one else would see him?

It was definitely not something he could report to the police, even if he could overcome the embarrassment of trying to explain in his complete lack of Portuguese who he was, his connection to Celia and what exactly he thought he had seen on the boat. Raising the issue of the man also having shoved him down some stairs the night before seemed an overcomplication too far. He wished he had someone to share his wild thoughts with as simply recording them in his notebook tonight was not going to cut the mustard. Stuart was the most obvious candidate, but his lack of follow-up interest after the sighting in *Parque das Nacoes* and the strange change of his temperament later on made Palmer return to his usual state of isolation.

He reached the highly polished glass doors of the hotel and stopped abruptly.

Sitting in the foyer, reading a local newspaper, was Stuart. He hadn't seen Palmer yet and wouldn't, if he could sneak in, but it was a good five metres to the turn off to the lifts and if Stuart were to look up for just a moment, he would catch Palmer looking shifty and evasive. He could keep his head down and feign ignorance were he caught, or he could just pass on by, find somewhere nearby to eat and return later, when Stuart had retired to his room. He hadn't entirely believed the builder's yelled revelation that they were staying in the same hotel until now and whilst he yearned for someone to confide in, now was not the time.

Keeping his head down, he continued past the doors, past the next hotel and on down the road, crossing over to where the children's park and the cycle path began. Whilst he hadn't noticed any restaurants in this direction on his dark and drizzly trudge last night, he hoped to stumble across something quick and easy before his leg or his will gave in. Possibly the fashionable kiosk could prove a good source for a bite to eat if he could remember where he'd seen it, and muster up the nerve to navigate past the cool-looking kids sitting around it. Thankfully, this evening was drier and away from the waterfront, fairly mild and after making a few hasty turns which didn't look at all familiar, he found a dark and deserted street with a swanky looking restaurant on one side and a more reasonable pizzeria on the other. Back at home, the restaurant would always have been his choice, but once more the terrifying idea of navigating a foreign menu and staff who couldn't understand him was too much and this street was just far enough away from the tourist trap that it might be harder to rely on multilingual options. At least pizza names were generally the same around the world, he fathomed, mostly a variation on Italian. He managed to get himself a table, order a four-cheese pizza with a bottle of Sagres and pay without too much fuss or embarrassment. The pizzeria was quiet, with what seemed to be mainly locals minding their own business and staff who showed little interest in who he was or what he was doing.

Returning to the hotel, Palmer was pleased to find the lobby empty, with just the same man who'd checked him in the night before on the desk and the trickling water which made Palmer feel like he needed the toilet. He hurried to the lift entrance and jabbed the summon button, standing with his back to the doors as they opened, should there be anyone he wanted to dodge as they emerged. Even with his back turned, he could sense the lift was empty and he hopped in and rose to the fifth floor. On exiting the lift, he could immediately sense that something was wrong. His room door which was just a few steps from the lift, was wide open and both flickering shadows and scuffling noises were bouncing down the hallway.

Palmer was rooted to the spot with fear, but also anger that someone had broken into his room and violated his space. He edged to the doorframe and was able to see that the door had not been forced in any way and that the card holder where you placed your room key in order to activate the lights had a card already in it. Whoever had let themselves in, had done it with a key and was still there, caught in the act! His initial instinct was perhaps an opportunistic hotel employee misjudging the time of his arrival, possibly having watched him from the windows of his room which overlooked the main street he'd just walked up. Shaking, he shuffled down the hallway, not entirely sure of what he was going to do once he rounded the corner and caught the intruder in the act. He had already taken a savage beating before flying out to Lisbon and had not expected to face more violence, certainly not in what he had considered the sanctuary of his hotel room. A terrific rustling of papers and knocking over of items confused Palmer as he really hadn't thought there was that much in his room to disturb.

Going against every fibre in his being, he reached the corner and before he had really rounded it, he called out "Hey!" hoping to avoid confrontation and scare the invader away. The sight that awaited him almost made him laugh, it was so incongruous. In the pleasant, warm light of the plush room was a figure dressed in camouflage army gear, a jacket and matching trousers flocked in forest-like shades of green, with a black balaclava on their head. The mouth visible in the ragged hole was cruel and snarling and definitely more like that of a man, and the eyes glinting in the mask were angry and wild. The figure froze in the act of shaking the contents of a holdall onto the floor and glared at Palmer, menace oozing from every pore. Palmer's plan extended no further than his cry and the hope that the robber would turn and flee, although this would mean having to come at him, or worse, through him, to the exit. A moment passed which seemed like an eternity during which pure hatred radiated from the invader and fear seeped from Palmer, despite his pretence of aggression.

Finally, the intruder let out an animalistic howl and charged straight at Palmer, catching him totally unawares and dashing his head against the wall. He crumpled to the ground, his knee sending blinding flashes to his pain receptors and his eyes rolling back in his head. The figure stamped over him, heavy shiny army boots coming down like cannon balls on Palmer's groin and chest before he fled down the hall and out of the door, slamming it shut as if that were an end to their meeting. It took Palmer minutes to force his eyes open, clear the sickening spots which dotted before his face and try to adopt a comfortable sitting up position. It felt as if his knee had completely popped out of its socket although he knew that was highly unlikely and his groin throbbed and his chest felt like he'd been stabbed. He needed either a stiff drink or a splash of cold water, or both, and so limped to the nearer bathroom to try and revive himself, preparing himself for the view in the mirror which would no doubt be shocking.

He wasn't wrong. His normally-light-brown face was red and blotchy and he had a nasty red patch on his head where the skin had broken against the sharp corner of the wall and was threatening to bleed through. He ran the taps and dabbed himself with cool water which did a lot to lower his temperature and anxiety, but nothing to improve the physical appearance. Rolling up one of the smaller bidet towels, he moistened it and lightly dabbed at his injured head. He then reached for the bottle of painkillers at the side of the sink and tossed a few into his hand, then his mouth, washing them down with more water. It was only then that he remembered that he still needed to buy painkillers, having not brought any in his hand luggage. He looked down at the shelf at the side of the sink where unfamiliar after shave, deodorant and a toothbrush stood. These were not his things. He dashed back to the main bedroom. Scattered on the floor were clothes, papers from a leather holdall and money which was spilling out from a brown envelope. These were not his things either.

This was not his room.

10.

Staggering back out onto the corridor and making every effort to touch nothing on the way, he looked at the hotel door which now swung to behind him, the folded up 'Do Not Disturb' sign having been used to prop it open but now symbolically giving up. 507 said the door. Palmer winced. His room was 502 and he now realised that he had previously taken the other of the hotel's two lifts, stepped across the corridor and found his room whilst tonight he had taken the other which led to a similar, yet crucially different aspect of the fifth floor landing. He dashed around the corner to where the other lift opened up and spewed forth a group of chattering Portuguese women. If they saw him, they didn't acknowledge him and continued to their two adjacent rooms, next door to Palmer's actual room of 502. He was reeling from the head wound and the general shock and although he'd accepted that the intruder wasn't raiding his hotel room, it seemed just another awful coincidence that he'd stumbled upon him. There was no way on earth he would report this crime, even though he'd been an innocent bystander, as it was too strange to fabricate a reason for him to be in the wrong room or to explain just how he'd gone into a room he thought was his but uncovered a burglar.

No, he would retire to his own room to calm down, take a proper look at his head wound and rest his inflamed knee. Whoever 507 belonged to would have to sort out their own mess and if the hotel had recorded the criminal on CCTV, then and only then would Palmer step forward to explain his appearance on the footage. If he'd disturbed the robber before he got what he wanted, as it had seemed, then perhaps no crime would ever be reported and the matter would end with a disgruntled Trip Advisor review about problems with the housekeeping staff.

Palmer got out his wallet where he'd stashed his hotel key and blindly let himself into his room. He staggered down the identical hallway, almost tensing himself to find the balaclava-wearing maniac mid-rummage, ready to attack him on new turf. But the room was empty. Tidy, sparsely showing evidence of there even being a guest, let alone an intruder and empty. He flopped down on the bed and kicked off his shoes. He hadn't realised his feet even hurt until he did this, perhaps the act of freeing them from the shoe made them awaken, or perhaps he'd simply got enough pain elsewhere in his body and they hadn't stood a chance of being noticed earlier. He threw his shoulder bag onto the bed next to him and lay back on the duvet, shuffling until his legs and arms could spread out in a star shape. He closed his eyes and the world went black.

He awoke, confused, momentarily forgetting where he was, as he always did in hotels, panicking that things were not where they should be and that the light felt all wrong. It was dark outside and only a bedside lamp was on, so he initially feared it was the middle of the night rather than just an hour or so later. Checking his phone, he saw that it was nearly a quarter to eleven and that he'd received a couple of texts and emails whilst he was asleep. The first text was from his mother: brusque and strangely formal as always, asking about his health and progress with her strange level of detachment in message form. The second was from the same unknown number as before. It simply said:

'ENJOY THE TRIP?'

He again tried dialling the number, but it wouldn't connect. Someone was definitely watching and taunting him. It had to be the red-haired man and whilst he was certain he hadn't been spotted when he saw him on the boat, the man could easily have seen him riding around on the bus after he'd encountered him at the ticket stand that morning. 'TRIP' was vague enough to suggest any mode of transport at a stretch and Palmer even wondered if it could refer cruelly to the shove he'd been given down then metro station stairs. His mind flashed back to the camouflage-wearing burglar and he mentally tried to match the man's stature and demeanour with the red-haired man. It was definitely not a match. The burglar had been much stockier, perhaps shorter too and his eyes had been dark and cold unlike the red-haired man's pale blue eyes. So there were two men possibly interested in physically harming him now wandering about Lisbon. He had done nothing to conceal which room he was staying in following the attack and it only now occurred to him that far from fleeing down the cobbled streets into the night, that the intruder could simply have hidden around a corner and waited to see where Palmer went, before returning to silence him. Well, an hour had passed and no silencing had yet occurred. The text had been sent during that time, but that made no specific reference to the disturbed crime, so it had to be unrelated.

He tapped into his emails and found he'd received the usual spam from Amazon about their deals of the day, a petition appeal about genocide somewhere in Africa and something he'd been waiting for a long time. His old school friend George Davis had finally replied to him after some weeks, with a very short and direct email which made him smile. It said:

'Palmer old pal,

Been terribly busy, sorry for delay. Finally checked and Celia's ex was admitted to Avondale Row as you suspected. Dates match.

Keep in touch,

G.D.'

George was a psychiatric doctor who lived in the Peak District, not too far from the Sheffield area where they'd both grown up and gone to the same high school. He was a pleasant enough man, although terribly unambitious which annoyed the hell out of Palmer as he was far too talented to waste his time dealing with the sorts of smackheads and loons who he dealt with on a day-to-day basis as part of his job working for a mental health crisis team. He could have done anything with his life, but was content to assist the disturbed and helpless for what must have been terrible hours for a decent enough wage. George was also one of the few friends Palmer had maintained after school and university and they met up from time to time to drink real ale, tell the same anecdotes about their youth and discuss the state of the world today. Palmer knew he had no true affection for the man, but he somehow anchored him to his past and the real world in a way which no one else did or could. He had asked him to discreetly check the whereabouts of one Gerry Payne, Celia's ex-husband around the time of Celia's disappearance as he knew the police weren't interested in pursuing the man and wanted to know why this was, what his cast iron alibi could be. It seemed from George's email that Gerry had been staying in the mental health hospital known somewhat anonymously as Avondale Row. Whether that stay was voluntary or involuntary, Palmer had no idea and he wished to press his friend's professionalism no further by asking more.

If Gerry was out of the picture when Celia upped and left, then he was another dead end of investigation, although for a time Palmer had nursed the budding idea of the woman's mentally fragile ex having had a psychotic break and kidnapping her, possibly even doing her in once and for all. It fitted neatly in Palmer's mind, certainly more neatly than any of the other possibilities, but this at least explained the police's apathy in investigating Gerry further. The man was a crackpot, but not a dangerous one.

Palmer reached for his notebook and added his latest updates. He made sure to take screen grabs of both the text and the email as back-ups and got up to look out of the window at the street below. There was no sign of a police vehicle and as he ventured onto the corridor, he could hear no signs of investigation. All he could hear were the muffled screams of the excitable guests in the rooms next to his, even from around the other side of the lift shafts. If he could be bothered to, he would complain about the noise. As he was about to turn back and possibly retire for the evening, he heard a familiar voice from down the corridor.

"'arry?"

He froze and grimaced. It was Stuart, now seeming bright and back to his chatterbox self.

"Well, well," replied Palmer, adopting a false smile. "You weren't lying about being in the same hotel then?"

Stuart was carrying bags from various souvenir shops and had a dopey grin on his face.

"Course not, mate," he said. "I told you, I saw you this mornin'. Funny that you got off at the wrong stop last night. If I'd known where you were stayin', I'd've told you!"

"I know, I'm a fool," said Palmer, starting to move backwards. Stuart had been about to let himself into his own room when he called out to Palmer and he didn't want to have to make an excuse as he sensed a coming invitation.

"Fancy a quick drink?" Stuart asked, before Palmer could take another step. "Either in 'ere, or down in the bar, if you prefer?"

Palmer allowed his inner hidden grimace to show on his face now. "Sorry, Stuart, I've got a banging headache and my knee's still no better," he said, not entirely lying. He'd made sure to put one hand to his temple to illustrate the half-truth, but also to cover up the missing chunk of his head.

"I won't keep you!" cried Stuart, beckoning with his head for Palmer to come in as he opened the door and stood with it open. "Just a quick one. Please."

He wasn't taking no for an answer and his big fat face looked suddenly saddened at the idea of rejection. Palmer had no guilt about rejecting him, but did feel perhaps that he should humour the man, possibly find out what he had been up to that afternoon and also have a drink from the builder's minibar rather than his own. Palmer relented and headed towards him, casually noting the room numbers as he passed. Stuart broke out into another happy grin as he stepped aside, bowing slightly to let Palmer go first. Palmer tried not to react as he noted the room number on the door: 507. The room he'd been in just an hour ago. Barely even reacting, he swept to one side of the dimly-lit hallway, holding the edge of the open door to allow Stuart to pass him. There was no way he wanted to be the first one into that room if he could help it. Stuart laughed a throaty laugh and inserted his card into the card holder on his way. Interesting, Palmer noted, that the holder was empty.

The lights flooded the room and as Palmer followed Stuart around the corner into the bedroom proper, Palmer was bemused to find no trace of the earlier intrusion. Had he mixed up room numbers again?

"How weird you're just up the corridor from me here in 507!" said Palmer, gritting his teeth at the clumsiness of his statement and realising now that he was inviting the chance to share his own room number.

"Yeah, innit just!" replied Stuart, missing the obvious opportunity to ask.

He put down his bags on the dressing table and stooped to open the minibar below it. He reached in and pulled out two bottles of Sagres which he opened and held one out for Palmer who had lingered by the corner at the end of the hallway. Palmer noticed a few flecks of blood on the paintwork, his temple flaring with pain as if to corroborate the evidence, before moving to accept the drink.

"Cheers mate," said Stuart, sitting heavily on the edge of the bed and tipping the beer in his direction for an imaginary clinking before he swigged greedily.

Palmer looked around, already knowing there was nowhere else to sit but the bed as the sole chair in the room was by the dresser, even closer to Stuart than the other side of the bed would be. There was something odd about being in a hotel room Palmer always found, especially someone else's as despite attempts to put in desks, armchairs and so on, it really boiled down to the fact that it was a bedroom, a room that ordinarily only those most intimate with you would be permitted and here was, sitting in that intimate location with a near-stranger.

"Cheers," Palmer responded, realising he'd left too long in his response and it now sounded odd. "Did you have a good afternoon?" he asked, segueing into

54

his interrogations.

"Not really mate," said Stuart, taking another hearty swig which almost emptied his bottle. He hadn't been kidding about it being a quick drink.

"Oh?" said Palmer, favouring economy of words.

"That's what I wanted to talk to you about really," said Stuart, putting down the bottle on his bedside table despite there still being another half-gulp left.

Had his miserable afternoon been capped by returning to find his hotel room ransacked and a stripe of mysterious blood on his wall and yet he'd still ventured out with bags of souvenirs in his hand for some reason? None of this stacked up. Either Stuart or the hotel staff had tidied his room or else the intruder themselves had done so. Stuart seemed vaguely troubled, but not 'someone's broken into my hotel room' troubled, and he'd been despondent hours earlier for another reason entirely.

"Oh?" repeated Palmer, his eyes working overtime as he scanned the room for some further clue that the earlier burglary had even happened.

"Yeah mate," said Stuart, now becoming visibly distressed. It was possibly to see the very thought processes going on in his head as he struggled to vocalise his feelings. "We need to talk about Celia. I know what you did to her."

11.

Palmer sat in his own room, shaking uncontrollably, feeling furious with himself for losing control. He limped to the minibar and took out two small bottles of wine, one white, one rosé and managed to stop shuddering for long enough to uncork both of them with the complimentary corkscrew before glugging out the contents of the white first into a glass. He reached for the glass, had to stop as his jittery hand threatened to slosh the contents everywhere, then gave himself a quick, frustrated pep talk.

He was being ridiculous, feeling anxious and fearful over nothing concrete. He hadn't heard some big devastating revelation from Stuart, nor had he got anywhere closer to solving any of the many mysteries he sought to untangle, but what he had discovered had still sent him into a spiral of tremors and gut-gurgling which he needed to settle before he could decide what to do. He held out his hand to see if the shaking had subsided enough to reach again for the glass and decided to go for it anyway, taking a huge swig, nearly draining the glass in one movement. His stomach made sounds of protest but the booze had an almost immediate effect of lowering his tension, in the same way a cigar might have done were he out on the street. He was collected enough to pour more wine, draining the small bottle and topping up the rest of the glass with some of the rosé instead. Heathen, he thought to himself before quaffing the mixture too.

Looking at his phone, he saw that it was half-past eleven and he suddenly felt very tired and very drunk. Adding up the various drinks he'd consumed today, he realised he'd had enough that evening to certainly get him merry, if not tipsy as he now felt. He reached for the television remote and flicked it on, the channel still being the classic British sitcoms of yesteryear channel and him being rewarded with an episode of "*Last of the Summer Wine*". He'd have turned it straight over, or off, back at home, but here, strangely cloistered in his plush hotel room in a strange city with much to mull over, it stayed on in the background and whilst his eyes occasionally took in the vaguely amusing antics of the geriatric ne'er-do-wells, his mind was firmly on recent events.

Stuart had gone from being an amiable travelling companion and occasional saviour, to a full-on problem in just one brief, awkward conversation. Their strangely tangled relationship was far more complicated than a new accidental friendship and Palmer wasn't entirely sure what to do about it. The builder had revealed that he had first spotted Palmer in the airport departure lounge and recognised him from a salacious story in a tabloid newspaper some months ago when it had been suggested that he had much more involvement in Celia's disappearance than he would admit. It was all entirely fabricated of course, full of innuendo, hearsay and 'a source close to the missing woman' style gossip. Thankfully, a mildly spicy story of a missing teacher, her ex-husband, their mutual friend and a drunken night on the tiles didn't make for much of a headline story, being a few inches of tittle-tattle sandwiched alongside bigger scandals of celebrity gropings, political downfalls and the ever-popular speculations on Brexit. What the paper had managed to do, which had offended Palmer the most at the time, was to source a photograph of him, Celia and Gerry which must have been from Celia's own social media pages and this had led to an uncomfortable discussion at work about whether he needed some personal time to deal with the goings-on.

Palmer had never officially been a person of interest in Celia's disappearance as he had no official ties to her, hadn't been the last to see her and had what he considered a rather cast iron alibi for the hours after she was last spotted on CCTV waiting for a taxi. The authorities had been more of the opinion that she had taken off, with searches of her flat revealing she'd taken most of her clothes and make up apparel with her, or at least, someone had removed them from her flat, if not her. A friend of Celia's had vouched that she had seemed keen on taking a break, just getting away from it all, somewhere warm, but it was just unfortunate that she had chosen to disappear without telling anyone exactly where she was going, when she was coming back, without taking her passport and right before a new school year without any warning.

Stuart had had his memory jogged by the latest development in the story, that of the red-haired man on the front page of his newspaper, and had stuck close to Palmer, managing to swap seats to sit next to him on the plane and spurred on by morbid curiosity to find out more. He'd shame-facedly admitted to noseying in Palmer's things whilst his eyes were closed, to see a hotel booking headed 'Sana Hotels' and gently probing to try and find out more.

He'd then stuck close by him, and even changed his hotel booking once he'd deduced which branch Palmer was staying in. If Palmer had paid more attention to him on the plane, he might have realised that the man had nervously contradicted himself several times, and the burly builder confessed that he was basically a bullshit merchant of the highest order, capable of spinning lies as easy as he could plaster a wall or knock up an extension. Worse than that, he admitted to having a macabre interest in real-life crime and whilst his trip to Lisbon had nothing to do with the Celia Payne disappearance, he had quickly decided to make it the focus once he'd spotted Palmer and had conspired to get close to him and learn the truth if possible.

Palmer had a million questions to ask in response, the biggest of which was a huge, bewildered "why?" which he never vocalised, but he had across a few tense minutes learned that Stuart had watched him leave the hotel with the Yellow Bus tour leaflet, then pursued him at a distance, keeping behind or on parallel streets, able to cover distance more quickly than he could limp, and making it to the bus stand ahead of him. Palmer had pressed him about the man in the queue at this point, unable to believe that he hadn't truly known the red-haired man was behind him, but Stuart was so embarrassed and apologetic that whilst Palmer was loathe to trust the man, he seemed to genuinely have no idea why he was asking. It tickled Palmer, deep beneath the confusion and anger, that an amateur sleuth had missed a key player in the drama in such a hilarious fashion, but he didn't elaborate on his reasons for asking. Stuart was many things – a slightly sad and obsessive fantasist for one – but Palmer couldn't imagine him being involved in the disappearance itself, or with the red-haired man either. He was just too odd and open with his emotions to be capable of hiding any further revelations. Palmer had realised that his sudden mood change that afternoon had been through guilt, of realising Palmer was no more a secretive killer than he was and through the angst at needing to tell him the truth.

No, Stuart was a bit of a loser all told. A man who spent hours at the gym each evening in lieu of any relationship, who then went on to eat unhealthily, spoiling his fitness progress and explaining his strange body shape and stayed up half the night visiting conspiracy theory websites and trawling through online discussion groups about unsolved crimes or miscarriages of justice. He lived alone, worked six days a week and had few friends. His trip had only been because his current employer had forced him to use up some of his holiday days before the year end and he'd been advised that Lisbon was pleasant at this time of year by one of his online acquaintances. He'd ended his awkward confession by stating that he genuinely didn't believe Palmer had anything to do with Celia's disappearance, but if he could be of any help, Palmer had only to ask. He felt he owed it to him, the builder had said, for misleading him and being generally a little stalkerish. Palmer hadn't felt the man needed to apologise or to make anything up to him, as after all, he himself had told enough lies, not the least of which had been telling him his name was Harry when surely he already knew it wasn't. What Palmer had felt though was exhausted. Mentally and physically. He didn't even want to poke at the particular hornet's nest which was the room mix-up and break-in, so he excused himself in as few words as he could and said that he might see Stuart tomorrow, but not to expect anything.

Whilst Palmer believed Stuart's new version of events and had already googled the full name given to him – 'Stuart Evans' – and found a Facebook profile which displayed the same burly face and piggy eyes as he'd just left in room 507, he had mixed feelings about associating with the man any further. He hated people who lapped up the scandal and drama of true crime and scoffed at the racks of magazines in newsagents devoted to the topic. He had enough going on in his life at the moment without dealing with a stalkerish hanger-on, but on the other hand, Stuart was into this kind of thing and might actually help with his investigations and was certainly a considerable asset to have on-side, should he need protection. He decided he would sleep on the matter and was about to strip off his clothes and roll under the duvet when he heard a faint scraping sound, like someone rubbing paper against stone. If he'd been at home, he would have assumed it was a leaflet sliding through his letterbox, so he leapt up painfully and turned down the hallway to the door.

On the floor, clearly having just been slid through the tiny gap between the door and the floor was a pamphlet. Surely not junk mail, here in a nice hotel? He stooped to pick it up and saw that it was a flier for the local custard tart emporium '*Pasteis de Belem*' which he recalled passing near to on the afternoon's bus tour. Strange for someone to post this under his door. He had thought to visit the district if the weather were fair tomorrow. He flipped the leaflet over and on the back, scrawled in scribbly red biro was the message:

'Tomorrow. Meet at noon.'

He doubted Stuart Evans would be so cryptic, not when he was hoping to still keep Palmer onside and be a part of his investigations. No, this was from someone else, someone who knew Palmer and more worryingly, knew which room he was in.

12.

Palmer watched with grim amusement as Stuart returned to the breakfast buffet for a fourth round of browsing. For some reason, the plates on which one could help oneself to food from the generous array of dishes were smaller than the saucers on which their oversized coffee cups sat but that didn't stop the burly builder from loading his up until he had to slow to a crawl to prevent anything slipping off the side. He had already devoured a hearty plate of scrambled egg, salty bacon, hash browns and for some reason, broccoli and carrots, along with hot buttered toast and more bread on top of that, and now returned with his inadequate plate heaped with Danish pastries. Palmer had nibbled on some granola with yoghurt, had a glass of some sort of carroty fruit juice and was enjoying another refill of his coffee cup when his companion sat down and began to tuck into his next course.

"What?" asked Stuart in mock surprise, the exact same reaction he had had at the second and third helpings. He had a goofy sheepish expression on his face and was enjoying the food and the company.

Palmer had lightly rapped on his hotel room door at 6.55 that morning, knowing full well that Stuart would be up and dressed and waiting for a sign that he was at least temporarily forgiven for his odd deception and sort-of betrayal. Like a puppy who has forgotten his training and befouled the hall carpet but still waits expectantly, eagerly for his master, Stuart may as well have had a wagging tail when he answered the door.

"Am I forgiven, mate?" he'd asked excitedly. "Well, 'arry, am I?"

Smiling at his use of the Christian name he surely knew was fake, Palmer nodded, trying not to give away that he saw that there was very little to forgive.

"And I can 'elp you out?" he continued. "A bit like yesterday only with both of us in on it this time?"

Again Palmer nodded, not wanting to make too much out of it. He trusted very few people in life and the two of them beginning their relationship by both lying about their intentions was not the healthiest of starts, but for some reason he saw Stuart as a simple, genuine person at heart. The deception had obviously pained him, hence his mood change in the afternoon and he'd quickly confessed and offered to help out. Two heads were better than one and Palmer didn't doubt that Stuart could handle himself if things got sketchy and the red-haired man resurfaced. Palmer still hadn't confided in him about the message he'd received last night, nor the encounters with the strange redhead who seemed to be stalking him as frankly, it all seemed a little too odd and unnerved him to dwell on it.

He'd needed no convincing to get Stuart on board for a trip to Belem, briefly noting it was a possible place to look for Celia and saying no more. Stuart was so keen to be involved and make up for what he saw as a terrible betrayal of trust, that he didn't ask at all about the location itself, only about their method of reaching it. Palmer had intended to walk as little as possible when planning this last night, but on waking that morning, had found the pain had all-but-subsided and so he proposed they walk part of the way, taking the route to the Basilica past which the Yellow Bus Belem line passed. Stuart was very concerned about Palmer's mobility, needlessly so, he thought, but it was strangely refreshing to have someone to fuss over him that wasn't his nag of a mother.

"I'll just eat these and we can get off," said Stuart, almost apologetically as he tore apart one of the pastries with his big bare hands and stuffed it into his huge mouth. "I dunno what's wrong with me today. I'm bloody starvin'. Must be the thrill of the chase, eh?"

Palmer nodded, hoping his new sidekick was going to take things a little more seriously when push came to shove and he was needed, although on reflection, did Stuart or even Palmer himself truly know what they were walking into?

The walk from the hotel was pleasant and as it was still barely 8am, the streets were quiet and bathed in the first light and warmth from the rising sun. Stuart despite his massive size was a fast walker and he was dressed for adventure it seemed, wearing a tan shirt with khaki cargo shorts and sturdy boots. If he'd topped the look off with a fedora, Palmer wouldn't have been surprised, but would have had to say something. He wore a leather shoulder bag, something a lot more fashionable than Palmer's and the words 'man bag' floated into his head as he contemplated it, and sunglasses which were sitting on his on the top of his head until he needed them. Palmer was wearing his dark jeans again from the day before, having packed very little in the way of clothing, and a sober grey shirt which he had made one concession to the heat and location with by rolling up the sleeves. Palmer found that Stuart was incredibly useful when it came to map reading as not only could he instantly track their progress, but he could memorise their options and apply them to the reality they were presented with, which often differed from the tiny dots and lines on paper.

Stuart was also capable of making Palmer feel incredibly at ease by distracting him with the most mundane conversations which had irritated him on the plane when he wanted nothing but peace but now actually helped to take his mind off the whirling mess of conspiracies which presented themselves to him. They discussed all manner of topics as they made good progress towards the busy Pombal roundabout at the end of the *Avenida da Liberdade*, from the housing market to what box sets were good on Netflix, all the time avoiding anything too specific or personal. Palmer loved it. What he didn't care so much for, despite the company and the lovely setting, was the random topography of the city again, where a left turn took them down a desperately steep slope down followed by a right which required them to ascend something nearly vertical. He could see why the city relied so much on trams and elevators to get around.

If he hadn't trusted Stuart's navigation skills, Palmer would have stopped several times over, surreptitiously checking his map without anyone seeing and doubling back or crossing over until he could read a familiar street sign. With him in the driving seat, their wending, winding path down some seriously narrow streets and seemingly far away from the beaten track didn't seem so dodgy, and they rounded a corner which presented them with the dome of the Basilica before it reached 9am. There was the small matter of a park, the *Jardim da Estrela* – or garden of stars – to traverse before they reached their destination and as Palmer's shin was beginning to needle him, he suggested a brief rest on one of the lovely park's benches. There was some sort of school sports day going on in the park and the noise of excitable children echoed around the twisting paths which occasionally were taken over by hordes of small giddy runners keen to beat their peers or a couple of teachers with a makeshift finishing line temporarily closing the way in order to set up another race.

As Palmer sat and began to subconsciously massage his knee and shin, he found Stuart's eyes on him, watching with concern and a degree of intrigue. He found he could ignore him for a few minutes as he pretended he didn't know he was being scrutinised and watched a group of titchy girls squabbling over a race result, but after a while it became necessary to address it.

"What's up, Stuart?" he asked, ramping up the joviality and even managing a half-grin.

"Oh, nothing, 'arry," replied Stuart. "'Cept, I was wondering how you 'urt your knee. I mean, I know you fell down those stairs, but you were already unsteady before that…" He trailed off, now slightly embarrassed. "…And obviously, there's the bruises and so on…" He jerked his head as if identifying Palmer's facial injuries.

"I was mugged," said Palmer quickly and for once, truthfully. "Last week. In Rusholme. Some hoodie with a knife and a smack habit no doubt, demanded I give them my phone and wallet. I suggested he politely fuck off and he headbutted me, threw me to the floor and stamped on my leg."

Stuart winced as though the pain were his own. "Rusholme, eh?" he said sympathetically, as if the very name of the Manchester suburb were enough to explain a brutal mugging. Truth told, you could be mugged anywhere in Manchester if you went looking for it, as Palmer had. "Been there mate. A gang of twats in Levenshulme 'ad a shooter one night and tried to tax me phone and a laptop bag."

Palmer couldn't hide his shock and seeing it, Stuart broke into fits of throaty laughter.

"I knew it were fake," he explained. "Little shits. I were on me way back from the gym after work and just sorta flexed me muscles a bit to scare 'em off."

He laughed again and Palmer knew that he wasn't being cocky or arrogant, but was very matter-of-fact about the incident.

"Did they catch the bastard that did that to you?" asked Stuart.

Palmer shook his head. "I didn't report it," he said. "Wasn't worth the trip to a police station if I'm honest. Once I was on the floor, the guy panicked and ran off. Didn't even take anything in the end."

"'ospital then?" asked Stuart with concern.

Again Palmer shook his head. "Same deal," he said. "Too many queues and questions. Just limped home, took some seriously strong pain killers and slept it off like a hangover."

Palmer didn't add that he'd made sure to take lots of photos of the horrific-looking injuries as the beautiful colour palettes of the bruises had blossomed or that he'd made sure both Mr. Singh in the local off-license and his snotty neighbour Mrs. Clarke had got an eyeful of his shambolic, hobbling self without giving either the chance to ask what had happened. That, he had left to their imaginations.

Stuart looked concerned again and pointed at his leg.

"You should let me have a look at that, mate," he said. "I've done enough damage when I've got carried away trainin' to know what's bad and what's not. You might be doin' more damage ignorin' it."

Palmer imagined for a moment the scenario in which he would either painfully try to roll up his stiff jeans or else take them off and sit in his underwear with this hulk of a man so close at hand, in order for him to look closely, or worse, to touch his bare and battered flesh. How close would Stuart be sitting or standing to do this? Would he be kneeling in front of him, worry etched into that blunt, fat head of his? Palmer felt a frisson of something unexpected and shrugged off the offer.

"It's alright thanks Stuart," he said. "I'm coping now. It's been a while. Although, this-" Here he pointed to the missing chunk of his temple. "-This is a brand new one and partly your fault."

He had already decided he needed to explore what had happened in Stuart's hotel room last evening and his segue here was not as awkward as he'd expected it to be.

"Whaddaya mean?" asked Stuart, raising an eyebrow.

Palmer proceeded to tell him all about his room mix-up and the balaclava-wearing intruder and how he'd left the room in a daze, sorry that he'd helped himself to someone else's painkillers and bloodied one of their towels but hoping that whoever the room belonged to would understand his accidental presence there and possibly even be grateful that he'd disturbed the thief in his ransacking. He ended by explaining how he'd fallen asleep and returned hastily to see what was going on, leaving the onus on Stuart to now explain what he already knew. Whilst Palmer had spoken, Stuart's face only showed surprise and now it was his turn to contribute, he looked confused more than anything else.

"I literally got back to the 'otel as I bumped into you," he said. "I'd wandered around the *Baixa* bit of town tryna take me mind off 'ow I'd just followed you around like an ambulance-chasin' weirdo and ended up in a few bars. I got mildly pissed to put it bluntly, ordered some disappointin' food, bought some questionable souvenirs and got a taxi back to the 'otel. Me openin' the door when you were there was the first time I'd been back to my room."

"So someone, possibly our camouflaged thug, went back to your room and tried to tidy up," theorised Palmer. "And they definitely had a room key to do it." He paused to let that idea sink in with Stuart. "The question is, was this random or not?"

"'ow'd you mean?" asked Stuart and Palmer feared he would have to launch into a lengthy explanation of the red-haired man and other possible parties out to hurt him or frame him or worse.

"I just mean that the first night, in the metro station, I was pushed down those stairs, Stuart. I didn't trip."

He could see the alarm in Stuart's face now and he looked around the park, as if sensing that they were in a lot more danger than he'd thought.

"You sure mate?" he asked, not sounding as if he doubted Palmer per se, more that he needed to hear the reassurance.

"Definitely," said Palmer. "You've met the man I think did it. That Scottish man in the bus queue yesterday."

Stuart's jaw dropped at this revelation, but his eyes were not on Palmer anymore. He was staring off across the park, beyond where the teachers were now giving out some medals to some of the race winners.

"He seems to keep popping up around town," Palmer continued. "I don't know what his angle is exactly, but he's up to something. He's potentially quite dangerous."

Stuart didn't reply. He was still gaping.

"Look, I'm sorry if this is a lot more trouble than you bargained for," Palmer said, wondering just how to break the builder from his spell. "He's something to do with Celia I think, I'm certain he's the man on the paper you had with you and he was on a boat..." Palmer stopped, getting annoyed now. "Look, are you listening to me, Stuart? That man is-"

"That man," interrupted Stuart, now raising one hand to point across the park.
"Is 'eadin' directly for us."

13.

Jon Scott Campbell wept openly and bitterly into his hands. People were beginning to stare at him now, but he didn't care. Moments earlier, an elderly lady with a head scarf wrapped tightly about her had approached him and bravely reached out with a spindly set of fingers towards his shoulder, but sensing her near, he had shrugged away and continued his silent convulsing. She backed away, startled by the intensity of his outpouring and shook her head to the others who were standing watching her bold effort as if to say he was beyond help. He was sitting, cross-legged in the middle of the arrivals lounge at the Humberto Delgado airport and had been silently rocking and shivering for close to ten minutes now. The airport was quietening down for the evening and the bulk of travellers were in the departures area ready to catch their evening flights. Far fewer people were trickling through from the later arrivals and even fewer waiting for them in the dimly lit hall. It had taken a few minutes for anyone to notice the distressed man and a few minutes more for anyone to consider doing anything about it.

An approaching security guard took the arm of the elderly lady and they conversed intensely for a few seconds as she gave both her report on the man and his response to her intervention and still unsure whether the man was dangerous, he radioed for assistance. The last thing anyone needed was an airport evacuation over a man who had possibly drunken too much and was feeling sorry for himself, and yet the alternatives and potential scenarios for loss of life didn't bear thinking about. Watching him over CCTV, the man had walked in, carrying no baggage or visible weapons and looked at the arrivals board. He had then sat for a while looking at nothing in particular, before getting up, checking the board again and pacing. Finally, he had picked up a discarded newspaper and just moments later, had slumped to the ground and begun his strange, sad outburst. The guard received word that he should approach the man with caution and so he called out a few times to get the man's attention. He tried at first in Portuguese, then in English. As he switched languages, the sitting man looked around in alarm, saw the guard and sprang to his feet. He sprinted blindly ahead, skidded to a halt looking for an exit sign and then disappeared. The guard gave chase half-heartedly but came to a panting halt at the main doors, seeing the man disappear into the falling darkness.

The reason Jon Scott Campbell was so upset was complex and surprising, not least of all to the man himself and he could only theorise in his frantic subconscious that it must have been something like the fugue state he'd experienced earlier that year and that he shouldn't dwell on it too much for fear of triggering another bout. He finally came to a halt when he reached a busy series of roundabouts leading out of the airport and certainly not a route for a pedestrian. He'd darted across a road or two, dodging a taxi's powerful headlights and risking both injury and the driver's wrath, and now needed to reassess his situation. He looked around and saw no possible sensible route other than to head back to the airport. No one seemed to have followed him and aside from maybe scaring a few people, he hadn't committed a crime as far as he could see. He trudged back across the network of roads he'd barely registered during his flight and decided to veer off towards the metro station rather than risk nearing the airport entrance.

He hadn't taken the underground rail system to arrive at the airport, favouring a slightly expensive and bowel-clenching taxi ride, and found it odd than in all his time in the city, he hadn't once ventured down any of the inviting stairways to explore the metro. Back in his hometown, he always used public transport and whenever he visited London, he enjoyed the thrill of descending the steep escalators with their warm gusts signalling a tube's arrival. Here in Lisbon, he had stuck to wandering about on foot, occasionally taking a taxi when needed and a boat ride on the river on one or two occasions. He found the metro station airy and light compared to those of other cities and seemingly a lot newer and better designed than most. He had no intention of taking a train although it would certainly pass the time he now desperately wanted to speed up or disappear.

Jon was an impatient man at the best of times, hot-blooded and short-tempered and prone to fits of pique when things didn't go his way and his pink face would flood with red at the slightest test of his nerves. Right now, without the benefit of a mirror, he couldn't see that his face was glowing crimson but he could feel it, a palpable heat emanating from his tingling cheeks and rising from the top of his head. He raked his fingers through his hair which was damp with rivulets of sweat and wiped his hand disgustedly on his shorts. He had dressed in a hurry and hadn't put much thought into his outfit, not that he ever truly considered fashion as a high concern before leaving the house, but tonight he felt slightly foolish in his selection of shorts as the temperature had dropped. He looked a lot like a tourist which was the last thing he wanted to do, but equally, he had seen no mileage in disguise or deception. He sat down on the edge of a bench, which caused the fussy-looking couple further along it to get up and move on in somewhat of a huff and wondered if he looked as bad as he felt.

He took out his phone, only to look at his reflection in the black surface and saw that he had received a couple of texts and missed a call. *Julie and Jeep no doubt.* Ignoring them for the moment, he looked at his dark mirror image, seeing an angry-red blotch of a face beneath a fiery shock of hair. This was no different from his usual reflection, but he did acknowledge that tonight he looked particularly unapproachable with teary stains down his lightly freckled cheeks and a tiny dried trickle of blood at the corner of his mouth from where he had bitten his lip so violently and repeatedly as he often did when frustrated. He would have got up and moved if that furious scarlet demon of a man had plonked itself down next to him with no warning. He licked his thumb and dabbed at the dried blood, gurning slightly as he twisted his face to check if he'd wiped it clean. Looking up he met the inquisitive eyes of a frizzy-haired girl being dragged along by a stressed-looking father. She was gawping, mouth open as if she'd never seen such a sight and whilst Jon knew children could be harsh in their judgments, he didn't appreciate it and poked his tongue out at her. Shocked, she tugged at her father's arm, babbling something to him that Jon couldn't hear and he didn't hang around to see if the parent paid attention, heading back up the steps into the chilly evening air.

A group of worn out students laden with bags of what looked to be souvenirs were dragging their wonky-wheeled cases towards the main entrance as Jon reached the top of the steps. He paused to watch them repeatedly try and pull the bulkiest of their cases without it tipping one way or the other, as if resisting the journey, desperate to hang on and not have its holiday end. Being a helpful man and also unable to watch someone making a hash of something like they were, Jon's instinct was to dash over and help them sort out the wonky wheels and get safely in the airport, but as he contemplated the gesture, he saw the security guard from earlier, standing beyond the glass of the main doors, deep in conversation with a colleague. The last thing he needed was to be chased away from what he had come to do, especially being a good Samaritan, so he watched the students struggle and tried not to laugh as one girl got in such a tangle that she tripped over her own feet and dropped her bags, spilling the contents across the ground. Postcards, a bright cuddly fish which Jon assumed was a sardine and some miniature bottles of liquor clattered across the concrete and the other girls shrieked and giggled. The lead member of the group barked something suddenly and urgently from the head of the pack, most likely that they were late for their flight, and the remaining girls tried to gather together the spilled possessions. A light breeze had caught some of the postcards and after a couple of attempts, the girl who had dropped them gave up and let them skitter away. A second even more urgent cry came from the group leader and the girl now grabbed her things and ran inside. She hadn't noticed her hat had fallen from her head in the kerfuffle and this too was abandoned to the night.

Jon walked over to the first postcard which had blown in his direction and saw it was of the *Castelo de Sao Jorge*. He stepped lightly on it to stop it moving away and knelt to pick it up. The next was only a few yards away, so he made a move. This card was a more generic 'highlights of Lisbon' card with images across the city in glorious sunshine. Again, he halted its wind-blown progress and pocketed it. He was now only a few feet away from the girl's hat, which was an oversized straw hat, something incredibly touristy and reminding Jon of something his drunken old aunt would have brought back from the Costa Del Sol when he was a youngster. He looked at the terminal entrance and saw no sign of the guards or of the students, so he bent and picked it up, putting it straight onto his head as if it had been his all along. He turned quickly to leave the scene and saw the head scarf woman from earlier who was now joined by a very sober-looking husband. She was chattering away to the man and he pulled her away from Jon's direction, nodding as she no doubt described the sobbing, hat-stealing lunatic who had lashed out at her in the arrivals lounge.

The hat fit and the old adage agreed, so Jon sauntered back across the windy plaza feeling lifted by his newfound acquisition. He'd always felt an immense thrill when stealing and even though this was more salvage than theft, it made his pulse race slightly to know that someone somewhere would eventually be missing the object he now possessed. He felt very silly for his breakdown not half an hour ago and strutted cockily in an arc around the front of the terminal, no longer feeling the chill despite his too-short shorts and lack of coat. He knew he was something special, was close to achieving his mission for the day and it now gave him a surge of confidence to imagine the look on his target's face when they locked eyes, just like that, across the distance. That whimpering wretch would get what was coming to him, if not now, then very soon indeed and Jon's heart would swell like a soaring balloon. He was so busy swaggering around the edge of the taxi rank that he hadn't kept an eye on the doors.

A steady stream, not quite a surge, of people was coming out, meaning that a flight had recently landed, most likely the flight he was meant to be monitoring. Crossing the edge of the shadowy plaza, he spotted his mark emerging from the doors and looking around for where to go next. Clueless as ever. Jon smiled a devilish grin and crept after him with murder in his eyes.

14.

Heart pounding and lungs searing with pain, Jon hadn't even looked back
once or stopped at one of the many roads he had crossed, instead heading
away from the airport as fast as he could. If a road was busy, he ran along it
rather than cross it. If lights were green for him to cross, he did so, without
considering where he would end up next. Before he knew it, he was far from
the airport, on a well-to-do looking *avenidas* with villas set back from the road
and pretty gardens. Swiss chalet style homes ran the entire length of the
considerable tree-lined road ahead of him and Jon instantly calculated where
he was. He course-corrected and skipped to the next junction, heading towards
what he thought was the *Teresinhas* district of the city. He had never travelled
on foot from the airport or passed through these *freguesias*, but he knew if he
reached the more familiar *Campo Pequeno,* the way from there would be
more familiar and less frantic.

There were few people out on these streets at this hour but the odd car lazily
crawled along the street, each time making Jon question whether someone was
already onto him, something he knew was ridiculous. No one was following
him and certainly not in a car coming from the other direction and he allowed
himself a brief rest, leaning on the low white stone wall of one of the
impressive houses at the end of the street. He was young and fit and quite used
to crazy early morning runs and sprints on a number of different terrains and
so this was no trouble for him, aside from his too-short shorts chafing around
his crotch and the hat and sunglasses, the former of which had fallen from his
head outside the metro station, as if the airport wouldn't let it leave, and the

latter which he'd hastily stuffed into his breast pocket in order for him to see where he was hurtling. He could see high-rise buildings looming on the horizon but the street itself seem to stretch on to infinity.

Before he made to set off again at close to his fastest pace, he remembered the texts and missed call on his phone and took out the device to check. In his fervour to complete his task for the evening, he'd completely forgotten them. The first text was from Julie, his homely but utterly dull wife. The second, much to his delight, was from Matilde, an incredibly sexy waitress he'd got chatting to in a restaurant in the city centre. In all the excitement, he'd forgotten about her, but an erotically charged vision of her drifted back into his keen mind, with her curves, her figure-hugging uniform and her gorgeous dark tresses of hair which she kept flicking around playfully. Jon was always on the lookout for a beautiful face, particularly one who was so easy and hedonistically minded. Anything to take away from the sheer drudgery he faced each night with the woman he should never have married. Jon now felt the blood rushing somewhere else entirely and staved off further thoughts of the desirable woman, simply re-reading her text one last time:

'Will you meet me again tonight? Xxx'

Regretfully, he hadn't seen the message until hours after it had been sent and whilst Lisbon and many Mediterranean cultures would not see the current time as being especially late and probably early yet for a good night out, Jon knew it was far too late to arrange anything with her. He cursed his timing and hoped that she had not met another admirer this evening to replace him. He would reply once he'd got back safely, he decided. Julie on the other hand, required an answer. He could hear her vaguely moany tone which was often said with such an innocent look on her face, but could never be read as anything short of passive aggressive to the point he often had to leave the room to avoid wanting to rid himself of her. Her text read:

'Take it you're not coming home tonight. Would've been nice to know. Dinner is ruined. J x'

It was the kiss at the end which really irritated him. Sure, she had every right to be annoyed at his sudden elusiveness and horrendous punctuality, but to add the final snide comment about dinner then end with the initial and the kiss was just part of her terribly boring routine. He could have called her earlier to let her know his plans and he could have called her now to reassure her. Instead, he simply jabbed at the screen and sent a brusque reply:

'On my way. J xxx'

He never usually sent so many kisses, but it felt like an active way of pointing out how stupid her own sign-off was and he knew it would cause her to make that little tutting noise she was so fond of or else that small, impotent sigh which signalled her annoyance at having to give up on something. By refusing to elaborate any further, Julie would take this as a sign that he had won his little power game and she should stand down for the evening. He wasn't going to tell her where he'd been or why and he wasn't going to give her a specific time for getting back, just in case he had second thoughts and swung by the restaurant Matilde worked in. But the bistro was all the way down in the *Bairro Alto* area, the opposite way to that Jon was supposed to be ultimately taking and he still doubted the lateness of the hour. Besides, he would definitely need to change out of his shirt and shorts which now felt quite sweaty and not the garb he would normally don for a night on one of Lisbon's fashionable streets.

Feeling smug at his response to Julie and aroused by Matilde's interest with him, he charged at breakneck speed along the endless *avenida* until he left behind the tranquil suburbs and finally came to a row of twee pink buildings on one side of the road and a wide open gully between the office blocks and apartment blocks which signalled he should veer off to the right. He knew this area better than the last, glancing up at a sign which read *'Avenida Sacadura Cabral'* and within minutes he'd arrived drenched and developing a stitch facing a line of pretty, uniform trees beyond which he could see the exotic domes of the *Campo Pequeno*. From here it was a fairly straightforward route down the *Avenida Da Republica* to the *Saldahna* area where he needed to meet his contact before retiring triumphantly to Julie.

Jon had run several marathons in his time, thriving on the painful training regimes he threw himself into, the hours he could spend out of the house getting race fit and then there were the overseas jaunts to participate in the best marathons the world had to offer. New York, Boston, Paris, Berlin. You name it, Jon had run it. He loved the near empty feeling which took over his body as he pushed it beyond its physical tolerances and the zone his mind settled into which separated the mental from the material and allowed him to push through into the final stretches. Then there was the buzz he got from the cheering crowds, making him feel like the celebrity he'd always felt he should have been which finally sent him into raptures. Right now, as he ran at full pelt along the glistening cobbled streets, he could have been in mile thirteen of twenty-six, feeling like a superhero, like nothing and no one could touch him. Even the rain which suddenly started to come down in curtains of bejewelled misery couldn't spoil his mood. He looked up at the dark sky as he ran, letting the raindrops fall into his eyes and refresh him, before wiping them clear and coming to a halt at his destination.

The street was deserted and only eerie pools of lamplight lit the way ahead. The darkness which had fallen over this part of the city was consuming and intense. Even the lights on the opposite side of the street seemed a million miles away and the gloom in front of Jon concealed the edge of the park that he knew was there. Lurking at the fringe of the dark was his contact, tossing a cigarette end into the bushes. Jon felt immediately serene. The figure in shadow was briefly illuminated as a lighter flashed and another cigarette was lit and nodded across the street. Jon looked in the direction suggested and saw the warm inviting lights of a hotel. The Sana Reno.

15.

Jon slept soundly and felt not only refreshed, but somehow supercharged, invigorated by last night's goings on. He woke to the slamming of the door – Julie leaving without saying a word – and padded about in the apartment in his underpants, something his wife would have shaken her head at. Sunlight streamed in through the apartment windows and he could smell fresh coffee in the kitchen. He was pleased to see the cafetière three-quarters full of strong coffee. Julie was many things, but she was dutiful. She would probably even text or call later to apologise for her behaviour last night and her leaving without speaking to him this morning. Jon poured himself a thick black mug of coffee and added a dash of skimmed milk until the ebony liquid was suffused with mahogany clouds. He took a sip and was pleased to find it had cooled just enough to drink quickly. He drained the cup and poured a second, emptying the cafetière, then prowled around the kitchen looking for something to sate his raging appetite. Thinking about it, he had missed dinner and only had a light lunch of salad and after the number of calories he must have burned during his late-night run, no wonder he was hungry.

Sitting on the sofa with a tin of tuna fish, he ate his strange breakfast in short, robotic mouthfuls until he felt his stomach signal it was happier. On the coffee table in front of him were an array of Julie's banal lifestyle magazines – all in English. She was hopeless at languages and always reasoned that most people spoke English anyway, so what was the point? She relied on Jon's own excellent grasp of Portuguese whilst they were in Lisbon and had similarly depended on him in other world cities they had visited. Jon often left her at home when he travelled either on business or as part of his globe-trotting series of marathons, but sometimes he just couldn't shake her off. Thankfully, they lived separate lives most of the time and Jon was glad of having his own room, even here in the rented apartment. He had been able to sneak in late, noting the light showing beneath Julie's bedroom door and slide into his bedroom, taking a much-needed shower in the en-suite. It made sense for him to have the master bedroom after all.

Amongst Julie's magazines was an awful low-rent women's magazine full of real-life stories which were generally horrific in their nature, presumably to make the readers feel better about their own miserable existence. Stories like *"I married my rapist!"* and *"Dead on our wedding day!"* screamed sensationalism and little tact. What caught Jon's attention was a headline which read *'I didn't murder my wife!'* and it made him smile. He made a mental note that he would thumb through the magazine later, purely for research purposes and check out the article. Who hadn't considered murdering their wife from time to time?

He finished his odd breakfast and dumped the mug and tin in the kitchen for Julie to deal with then returned to his bedroom. Catching sight of himself in the full-length mirror, he couldn't help but take a moment to admire his lean physique. His pale pink skin was mostly covered with freckles and red hair which he trimmed on his chest and waxed elsewhere, but aside from that, he thought he was in excellent condition. He worked hard at the gym and on the running routes he pounded, to maintain nice pecs, firm abs and lean thigh muscles. His underwear was tight and had a large bulge which he knew was growing as he checked himself out in the mirror. He felt secure enough in his own sexuality to look at other men in admiration or disgust and knew that whilst he may have occasionally been aroused by what he saw, he would *never, ever* act on it. A cold shower would set him up for the day in many ways.

In the gorgeously tiled wet room which adjoined his bedroom, Jon stripped off his pants and tossed them carelessly over his shoulder. Last night's clothes were sitting on the wet tiles and he noticed the ruddy puddle of water underneath them. He hadn't quite washed all the blood away not even to the degree of fooling anyone giving the room a cursory glance, let alone a forensic sweep.

'Yet who would have thought the old man to have had so much blood in him,' popped unasked-for into Jon's mind. Macbeth, he thought. It had been years since he had taught Shakespeare but the sheer drill-like nature of getting students ready for exams meant that so many chunks of text were lodged in Jon's head, if not in the heads of the poor kids. A scene of the eponymous hero and his wife came sharply into focus and Jon was certain he was right. He knew who would definitely have known the answer, but she wasn't around

to question.

He gathered together last night's clothes along with his recently shed pants and took them back through into the kitchen where he set about trying to find a bin liner to put them in. Julie knew where everything in the kitchen was and she was always moving things around to give herself something to do, something to proudly announce on his return to the apartment as if cleaning a cupboard or rearranging a drawer or two were the height of her achievements. He finally found a roll of black bags under the sink and stuffed the yellow shirt, pinkish shorts and undergarments in, all now splashed with the reddy-brown water. He had no idea what day, if any, the bins were emptied around here, but he knew plenty of places he could offload the offending bag. Lisbon was full of building sites and skips at the moment, he thought cheerily.

His shower was long and languorous and he couldn't help further arousing himself under the torrents of warm water, deciding against a cold shower, thinking about Matilde's supple young body. When he finally set about drying himself and getting dressed, he noted that it was almost 9am and he should probably think about heading back into the city centre. He had no idea where Julie had gone so early – possibly the nearby supermarket, or else for a walk along the river somewhere – as her normal excursions were purely shopping-related and nowhere would be open at the time she had departed. Perhaps she had met one of her awful friends for breakfast at some pretentious café or maybe – here Jon stifled a laugh – she had left for good, run off with another man, a handsome bronzed and bearded local. Jon thought of Aleixo now for some reason, the chiselled man who serviced the apartments who had flirtatiously introduced himself to them both as they arrived, standing bare-chested in the beautiful afternoon sun with a tool belt around his waist and a rakish smile on his face. Not Julie's type at all.

Jon selected a pair of mint green shorts to wear today, the same cut as the salmon ones from the previous night and remembered the sexy sales assistant at *El Corte Ingles* saying how much they suited him and him choosing four different coloured pairs out of sheer vanity. He liked how much of his muscular legs they showed off but knew they were quite impractical in anything other than blazing sunshine and that the sales assistant would have said anything to get a sale. Julie had hated them, he could tell, not that she would ever have said so, but he caught her eye-roll in his peripheral vision. She'd have been happy if everyone wore polo necks, trousers or maybe even a burka. She hated showing off her body outdoors and wasn't especially keen on showing it off indoors either for that matter. Annoyingly, she had a good body for her age, which was part of what had drawn Jon to her. She was trophy-wife material and looked good on his arm, but he'd soon found her to be offensively devoid of personality, not even having the accidental hilarity of some of the bimbos he'd attached himself to previously. Jon completed his look with a Hawaiian shirt he'd bought in Florida, a rather loud number, but far from being baggy, it was skinny fit and showed off his body, especially his tight biceps.

Finally leaving the apartment at 9.15, snatching a designer flat cap as he spotted it hanging on the back of a chair on his way out, Jon was pleasantly surprised to find it was a glorious day. The sun was already beating down its welcome rays and there were no signs of the drizzle of the previous night. He quickly hailed a taxi and during the ride kept an eye on the driver's choices of streets as he always did, knowing that some taxi drivers around the globe would see a tourist and their lack of local knowledge as an easy way of making extra money on a needlessly complicated route. Luckily for this driver, he took the fastest route, knowing which roadworks to avoid and didn't extend the journey beyond what was required. Jon almost felt like tipping him, but didn't. He never tipped. Exiting the taxi he merely said a cheerful 'obrigado' and put on his sunglasses.

The *Praca do Comercio* was already starting to come alive with tourists flooding down the many *avenidas* which led to it and stopping to marvel at the sunny, open plaza with its beautiful columns and archways, vivid yellow paintwork and impressive statue of King Jose I and the mighty Tagus beyond. Jon took a seat at an outdoor table at a glossy new bar restaurant on the corner and enjoyed another coffee as he waited, with a perfect view of the square. As he wondered how long it might take to set up the next part of his plan, he felt his phone buzz. Jon may have been of the generation who lived via phones and social media, but he could easily go for hours without checking his phone, something which he knew irritated Julie, although again she never vocalised her annoyance aside from her blunt texts. He realised he hadn't once looked at his phone since last night and was pleasantly surprised to find two messages from Matilde and one from Jeep.

The first Matilde text was from 1am, around the time she'd probably got in from either a night out or a late shift and it simply read:

'Too busy Jon? Matilde X'

He could imagine her delicate fluttering eyelashes and pout as she playfully, jealously said this out loud to him. He had completely forgotten to reply to her other message last night either, but it hadn't deterred her and the second message was from 7.25am, most likely once she had woken up and found she had still not heard from him.

'I slept alone and sorrowful. Call me. Matilde XX'

Where she'd picked up that particular turn of phrase he had no idea, but he loved the idea of her being 'sorrowful' over missing a date with him. She was sexy and needy in all the right ways. He decided she deserved a response, despite him not being fully sure of his plans for the day and evening.

'Sorry Matilde, was working late with phone off. Would love to see you again. Jon XX'

He knew she'd believe him, her wide chocolate eyes were pools of innocence and he enjoyed the idea of corrupting her a little, slowly at first with his lies, then finally in the bedroom. Smiling at the thought of her hot brown body on top of his, he had taken his eyes off the street, but now looked up to see a queue had formed at the Yellow Bus company stand. It was time to act. Someone at the stand spotted him and waved eagerly across the road. Jon cursed the lack of caution and borderline idiocy and sprinted over the road to get the ball rolling on the next part of his plan.

16.

The *Feira da Ladra* was a sun-drenched paradise of the rare, the collectable and the downright bizarre and Jon whiled away a pleasant morning of browsing at the many varied stalls at the flea market. Even his raging impatience couldn't alter the fact that there was nothing he needed, nor wanted, to do until later that afternoon and so he had taken a leisurely stroll across the city, passing by the beautiful tucked away *Se* cathedral, following the crazy-complex tram route up the steepening hills towards the *Alfama* district before heading on past the *Sao Vicente* monastery beneath a strange, overlooked bridge of sighs and down into the flea market which exploded as far as the eye could see in bursts of sound and colour. Stalls both official and simply scattered goods on a shawl on the pavement filled every corner of the space and Jon took his time, winding his way in a leisurely fashion around all of them.

Like a cross between a car boot sale and an antiques market, the variety of goods on sale varied from priceless looking clocks and lamps to worthless looking bits of broken watches and toys. On one stall one could purchase an array of doll limbs for a few cents, at another boxes of sinister black and white photographs from the early days of photography were stuffed with no sense of order whilst at another stall myriad plugs, cables and chargers from close to thirty years of electronics advancement were heaped with a lucky or perhaps carefree plunge into them the only way of working out what might have belonged to what. Jon paused at one book stall to look at international editions of some of his favourite novels and flicked through a Portuguese edition of a Tin Tin adventure, knowing the story well enough to translate the text even without his excellent grasp of the language.

At the lower end of the market, things were even less organised, with blankets laid out on the grass by the National Pantheon, a stately white domed building seemingly at odds with the chaos of bric-a-brac heaped on its doorstep. Here, anything went, with all manner of cheap tacky goods and random odds and ends on offer. Jon stopped to look at a hideously bad taxidermied creature which in another life might have passed for a fox. As he grinned at its leering face and popping eyes, the dark-skinned man standing by it, who may have been its lucky owner or simply exhibiting the poor creature, chuckled at Jon's interest but made no attempt to offload the beast. The way the animal's eyes, or rather, the strange glowing spheres which now replaced them, bulged in its head was obscene and reminded Jon of someone having the last breaths of life strangled out of them. He smirked and moved on.

Heading along the bottom edge of the market and then swinging back up the steep incline, Jon passed stalls selling what appeared to be Frida Kahlo motif rucksacks and whilst he found them to be cheap and hideous, he stopped and negotiated the price of one down from €20 to €10 and begrudgingly handed over the money. He then headed on up past a sequence of stalls selling strange glam rock style shoes in many eye-watering colours and styles and finally found a second-hand clothes stall. He selected a few cheaply made unpleasant blouses which he would have thought more appropriate for throwing away or turning into household rags rather than selling on to a new buyer, but was pleased that his haul including some women's trousers and shoes, cost less than €30 in total. As the jolly gap-toothed woman on the stall took his money, she began rummaging for carrier bags in which to place the sold items. Jon shook his head and showed his new rucksack. Even though he spoke fluent Portuguese, he said to her in the plummiest English accent he could muster up, "I'll put them in here. You see I'm pretending to murder my wife. She's awful." The woman nodded along, understanding he was speaking English but very little else and from his pleasant upbeat tone, that he was happy with the purchases and the arrangement for carrying them. He laughed at her and she laughed back as he left.

On his way back up and out of the market, he briefly stopped to look in the window of one of the more permanent retailers which operated out of a central building of shops and cafes amidst the unbridled craziness of the flea market proper. The window displayed what appeared to be World War II memorabilia and on closer inspection, Jon saw a whole proud selection of Nazi regalia further inside the shop. Now wasn't the time or the place for random browsing but he pencilled in a return visit for another day after things had calmed down a little. He could feel the sun starting to burn the back of his neck and decided to get out of the heat for a while, stopping at the nearest café and enjoying a cool lemonade with ice and sprigs of mint in the top whilst surveying the bustle of shoppers and tourists. By now, it was heading into the afternoon and he pondered whether to enjoy some lunch out here or wander back into the city centre where his next task took him. Nothing on the café's menu inspired him particularly, so he paid his bill and left, ogling the frumpy but well-endowed girl who accepted his exact-to-the-cent payment.

Heading back into town, his stomach began to rumble, perhaps from the brisk pace he was maintaining or the simple fact it had been close to five hours since his fishy breakfast, so he gave in and stopped at a street side café in the *Alfama* where he ordered some *pasteis de bacalhau*, native fish fritters, which he wolfed down with a glass of sweet rosé. He knew he shouldn't drink on the job, but there was something terrifically authentic about dining on the labyrinthesque streets of this part of the city which put him in a devil may care mood. He checked his phone as he dabbed at the last morsels of fish and found that Matilde had replied again.

'Tonight? M X' was all that the message read and Jon began to calculate where he hoped to be at what time, to see if he could safely arrange a time to meet the sultry girl.

He was less enthused to find a message from Julie which was so boring he couldn't even be bothered to finish reading it and deleted it before he had chance, knowing he could fob her off by stating that he'd never received it, should she later mention it or question his lack of response. He was even less happy to see his third and final message from an unknown number. It simply read:

'Fuck with me, I fuck with you.'

He read the message three times over trying to hear a tone of voice to work out who it might have been from. Jon had several candidates in mind, such was his life these days but couldn't pin it down to anyone in particular, certainly not anyone whose number he didn't have or that had his number without him knowing. He tried dialling the number, expecting nothing and was shocked when it was answered on the second ring.

"Yes?" came a deep, surly response.

"This is Jon Scott Campbell," said Jon, calmly, figuring there was no point being evasive if this person already had his number. Perhaps it was a text sent his way in error and this call would clear things up.

"I know who you are," came the reply.

Jon couldn't be sure, but the low register, beyond gravelly or smoke-ruined, sounded as if it were altered in some way by a voice changer, like something you would hear on a documentary where a participant wants to keep their involvement anonymous.

"How may I help you?" asked Jon, feeling that by staying as polite as possible it might cause the recipient of the call to lose their temper and give more away. "I received your pleasant text," he added.

"Let's get things straight, Mr. Scott Campbell," came the terse response. "The game you're playing is a dangerous one. I suggest you retire from it before you are actively retired by someone else."

Jon couldn't suppress a laugh at this. "Am I supposed to feel frightened? Threatened?" he asked, grinning at the ridiculousness of it all. "I'm not even sure I understand what you're referring to."

"Oh you know very well what I'm referring to," continued the creepy voice. "I've been watching you for some time."

At this Jon looked around, almost involuntarily. There were a few other diners enjoying their meals on the wooden terrace by the café, a few tourists meandering down the hill and an old woman with a headscarf struggling up the hill with a heavy wicker basket.

"Are you watching me now?" he asked, intrigued.

"Of course," said the voice. "Did you enjoy the *pasteis*? I find them a little bland."

Jon couldn't help dropping the fork he'd been holding in his free hand and sitting bolt upright in his seat. He quickly began to properly assess those around him, looking for anyone possibly on a phone, anyone who had been looking his way at any point during the meal, then cast his eyes further afield, to a yellow tram which had idly been awaiting a points change before clattering off, to the upper windows of the buildings on both sides of the streets which could easily have been hiding a watcher behind the distant curtains.

"Got you looking now, haven't I?" rumbled the voice.

"Look, what do you want?" demanded Jon, more irritated now at someone trying to mess with him and potentially interfere with his afternoon plans.

"I want you to stop what you're up to, as I suggested before," replied the voice.

"There's no possible way you could know what I'm up to," argued Jon knowing that even the best surveillance couldn't have tracked each and every one of his moves over the last few days. A private investigator wouldn't have the resources and a police detective wouldn't alert him to an investigation in this bizarre manner. No one could possibly have kept track of his various movements. Even Jon himself couldn't keep track for many various reasons. In addition to that, he hadn't stuck to plans, had acted on impulse, had hurtled off, turning his original idea on its head and no one could have kept up with him. No one.

"You'd be surprised," said the phone voice. "You're not as unpredictable as you like to think."

Jon got up now and walked around as he spoke, circling then table, looking who was outside his peripheral vision, scouring every last detail of the terrace and its surrounds.

"Who are you?" he demanded. "I'm willing to bet you're someone I know, given your so-called knowledge of me?"

"Who I am is of no importance at the moment," came the reply. "And you won't find me looking around so haphazardly. I'd settle your bill if I were you, I think the waiter thinks you're trying to scarper without paying."

Jon whirled around to see the little old man in the black waistcoat who'd brought him his lunch scuttling over with the bill in his hand, hoping to intervene before Jon left the café. He was muttering about the '*conta*' as he approached and Jon turned his back on him, not wanting the distraction. He lowered his voice and said through grit teeth, "Look, you have no idea who you're messing with. I'm a dangerous man." He almost believed it.

He wasn't expecting a laugh, but that's what echoed through the speaker on his phone – a deep, distorted, burst of laughter, mocking him, angering him. He knew his face had reddened as he could feel his ears burning, not from the sun this time. He could sense the waiter right behind him now and it took every ounce of restraint he could muster to not spin around and strike the little man out of sheer impotent rage.

"I suggest you take the next flight out of Lisbon," said the mystery voice. "Before things get too ugly."

Jon could feel himself shaking with rage now. He blood was boiling and he was ready to erupt.

"AND WHAT IF I DON'T?!" he roared into his phone, not caring that it startled the diners around him, made the waiter stumble back a few paces from him, made a passing woman drop her bags in shock.

More laughter followed. After it dissipated, the voice replied, "I shall be forced to rock your pathetic little world with just a few calls to a few interested parties."

Jon wanted to ask who, to ask what and why, but no words would come forth from his twisted mouth. Fortunately, the voice continued, elaborating, "Starting with telling anyone who is interested that one Celia Payne arrived in this city very much alive, although I can't say for certain that that's still the case any longer, is it, Jon?"

17.

To say that Jon's afternoon had been ruined was putting it mildly. As he stalked along the riverfront in the strange juxtaposition between the intense rays of the sun and the cooling breeze from the Tagus, he felt for all the world like simply sprinting across the dock in front of him, vaulting over the chain railing and hurling himself into the deep waters. A suicidal impulse was something new to him, usually his intense feelings of self-preservation meant he was more likely to push someone else to their doom ahead of him in order to save himself and yet here he was considering the mesmerising azure lure of the river. Behind him, above the colourful stack of waterfront buildings he could see the upper reaches of the cathedral and somewhere below, amongst the twisted streets of the *Alfama,* his nemesis was lurking, no doubt now gloating at his wild outbursts and near meltdown only an hour or so ago. Ahead of him lay the *Terreiro do Paco* boat terminal, a busy location for those wishing to cross the Tagus more for business than pleasure as the ugly ferries churned their way back and forth through the choppy waters from its jetties. Times like this, he turned to his trusted friend Jeep, but not right now.

He imagined Julie's docile, cow-like expression upon learning of his death suddenly betraying the strength of her feelings for him, now let loose despite months, if not years, of burying them. She'd try to maintain the façade of a woman who was untroubled by major disaster in her life, choosing instead to live vicariously through the scandals in her trashy magazines, but she wouldn't be able to help revealing her inner shock at hearing the news that her so-called beloved husband's bloated corpse had been pulled out of the river's depths after days of him being missing. A small twitch at the corner of her mouth or a sudden jerk of an eyebrow. The glazed-over look of a woman who medicated herself beyond what was acceptable or healthy in order to cope with life and knew more about the latest offers at the nearest mall than she did of her husband's business affairs. Jon smirked at the inevitable questions which would ensue such as why she hadn't reported his disappearance, or what she understood about the reasons for him being in Lisbon, or exactly who the lease on their apartment said was supposed to be paying the rent. It would be delicious. Almost worth tossing himself in to know it would all happen and ruin her day. Almost.

He veered away from the water's edge and headed towards the terminal. He ought to leave the city for a while perhaps, if not on the flight as his aggressor had commanded, then on a boat bound for the south side of the river where he could no doubt lay low for a few days. But before that, he needed to rid himself of his current apparatus. A bin or a skip wouldn't do this time. His stalker knew he had the bag as they had watched his every move at the café and perhaps had been following him earlier, seeing him acquire it and fill it at the flea market. The river was as good a place as any to dump it, but not on the tourist-filled quayside or the commuter-packed jetty within the terminal. Then he spied it – the sign advertising the Yellow Bus boat tour departing just ahead. He could take the boat to Belem and dump his things overboard in the middle of the vast river as they sailed. If anyone saw him, he could pretend it was an accident, that he'd lost his balance momentarily and dropped the bag. There'd be no stopping or turning back to retrieve it and sufficiently weighted, it would sink forever. It was late afternoon now and as the wind was getting up here by the water, he doubted there would be many tourists looking for a pleasure cruise.

Checking out the entrance to the boat tour's own jetty which was firmly locked and gave nothing when he rattled it, Jon reasoned that it would only open when a boat was ready for arrival or departure, but that he could easily shimmy over and see what lay on the other side. He could even possibly sneak on board without a ticket or find a good place to lose the bag without having to get on the boat. The area was momentarily deserted so with his back to the high fence and gate, he casually tossed the Frida Kahlo rucksack over his shoulder. Hearing nothing other than a muffled thump as it hit the ground, he smiled and waited for his chance to join it.

He looked around and saw a few milling people near the main terminal and was about to look the other way when he came face to face with a group of four people, two middle-aged, two old-aged, who looked quizzically at Jon as though he had just manifested from nowhere and scrutinised his appearance. The younger of the two women, her hair curly and her manner playful, asked him in French if he worked for the boat company. He realised that they must have seen him trying to open the gateway and assumed he had proper business doing so. In damn good French, he explained that no, he wasn't an employee, but if they headed back the way they'd just come to the little booth on the corner, that someone who did work for the company would be able to advise them. He wanted them to move off and give him the few seconds he needed to disappear over the gate before anyone else came along. The woman thanked him rapturously for what was little more than a rerouting and the others added their chorus of *mercis* as they turned around.

He had mere seconds with no one directly watching him, even the busy road which ran not metres away had suddenly calmed. It was a sign. He sprang athletically over the gateway and landed gracefully on the other side, the rucksack lying on the dusty ground alongside him. He grabbed it and began to jog along the path which led into a slightly dilapidated looking dock which comprised a wobbly pontoon bridge and a further area with mooring points and a small shack with the tour company logo on. Thankfully there was no one around so he continued right up to the shack and peered in at one of the filthy windows. His heart skipped a beat as he realised there was someone inside the shed, sorting and coiling various ropes and tucking them neatly onto a shelf within. He ducked down out of sight before they had a chance to turn and in one continuous movement ran like an animal on all fours until he reached a side of the corrugated metal building which had no windows.

This was the side most exposed to the wind which was really rather bracing this close to the river and as his face began to be whipped and become chapped, he spotted a small yellow shape bobbing along the river in this direction. It would take a while to arrive, but if it were to get any closer, he ran the risk of being spotted by someone on the boat or being caught by whoever was in the shack as they would no doubt emerge to greet the vessel. He ran to what was the back of the shed and crouched, catching his breath. He heard a walkie talkie crackle from inside and the painful creak of unoiled hinges as someone left the shack and then a brief one-sided conversation about arrival times and a shift change. Jon reckoned he could lurk behind the shack until the boat arrived, then once the crew were busy anchoring it or whatever they did, he could slip out unnoticed and board the boat. Ideally, although he hated the idea of the journey being busy, there would be other travellers to mingle amongst. It was then that his phone began to vibrate in his pocket. Ordinarily it was a subtle *vrrr vrrr* which went unnoticed amidst the other ambient sounds around, but here, for some reason, when he needed discretion the most, it rattled and groaned like a stuttering foghorn in his pocket.

He heard footsteps and knew that the person out the front of the shack was moving to come around to the back, but could not make out which direction they were approaching from. Taking a gamble, he ran to the fourth and final side of the shack, the one he had yet to explore and was pleased to not run headlong into anyone. The member of staff had taken the riverside way and he now heard them clicking a lighter and the pleasing sound of a cigarette paper crackling as it caught light. The crew member possibly hadn't heard him, but had rather taken the last chance for a crafty cigarette, out of sight of the approaching boat, whilst he still could. Jon took a risk and pulled out his phone to silence it.

'MATILDE CALLING' it read.

Strange. She knew full well that he was as reachable as he was and not to push things further with calls or demands on his time. For heaven's sake, his wife had been there when he first met the intoxicating girl and it was only when Julie had taken one of her many trips to the powder room, that he'd been bold enough to flirt openly with Matilde and finally ask for her phone number. She knew he was married and often not able to reply. Okay, so she didn't know the full gory details about why he was so often unreachable, but she was content with the idea that she was dabbling with an attached man and au fait with the inherent pitfalls and setbacks that presented. For her to be ringing like this, in the early evening, was odd.

He'd considered for a brief nanosecond at the café that the threatening message and subsequent call could be connected to Matilde. Possibly her own love interest taking the initiative and warning him off. He knew Matilde had a boyfriend, maybe even a fiancé. He thought it quite quite possible and indeed probable that she had many boyfriends. She seemed that sort of girl who loved new attention in as many bursts as she could get, but he severely doubted that any of her lovers would be jealous or bothered enough to track him down and warn him off. The final mention of Celia Payne had totally destroyed that idea and he realised in that moment that he would have been far happier to have to deal with a spurned and bitter love rival on his heels than what he was actually now facing.

Now he could hear the smoking crew member talking on the walkie talkie, reassuring whoever was calling that he was in fact there, just tidying things on the jetty and not to worry. The boat must be almost there. He pressed himself flat against the side of the shack and waited to see what would happen, straining to hear footsteps or the door creaking again to give him an indication about where the man was. No clues were given and the first Jon knew about it was when the crew member himself darted right past him, thankfully headed over the pontoon to the gate, most likely to open it ready for customers to enter. He was so engrossed in his task and finishing his cigarette that he didn't notice the oddly dressed tourist who had no business lurking alongside his shack. Jon watched him disappear over the swaying pontoon, his painfully thin legs and not-quite-there bottom encased in the skinniest jeans he'd ever seen. This caused Jon to shiver slightly as it reminded him of his too-short shorts and he began to feel the chill.

Not ten minutes later, there were all kinds of noises from the jetty and Jon, who had retreated back behind the shack where he couldn't be seen by either arriving tourists from land or the boat on the water, knew this was his moment. He went back around the far side of the shack to find three yellow top wearing crew members guiding the last of the queue of tourists across the gangplank whilst the skinny-jean wearing man stood and now smoked openly, clearly no longer fearing reprisals. He was a stunningly handsome young man Jon noted, with a thin beard along his square jaw and the pleasing tan which most of the locals sported and Jon found a turn on. By this point, he'd added himself to the end of the stragglers and was waiting for his turn to board and so when the skinny jeans man noticed him staring, he simply gave Jon a cheeky salute and a smile which gave away no sign of having noticed him earlier.

Jon climbed up the narrow steps to reach the upper deck but before he even stepped out on the open level, the wind blew so strongly, he realised he didn't want to sit exposed to the raw chill for an hour or more, so he returned to the lower deck and found an empty booth with such a poor view of the river that no one wanted to sit there or even near it, which was ideal for him. The voyage itself was uneventful and the deafening voice of a bilingual pre-recorded tour guide made him jump every time it burst forth from the crackly white speakers all around the ship. He knew the story of Lisbon well enough to have given such a narration himself and hearing it in two languages he understood didn't help or make the journey go any quicker. As the boat chugged into the terminal at Belem, where it would pick up its last travellers of the day, Jon waited for the departing tourists to come down from the upper deck, then went up to see for himself what his options were. There were still too many people on this deck, on both sides, meaning he would have to lay on the theatre were he to convincingly lose his bag overboard. He noticed a further set of steps leading up to what must have been the uppermost deck, chained off to members of the public, but no one was around, so he climbed over the chain and ascended.

Reaching the top, this was the perfect spot to lose the millstone that the bag and its contents had become. No one else was up here and if there had been, Jon was perfectly prepped to make his apologies, explain his short-sightedness and descend, hopefully without suspicion. This was simply a viewing deck, quite small in area and guarded around with a metal rail. Only a small two-seater bench and some sort of tall spinny funnel-like apparatus was up there and there was no way anyone lower down on the boat could see his actions.

He placed the bag on the bench and unzipped it to remove the smaller carrier bag he'd placed in once he first bought it. He wasn't overly sentimental, but he was sad to lose the contents of the bag – one ring, a silver watch, a thin gold chain and a long kitchen knife which still bore beads of dried blood. He inspected the knife, wondering just how little blood had remained on it despite the volume it had produced. Having checked everything was present and correct, he was about to return the knife to the carrier bag and stow it deep within the rucksack amongst the second-hand clothes, when suddenly he heard voices coming from the stairway up. He had no time to replace the knife in the bag and the bag in the rucksack and definitely not enough time to move or come up with a reasonable excuse, so he chose to dive behind the large funnel, still clutching the knife and carrier in hand.

He could hear breathless flirty voices, deep in their own world of seduction, broken only by a question as to the strange rucksack sitting on the bench, before he heard it being tossed onto the deck and the soft, wet sounds of kissing ensued. Jon didn't dare peer out from behind the funnel and was irritated that he knew so little about boats that he didn't even know what he was hiding behind, so he simply waited, wondering just how long a couple could kiss for in this chilly air or whether two people would really have full intercourse on the top deck of a boat. All the while, despite the freezing temperature, his blood seethed and boiled.

18.

"Marijuana? Cocaine?" hissed the shady-looking man as Jon stalked up the busy high street.

It was getting dark on the *Rua Augusta* which ran from the *Praca do Comercio* to the *Praca do Rossio* but the hordes of shoppers and tourists hadn't yet thinned out and were now joined by people preparing for a night out, looking for something to differentiate between the near-identical restaurants with their pleasant outdoor seating and eager staff. This was the third time Jon had been approached by someone looking to sell him drugs and he wondered just what it was about him that suggested he might be a potential buyer. The touristy outfit was one thing, but the look of pure thunder on his face and the purposeful way he was marching down the street would surely have been enough of a clue to leave him alone. But no, three separate men had sidled up to him and whispered not that discreetly that they had a variety of drugs to sell. The first, although Jon wasn't especially prejudiced unlike some of the people he knew, had been dark-skinned and looked like the sort of man who might sell drugs or at least be portrayed as selling them in a tawdry drama, the kind Julie lapped up. The second and third however had been far more respectable looking and Jon had been bemused by the first of these who was a jolly-looking fat, middle-aged man in a cheap striped suit, not the lithe athletic drug-peddler who would be ready to sprint away at the hint of a police siren or the revelation he was an undercover cop.

Jon had politely declined the first, actually rather stunned into reticence, but was ruder to the second and now barely acknowledge this third lad, a young, north African man who looked to have been sampling the goods from the wild

92

look in his eyes. Jon was torn between telling him to shove off, possibly in Portuguese if he could remember a rude enough term, and actually shoving him away, or acquiescing and inquisitively finding out just what the man really had to sell and how much it might set him back. He doubted the man himself had anything illicit on him, and having seen the odd American drama set in the drug-riddled projects, he imagined a network of hawkers and street rats who would relay a message along to the source before he'd finally be approached with an innocuous brown paper bag, maybe even a fast food branded one, which contained his request. Jon hadn't sampled drugs in a long time, since his university days, but he wondered just how he'd feel about poisoning his perfect body with them now. It might help with his mood and it certainly couldn't make him feel much worse. He buried these wild thoughts and simply ignored the man, pressing on until he reached the next square which opened up ahead.

He had finally, clumsily managed to rid himself of his accursed rucksack after the canoodling couple had descended from the uppermost deck of the boat, but only once the boat had practically arrived back at its jetty. He might as well have thrown the damned thing in the harbour from the docks and saved himself the hassle and the discomfort of being cramped behind the cold metal funnel, ensuring he was hidden from the view of those on the same deck but also not visible to those below. As he'd hurled the carrier bag into the inviting depths of the Tagus, he'd silently mouthed goodbye to the knife and what it had caused, such an ugly, violent act. Then he'd made to swing the rucksack over, but had forgotten it was still unzipped and the bag flew obediently over the rail but its contents spilled everywhere, forcing him to stoop and pick up every last shred of clothing and throw it separately overboard. The various coloured items of material looked very conspicuous as they were churned by the waves and frothed around in the wake of the boat. He could hear the sounds of people disembarking and hoped that no one would cast a glance back to the riverside view windows to see the strange fluttering of garments being hurled into the water. It was too late to worry about that now. For a moment he felt as if there had been a pair of eyes on him, that rising, prickling sensation on the back of his neck but as he looked around, he saw that it would be quite impossible for anyone to see him without ascending to the same level and everyone else on the boat was doing the opposite.

Having delayed so long in disposing of his things, this now left Jon with the unenviable task of getting off the boat without being spotted or questioned. He had no doubt that his appearance would be memorable to the boat hands should there be any investigating of the items thrown into the Tagus, especially trying to disembark so long after everyone else from a level he shouldn't have been on, and worse, the skinny jean wearing crew member might have his earlier memory jogged of a possible trespasser lurking around his shack should he have also caught the briefest glimpse of him there. All in all, things were not looking great and Jon also worried that if he delayed too much, the boat may in fact set off for wherever it was stored during its downtime, possibly far away from the main harbour or even beyond security fences and cameras. So, he decided to use his athleticism to his advantage and dropped over the rail which led to the upper passenger deck, avoiding the stairs for fear of being spotted. He could hear the roguish banter of the crew and as he crept to the rail which showed him the quayside, he could see them undoing the mooring ropes and sliding the gangplank back onto the vessel. Two of the crew seemed to be staying on the jetty with their skinny jeans comrade leaving what Jon estimated to be just the boat pilot and at most, two others on board. He would have the narrowest of windows between the landward men turning and leaving and the boat drifting too far away from the dock to jump and he needed to time it to perfection.

Jon realised he hadn't breathed out in minutes, crouched peering through the railing, not feeling the growing chill of evening, but tensed like a wild animal ready to pounce on its prey. Finally, as the boat began to bob sickeningly and drift from the dock, Mr. skinny jeans pulled a pack of cigarettes from his pocket and offered them around to his colleagues. They all then turned to walk towards the shack, although Jon wondered what the three of them could possibly get up to in such a small building, and Jon seized his chance. He vaulted over the railing and even though the height was much worse than he'd anticipated, he still managed to soften his impact on the hard concrete by converting his dive into a forward roll and skidding to a halt on his backside on the cold ground. He had skinned his knee on the railing he thought and it was bleeding quite profusely. More D.N.A to signal his doom, he cursed. The three crew members had gone into the shack, possibly only to retrieve belongings as he couldn't imagine them all staying in there and certainly not smoking in the enclosed space, so he figured he had mere seconds to escape. He leapt up, ignoring the blood which trickled down onto his white socks and sprinted back along the swaying pontoon and was grateful that the entrance gate had not yet been closed. As he finally allowed himself to slow, then finally stop, he sat down on a bench with a view of the river, straining his eyes for evidence of his river-bound dumping, but could see nothing in the swirling white foam left by the departing boat. He turned to look across the wide plaza at the glorious *Rua Augusta* arch which towered over everything else and invited travellers to head away from the river towards the numerous shops, bars and experiences and thought he saw someone he recognised.

A hobbling man was heading away across the busy square, not especially different from the other milling tourists and Jon had no idea how he'd even managed to single him out from such a distance. He had keen eyes, but this was remarkable. It simply couldn't be. The man he was watching grow smaller and smaller and disappear amongst the busy traffic of people, buses and trams, ought to be thousands of miles away, in England, possibly Manchester, maybe Sheffield, he wasn't sure. Jon had even felt certain that he might have been in prison by now although he had heard nothing of it in the newspapers Julie left lying around the apartment. Him being here couldn't be a coincidence though. This changed everything. Jon dashed across the square, keeping behind the towering statue of King Jose but trying to scan and locate the man as he moved. He reached the busy transport hub with its busy lanes separating him from the columns and arches of the gateway into the city and stopped in a bus shelter. There was no doubt that the man was who he had thought he was now that he could see him more closely. Limping along he had made poor progress compared to Jon's quick bursts of sprinting and it was clear to see his face as he turned to look shiftily over his shoulder before he moved on.

The man was Edward Palmer and Jon knew for certain that he had raped and murdered his former colleague and schoolteacher Celia Payne.

19.

Jon's hunch had been right all along. Things were a lot worse than he could possibly have imagined. Not even the subtle charms of Matilde could distract him from the hurricane of trouble heading directly for him. He met her for a solitary drink in a bar on the edge of the *Bairro Alto*, not too far from the restaurant she had just finished her shift in and whilst she bubbled with excitement and displayed every sign of wanting to go to bed with him, Jon's mind was elsewhere. He'd hoped that just the sight of her would settle his fluttery stomach or calm his fiery temper, but he was almost disappointed when she breezed in through the glass doors, wearing a gorgeous black dress which showed off her wonderful figure and made other men in the bar turn to ogle her. She wasn't quite as stunning as he remembered, her lips not as full, her stunningly mesmeric brown eyes seemed not to sparkle as they had in his memory. All in all, the idea of Matilde was far more desirable than the reality. He listened boredly as she spoke of the banalities of her evening shift, of a man who was so rude she had deliberately brought him the wrong order and then taken even longer correcting it, and of a trip she was thinking of taking with some of her girlfriends along the coast to Estoril that coming weekend.

All through what should have been a pleasant hour or so, Jon could only imagine how he was going to extricate himself from the tangled mess he was now embroiled in and just how much toil, or blood or money it would cost him to do so. If Matilde sensed his mind was elsewhere, she didn't comment or ask about his problems. In fact, she barely spoke of anything that wasn't directly connected to her and Jon found that she was a little more shallow than he had thought and rather self-absorbed. If he had been sitting opposite someone who displayed the signs of a troubled mind like Jon was doing, he

96

knew he would have picked up on it and probed to find the source of their problems. But not Matilde. Jon was on the verge of politely cutting short their rendezvous more out of spite than necessity, when Matilde herself suddenly stood up and declared that she had a second engagement she was running late for in *Graca* and with a quick, chaste peck on his cheek, she was gone. Jon didn't know if she had just invented the meeting or if it was a manoeuvre designed to test his resolve, but he didn't care. She could have been meeting one of the waiters he knew was sweet on her or she could have simply gone home to wait for his response, but Jon had no desire to waste time or effort on pursuing her. He finished his drink, noted that she hadn't finished her vodka tonic either, so downed that too and left.

He wandered aimlessly around the district for a while, losing track of time and direction and only coming to his senses as a tuk tuk whizzed by only inches from him as he'd inadvertently stepped into the road. He realised he had missed another mealtime but had no appetite for food at the moment, his stomach feeling like a hollow pit of bile which bubbled and frothed with anger and anxiety. The alcohol had made him lightheaded to the point that he had not been paying attention to anything or anyone around him. After his narrow miss, his thoughts cleared a little and he stopped on a street corner to take stock of where he was and where he needed to go. He didn't recognise the road he was on, but could see tram lines ahead and soon found himself at the square by the church of *Sao Roque* and able to navigate his way back to *Rossio* where he would have to make a big decision. The evening was cooler now, though not unpleasant and whilst the streets were well-lit, shadows clung to every corner, every less-traversed side street and Jon began to run again.

Barely out of breath but still in need of a rest, he threw himself down on a stone bench in the marble mosaic-tiled square. By day the square was sun soaked and bustling, by evening it was still busy, especially for a Tuesday night, but cooler and hanging beneath a strange weight of expectation as if the people around were expecting something big or magical to happen. Traffic was racing around the outer edge of the square with the swinging beams of headlamps occasionally caught Jon full on in the face and made him lower his head, the beginnings of a migraine manifesting in his head and behind his eyes. He had choices to make and not much time to make them. He quickly checked his phone, hoping that somehow someone might have been in touch with some world-changing news which would save his skin. The only message he had was from Julie. It read:

'I don't know if you're planning on coming home today at all, but if you do, please bring milk. Julie X'

Jon couldn't stop himself laughing out loud, despite the other churning emotions challenging his mind. What a bizarrely casual approach to life to be utterly fine with the idea one's husband might not return home at all and beyond that, to request that if he did, to issue an errand! Without even thinking about it, he fired off a text of his own and his finger hovered over the send button.

'If I do return home, dearest, it will be to pack my things to leave you. I won't be bringing you milk but as you are a fat, disgusting cow, perhaps you could produce some of your own. Jon XXX' he had typed.

Of course, he had no intention of sending the message, it was simply his way of channelling his loathing of his supposed better half and was part of the reason Jon rarely engaged in conversation with her, just in case feelings like this drifted from his carefully guarded subconscious into his actual spoken words. Julie wasn't even fat or particularly disgusting and she'd have been mortified at the bovine comparison but Jon didn't care. He moved his thumb to delete the message and accidentally caught the 'SEND' key. There was no way of undoing or cancelling the text and before his very eyes, the word 'READ' appeared after the offending message. *'JULIE IS TYPING A RESPONSE'* appeared, disappeared, reappeared and then disappeared for good alongside the conversation and Jon imagined Julie beginning to send him a reply which was at first outraged and shocked, then realising how silly she was and that it was obviously some sort of very clever, subtle joke of her husband's and deleting her words. She would then have re-read his insults, set to in typing an optimistic-toned question asking what exactly he was talking about, if he was okay and so on, before realising that perhaps, finally, Jon had shown his true colours and realising there was no way she could respond to his attack. She would again delete her message, exit the messenger app and put her phone away. Maybe even reach for a bottle of rosé – there was always one at hand.

Whilst Jon was simply imagining all this, he knew Julie all too well and knew he wouldn't be too far away from the truth when it came to her actual reaction to his accidental text. He had shown her his ugly, hidden true nature which so often wanted to float to the surface of his feelings, sometimes flashed behind his eyes if you caught him at the wrong moment and which he had sworn never to reveal to anyone ever again. Acting came so naturally to him, he scoffed at the appalling actors who stunk up the screen in Julie's beloved soap operas. None of them could so effectively carry off the role of certified lunatic masquerading as regular sane person and loving husband. For five years he'd convinced everyone around that he loved Julie, that he was a hard-working well-adjusted, occasionally stressed but otherwise all-round good egg and it had worn him out. Well now all that was over all thanks to technology.

He put Julie and the inevitable fall out far from his mind and focused on what mattered, what he had to begin to sort out in the next few hours. There were several courses of action available to him, all of which involved an element of danger and getting far too close to people he despised but needed something from and he wasn't sure how he could even begin to decide which option to take, or which order to attempt to do more than one of the courses. He needed advice, an ally to sound off against, to bounce ideas around with and to give him guidance, even though he utterly rejected it most of the time and found those who came crawling for a shoulder to cry on or a sympathetic ear to be totally weak and lamentable. Jeep was the obvious candidate but wasn't answering his phone. The only person who'd even come a close second to having that role in Jon's life had been Celia, his friend since the days of university and teacher training, the woman he might have married at one point, had he realised the strength of her feelings and been able to mask his own disgust at her clumsy advances and feigned the attraction he discovered she assumed was mutual. But she was gone and somewhere in the city tonight, there were three people Jon could tackle. One was looking for Celia, despite the distinct possibility she was gone, or dead. Another was trying to tidy up an unholy mess that Jon himself had caused. The third knew exactly what they had done, was seemingly playing games with everyone around and maintaining the pretence that they were entirely innocent of blame. In the next 24 hours, Jon would need to take care of all three, threatening, intimidating and ultimately killing if he had to.

But best of all, he would enjoy himself.

20.

Breakfast was a rather perfunctory affair for Jon. He ate because he knew he ought to, but Julie had not brought in any fresh groceries for a few days now and so the cupboards and refrigerator were sparsely populated with nothing he truly craved. So he sat and ate the last remaining tin of tuna fish, but feeling a sense of occasion, he tipped it into a bowl, ground some black pepper onto it and ate it as if it were the key ingredient in a more interesting meal. He would have made coffee but the cafetière was still sitting on the side by the sink, waiting to be emptied and cleaned from yesterday along with a number of other dirty plates and dishes which Jon was sure were from the day before that. Julie had seemingly gone on strike. It suddenly occurred to him that he hadn't heard from her since her text yesterday and there was no sign of her around the apartment. Out of sheer curiosity rather than concern, he ventured into her bedroom. The floor was littered with what he thought were discarded costume choices, which was something he'd seen Julie do, back when he cared enough to watch her get dressed or notice what she was wearing. She would select a dress, slip it on, look at herself for anywhere between five and ten minutes, striking different poses, looking in various angled mirrors and sometimes even taking an array of selfies with a pouting face like a teenager, before deciding she hated what she had on, sliding it over her head or down and onto her feet before hurling or kicking it across the room. Lather, rinse, repeat.

Jon couldn't imagine what purpose she'd had for being so selectively fussy about her outfit. She hadn't mentioned any plans either for the day or a tedious social gathering in the evening. None of her dull friends had called around recently or disturbed his work by phoning the apartment number and she hadn't dropped any totally unsubtle hints about needing more perfume or a new wrap or a scarf or whatever passed for fashion accessories on that particular day. She knew that Jon cared very little these days, but would not question the extra money missing from the joint account or outrageous sums amassed on the credit card as long as she had alluded to what she was going to buy ahead of time. Jon acknowledged that he hadn't paid her even the tiniest bit of attention over the last few days and that it was quite probable she had mentioned some meeting she had, or some shopping trip she'd lined up and he had failed to register it. Perhaps she had left her clothes strewn about on this occasion as a deliberate protest at his especially ignorant attitude with her, knowing that curiosity might draw him to look in her room and find the mess and begin to wonder where she was.

Sadly, Jon doubted that Julie had done the one thing he really wished she had done which was to disappear entirely. If she had gone off, in a huff or otherwise, she would definitely have taken her clothes and travelling cases and they remained on top of the wardrobe where she'd struggled to place them when they first moved in. Jon racked his brain for clues as to her whereabouts. He hadn't received any texts from her, couldn't recall hearing her presence in the flat during the night, or hearing the door slam that morning. Perhaps one of his enemies had stolen in and spirited her away. Well, more fool them if that were true.

He checked his phone and was disappointed to find no messages and no missed calls. Not even a message of reassurance from Jeep. His aggressor had not followed up on yesterday's call and subsequent threats and even the playfully needy Matilde had seemingly given up on him. Well, if today had the potential to be Jon's last day on Earth, he would waste none of it on the undeserving. A random idea surged into his brain, one of heading into the *Bairro Alto* to a certain innocuous-looking building which he knew for a fact contained a seedy sauna where the flightiest and most vapid homosexuals sought to massage one another's egos and more. If Jon was going to end up dead or wounded, or in prison, the idea he should do something outrageous, something he'd often thought about but talked himself down from in a litany of self-loathing and disgust, was very attractive. He thought briefly about a young man at university who had one night after too many drinks tried to take his trousers off and pleasure him. He remembered a sixth former he'd taught who he knew was watching him with far more than academic interest and would gossip with his female friends about what they'd all like to do with Mr. Scott Campbell. He thought of the skinny jean wearing crew member on the Yellow Bus tour boat dock. Jon realised he had stiffened and felt appalled and sickened at his weakness.

He knelt amongst Julie's garments and grabbed one at random, holding it to his face to inhale a deep draught of her perfume and possibly her natural feminine fragrance. It smelled merely of fabric conditioner and Jon knew deep down that even if it had carried her particular delicate scent, then it would have done nothing for him whatsoever. Whether it was Julie or all women, whether Jon had deeper issues than any of this, he didn't know and now wasn't the time to find out. He threw Julie's blouse to join its cohort on the apartment floor and turned and left her bedroom. He doubted he would ever see his wife again.

As he was preparing himself to leave the apartment, again imagining this to be the last time he would see it, his mobile phone rang. The display simply, unhelpfully said '*UNKNOWN*' and he considered rejecting it as he would have done any other day, but today he sensed it was not simply a cold-caller chasing an insurance claim or a P.P.I. investigation. He accepted the call and was chilled by the voice but also had his nerves settled by learning it had been the right decision to make. It was the low, aggressive voice of the mystery caller.

"Still here, I see?" the voice rumbled.

"Just how do you see?" asked Jon, feeling energised, knowing the caller had no real power over him.

"You're not as careful as you think, nor as clever," said the voice. "*Jardim da Estrela* at 9. Be there."

"And what if I don't?" dared Jon.

"Then you'll miss out on the perfect chance to settle your scores," said the voice, sounding suddenly less hostile and almost benevolently helpful. "This has been set up for you to end things once and for all, Jon."

Jon caught his reflection in the hall mirror and saw the stunned look of bewilderment he knew had crinkled up his smooth flawless brow.

"Who the hell are you?" he asked, exasperated. "What do you get out of any of this?"

The caller laughed and Jon had to move the phone away from his ear as the throaty cackle rumbled through the speaker loudly and irritatingly.

"I get my own level of satisfaction, Jon," came the reply. "You'll soon see why. Since you wouldn't leave, you can face your demons. Be there of your own free will and you'll feel far better than if you are dragged there kicking and screaming."

Jon wondered who the hell this caller thought they were to make such repeated threats. How would they even achieve what they were suggesting? He could sense that the caller was almost done and knew his time was limited.

"Is that you, Palmer?" he ventured. "I know it's you, isn't it? I saw you near the river front."

If the laugh had been awful before, it was ten times worse now. Great whooping cascades of laughter deafened him before he had a chance to move the phone away and he cursed himself silently again for triggering it.

"No, no," boomed the reply, when the laughter had finally subsided. "Not he, sir. Not he. 9am. *Jardim da Estrela*. Be late at your own peril."

The line went dead before Jon could take a second guess at the caller's identity and he threw the phone angrily to the floor where it smashed and burst apart into case, battery and SIM card. He hated the way the caller spoke to him and manipulated him and to have made them ridicule him so much after his guess made him feel pathetic. For all he knew, it could still be Palmer. Why would he own up to being that maniac? Why would anyone? He looked at his watch. It was nearly half past eight and he would be hard pushed to make it to the destination in that time. If the caller intended on joining him there, they too must be nearer the venue and not simply stalking him on the streets outside. He grabbed a lightweight jacket, checked himself in the mirror once more – he was wearing lilac shorts, a tailored khaki shirt, white socks and the hiking boots Julie had bought him when he travelled to Morocco for a desert marathon a year or so ago – and was as satisfied with his appearance as he could be. He was aroused again and questioned whether he was truly turned on by the jeopardy he was facing or by his own appearance, alluring as he found himself. It was odd, whichever way you looked at it.

He was lucky to hail a taxi on the street outside the apartment without having to walk to the main road as he normally had to at this hour of the day and the driver made great time, pulling up outside the basilica by the *Jardim da Estrela* with a good five minutes to spare. He paid the driver the exact amount and entered the park. Children were haring here and there doing some kind of sporting challenge and Jon veered instinctively away from them. He regretted not picking up the components of his phone and reassembling it as there was no way he could be contacted by his mystery caller or anyone else for that matter. He would simply have to stalk around the lush surroundings keeping out of the way of any of the teachers or students, or sit somewhere with a good view of the park without seeming like he was watching the school activities. Before he could make a decision, he saw two men sitting on a bench in the shade of a huge, prehistoric-looking tree, away from the rays of the sun which were already quite intense. To his horror, he realised he knew both of them and that this had been a bigger trap than he'd anticipated. Checking that the knife was still in his jacket pocket, he walked slowly towards them.

21.

Stuart Evans giggled nervously as he paid for his sandwich at the self-service till in the busy branch of WH Smith's at Manchester airport. It didn't take much for him to be freaked out by a brush with celebrity and given his idea of a celebrity was often much vaguer than most, he became a bag of nerves when confronted with someone he considered to be famous. Someone actually famous made him shiver and sweat like he was in the grips of a terrible bout of flu. Luckily in his line of work he rarely met the very really proper famous but had once done an extension on a house next door to a rather famous footballer and had spent the entire project having out of body experiences every time he saw the Bentley glide up the neighbouring drive and the sharp suit-wearing god of a man hop out. Stuart's idea of famous was what other people would have charitably categorised as infamous. Whilst people he knew around him seemed to worship any kind of fame, be it a Hollywood megastar or that peculiar new brand of celebrity – those famous simply for being famous and boomeranging from reality show to reality show, channel to channel, from hot to not and back again – Stuart was fascinated by those not relying on a vaguely attractive body, a passable singing voice or the willingness to do anything on camera. He loved true crime. The victims, the accused, even sometimes the law enforcement officers involved if there were sufficient details, were all immensely interesting.

The man at the next till along, struggling with a packet of crisps which wouldn't scan despite his repeated attempts to flatten out the barcode and repeatedly offer it to the uninterested scanner, had seemed vaguely familiar to Stuart and at first he had thought it was perhaps someone whose house he had worked on. As the man, who had short white hair and a neat beard, turned to look around for help from any sales assistants within range, Stuart got a good look at the weathered face, the sad crinkly eyes and the perturbed pout and realised that if he mentally took 10-15 years off the man, that he knew exactly where he'd seen him before. In the mid noughties, there had been a particularly nasty series of assaults in the Rusholme area with young female students being accosted late at night for their handbags, phones and dignity. Thankfully the attacks had stopped short of sexual assault but that didn't help the poor traumatised girls, the hysteria which broke out around the university or the reputation of the local police force for not being able to reassure the populace. Fronting every local news bulletin had been the fraught features of one Chief Inspector Wrigley who had tried his best to assuage the fears of the people but had very little in the way of hard proof that the attacker's days were numbered or that he could protect the young women of Manchester.

Now much older, but carrying the slightly haunted look in his eye of a man who never cracked a certain big case in his career, he was still unmistakably Wrigley. Stuart appreciated that he might have been over romanticising the whole thing and for all he knew, the man might have long forgotten the travails of a decade and a half ago. Heck, he'd probably had dozens, maybe hundreds of similarly challenging cases which tugged at his concentration and undermined his confidence, but for those long months in 2006, Stuart had repeatedly seen the inspector fronting appeals, re-enactments and being taken to task by the public and politicians who abandoned their loyalties and made a scapegoat of the local constabulary to win the favour of their constituents. To Stuart, this man with his steely grey eyes and prematurely greying hair, had been a legend. He'd looked him up online and found out as much as he could about the man, about his training, his early career and even what little he could find about his life outside of the force. As much as the criminals themselves were fascinating to study, there was something about this cop who wouldn't quit which made Stuart happy. At least one of his internet chums would be chuffed to hear of this sighting and he couldn't wait to share the news once he hooked up to the airport wi-fi.

Stuart took his sandwich and drink and followed Wrigley for a short while, keeping far enough behind him so as not to look as if he were stalking him, but interested in where the man was going and with who. He trailed after him as far as one of the gates where the old man was met by a similarly grey wife and what must have been grandkids. Three eager young children who were excited to be reunited with their grandfather and more importantly, the crisps and sweets he had brought for them. Stuart had almost expected to find Wrigley travelling alone, abandoned by his wife and family for his failings in his career – a rather ridiculous idea he knew, but in his mind all detectives with unsolved cases were inevitably plagued by thoughts of what might have been, right through until their dying days. Just like in the movies. Seeing

Wrigley so happy and off on a foreign adventure with his loving family made Stuart feel rather jealous at his own life failings but ultimately he thought he couldn't hold that against the man. So, he turned and headed back to the shopping concourse and ate his sandwich on a seat with a view of taxiing planes. He ate quickly and hungrily and still felt hungry so headed to Starbucks to get himself a warm panini.

Queuing idly, Stuart's thoughts raked back over the details of what he had termed 'the Wrigley attacks' in his mental files and he boredly stroked the hairs on his muscular arms as he waited. It was then that he saw another celebrity. A big one in his online circles, but not so much in the real world. Stuart's internet contacts met in the discussion forums of a website sensationally titled miscarriagesofjustice.com to mull over unsolved crimes, mysterious cases, crooks who got away with it and the incompetence of police professionals. Their latest favourite topic of conversation was the Celia Payne case, something the police were barely interested in, but his online friends were obsessed with. A woman in California, username *Derek_Bentley_was_innocent* had pored over every last detail of the case, the most-likely made-up sightings of the missing teacher and the most probably candidates for her kidnapping, murder or selling into slavery. Ex-husband Gerry Payne was the discussion group's favourite for the crime, whichever crime it actually was no one could agree, but for *Derek_Bentley_was_innocent* it was a different matter. She was certain that one Edward Palmer was at the heart of things. His alibi was 'hokier than a thrift store diamond' in her words and she'd slowly got the rest of the group round to her way of thinking. Now, said suspect Edward Palmer was sitting just a few metres away from Stuart. His group would go crazy.

As Stuart wondered what he could do to corner the man and get some answers, the tannoy announcer's nasal voice informed them that the gate for the Lisbon flight was now open. Palmer cocked his head to one side, registering the announcement and Stuart's heart raced to see the man's light brown face all beaten and bruised as if he had recently been fighting, perhaps defending himself against his female hostage's escape attempts. Palmer got up, checked his shoulder bag and headed off towards the gates. Could he really be heading for Portugal as Stuart himself was? This could be a priceless opportunity. Whilst Stuart looked like he meant business, being as tall as he was wide, having arms with wider circumferences than many people's waists and the look of a wrestler fallen on hard times and gone slightly to seed, the truth was he maintained his musculature by heavy sessions at the gym and working hard in the construction industry, that he ate far too much, feeding his misery and insecurity with food rather than the drink he would have rather had and that he had managed to avoid ever properly being involved in any sort of serious physical fight in his life by being both generally opposed to violence and highly persuasive, somewhere between charming and obsequious, he'd been told. He couldn't let this one get away though.

Palmer stopped at the exact gate Stuart himself was bound for. His rather randomly chosen holiday destination was the same place of choice as online person of interest Edward Palmer. If he had Celia locked away somewhere, or better yet, her body stowed in a lost luggage locker or something, then he had no worries about jetting away to another country. In fact, it had been suggested that the missing schoolteacher might have simply upped and left, tired of life and its disappointments and fled to the warmer climes of the Mediterranean, with the small problem of her passport being found in her belongings at home. Perhaps, as one jittery student from Brighton speculated in the forums (username *Brightonandhoes*) the two of them had eloped together, possibly for insurance money, definitely for love. She might be nicely set up in a Portuguese love nest whilst Palmer covered their tracks in the UK, only feeling confident enough to join her now the heat had died down.

Stuart's stomach gurgled now and he realised he had walked straight out of Starbucks with the shrink-wrapped panini still in his hands, stolen in fact. Perhaps he would one day become the topic of conversation on his own forum – *the phantom panini pilferer!* He laughed a rough, throaty laugh to himself which inadvertently got Palmer's attention. He spun around to investigate the source of the rasping and Stuart ducked to pretend to tie his shoelace. Even though there was nothing to hide from, he felt self-conscious that he had been following Palmer and that potentially this slight, damaged man could have been a cold-blooded killer. Looking up as he mimed tying a final bow in his laces, he saw that Palmer had found himself a seat near the gate entrance and was massaging his left knee, wincing all the while. Another injury caused by his misdeeds no doubt. Stuart stood back up and allowed a group of shuffling old ladies, chattering away in what sounded like Portuguese, to pass him. He drifted back behind other people, keeping an eye on his target. If he were a movie detective or a spy in a comedy he would have a newspaper with eye holes cut out of it through which to monitor Palmer. He spied a paper abandoned on the arm of the nearest seat and he took it. He could always pretend to read it and get closer to his mark, or simply while away some time on the flight.

He glanced at the sports page on the back cover, then flicked aimlessly through the entertainment pages and a story about a local election. It was only when he reached the end of his backward odyssey through the newspaper that he saw the cover. 'MAN SOUGHT IN CONNECTION WITH WOMAN'S DISAPPEARANCE' read the headline and underneath was a picture of a man he knew as well as any of the people whose lives he dissected and placed underneath the microscope on miscarriagesofjustice.com. This was his own personal favourite choice in the Celia Payne disappearance and the story was all about the latest developments in the rather lukewarm investigation. The man was beaming out from the front cover in a photo surely taken from his work I.D. badge and the story was strangely vague about the reasons the police wanted to speak to him, but Stuart wasn't fooled. This man, Jon Scott Campbell, was the man he had pegged as key in the Celia Payne disappearance, but more importantly, weirdly, improbably, he had been the boyfriend of the first woman assaulted in the Rusholme case and the man Stuart knew had been responsible for every last one of the attacks.

22.

Stuart watched intently as Palmer pretended to sleep. It was clear that his initial clumsy attempts to befriend the man had gone spectacularly wrong and now he was feigning sleep in order to shut down further conversation. Stuart had caught him scrunching up one eye in order to peek out of the corner of the other to see what he was up to and so politely, Stuart had pretended to be looking out of the window, even though it was too dark to see very much at all. Palmer had resented him choosing a seat next to him – something he'd had to clear with the air steward after making out he had an issue with the man he should have been sat alongside – and been as abrupt and unfriendly as he could be, and Stuart acknowledged that he probably deserved it. He could make inane small talk with his customers, chatting away to elderly ladies having their lofts converted about biscuits, poodles and fly tipping and he could match the more macho banter of the other labourers on a building site, meandering between football, women and tabloid politics. What Stuart had never mastered was the more subtle, somehow deeper art of conversation which allowed someone to open up and also revealed your own true nature. He did most of his interacting online where a mood was easily conveyed with an emoticon or an acronym but rarely did his face ever match the poking-out-tongue emoji and he had never once rolled on the floor, laughing out loud.

Palmer didn't seem like a maniac, he had to say, more of a poor people person. The irony wasn't lost on Stuart, but whereas he was clumsy and inexperienced with real people and real conversations, Palmer seemed wilfully resistant to prompts to talk and genuinely rather uncomfortable having to be in the company of someone he hadn't prepared for. That didn't make him a kidnapper or a murderer though, although Stuart remembered

110

Brightonandhoes sharing a Venn diagram on the topic of personality disorders and violent crimes. Anything could be proven with poorly researched facts on the internet. Perhaps he was judging Palmer unfairly and he really was just trying to sleep, just trying to get away from a potentially rather stressful and upsetting situation back in England.

Stuart decided to conduct a small experiment and got out the Manchester Evening News he'd found at the airport. He flapped it open slightly dramatically and angled the front page so that Palmer would see it, if he were really awake. He pretended to read an article on community policing and waited to see if anything happened. It wasn't quite the espionage eyehole ruse he'd envisaged, but the paper also allowed him to hide away from the world for a few moments. His experiment had borne no fruit, so he folded the paper shut again, chanced a quick study of his neighbour's face and bruises up close. They looked particularly nasty, with a swollen lip something he hadn't noticed until now. Maybe the guy really did just want a snooze. Well, while he slept, Stuart would satisfy his hunger with a bag of miniature Toblerones he'd bought when he first arrived at the airport, then the biscuit offered around by the air steward. He took a second, claiming responsibility for handing it to Palmer when he awoke as if they knew one another, but ate it himself. They were flaky palmier biscuits and that seemed to be a near enough reference to his target for him to chuckle a throaty laugh to himself.

Palmer seemed to be genuinely asleep now, his head slumping slightly in what would have been an uncomfortable position were he awake, so Stuart felt a quick surge of adrenaline, willing him to make use of the situation. Palmer had a lightweight jacket across his lap with his hands resting over it, but it was angled so that the bottom end where the pockets were was right next to Stuart. He slowly inched his hand towards it and patted the pocket on the top of the garment. It was disappointingly flat and empty. He retracted his hand then burrowed it under the jacket this time, seeking out the other side pocket. Squeezing his thumb and fingers together around the edge of the material, he found a slight bulge, like a piece of folded paper. He sneaked a glance at its owner who was still either sleeping or pretending so consistently that he wouldn't notice then quickly manipulated his hand, bending it awkwardly back on itself to reach into the pocket and remove the paper. Breathless, he slid it out from under the jacket and saw it was a hotel booking sheet headed with a Sana hotels logo. He had only just clocked this and the word 'Reno' when Palmer began to move restlessly, keeping his eyes closed but moving the jacket aside. Without thinking, Stuart grabbed the edge, slid the paper back under and into the pocket and then let go. Palmer opened his eyes, looking puzzled as someone who had fallen asleep and forgotten where they were, but if he had felt the slight resistance on his jacket, he didn't seem to show it. He simply leant forwards and put the jacket into his hand luggage,

111

zipped it up and fanned himself a little, indicating he had stirred due to being overly warm. Stuart was glad that for once the man's avoidance of him was an advantage.

By the time the plane touched down, Palmer had resisted every subtle and even a fair few blunt invitations to reveal more about himself to Stuart and the builder was growing weary. Only once or twice before had he ever actively got himself involved in a bit of detective work and even then it tended to be asking questions to elderly eyewitnesses with unreliable memories about events from decades ago then matching them to statements they'd made at the time. Cold cases, those long abandoned and forgotten, were meant to be the crux of the miscarriagesofjustice.com site, but this Celia Payne business was irresistible to him as it was both uncategorised as yet as a particular crime, but also still hot, still live and unfolding before his eyes. Stuart also felt sick to his stomach at the idea that he could be potentially cosying up to a brutal murderer and even embroiling himself in their crimes, but something kept telling him that Palmer wasn't the awkward weirdo the press had labelled him. The inclusion of Jon Scott Campbell into the equation made Stuart excited. A man who had surely got away with a string of assaults could easily have grown smug and overly cocky and moved on to a more serious crime, but how was he linked to Celia? The sooner he got near some free wi-fi, the better.

Stuart hadn't been able to find out where Palmer was going once they landed, or where the specific hotel he might have been staying at was located. For all he knew, the man could have been moving on elsewhere and so when he finally parted ways with him before the baggage carousel, Stuart felt deflated. Even leaping to his aid as the man stumbled on the exit ramp failed to bring him into his confidences. As Stuart waited for his luggage, he wondered what was going on back in Manchester and whether anyone would have missed him yet. Being practically self-employed, he could take holidays as and when he saw fit and he had just finished a rather tedious job of fixing another cowboy builder's work on a middle class social-climbing housewife's extension. His trip had been fairly spontaneous, to the extent that he hadn't told the few people who might notice his absence – the man, *Don he thought*, at the building merchant's yard, a couple of lads he sometimes chatted to at the gym who also kept the same hours, and the people whose company he spent most time in, those in the discussion forums. It was close to 10pm, handily the same time as back in the U.K., and by now Stuart would normally have returned from the gym, showered and changed into a vest and sweatpants before retiring to the back bedroom which he kept as his office, in reality, a place where he sat at his laptop most of the night expounding theories and occasionally masturbating.

As he waited for his suitcase to manifest itself on the conveyor belt, Stuart got out his phone and was pleased to see that there was free wi-fi at the airport. He opened the internet browser which automatically took him to the miscarriagesofjustice website, but before he checked in with his soon-to-be-very-jealous contacts, he needed to do a hotel search. He'd never heard of the Sana hotel chain and had felt sure he'd mangled the pronunciation of it when trying to probe Palmer, but he found there were far too many branches in and around Lisbon for him to be randomly trawling through. Then at last, he remembered the additional word 'Reno' which he'd mistakenly thought might be another place, when in fact it was a branch of the Sana hotel chain located a mere taxi ride from the airport. He clicked onto the hotel's website, found there were still rooms available and impulsively booked one for the next three nights. By the time his battered leather case hoved into view on the busy carousel, Stuart had cancelled his existing booking at an aparthotel in the city centre, forfeiting €40 in the process, but it was worth it in his view. He may have lost Palmer here at the airport, but he would find him quickly enough at the hotel. Maybe he would even prove the man's guilt or innocence, depending which way things went.

Stuart had a huge wad of Euros in his pocket, having simply withdrawn the available balance at the cash machine at the end of his street, then gone to the Bureau de Change in Sainsbury's and exchanged the lot. He hadn't taken a proper holiday in ages and it felt liberating to not think about money. Besides, he had plenty more and unused credit cards to chip into too. He left the airport via the main exit and was about to look for a cab when he saw something very odd indeed. A suspicious looking figure was moving rapidly and stealthily across the wide-open space between the terminal and the entrance to the underground. A few other travellers were milling about, most of them from the same flight, Stuart noted, but not this man who was closing in on another figure near the steps down into the metro station. Stuart watched, open-mouthed as the man reached his target, a woman wearing a head scarf and long dark shawl and grabbed her by the wrist, twisting it painfully back on itself. Before the woman could do anything, let alone emit a scream, the man had slapped her face and begun to pull her with him. She still didn't make a noise, but managed to twist out of the man's grip and stumbled back towards the staircase. She collided with someone already on the steps who tumbled down out of sight. The woman's assailant closed in again and hauled her to her feet as if she weighed nothing at all. From this distance it was impossible to see the age of the woman, especially beneath the scarf and shawl, but if she were elderly as the outfit suggested, this rough treatment was even more horrific.

Looking around, Stuart could see that no one else was motivated to act, so he began to charge towards the violent-looking scene. The man, who he could now see was slim but muscular, young and red-headed, wearing a shirt and shorts, was furiously dragging the woman off towards the taxi rank. She was only slightly resisting now as if the shock of bumping into whoever was on the steps had knocked the life out of her. She had her back to Stuart now and looked bizarrely like a nun or Muslim woman in a burqa being cruelly persecuted by the athletic man. By the time Stuart got anywhere near them, the man had bundled the woman into the back of a taxi, thrown some money at the driver and barked some instruction in what sounded like Portuguese. He could hear now that the woman was sobbing, but the door slammed shut and the car drove off before he reached the kerb. The man was standing, watching the taxi leave and didn't notice him creep alongside him. Stuart couldn't believe his eyes. There, standing casually alongside him as if they were two men enjoying the scenery or using neighbouring urinals, was the Rusholme attacker, Jon Scott Campbell. He opened his mouth to accuse the man, but faltered, realising he could be placing himself in danger and that his accusation would most likely mean nothing to him. He was now very self-conscious about standing so close to this stranger who would surely look to his right and see him standing far too close, not exactly queuing for a taxi.

Jon Scott Campbell did look around eventually and far from giving Stuart a look of 'what the hell do you want?' which was what Stuart expected, his face became a mixture of emotions, showing shock, recognition, fear and disbelief.

"Stuart Evans?" asked Jon.

Stuart froze rigid. How did this man know his name, let alone recognise him? Before he could find out, Jon fled with a look of absolute terror on his face and disappeared into the night.

23.

Stuart had waited for as long as he could in the hotel foyer. Whilst he was ordinarily quite the night owl, surviving on only a few hours of poor-quality slumber after half the night on the internet or winding down after a ferocious session at the gym, tonight he was worn out. His further attempts to ingratiate himself with Palmer had failed and the man had slipped off the metro a stop earlier than he'd anticipated and was yet to show his face at the Sana Reno. The hotel was lovely and Stuart appreciated the receptionist's efforts to make him feel welcome, obviously registering a certain amount of distress on his face. He'd checked in but not gone up to his room yet, explaining to the smiling man on the desk that he was looking out for a friend. He didn't want to push the employee's professionalism by asking for the private details of a guest, but he didn't dare ascend to his room in case he missed out on seeing Palmer arrive. So he sat with a large delicious mug of hot chocolate which the receptionist had kindly suggested might be brought to him as long as he insisted on waiting in the foyer and multitasked, scouring the Manchester Evening News for clues to Jon Scott Campbell's involvement in the mystery whilst also setting his online contacts to work doing the same via the internet and hotel wi-fi. Hardly anyone entered or left the hotel at this hour and as it began to rain, only a bedraggled woman stumbled in through the main doors, realised she had made an error and headed for the hotel next door.

Now falling asleep where he sat, Stuart admitted defeat and hauled his luggage up to his room, leaving his paper and his half-empty mug on the table and concluding that Palmer had altered his plans. If Palmer had come to Lisbon specifically looking for Jon Scott Campbell, Stuart found it bizarre that he had seemingly missed him by only moments, that he might actually have

115

been caught up in the sinister redhead's scuffle with the mysterious woman. As Stuart slept a deep but restless sleep, his subconscious misremembered the evening's events and had Celia Payne herself as the hooded woman caught in a tussle between two men who could have had a hand in her kidnapping and disappearance, almost a strange tug of war between two people intent on hurting her. Stuart himself became the taxi driver, speeding her off to safety where a resigned Inspector Wrigley gave him England's highest commendation for rescuing the victim of a violent crime. He awoke, startled by his own laboured snoring with a racing pulse and a crick in his neck which wouldn't shift, even after an early morning shower which left him even sweatier than before.

Jon Scott Campbell was clearly still up to his old tricks, attacking defenceless women, brazenly in public and getting away with it. Stuart had learned from *Brightonandhoes'* extensive internet research that the former teacher had given up an educational career some years ago following an incident at his school which seemed to be an allegation of indecent assault which had been made then swiftly retracted. He was married, though not to his girlfriend during the time of the attacks in Rusholme and now seemed to earn a living as the owner of an online literary press which specialised in tawdry crime novels. He had seemed to be ahead of the game, churning out cheap, easy to read fiction for the first owners of kindles and e-readers and it was thought probably wrote a fair few of the books himself under a number of aliases. Stuart was fascinated by the parallel between his interest in true crime and Jon Scott Campbell's predilection for imagined crime despite his own history and involvement with the former. *Derek_Bentley_was_innocent* had admitted to having bought and read a fair number of the man's works and had read somewhere that he travelled around the western world writing his books and enjoying the proceeds. Stuart was disgusted to find that many of the novels dealt with violent crime against women and at least one riffed on the Rusholme attacks themselves although he couldn't prove that the book was one of Jon's.

Just the very proximity of the man and possibility of his involvement in another unsolved case revolving around violence perpetrated against a woman made Stuart angry but it also made him feel less sure that Edward Palmer was involved. The man seemed too spooked, too ill-at-ease to be a single-minded criminal and was definitely more in the realms of the sociopath, blundering along with little forethought and no real plan. Whilst he still wanted to get closer to Palmer and find out what he could tell him about Celia and possibly even help the man, it was John Scott Campbell that now fascinated him. He had no idea how the man knew him or had recognised him, his trawling through criminal history usually being a 100% one-way street. He could pick out serial killers from their mugshots but would be appalled and amused if they had a clue who he was.

Before dressing and heading down for breakfast, Stuart checked his forum again and was pleased to see that *Derek_Bentley_was_innocent* had spent most of her evening in California unearthing some interesting trivia about JSC publishing, the company owned by Scott Campbell. There were holdings across a number of European cities but most intriguingly, a major shareholder in the company was listed as one Kulani Kanaka'āina, a name his contact was sure was Hawaiian, whose address was in an apartment block in the *Parque das Nacoes* region of Lisbon. If Stuart were to find the man at all, he was sure that this would be the right place and if not, then the exotically named woman and co-owner of his business might be able to point him in the right direction. His first mission was to locate Palmer and find what his plans were, but by the time he got down to the breakfast room where he felt he would surely be able to lie in wait, he spotted the hobbling form of the injured man heading down the stairs to the hotel lobby. Stuart had missed the chance of a leisurely breakfast over which he could attempt to bond with the nervy man and now felt that any attempt to accost him as he was leaving the hotel would be met with suspicion and rejection. So Stuart kept at a distance, observing him select a pamphlet for the Yellow Bus tour company and then head off in the direction of the city centre.

Palmer meandered around town and at one point Stuart wondered if he were doing so on purpose to shake off anyone pursuing him, but he soon recognised the perplexed look of a man who was lost but too proud to check his map and also seemingly in a great deal of pain. Stuart watched him from the corner of the opposite street as he ducked into a chemist's but he didn't stay inside long enough to make a purchase and when he emerged, he seemed even more agitated. Once they got within sight of the river, Stuart concluded that Palmer was heading for the bus company's ticket stand and quickly overtook him on a parallel street, reaching the booth whilst Palmer was still a speck on the horizon. There was a sizable queue forming at the stand and the attractive brunette on the counter seemed to be in no rush to reduce it. Stuart had no intention of buying a ticket unless Palmer caught him up and demonstrated that this was indeed his target for the morning, so he stood aside and let the queue shuffle past him. They would bond over their shared interest in the tour and be trapped together for a few hours where Stuart could get a proper measure of him.

He had lost sight of Palmer in the distance and for a moment feared that he could have ventured off down one of the many side streets, perhaps heading for a different destination and was craning his neck to scan the distant meandering crowd when he felt a shiver run down his spine. At the back of the queue and only a few metres away, a red-haired man in an unpleasant shirt and shorts, wearing a flat cap, was whispering something in the ear of a pretty young woman with tresses of dark hair. She was nodding as if he were giving her directions and Stuart noticed her slender wrist was locked in one of the man's fists. Jon Scott Campbell gave her one final insistent instruction it seemed, then released her and she disappeared across the busy road, barely taking care to cross safely. Stuart had reached him in seconds and it was his turn to lock onto a wrist, grabbing Jon's hand in one of his sizable paws.

"What the fuck are you doin'?" he growled with barely concealed hostility. "And 'ow do you know who I am?"

Jon Scott Campbell looked horrified again but showed no signs of running. His eyes were wide and when he finally closed his gaping jaw, a look of smug satisfaction replaced the fear.

"Take your hand off me you thick bastard," he commanded. "Before I cut it off."

He said the words with such venom that Stuart was slightly taken aback. He'd only grabbed him to stop him fleeing and hadn't particularly meant to suggest harmful intent. He let go of the man's wrist and stepped back in shock.

"'ow do you know who I am?" he repeated, waving his arms emphatically as Jon remained silent and his smirk grew. "I know who *you* are and what you did to those girls," he added, as if that might stir the man into action.

"Which girls? Where?" was all the man replied at first. Seeing the perplexed look on Stuart's face, he continued. "So many girls, so many places."

Stuart was about to try and compose himself, to remember his research, to present the monster with some cold hard facts which might make him think twice about running away or threatening him, when Jon Scott Campbell simply shook his head and turned away.

"Give my regards to *Brightonandhoes*!" he yelled as he vanished into the crowd.

Stuart was shaken. If Jon Scott Campbell knew the name of a member of his discussion forum, what else did he know about him?

24.

Stuart's day was becoming testing. He had barely had time to process this latest development when Palmer finally caught up with him and he had to bury all his worry and doubt beneath his bluff builder's exterior. He became the cheeky, charming tradesman everyone already expected him to be the moment they pieced together his appearance with what he did for a living and soon inveigled himself into Palmer's morning. He was glad of the audio tour guide available on the bus as his previous idea of finding out more about Palmer's movements took second fiddle to trying to work out how Jon Scott Campbell had invaded his life. So whilst his travelling companion seemed to be enjoying the slightly dull description of the route their bus was taking, Stuart was fretting over what the red-haired man had done, how much he knew and whether he was perhaps signed up to miscarriagesofjustice.com under an identity he hadn't spotted and perhaps had witnessed every last word of his discussions about those connected with Celia Payne. As security was so tight on the forums – applicants were vetted by location, I.P. and email addresses and made to pay a forum upkeep fee just large enough that it put off timewasters and ensured that only those who truly wished to meet like minds and discuss the intricacies of historic criminal cases made it through the process – Stuart had always felt safe discussing things in the open. The member count was tiny really, barely a hundred members of which only half posted at all and half that again on anything resembling a regular basis. Stuart shuddered as he thought about how open and honest he had been online to the friendly strangers he could confide in and how it felt a violation that someone like Scott Campbell could have been lurking amongst them.

It was slowly dawning on him that Palmer seemed to be more of a victim in this whole business, another name the tabloids and awkwardly Stuart himself had bandied around as just the right sort of misfit to have snapped and spirited away a vulnerable woman. If Stuart had been better at maintaining real-life friendships, he knew for a fact that Palmer, or 'Harry' as he'd bizarrely introduced himself the night before, would be his sort of acquaintance. It took his mind off things to chip in with the odd comment about the scenery they were passing and Palmer who had suddenly become a lot more convivial today seemed to appreciate the company. It was as if they'd swapped personas overnight. Stuart knew they'd both lied to one another too much to ever form the basis of a real friendship, but for a sunny hour on a tour bus in a foreign city, they'd become an odd couple, the stuff those cop buddy movies were spun from.

As the bus pulled up alongside a sprawling shopping centre over the road from the gleaming railway terminal, Stuart saw a group of young women chatting away on the pavement. They were typical local beauties and Stuart, being a good stereotype, would have ogled them from the vantage point of a construction site's scaffolding, but he felt certain that one of the girls, central and holding court over the others, was the girl from the bus stand that Scott Campbell had been ordering around. She was possibly even the head scarf woman from the airport he realised and then saw Palmer watching him stare. The man followed his gaze and a brief flash of disapproval belied the polite smile which he affixed to his face. Palmer just thought he was living up to the builder cliché it seemed. But before Stuart could think of something to say which would open up the mystery of the girl and her repeated appearances, Palmer himself got agitated and leapt up, hurtling down the steps of the bus, despite his injured knee. By the time Stuart had caught up with him, he'd been trying to get off the bus against the driver's advice. He calmed him and led him back upstairs and felt a swell of excitement as Palmer finally mentioned the name "Celia". Stuart feigned ignorance, feeling it safer to not act like he'd been a groupie to a potential criminal and also to allow Palmer to give him his version of events, but it soon dawned on him that Palmer was losing the plot. He had imagined seeing the missing woman getting off the very bus they'd been travelling on and Stuart couldn't fathom whether this was through guilt at knowing what had actually happened to her or temporary madness at not knowing. Palmer looked pathetic, sitting on the brink of breakdown, thin, drawn, covered in bruises and not built for this. He couldn't resist giving him a hug and realised he could feel every bone in his body as they embraced.

He needed to tell Palmer that the reason they had crossed paths so often wasn't a coincidence, that they were even staying in the same hotel, but given his state of distress and the imagined sighting of Celia, he thought it best to wait until their day was a little calmer, possibly even break the news to him as they parted for the evening. Palmer seemed to calm down, but Stuart couldn't begin to imagine what he was going through, fantasising that Celia was tantalisingly close but unreachable. It was a psychologist's dream. Stuart had quickly dismissed the idea that the missing woman was actually on or near the bus. Having studied this case for the last months, he would have spotted her a mile off and knew that the one thing people who had run off or been dragged off to another country rarely did was stalk or haunt the people actively looking for them.

At the end of the bus ride, Stuart took Palmer for lunch and watched as little by little his companion came down from the crazy level of anxiety and paranoia he had been experiencing earlier. It was very easy to feel paranoia in a strange city where every corner seemed to unveil another strange incident and potential danger and a couple of times, mid-bite into his fish sandwich meal, he thought he spied another woman like one of the victims of Jon Scott Campbell and took a photograph, pretending to admire the view of the square they were in. He knew very little about Lisbon and as he paid up and they headed for a second tour bus of the day, he realised that it had been the suggestion of *Brightonandhoes* to come here. The young man had posted a hyperlink to a comedy travel show which toured the city in just 48 hours and they had chatted at length about how picturesque and fascinating the city was. Before that, Stuart had considered an English seaside trip, possibly the south coast rather than the windswept but nearer Northwest. What if he himself had been manipulated the whole time? He began to flick back through his memories of one of his closest online friends, wondering just how much he truly knew about him, whether the lad had been coerced into playing this game or whether it was his own design. Stuart shook his head as if to loosen the fog of suspicion. He didn't even know if there was a game to begin with.

During this second bus ride, Palmer had seemed more at ease but Stuart had been distracted and began to feel foolish. The only person who could possibly even begin to understand what he was thinking about, who he could possibly trust, was the man he'd spent 24 hours stalking, believing him to be a kidnapper or murderer. Imagine how that would sound if he opened up to Palmer! So as the bus reached the terminal, Stuart remained seated and allowed Palmer to hobble off on his own adventures for a while. Stuart had also realised that the one thing he had been supposed to look out for on the first bus journey was the apartment block in *Parque das Nacoes* where Jon Scott Campbell's business partner had an address. Perhaps the brunette he was now convinced he had seen twice could actually be her. The shopping mall was probably within walking distance of the location. He needed to explore this avenue. As Palmer waved to him from the street, Stuart felt brave enough to drop at least one bombshell, suggesting they meet at their mutual hotel's breakfast room. The bus pulled away before he could work out what the expression on Palmer's face meant. It looked like horror from where Stuart was sitting.

He changed buses at the next stop which overlapped the two routes and got on another bus headed along the *Olisipo* route, back along the river to the *Parque das Nacoes* area. He didn't bother plugging in the headphones this time and sat downstairs, not caring to take in the view, merely using the vehicle for transport, not sightseeing. When the bus reached the stop where Palmer had had his episode, Stuart alighted and looked around, considering it too much of a gift from the universe that he should bump straight into the woman he was looking for. He took out his mobile and stood by the entrance to the huge shopping complex, hoping for some free wi-fi. Thankfully there was and he dismissed the discussion forum home page which popped up, to access a map application instead. The apartment block was just a few hundred metres from here. He took note of the route, committing it to memory, then closed the app and set off walking. He was becoming quite sweaty in the intense afternoon heat and wished he'd stopped for a break or a refreshment before moving away from the commercial streets onto the more residential blocks.

Standing outside the correct skyscraper, Stuart looked up to see at least fifteen floors of metal and glass telescoping into the brilliant blue sky and a smart, upmarket lobby which needed no keys or access cards to enter, serving as the way in for several businesses too. Mailboxes lined one wall and an unmanned reception desk the other. Beyond, there were several elevators which even from a distance Stuart could tell needed an access card to activate. This was as far as he could wander without sneaking or trespassing. He took a quick look at the mailboxes, hoping for names, but finding anonymous numbers instead. The lift doors opened and a glamorous middle-aged black woman wearing a brightly coloured kaftan exited. It Stuart had been closer, or more prepared, he could have made it to them before they closed again but as it was, his mad dash would look suspicious and would leave him several metres shy of an entry method. If the mysterious Kulani Kanaka'āina was here, Stuart wasn't going to find her or, he admitted somewhat sheepishly, even recognise her if he did. The African woman could have been her for all he knew. He cursed himself again, thinking how underprepared he was and how long it had been since he'd ventured outside into the real world on his investigations. He thought he could hear the voice of the receptionist fussing around in the office behind the desk and wondered how it would go down if he tried to schmooze his way into the building, or at least find out if the woman, or Jon Scott Campbell himself, was here.

He moved to the reception desk and waited, but no one seemed in any rush to appear. As he waited, boredly, he checked his phone and found that there was an open wi-fi network he could hijack. He checked into his forum inbox and found a new message from *Derek_Bentley_was_innocent*. He read it twice before quickly leaving the building and hurrying back to the bus stop. The Californian's usual cheery tone was absent from the message and the whole thing read like a chilling threat. The message simply said:

'THE GAME'S UP. JON SCOTT CAMPBELL IS ONTO YOU."

25.

There was only one thing for it, Stuart concluded, after polishing off another plate of food. This particular plate was now swimming in oil and the discarded fish bones of his rather disappointing *Bacalhau a Minhota*. Bizarrely, the dish had been both too wet and too dry, with the overcooked and chewy piece of dry fish being symbolically drowned in what felt like a gallon of olive oil. The picture on the laminated menu had looked so promising and Stuart had been so hungry that he'd ordered several different dishes of things he knew and others he had never had before in order to satisfy his stomach. When he was nervous, he ate more and he always ate to excess before the regret kicked in. This dish had come topped with tasty slices of fried potatoes but also a tangled mess of fried onions, unpitted olives and cherry tomatoes. Stuart had munched through several smaller crunchy pieces of onion before he realised they were in fact huge chunks of raw garlic. Hating himself, he devoured the dish, pausing every few moments to extricate another ridiculously large fish bone from his mouth of food and toss it on the side of the plate. He'd already eaten a salty fish soup, a plate of sardines on toast and a salade niçoise but needed both the calories and the reassurance that overeating always temporarily brought him.

He'd made the important decision during a rather unpleasant cab ride back from *Parque das Nacoes*, cursing that he'd failed to read the bus timetable accurately and had missed the last Yellow Tour bus which could have returned him right to the district his hotel was in. Hailing a taxi, he'd suddenly changed his destination on a whim, thinking it better to line his stomach and make some quick purchases before returning to his room and putting his plan into action. The cab driver had overcharged him and he'd been too distracted to say anything about it, stepping out in the shadows of the bustling square and into the first restaurant he saw. It was overly touristy, reflected in both the prices and the selection of food available and the waiting staff seemed to have an air of snobbery about them which didn't really fit with their clientele. The sneering waiter showed Stuart to a seat, visibly gurning when Stuart said he was dining alone, and then disappeared for the best part of a quarter of an hour without enquiring about drinks. Stuart ordered a bottle of Sagres and then changed his mind and ordered a bottle of the house red. The waiter could be seen to roll his eyes at the choice and when he returned with the cheap looking bottle, it was as if he couldn't uncork it, pour it and get away quickly enough.

One thing Stuart had learned over the years of studying true crime was the passion with which the wrongly accused fought against their accusers, summoning a strength of character Stuart could only marvel at with envy. These struggles could go on for years with defendants striving to clear their names and sometimes even to seek out the true perpetrator of the crime and see them brought to justice. Of course, often the falsely accused simply gave up under the weight of accusation and the seeming inevitability of the legal process which thundered along at times like a derailed train, screeching onto the wrong platform and hurting everyone in its path. In those cases, often the innocent ended up charged or in prison and despite campaigners or online busybodies getting involved, it was all too late. Stuart had long mulled over a case in the late 90s where a scout leader had been falsely accused of inappropriate behaviour after a troubled youth had taken his dismissal from the pack badly. The initial allegation snowballed into a whole raft of testimonies, all spurred on by that first lie which was intended as a spiteful prank, with other youngsters bullied into adding their own lurid inventions. The accused had been dismissed from his job and whilst the case fell apart in court due to the unreliability of some of the witnesses and contradictory bits of evidence, his reputation was ruined. He was later found hanging from a tree in the woods he'd used to take the boys camping.

Imagining Palmer facing charges of killing Celia, Stuart knew that he wasn't built for it, physically or mentally. He was literally falling apart just investigating the woman's disappearance, let alone being dragged through police interrogation, the court system and a trial by media. And yet it seemed like someone somewhere was intent on this happening and they had dragged Stuart into their web of lies too. He now knew for certain that Jon Scott Campbell had infiltrated his online haven, most likely posing as the Brighton teenager who had bonded closely to Stuart over the months they'd picked apart the case. His other trusted source of information, the Californian whistle blower, had not resurfaced as yet to elaborate on her brief warning and neither of the two had logged into their accounts since earlier in the day. Stuart knew that he had to warn Palmer about all of this without sounding like some conspiracy nut which was difficult because deep down, he knew that that was exactly what he was and exactly what his story would sound like. Perhaps he could reveal what he believed a little at a time, winning Palmer's trust and protecting him from whatever Jon Scott Campbell had in mind. He needed the man to feel like they were both in it together, which was why he had formulated the plan to make himself appear to be a victim in the proceedings.

Leaving the disappointing restaurant with a tip he knew they didn't deserve, he quickly made his way back up the *Avenida da Liberdade* towards his hotel, keeping an eye out for either Palmer or Jon Scott Campbell as he went. Lisbon was a big, sprawling city and yet it felt inevitably cosy and despite the fairly impressive crowds of tourists, he knew that the city was empty compared to the peak of its popularity in the summer months. Running into someone he knew would never be easier. He reached the hotel fairly certain he had seen neither of his marks and slipped through the lobby to wait for a lift. A noisy group of women were already waiting and as the lift doors opened, they poured in before turning and asking if he were joining them. Their giggly excitable din was not what he needed as he tried to think clearly, so he shook his head politely and waited for the other lift. It took its time to arrive and thankfully he had the lift to himself for the whole brief journey.

He knew his plan was slightly silly and even now, on the threshold of beginning to put it into action, he wasn't quite sure of the details. This was one occasion where it actually seemed prudent to do less than he intended and yet it might be more believable if he properly saw it all through in its ludicrous detail. He was going to fake a break-in of his hotel room, but ensure that Palmer was the one person he turned to and confided in, not wanting to let the hotel staff know, for obvious reasons. Palmer was just jumpy enough that he would agree and probably advise him not to report it and together they could theorise about the reasons for it happening. The issue of their red-headed nemesis would come up and Stuart would ally himself with Palmer, aiming to bring Scott Campbell down together and help him find the truth about Celia Payne, wherever she was. The plan was just silly enough that it might work, but once more Stuart was doubting the level of commitment to it required.

Given Palmer would be unlikely to ask to see the crime scene, there was no need for Stuart to fabricate one and yet he felt like it would be more believable to actually mess his room up a little just in case. Putting on a disguise and wearing gloves would make it seem even more authentic. At one point he had even considered pretending he'd caught the thief in the act and been roughed up a bit during their escape, perhaps darkening an eye with make up or bruising his own cheekbone to fit the scene, but this was a step too far. Also, thinking about Palmer's real facial injuries made him feel like it would be faintly mocking to conjure up some of his own. No, he would simply throw a few things around in his room and then rush to Palmer's room where the man must surely have returned by now, and ally himself to the man through their shared experiences. Stuart could almost envisage the red-haired man's hateful eyes as he rifled through his possessions in mild disgust.

As he stepped out onto the corridor, he noticed a crumpled-up bit of card on the floor by his room door. It was a Do Not Disturb sign which had previously been hanging on the back of the door. He rummaged in his pocket for his hotel room key but couldn't find it. There was no sign of it amongst his slightly sweaty wad of banknotes, nor in his shirt pocket, rear trouser pocket or inside his wallet. It had gone. Had he possibly dropped it during one of the many occasions he had clumsily fished in his tight pockets for money, possibly as recently as the restaurant or taxi ride before that? A trip down to the foyer would be embarrassing, but necessary. It was then that he noticed that the room door wasn't as closed as he had assumed, as shut as he had left it. He gave it a push to test his suspicions and it swung open at his touch. Nervously, he entered and saw a room key, possibly his own, already in the holster by the door which activated the room lights and air con. Was his memory playing tricks on him? Had he in fact left without his room key and not closed the door properly? Had a slack maid done this instead? He rounded the corner to the main sleeping area and found that his crazy plan to draw Palmer into his confidences had been thwarted. Someone had already ransacked his room. His envelope of money was on the floor, somehow not tempting enough for the thief, but he quickly realised one thing was missing from the room, the single most important piece of evidence he had – Celia Payne's passport.

26.

Drunken tidying was not a good idea Stuart noted. He was sitting in a heap on the floor in his hotel room surrounded by random piles of his belongings. Unable to face a thorough investigation of his room, he had wandered out of the hotel in a daze, putting one foot in front of the other but not really paying attention to direction or destination. He was lucky that the streets were fairly deserted at that hour on a Tuesday night but his wandering had finally taken him to a late night supermarket within which he found himself stunned at the prices of the gleaming rows of alcohol and almost without thinking about it, had exited with two plastic bags full of wine at barely a Euro a bottle. Nearby he had noticed a play area, even though he wasn't really paying attention to anything around him, and was confident it was too dark and cold for anyone to be sitting around at that time of night, so he clambered over the railings and plonked himself down heavily on a damp bench, clinking his bags of bottles noisily by accident. There was no one around to see or hear his antics, so he had grabbed the first bottle at random from the bag and laughed so hard that he almost wept, shaking with spasms of disbelief as he discovered it was a bottle with a cork and he had no corkscrew. He selected another bottle. That too had a cork. Rummaging through the bags he quickly discovered he had bought six bottles of wine and not a single one had screw cap lid. Bloody backwards country, he chortled to himself.

He considered returning to the shop to see about buying a corkscrew or even to his hotel room, but figured if he could face the latter, then there was no point sitting in a strange unlit park freezing his arse off and drowning his sorrows. He tried cracking the thin glass neck of one bottle on the edge of the nearby wall, but the glass was so cheap and fragile, that the entire bottle fell apart in his hands and wine gushed all over the bench and floor, though thankfully not on Stuart himself. Looking around the play area for something else to assist him in his fruitless endeavours, he wandered to the railings at the other side which led into a park overlooked by a busier street than he had thought. He wasn't sure how far he'd walked, but it had been far enough to leave the quieter streets of the *Sao Sebastiao* area behind and to have stumbled onto a busier neighbourhood. He could hear busy traffic somewhere very nearby and wondered if he had inadvertently wandered back towards the city centre in his absent-minded state. Either way, he figured he might as well make use of the situation and found a gate which took him onto the street, then around a corner and down a long sloping road which was busy with speeding traffic. He knew he wasn't far from where he'd ventured earlier that day and that there were souvenir shops nearby. Still clutching his plastic bags, he strode purposefully past the pretty blue tile fridge magnets, the cuddly sardines and the revolving racks of postcards and found himself a novelty corkscrew, the handle of which was in the shape of Portugal. He flipped it over and found the price sticker said it was €5. Now was not the time to be blanching over an inflated tourist price. He grabbed a few postcards from next to the counter to add to his purchase and not make it look like he'd come in solely to open his booze, paid and left.

Before retracing his steps, he ducked into a neighbouring *Ginjinha* emporium. Here he bought himself a couple of nips of the warming cherry liquor which was so popular in the area and packaged for tourists in every possible way. The man serving behind the counter was jovial and offered Stuart a taste of some of the different varieties he had on offer. Stuart chatted in what little Portuguese he could manage before the man switched to his broken but highly persuasive English repertoire. Loosened by the alcohol, Stuart forgot his cares for a pleasant twenty minutes and he knew that the shopkeeper had noted his clanking bags of alcohol and figured him for a man on a mission, or at least, one who was up for buying plenty of alcohol that night. Stuart wasn't easily scared, but he was nervous about returning to the hotel and discovering what his burglar might have taken or worse, left behind, and the drink made the idea slightly more palatable. He still needed to win over Palmer and whilst he had momentarily considered that he could have the man all wrong and perhaps it was he who had ransacked his room, found Celia's passport and was now looking for blood or just answers, he thought it more likely that Jon Scott Campbell was the culprit. Stuart must tell Palmer just enough to get him onside but without totally freaking out the man with his insane conspiracy theories. Was a conspiracy theory insane if it was actually all true, Stuart mused?

Now starving, he bid his persuasive new friend goodbye after buying a few more miniatures of the moreish drink and left the emporium, heading back up away from the busier streets, past the theatre district and fashion boutiques to where he remembered seeing a good old fashioned kebab shop, almost identical to those he would frequent back home in Manchester. He ordered himself a disgustingly large doner meat wrap which oozed with garlic mayonnaise and dripped with grease as he tore into it. He ate whilst on the move, keeping his salty fries for later in one of his bags and when he reached the large mall on the corner of the block he knew his hotel was on, he veered off towards a quieter street where he could extricate the cork from the first bottle he pulled out of his bag and empty the bottle down his throat. He had always been a heavy drinker, from the days of rugby training and tours as a teenager but as he'd got older, it had become less social and more a solo activity in his own back bedroom whilst surfing the internet. He knew it was empty calories, he knew the others at the gym thought it ridiculous to be training so hard and then shovelling crap and poison down your neck, but Stuart had few other vices he reasoned. The wine was gone in minutes and he managed an almost comedic burp before he tossed the empty bottle into a bin. There was no way he was going to drink the other four bottles and given they had cost so little and he was already getting tipsy, he tipped them out of his bag into the bin with a crash which made a couple on the other side of the street look around in surprise.

Now faintly drunk, he felt quite angry about his room being violated and his things rummaged through and it took him all his restraint to not go to the front desk and report the crime. He knew that would open a huge can of worms and leave him facing many awkward questions, the most uncomfortable of which would be what he was doing with Celia Payne's passport in the first place, and before he knew it, Edward (or whatever he was calling himself these days) Palmer would be hauled in too and discover that he was a huge creepy charlatan. He stormed up to his room and set about doing a mental inventory of what he had brought, what he had unpacked and what was missing, aside from the passport. Then he looked around for any evidence the ransacker might have accidentally or deliberately left for him. Only a blood smear on the corner of the wall stood out, but he couldn't honestly think why a burglar would leave something like that behind and couldn't rule out that the mark had been there before he checked in. He wiped it with a damp cloth from the bathroom, noting that a few of his things seemed out of place in there too. He emptied out every drawer and compartment of his luggage and sat amongst the piles of clothes and possessions and wondered what the hell he was doing.

It suddenly occurred to him that he should go and seek out Palmer, to draw him into his confidences as soon as possible. The macabre thought passed through his head that Jon Scott Campbell could already have paid him a visit, threatened him, roughed him up or worse, if he knew that they were both staying in the same hotel, just doors down from one another. He quickly tidied away his things so that the room looked as it had when he'd first checked in, tidier even than it had been when he'd departed that morning, and clutching only the bags which contained his souvenir purchases, he left. He paced the hall, at one point pressing his ear gently to Palmer's room door 502, just around the other side of the lift shaft, but hearing nothing. He had paced as far as the other end of the corridor when he turned and saw Palmer moving quickly away from him. Only half an hour later, they had both drunk several bottles of Sagres, Stuart had owned up to at least part of his backstory, explaining how he had basically been following him guiltily around for the last 24 hours, but couldn't help but notice now that Palmer seemed oddly distracted, looking around Stuart's hotel room as if something were amiss. He took the news rather well, Stuart thought, all-considered, but there was no way he could bring up the added complication of Jon Scott Campbell or his unauthorised meddlings in the Celia mystery. Stuart couldn't be sure, but he thought he saw a look of pity flash briefly across Palmer's usually guarded face and he thought it ironic that they both pitied one another in different ways. Plans were tentatively made for the following morning and Palmer tiredly, drunkenly bid him goodnight.

Stuart considered the latter part of the evening a success, especially when compared to the earlier disaster and as he plugged in his phone to charge overnight, he checked the pages of miscarriagesofjustice.com, wondering how he had coped not spending the hours online he ordinarily would have at home. Neither *Derek_Bentley_was_innocent* or *Brightonandhoes* had logged on which was highly suspicious. There were only a few members online, most just lurkers who rarely posted. But the thing that drew his eye was a new discussion thread which had been opened, little animated starbursts exploding either side of the title to alert posters to its status. It had been started by a forum member called *GepettoPsych* which Stuart found odd as it wasn't a username he recalled. Possibly someone had changed their existing name, but it couldn't be someone brand new as he alone could authorise membership. The title of the discussion was the real shocker and without even opening it to read the contents, he knew things had fallen apart completely. The thread's title was '*HOW STUART EVANS GOT AWAY WITH MURDER*' and as Stuart dashed to the bathroom to be sick, he wondered who had betrayed him this time.

27.

Stuart's head was splitting when he finally rolled over to turn his alarm off. He was lucky that he was used to consuming enormous amounts of alcohol, sleeping very little and then being able to get up with a relatively clear head or else he wouldn't be able to function most days on the construction sites and his silent business partner and sometime boss would have rumbled him and sent him home. On a day to day basis Stuart could drink just enough to drown out the underlying misery which crept into the corners of his life. After a frustrating day of hard labour, he would punish himself at the gym, straining his already aching muscles in acts of self-loathing at how empty his life was. Returning to his deserted home, sometimes he would then undo all his good work with unhealthy takeaways and booze, immersing himself in the grubby world of petty, violent and sordid crimes, seeking to solve what he had decided himself to be miscarriages of justice. And yet one of the biggest miscarriages of justice that he knew about and was directly involved in must remain ever a secret. The dawn would arrive, sometimes he would not have even managed an hour of rest, and he would face the day, as sober as could be expected, but with the slightly dopey smile on his face that the public expected and which masked his true nature.

For some reason this morning, nothing could shift the painful stabbing behind his eyes and he'd snoozed three or four times past his initial early alarm hoping it would fade. It was probably the sheer amount of alcohol he'd consumed in such a short period of time on top of the levels of worry which had been heaped upon him across the day which totted up to a stress migraine. He knew that a good breakfast would sort him out at least a little, as long as he could keep the food down. It could very well be the last breakfast he enjoyed before all hell broke loose, if he could enjoy it at all. He'd have to face Palmer and the potential that he might have slept on the news of his pseudo betrayal and decided to reject him. What he really ought to do is go straight home and sort out the mess he was potentially in. Getting away from Jon Scott Campbell would be a start, although given the global nature of the internet, it seemed his reach was far.

His phone was fully charged but no one had been in touch, no one that he knew in the real world. The sensationalised story splashed across his discussion forums had not spread any further it seemed. The slightly secretive nature of most people who visited the site combined with the fact that a lot of their ideas were definitely 'out there' meant that he still had some hope that no one had believed what *GepettoPsych* had posted. The fact that there were scanned images of newspaper reports from back in the day and links to other corroborating sources tarnished whatever hopes he had deep down. For a crackpot to make up a slanderous story was one thing, for them to find an unreliable tabloid from years ago to back up their claims was another, but to find three different accounts of what had happened all that time ago and a few other eyewitness statements to add extra weight seemed to be a mammoth task, a perverse labour of love with no real benefit to anyone. No one had commented after the five posts from *GepettoPsych* but Stuart could see which members had visited the thread and most likely read the stories. What he had done to deserve any of this was uncertain, but if Jon Scott Campbell was trying to break him, or stop him from exposing his own crimes, then this was tantamount to mutually assured destruction. Stuart would see Scott Campbell similarly ruined if it was the last thing he did.

He showered without bothering to adjust the temperature and found the chill to be majorly reviving, despite it making him shiver as he shuffled and dripped his way back into the bedroom. An unanswered pair of mysteries from the previous night suddenly seemed connected and wrapping an enormous fluffy white towel around his midriff, he perched on the side of the bed and checked his phone where it was still plugged in. The idea that had floated into his head during the freezing torrents was that perhaps the new forum member *GepettoPsych* had actually been authorised by his own hand, or at least, someone hijacking his account, and sure enough, as he entered the moderator functions of the forums, he saw that someone using his log in had okayed the membership yesterday afternoon, Stuart knew he was careful with his passwords, used all the right antivirus and malware defence stuff and wasn't especially vulnerable to attack and yet it had happened. The other mystery was that of his room key card seeming to return to his room to aid the break-in. As he slowly dressed and placed his possessions where he always did about his person, he confirmed that he usually, without even thinking, kept both wallet and phone in the same pocket, his right-hand jean pocket. He laughed his throaty laugh at the silliness of him having to re-enact this in order to confirm it, when he knew for a fact that this was where he always kept them. Someone must have got at his wallet and removed the key card and also most likely accessed his phone and authorised the new forum member all in one fell swoop. But who?

Palmer had had the most access to his person, spending most of the day close by his side, but Palmer had no reason to do any of these things and certainly no reason to be in league with the man who had already taken steps to ruin his life and was actively patrolling the city monitoring them both. Jon Scott Campbell was the only real contender, but how on earth had he managed to purloin his possessions and also return them without him noticing? Stuart's headache had begun to clear but as he tried to run back through the previous day's events step by step, the throbbing returned and his eyes began to ache. It was nearly ten minutes to seven and in a while he would get up and wait faithfully outside Palmer's room for him to rise, to begin his service. He needed to push a little further with his efforts to dispense the full truth to the man, but as each hour passed in the beating sun and clinging shadows of Lisbon, the amount of truth he had to tell kept shifting and twisting like bubbling sugar in a hot pan, threatening to froth up and out and scald those in the vicinity. This culinary imagery served only to make Stuart's stomach gurgle and he knew he'd be able to face breakfast in spite of everything.

Before Stuart could make his own efforts to leave, Palmer had knocked on his door and soon enough they were down at breakfast together. Stuart ate to settle his guts and take his mind off the number of different dilemmas he had and Palmer seemed pensive and reserved, though not as prickly as the previous days. He even seemed amused at Stuart's repeated trips to the breakfast buffet to stock up for the day, though he himself was more restrained. Palmer was insistent that they head to the area called Belem, one they had passed through on the second of their bus trips, though he gave no more information as to why he had chosen this place. Stuart was pleased that Palmer was allowing him to accompany him and knew that he clearly hadn't taken it badly that he'd been following him previously or learned anything else unsavoury about him in the intervening hours. Well, Stuart would find out everything eventually he thought, and little by little win Palmer over completely, whilst also telling him as much truth as he could palate. The thought of more of the deliciously sweet custard pastries he'd only just finished munching on was another draw for the location, as Stuart knew it was the only place you could purchase the variety of tart named for the area. Yes, Stuart would ply Palmer with flaky pastry and cinnamon-sweet filling and they would become firm friends and allies and Jon Scott Campbell would be thwarted as every movie villain should be.

The journey to Belem was a complicated one, around the confusing up and down streets of the city but Stuart was confident with his memorising of the map and felt he could easily lead them, even with Palmer's injury, to the basilica where they could hop on the Yellow Bus to their destination. As they walked, Stuart mentally mimed the action of slipping a hand into his trouser pocket and sliding out his wallet or phone or both and wondered how close Palmer had been to him, how close anyone could be without him noticing or feeling the proximity or absence of his things. It seemed very unlikely and yet it must have happened somewhere along the way. He kept patting his pocket when Palmer wasn't looking, ensuring it didn't happen again. He'd gone into the moderator-only higher functions of the site and closed the whole place down that morning, not risking anyone else seeing the dreadful revelations *GepettoPsych* had posted and hoping that if Jon Scott Campbell was monitoring the site, that it would throw him a curveball to find it deactivated so suddenly.

Once they reached the park near to the bus stop they were heading for, Palmer needed to rest and Stuart had been watching him carefully to see how he was doing. It was clear that he was in a lot of pain and not just the injuries he had when they'd first met. Stuart had noticed a new wound on the man's head. Now was as good a time as any to ask about it all and Stuart was disappointed to find that he didn't entirely believe Palmer's version of events, something ropey about a mugging in Rusholme. The very mention of a violent incident in that area set Stuart's teeth on edge and his mind racing to thoughts of Jon Scott Campbell's streak of terror fifteen years ago, but he was able to throw in an exaggerated anecdote of an incident that had happened to one of the brickies he worked with as if it had happened to him and keep Palmer entertained. Stuart was pleased to see Palmer was shocked at the casual way he relayed the story but secretly impressed at his no-nonsense approach. Stuart couldn't believe that Palmer had done nothing about his attack and when he told him how he'd acquired his newest injury, Stuart was floored. The idea that Palmer had interrupted whoever had broken into his hotel room and been hurt in the process made his own head begin to throb again and he trotted out a lie as to his own whereabouts the previous night, not fancying his drunken wanderings and search for a corkscrew as sounding especially believable.

As Palmer launched into a particularly fervent discourse about a man who he thought was stalking him around town, who had attacked him in the metro station and stalked him to the river front, Stuart realised that he was describing Jon Scott Campbell without really knowing who he was or the extreme influence the man had over both their lives at the moment. Worse than that, as Palmer rambled on and Stuart stared into space, he spied a red-head moving through the elegant trees of the park, dodging past children and teachers all engaged in a lively sporting event and oblivious to the violent, disruptive presence now close at hand. He reached into his other pocket, the one he had not needed to monitor during their journey and clutched at the corkscrew he'd put in there this morning. Jon Scott Campbell was approaching them and if he got near enough, if he tried anything to hurt him or Palmer, or even any of the innocent bystanders around them, Stuart would whip out the corkscrew and jam it into the bastard's throat, twisting it around until he was dying or dead. He wasn't going to get away with it this time.

28.

Matilde Marujo was a naïve little thing with too much time on her hands for the wrong sorts of men. She worked hard most evenings throughout the week and into the weekend and filled the small gaps in her schedule with rendezvous after rendezvous with the type of men who frequented the bar restaurant she worked in. She had lived her entire life in the bright and busy streets of Lisbon and had never left the area, not even to visit her father's family in Spain or her mother who had fled the country when she was a child too small to even remember her face. The furthest she ever travelled was along the coast or across the Tagus for a brief excursion with her girlfriends to sunbathe on the beaches or flirt with the sailors and fishermen they encountered. Being dazzlingly pretty and looking much younger than her age, she found herself the focus of attention in whichever circles she moved, be it the men she took drinks orders for at work, her father's friends who were always around at the family apartment or just the catcalls and wolf whistles of oglers on the cobbled roads she meandered along each day. Her hair fell in long, chestnut tresses which naturally curled and flicked into her eyes when she threw her head back and laughed her childish little laugh which she knew drove the men wild.

Her life was very uncomplicated. She rose when she felt like it, knowing she had hours before her shift started, in the spacious apartment her father owned and in which she had her own en-suite room. She would wander about in her silken nightgown, drinking coffee and looking at the newspapers her father left around hoping to entice her into a better way of life. He seemed to judge her as a silly child at times who was on the wrong path in life but reacted badly to any attempts to steer her, so he simply kept her at a distance, had learned not to interfere too much and hoped she would find her own way eventually. The newspapers were usually international or broadsheets as he judged the local tabloid press as worse than fiction. His work often took him away from town and after the first few times of trying to persuade Matilde to accompany him, he had given up but would return with wild stories of the places he had been in the vain hope something would stir within her and make her beg to be taken along on the next trip.

Once it reached mid-morning, she would shower and dress and sometimes wander down to the market to buy groceries for the evening meal, if she felt like cooking. If not, she would sometimes take a stroll around the neighbourhood park or visit a gallery where she would stare for a few minutes at each painting, knowing that the swirls and blobs of paint translated to nothing in her mind, stirred no emotion and the process was a waste of time. On days like this, she would grow frustrated and set off for work early, returning home after her shift to a darkened apartment, an empty fridge and a rumbling stomach. Most nights Matilde had an engagement with a man and if not one of the sleazy local boys who already knew she would take them to bed, then someone she had met in the restaurant who was just passing through and looking for an evening of company and passion. Matilde sometimes dwelt on the idea that she was effectively a very low-rent, low-priced escort who after a few drinks, a few more compliments and some gentle nudging would leap into bed with whichever man was doing the buying that day.

Matilde's horizons were narrow and her expectations low and she did not believe in love of any sort. She cared for her father when she saw him, but she also resented that he had driven her mother away who she felt sure she must have had some affection for as a child, but with no memories of the woman and her father having destroyed every photo of her, Matilde's imagination was not strong enough to conjure up even the vaguest impression of a loving mother. She had no desire to search for her on the internet, though some of her girlfriends had pointed out how easy it would be, and didn't even own a computer of her own. She kept a mobile phone but only for keeping in touch with her father, her friends, work and the men she eagerly gave out her number to. People found it odd that she had no smart phone, had no social media accounts and lived her life very simply and without the complications of the modern age. People found it more odd that she refused to take things any further with any of the boys who fawned over her and instead simply went on dates which invariably ended in the bedroom.

She had no type and had gone for drinks with men of all shapes, sizes, colours and backgrounds, often men who others coughed and spluttered over when they saw her on their arm due to their complete incongruity beside her. She dated men who reminded her of her father or his friends and saw nothing peculiar and she willingly slept with men she knew were already involved or soon to be involved. She had woken up in the house of a man on the morning of his wedding, discovering him getting his morning suit on as she stirred and had once been served breakfast cheerily by the wife of a man she had slept with, a wife too afraid of losing her husband entirely who had slackened the shackles of matrimony quite a lot. Her latest flame was another man whose wife clearly didn't satisfy or appreciate him any longer and Matilde had felt sorry for him, seeing his romantic efforts spurned across the restaurant table and the cold looks the woman had given him and indeed Matilde herself when she had tried to break the ice with a few questions about their stay in town. When the man's wife took her fifth trip to the restrooms, Matilde had been delighted when the man told her how beautiful she was and exchanged numbers with her. He had barely restrained his desire for her even when his wife returned and Matilde was thrilled that this British man with his passable Portuguese and loathsome wife would entertain her for the next few days at least.

They had texted the entire evening from the moment he had paid and left, making sure he placed the ridiculously generous tip into her tiny delicate hands and allowing her to feel the warmth in his own as he closed them around hers. Matilde would alternate between Portuguese and English in their messages but often didn't understand what Jon had said to her, relying on her limited vocabulary designed merely to communicate with the steady stream of tourists who found their way into her restaurant in the busy summer months. He told her he was a businessman with a sick wife (though Matilde felt no sympathy for the miserable shrew she'd clapped eyes on that first night) but would not say what his business was or what his wife's illness was and Matilde didn't care to ask. Whilst he rarely agreed to anything definite in terms of meeting up, the suggestion was always there and the tone of their messages was beyond flirty. Between these messages, Matilde continued to date local boys and drive them wild with her mercurial temperament.

It took Matilde a week to cajole Jon into bed and whilst their lovemaking had satisfied her, she was practically thrown out of his apartment straight after, with the definite suggestion being that the sickly wife was unexpectedly returning which seemed to anger Jon. Since then, Matilde had only heard from him a few times and whilst she desired him – his face was attractive, his body appealing and his charm undeniable – she adopted the same girlish silliness she used with all her courters which made them feel like they were all she was thinking about when often she was either thinking about all of them, or more often than not, none of them. Jon was often very late in replying to messages and Matilde didn't know or care whether it was his work or his awful wife causing the delay. She didn't much think of him between texts but when her phone buzzed and she saw it was Jon, she felt an undeniable stirring.

139

One afternoon on her day off, she had taken a long, decadent bath knowing her father was away and she could wander about the apartment entirely naked without reproach, but upon leaving the bathroom she discovered one of her father's business friends sitting in the kitchen, apparently waiting for her father, but more interested in her movements. He had picked up her phone where she had left it charging by the kettle and was thumbing through it disgustedly, reeling off the amount of male names in her contacts list, taking chunks of text messages already salacious enough out of context to make them sound disgusting and asking who this Jon character was. Matilde wouldn't show that the man's presence made her flesh crawl as one thing she knew about her father's friends was their thirst for power knew no bounds, so she simply asked him to leave and threatened to go into the street and call for help wearing not a stitch of clothing if he didn't obey.

Unfazed by her afternoon, she had been almost pleased to receive a call from her timid boss begging her to help out for a few hours that evening as her co-worker Beatriz had failed to turn up for her shift. Later as she was about to leave, she received a message from Jon arranging for them to meet that night and she was pleased that she had only agreed to a few hours and not the late shift her boss had really wanted her to volunteer for. She met Jon in a bar near work, changing into one of her sexier dresses in the restaurant toilets but found him distracted and uninterested. Attempts to provoke him, to make him jealous all failed and so somewhat despondently, she left, thinking she should probably seek out her father's friend and apologise for her earlier bout of melodrama. She tottered down the street, wondering whether to take a taxi across town or whether to walk. It was a pleasant enough evening.

The winding streets, so familiar to her, danced with the shadows flung by passing vehicles in the darkness but Matilde felt no trepidation. She was halfway to her destination before she even realised someone was following her. They were just far enough behind her that she had dismissed them as merely someone heading the same way, but after a few deliberate wrong turns and a hike up a ridiculously steep side street that no one in their right mind would attempt on purpose and then descend straight after, she realised the shadowy figure was not only keeping track of her, but was now gaining, perhaps emboldened by the lack of any other people around. Matilde had veered off the beaten track slightly in order to definitively decide if the dark shape behind was following her, but had now taken herself into a deserted and oppressive street that she didn't often walk down. It was narrow and the buildings rose high on either side, windows and doors boarded up, no side streets and a low bridge intersecting the way. High above, she could see the warm inviting lights of other bars and restaurants and hear the laughter of pleasant conversation and good company. The gloom of the tunnel beneath the bridge gave no hint of an escape and moonlight glimmered hauntingly in the puddles which barred her progress.

She broke into a run, kicking off her heels and splashing through the black water, disappearing into the gaping mouth of the tunnel. She could hear the echoing footsteps of her pursuer also speeding up and hoped that she had enough of a head start to make it under the bridge to where she hoped a steep stair would allow her to ascend to the safer level. The darkness of the tunnel consumed her; it was much longer and darker than she had anticipated.

She never made it to the other side.

29.

Palmer looked to where Stuart was gawping, his annoyance at his companion's lack of focus instantly replaced with mortal fear. Briefly in between these two extreme emotions there had been a moment where Palmer had assumed this to be some sort of strange joke far too subtle or too edgy for him to appreciate but now he could see that this was no laughing matter and that Stuart too was nervous. Stalking across the park, not fifty metres from them was the slender red-haired man, looking angry and determined and exuding a natural force so unnerving that even across the closing distance, Palmer felt intimidated. As he grew nearer, Palmer could tell that this was most certainly the man he'd seen at the metro station and on the boat, but was not a match for the intruder last night. His gait and body language was more cocky, more full of sang froid than the brutal blundering of the burglar. Stuart had leapt to his feet, though Palmer was not sure whether the big man's instinct was for fight or flight but he himself was rooted to the bench. Surely an attack in broad daylight, amongst the innocent play of children was beyond him?

"Stuart?" asked Palmer, breathlessly.

The builder merely looked around at the sound of his name but it was as if he couldn't see Palmer. He was blinded by rage or fear or some other all-consuming emotion as yet unidentified and his strange blank face made Palmer even more unsettled than the approaching stranger. Looking around, there was no one to summon for help, no obvious escape route, especially not with his troubled knee and within a few moments, the red-headed man would be on top of them. Just as Palmer had given up hope of any sort of intervention, out of nowhere, two square-jawed men in dark suits had appeared and barred the approaching man's progress. Palmer assumed they must have been just out of sight, perhaps themselves lurking in the picturesque gardens awaiting the man's arrival and as suddenly as they had appeared, they disappeared, hauling the man along with them. He showed no signs of protest or resistance and walked between them as they led the way to the far side of the park. As they disappeared amongst the trees, the red-headed man turned and shot such a glance of hatred in their direction that it made Palmer shudder. Once they had all vanished from sight, Palmer unfroze and painfully stood.

"What the hell just happened?" he asked Stuart, who was clenching and unclenching his fists as if in the midst of a terrible spasm. "You know who that man is, don't you?" he added, angrily, wondering just what else Stuart knew and had withheld from him over the last 36 hours.

After a long pause, when the rising and falling of his huge chest subsided, Stuart finally broke his gaze off from the edge of the park and it was as if his attack mode had been stood down. He turned to look at Palmer, sheepish and sorry.

"I don't really *know* 'im," he admitted. "But I do know who 'e is. 'e's a dangerous man. Someone who's got away with some terrible things over the years and I've been onto 'im."

Palmer gaped at this news, questioning in his head why Stuart had failed to disclose this information each time he'd had the opportunity, each time the red-haired man had been nearby and even when Palmer had expounded his insane-sounding theories about him.

"Trouble is," Stuart continued. "I think 'e's now onto me. Well, both of us, I reckon mate." He looked down at his feet, took a deep breath as if he'd weighed up the possible outcomes of what he was about to say. "'arry…" he began.

Palmer shook his head and raised a finger in objection.

"If we're being honest with one another at last," he interrupted. "Then you need to acknowledge that we both know my name's *not* Harry and stop calling me it. I'm Edward Lawrence Palmer, 37, born just outside Sheffield, single, no children and I'm here in Lisbon looking for answers in the Celia Payne disappearance."

He presented his hand to be shaken by way of introduction and was clearly indicating a fresh start. Around them, the occasional scream of excitement or enthusiastic cheer shattered the otherwise tranquil atmosphere. Stuart's face became the dopey default setting which both amused and irritated Palmer and he finally took Palmer's hand and shook it eagerly.

"I'm Stuart Arnold Evans, 28, from Levenshulme originally," he said. "Builder and co-owner of a construction company. I live alone and as you know I'm a bit of a true crime buff. I came 'ere on 'oliday, not business or owt, but I'm now thinkin' I've been steered into this whole situation by that man, that *bastard* we saw."

It was the first time the red-headed man's presence had been spoken of since his strange removal by the suited men and Palmer was keen to find out what Stuart knew. He suggested they get out of the area quick, sticking to their original plan of getting the bus to Belem, giving them the chance to cover some distance speedily, have a change of scene and be alone to share what they both knew. After all, Belem was where he had been summoned to, separately perhaps from this interception. As they left the park, the welcome sight of a yellow double decker came thundering down the hill and pulled into the bus bay ahead of them. Stuart chivalrously dashed to stop the bus and asked the driver to wait a few moments whilst Palmer hobbled as best he could after him. The driver looked at Palmer with pity as he hauled himself aboard and waved his ticket and whilst Palmer found a seat, Stuart bought another day ticket, removing more wads of cash clumsily from his pockets.

Once seated, the two of them had an awkward few moments whilst they caught their breath and Palmer stared intently out of the window as the park vanished from view and the bus drove past the magnificent Basilica on their left. He half-expected to see the red-headed man chasing after the bus, breaking free from the custody of the imposing goons in suits.

"So who *is* that man?" demanded Palmer after a while, impatient of waiting for his so-called comrade to fess up.

"Jon Scott Campbell I believe, 'arry," said Stuart and this time Palmer did nothing to correct him. It sort of felt right. "I think 'e might've been the one who did somethin' to your Celia. 'e's got form for it."

As the bus wended its way through the narrow streets, finally lurching onto the major road which ran parallel to the Tagus and under the colossal *25 de Abril* bridge, Palmer listened intently as Stuart told him about a string of attacks on young women around fifteen years ago in the Manchester area and how he felt certain that this Jon Scott Campbell character was responsible. Palmer was amused to hear about Stuart's discussion forums and how he had been their latest topic of conversation, but was astonished to learn that this dangerous man had most likely infiltrated these forums either recently or much earlier in order to monitor Stuart's progress but also it seemed to manipulate him. Palmer sensed there were still more things Stuart was holding back, but had been given more than enough to think about and felt that he should reciprocate, so he told Stuart everything about the messages he had been receiving, the key card, the texts, the birthday card and postcard and how he'd tracked the background of the image of Celia to the underside of the bridge they had just now passed under. He explained his half-formed plans to test the hotel room key on the various hotels around the city and expected Stuart to rubbish them, but found the burly builder nodding in approval.

"Best way, mate," he said. "Do it logically. Go 'otel to 'otel and test it. Maybe we could even access the 'otel records or guest lists somehow."

He trailed off, as if there was something he'd thought of, then immediately dismissed. Palmer hated the awkwardness of it.

"But what if it's all a trap set by that maniac?" asked Palmer, his heart racing again at the very idea of seeing the red-haired man's baleful eyes. "I mean, how come he was there at the park? You didn't discuss our plans online, did you? You said you'd already deleted your forums. And if he sent me the Belem message, why would he intercept us *there*?"

Palmer's head was beginning to hurt almost as much as his knee. None of this easily made sense. Whoever had shoved the pamphlet under the door, it wasn't Jon Scott Campbell or Stuart, unless both or either of them was playing a stranger game than he could even imagine. His biggest fear was that he was being framed and by playing along, following the orders and decoding the clues, he was in fact falling into their trap. The more bizarre theory which he couldn't shake off was that Celia herself was doing all of this. That this was her twisted idea of revenge, but the thought of her poor, broken body lying in a heap of rubble in a deserted alleyway somewhere in Lisbon made him feel guilty for suspecting her. She had been many things, but wasn't a Machiavellian mastermind. Palmer had caused her a hell of a lot of pain both directly and indirectly and the least he could do now was to track down what had happened to her and if she was in some sort of trouble, if she'd had the breakdown some suspected, he could guide her back to sanity and back to her home.

As the bus pulled into the vast open tract of land in front of the magisterial monastery, the two men got up and disembarked. Palmer knew that he still couldn't entirely trust Stuart, but their strange shared experience of being in the firing line of Jon Scott Campbell had somehow brought them closer together.

"Who do you think those men were?" Palmer asked as he sat on a stone bollard to massage his knee before the inevitable stress and strain it would be placed under during their search.

Neither of them had raised the question of what had actually happened to Jon Scott Campbell, the surreal sight of the two men resembling bouncers suddenly escorting him from the park almost too good to be true.

"I think," began Stuart, faltering slightly. "I think that could've been my fault. Sometimes I... sometimes my investigations online aren't always welcome and...well, to see men like that followin' me, followin' people that I'm followin'...well, it's not the first time. What I mean to say is, I *think* it 'appened again today."

Palmer didn't dare look up from his work manipulating his knotted leg muscles, didn't dare make eye contact with Stuart. If he did, it might be seen as validating his crazy statement and something might be given away in his look which said that he now believed the man to be absolutely 100% insane.

30.

Stuart knew that what he had just confided in Palmer would sound utterly utterly batshit crazy to anyone else, but he felt deep down that Palmer was a kindred spirit who would not laugh or scoff at his claim, but would be understandably surprised and perhaps concerned. Whatever world Stuart had stumbled into this time, it was unlike anything he'd experienced before, but at least he had Palmer with him to share the strangeness. Stuart remembered a book he'd read at high school set during the Great Depression where a miserable African American character lived alone and had reached the point where at times he no longer knew if what he was seeing was real or not and badly craved company, if only to have someone to share experiences with. He couldn't remember much else about the book other than it having a morbidly tragic ending for quite a few of the characters. He resolved to look it up when he got home.

Stuart hadn't worked hard at school despite a natural ability for education and his teachers constantly telling him he was much smarter than he gave himself credit. His English teacher in particular praised his imagination and creative writing, but Stuart knew it was born out of a troubled upbringing and didn't like the part of himself that it revealed when he tapped into it. He often launched into slightly off-kilter narratives, both written and spoken which seemed perfectly harmless at the beginning but soon made others around him wonder if he was altogether sane by the end of them.

Ultimately, Stuart was more inclined to practical matters and was good with his hands, hands which he now realised had blood spattered on them as he sat next to Palmer outside the huge monastery. He turned them over, keeping

147

them low, out of Palmer's eyeline hopefully and realised that he must have been squeezing the corkscrew so tightly in his pocket, that he had gouged a deep spiral channel into the palm of one hand which looked raw and painful and had transferred blood to the other during his later handwringing. He hadn't even remembered bringing the corkscrew along with them that morning, but there it was in his pocket. A knife would have been more use, something to brandish and warn an attacker off rather than something which suggests jovially opening a bottle together. He looked around for something to wipe his hands on and saw nothing and knew he had no tissues or wipes of any kind about him. He wasn't the sort of person to carry such things around with him. The leather shoulder bag he wore might have looked like it would be ideal for such things, but Stuart wore it more out of routine than practicality and when he wore it at work, he took stick from the lads who dared to comment on its stylishness with nothing but a mocking tone. It contained one of his most precious possessions, one too valuable to leave lying around unattended.

Palmer on the other hand looked like a man who carried things of use with him and Stuart had spied in his bag the previous day on the bus and seen practical things like water, suntan lotion and a notebook at the very least. He stared at the bag now, wondering if it might also contain plasters, antiseptic, gloves even, to treat and to hide his shame. Stuart realised that Palmer was now watching him as he stared at his bag and had spotted the injury to his hands. He looked nervous, but simply said very calmly that they had perhaps better find somewhere to wash and freshen up. How very British, Stuart thought. How very Palmer.

Stuart was keeping speech to a minimum now, fearing his own stupid blundering tongue either driving Palmer further away or else accidentally revealing something foolish or incriminating. On the bus ride he had been about to suggest he knew a contact who could easily hack into hotel records and help in their search for Celia, but then he realised that the youngster he thought of as a computer expert capable of accessing privileged information from a number of secure sources may in fact be the alias of the very man who had arrived earlier to menace them. He was already walking a very fine line between remaining calm about his breached security and going into complete meltdown about the idea that his prized forums may in fact be an entire fiction spun by an enemy. Palmer for his own part, seemed tired but unflappable. Stuart watched him intently as they walked in the shadow of the monastery.

His comrade had gone on to suggest that the nearby *Pasteis de Belem* bakery might be a good place for Stuart to find a bathroom to check out his hands and had nodded across the road and tram lines to a street where Stuart could see a queue snaking along from the front of a long blue shop front. Palmer had reasoned that whatever Jon Scott Campbell had planned, it had been derailed or delayed and they should use the time they had before he attempted to catch up with them again to do some digging. He was quite vague about what exactly that entailed and Stuart knew that he was keeping things back from him still. He knew that it would be hypocritical of him to pass judgement, given the amount of things he himself had yet to disclose. Palmer went on to say that here in the bright and bustling open spaces of Belem, he felt safe and that extended to the tourist trap tart emporium down the road. Stuart wasn't sure if he was overdoing things to make Stuart feel better or to reassure himself, but he said that he would wait, probably returning to sit on one of the bollards, whilst Stuart got cleaned up and not to worry about him.

Stuart carefully crossed the road, keeping his hands stuffed in his pockets – he figured there was probably already blood in one if not both of them so what the hell – and occasionally glancing back at Palmer who seemed to be engaged in browsing on his phone. The queue leading up to the custard tart specialist was long, longer than the shop front itself and was made up of all manner of tourists, though he noted the largest faction was a long group of Japanese-looking people who true to the stereotype were photographing the building and each other to within an inch of their lives. There were two entrances to the building, one for those wishing to dine in and one for those simply wanting to purchase and take out some tarts. The queue was heading to the latter of the two doors, so Stuart excused himself and made his way through the first door, hoping to find a bathroom without having to sit down or order anything.

The smell of vanilla, cinnamon and rich sweet pastry had wafted out onto the street, but once he stepped over the threshold of the building, it was all-consuming and mesmerising. Even though it hadn't been long since he'd eaten, Stuart found his mouth watering and his stomach gurgling persuasively that it needed some of the tempting treats immediately. He staved off the impulse for now and found a pretty blue tiled bathroom he could hole up in, veering away from a maître d' who looked as though he was heading over to seat him. It was an individual cubicle with wash basin and therefore no audience, so Stuart bolted himself in and ran some warm soapy water in the basin. The imprint in his hand would have been comical if it hadn't been so painful and it alarmed him that he must have been so worked up to inflict the injury on himself, but also to have not really felt the pain until he saw the severity of it. The drying blood rinsed away quickly from both hands and the sting of his right hand numbed slightly when immersed in the water. The pain was a real reminder of the dangers of what he normally only encountered online and even though the wound was self-inflicted, it was like his first taste of action in the field. He felt ambivalent about the whole encounter.

A gentle knock sounded on the bathroom door which Stuart barely heard as he was emptying the sink and running both taps on full to rinse away the traces of blood. He pulled several paper towels from a dispenser and dabbed at both of his hands, drying them but also checking if the wound was still bleeding, if further washing or soaking was required. A second louder knock made him jump and he now turned both taps off and stood silent, listening for who it might be. He asked who was there in English first, then something closely resembling that intent in Portuguese, although it could have been Spanish when he thought about it. There was no reply in any language from outside. Perhaps the person was simply keen to use the facilities but not to engage in conversation about it. Most likely they had moved off to find another bathroom. Stuart looked at himself in the mirror and was dejected. His face was red and shiny where he'd obviously caught too much sun the day before, with the worst areas being the tip of his nose and his ears and neck. He was sweaty and looked in worse shape than usual, his neck muscles hidden behind rolls of fat which only intensified as he frowned at himself. There was a sudden hammering at the door now, aggressive and impatient and Stuart panicked. There were no windows from which to leap, not that he'd probably have been able to get through them anyway, and his only escape was to face whoever was banging. He decided that there was nothing for it other than to confront them, so he slowly took the corkscrew out of his pocket, holding it in his uninjured hand, behind his back and then slid the bolt across.

He pulled the door suddenly towards him, jumping back and causing the person on the other side to stumble forwards in shock and almost land on the floor in a heap. Brandishing the spiral spike, Stuart glared down at the shape of a small Chinese boy who immediately burst into tears. He had his legs crossed and was jiggling urgently, clearly desperate for the toilet and unsure what to do about it. He saw the tool in Stuart's hand and began to wail. Stuart sidestepped around him and gestured as if to indicate that the toilet was now all his and moved quickly through the eatery, riddled with embarrassment. He hoped the child got over the sudden shock and had managed to reach the toilet before it was too late and managed to calm himself down, fight off the adrenaline rush as he stepped back onto the street. The queue had gone down somewhat in the minutes he'd been inside and he thought it prudent to satisfy his hunger and settle his stomach again with some of the sweet treats. He tried to picture Palmer's face when he arrived back at their seat with his arms laden with custard tarts. He really didn't know the man well enough to know exactly what his reaction would be. He barely seemed to eat and didn't look as if he looked after himself or ever indulged in such things.

Stuart couldn't help himself. Stress made him hungry and food made him calm. He bought six heavenly smelling tarts which were delicately placed into a cardboard box, then a see-through plastic bag with the emporium logo on.

Sachets of icing sugar and cinnamon were tossed into the bag, along with napkins and Stuart emerged from the building for a second time, this time feeling pretty upbeat, despite everything else going on. He marvelled at how uncomplicated life could be with a bag of calorific pastries in his hand and the sun beating down on him. Even if Palmer refused a tart, he'd persuade him to at least give one a try. The smell alone was irresistible. He reached the crossing to get to the monastery side of the road which was busy with a tram heading by and also a Yellow Bus parked up ready to embark on a different route around the area. Once these had moved off and the cars held up by them had cleared, Stuart crossed and looked around blinking in the bright sun to locate where he had left Palmer. He felt sure it had been the stone blocks by the edge of the grassy lawn which lay before the monastery, but there was no one there. The blocks further away were home to a group of what appeared to be nuns, possibly on a pilgrimage of some sort, he mused.

He reached the blocks he felt certain he'd been sitting on not that long ago and behind the second one, he found a tiny bottle of suntan lotion and a pair of shades, clearly from Palmer's shoulder bag. They were lying in the dry dust at the edge of the yellowing grass, as if the bag's contents had spilled onto the ground, as if they had been dropped or tossed aside in anger. But as for Palmer, there was no sign at all.

31.

Jon Scott Campbell was uncharacteristically worried. He wasn't an idiot and had known that a pretty young carefree thing like Matilde Marujo had exceptional baggage, and in her case, it was an entire set of Portuguese Mafioso luggage in the form of her psychotic father and his associates, but Jon had never expected to fall foul of them and their peculiar attitudes to justice. He knew Matilde was most likely an embarrassment to her father, being so flighty and getting about town with half the eligible local men of age and a fair few not eligible and certainly *not* of age. At worst, Jon had expected her to finish things abruptly by parental pressure, or for him to be rudely roughed up in an alleyway one evening whilst leaving her company, but he had never expected to be publicly kidnapped and bodily hauled away. He now assumed he was in one of the Marujo property lockups, the family business owning many random plots of land throughout the city and wider region, rather handy for Marujo himself, but not so handy for Jon who had lost all sense of geography once bundled into the car and given a severe slapping around to disorientate him. The awkward journey staggering from the car to the room he was now in was a further daze and he felt that whilst the heavies hadn't intended to hurt him much…*yet*…one of them had caught his right temple and eye and it was swelling up, limiting his vision. But what he *could* see was the dingy interior of some sort of junk room or storage locker. He could be *anywhere*.

Marujo was a hideous, sweaty man, lacking every positive quality his daughter possessed and in fact more resembling a crooked, inverse mirror image of the willowy beauty. His skin was liver spotted and pockmarked, his hair wiry and white in great tufts on his brows, in his ears and emerging from

152

his unbuttoned shirt at his chest. He wore huge, 1970s style sunglasses which made him look like a faded Las Vegas entertainer and he stank, a nauseating mixture of body odour and awful cologne – a really nasty vintage which smelled like stale piss and musk and cost him a small fortune to procure. Even though Jon's vision was impaired, he could smell Marujo a mile off. He owned so many properties around the town that it was invariable you had accidentally stumbled onto his turf, but it was impossible to tell normally, so varied was his portfolio, until a side door opened within the restaurant or gift shop and that awful, gut churning smell wafted through. Marujo was here now, which could only mean trouble for Jon.

"Where *is she*?!" roared the businessman from the shadows.

Jon realised that he had been sitting there the whole time, in the darkness, and it was only the whirring of a fan which someone had just turned on which had alerted his nostrils to the stench. He squinted around and realised that the items he had supposed were junk earlier, were in fact perhaps a little more valuable. There were vases, items of jewellery and even paintings, some wrapped in dustsheets, others leaning on shelves like oversized dominoes. This was a stash of some sort, Jon thought. Marujo had a filthy fat finger in every pie going, every area of crime, both petty and organised, and this had to be one of his secret storage houses. If Jon had been brought here, that didn't bode well. Marujo must be arrogantly assuming he would never walk away from this place.

"She who?" spat Jon through gritted teeth, figuring playing dumb might at least keep him alive a little longer whilst he figured out what to do.

"Matilde, you bastard!" cried Marujo, and the despite him being a good few metres away, Jon felt flecks of spit land on his face.

Jon's hands were bound behind his back and he had been tossed onto the cold stone floor like a discarded toy. There was nothing stopping him from getting up, if he could get his balance properly, and nothing stopping him from walking or running even. He took in his surroundings now as his eyes grew accustomed to the dark. There was a large garage door behind him which he didn't remember coming through, as he had heard no noise which would have accompanied it, but he noticed a regular doorway to the left, which light streamed under. It wasn't even closed properly. There were no guards in here, none of the heavies who had hauled him in. *The sheer arrogance of Marujo, to leave him here without being properly restrained or guarded!*

"I don't know," replied Jon. "I saw her yesterday." He raised his head now, trying to make out Marujo's repulsive form in the gloom, then changed his tone, to one of breeziness. "Have you tried phoning her?"

"She never came home last night," growled Marujo and Jon's stomach shuddered a little.

No wonder Marujo seemed angrier than usual. No wonder mistakes had been made in terms of allowing him chances to escape. Emotion made fools of people. He would use the man's sentiment as his way of getting out, but Jon too was interested in knowing the truth about where poor Matilde had gone. Logically, she had gone home with another man, or spent the night with friends as so often happened, but for Marujo to be this wound up, there must be more to it than he was saying. Still, Jon had no time to hang around being vaguely interrogated by an idiot like Marujo. He needed to get back on track with his plans.

Stuart Evans had looked rattled to bits when he clapped eyes on him in the park, and even though Jon hadn't organised the meeting, it was pleasing to see how paranoid he had been able to make him. Infiltrating his pathetic true crime forum had been simplicity itself. But seeing Evans and Palmer together had spooked him a little. The two men ought to be natural enemies. One was a pathetic defender of the vulnerable and needy, the other the cause of their suffering. What had Palmer done or said to get Evans on side? Jon would need to get in touch with his own ally, Jeep, and find out what was happening. But first, he needed to get out of this ridiculous kidnapping scenario.

Marujo was slavering on about some sort of pain he would inflict upon Jon, but he wasn't listening. He had shuffled so that he backed up against one of the shelves, using it to slowly stand. Marujo's tone barely altered which suggested that he wasn't even paying attention to him, behind those ridiculous shades. Jon was slightly thrown by the rev of an engine and the rattle of machinery until he realised that what he could hear was the car he had been brought here in and the mechanism opening the garage doors. No wonder there was no one guarding him, the goons had been sent off to bring the car in. The storage room was huge, almost a small warehouse and this was Jon's chance. He glanced quickly back to see light flooding in as the larger door whirred upwards and could smell the strong fumes of the car engine. Marujo was still ranting, but had raised his voice now above the motor noise and in seconds, Jon had lunged at him, knocking him from his chair in an outraged squawk. He had a good few seconds left before the door fully opened and the people in the car got a clear view of him, so Jon gave Marujo's torso a solid kicking which he almost immediately regretted as the sweaty blob on the floor seemed to latch onto his foot and refuse to let go. He extricated himself by stamping viciously on the man's arm until he felt something break and turned and headed for the side door. The garage doors were open now and headlights streamed in as the car shuffled slowly forward. Jon didn't know what lay beyond the door, or how quickly anyone would give chase, but he knew that this was his chance.

He had reached the side door in three bounds, having loosened his bonds, and was about to vanish when he spotted a large holdall practically blocking the way. Gold jewellery, candlesticks and even rolls of paper – scrolls perhaps – bulged from it. Someone had been very busy robbing or fencing it seemed. Jon considered it a tax for his inconvenience and a gift, given it was right there in his escape path. Barely pausing for thought, he heaved the bag over his shoulder, surprising himself at how heavy it was and how much more in pain he was than he had thought. Those boys had given him a better seeing to than he had thought. Well, next time he saw them, if there *was* a next time, he'd give as good as he got. But first, he needed to deal with Palmer and Evans. He was away through the door, down a corridor, up a flight of steps and found himself squinting in the sunlight on a narrow, steep street he felt certain was within running distance of *Rato* Metro station. By the time the idiots reversed their car out of the subterranean parking garage, he would be long gone.

32.

It wasn't that Palmer was suddenly freaked out by Stuart and had to get away. It wasn't even that he had seen this coming and chosen his moment to swerve his company. It was more the fact that something suddenly, terribly, urgently obvious had occurred to Palmer and he simply had to investigate. He'd waited a few minutes for his companion, had hobbled back to the road crossing to look for him, but it seemed the bluff builder was in no real hurry to get back to him, and without a way of contacting him, he simply had to ditch him. He was sure they would reconvene at the hotel before too long and if they didn't, then, no *huge* loss. Palmer didn't do proper, close friends and never really had. Even his supposed best friend Dr. George Davis was suitably kept at arm's length. He wasn't about to change now.

Clutching the pamphlet which Palmer had assumed was suggesting they meet at *Pasteis de Belem*, he scurried away through a rather charming ornamental garden with water fountains and much further away, a view out across the Tagus. He had been rummaging in his bag, checking his journal, then had decided to study the message, wondering if it compared to any other example of handwriting he'd seen previously. It was then that he suddenly noticed that far from simply being a scrawly red pen message, that in fact, some of the letters of the message were actually in *black* ink. He had read it as:

'Tomorrow. Meet at noon.'

On closer inspection, after underlining the letters, it actually said:

*'**Tom**orrow. M**e**et at noon.'*

156

The letters 'T' 'o' 'r' 'r' and 'e', which were in black ink, clearly spelled out the word 'torre'. As he limped along the path amidst the uniform strips of green lawn and immaculately clipped trees, the hazy shape of the southern side of the Tagus came more into view and directly in front of it, the gleaming white thrusting shape of the *Padrao dos Descobrimentos*, the monument to Portugal's brave historic explorers. Palmer remembered from the boat ride the day before that just beyond that, along the coast, was the *Torre de Belem*, the medieval-looking tower which was surely his true destination. The photo of the underside of the bridge was a steppingstone along the way to the tower, he now assumed. Someone, if not Celia, then someone pretending to be her or who knew the truth of her location or disappearance, wanted Palmer at the tower, and despite his lack of mobility, he intended to make the date they had set. It was already well after half past ten and Palmer thought it may well take him half an hour to drag his sorry self along the river front to the tower. He had also noticed on the river cruise that some sort of queuing system operated at the tower whereby tourists wishing to gain access to the relic were lined up along a wooden bridge leading up to the building itself as if the place were so popular, or its capacity so limited that it was one in one out. Arriving for the noon deadline might not be as straightforward as he imagined if he were still stuck in a queue at the allotted hour.

Palmer gave a brief moment's thought to what his new acquaintance's reaction might have been to his disappearance, but hardly knowing this Stuart character at all, he found it hard to predict. Sometimes Palmer felt that his brain was very much wired up in the way an early computer system might have been arranged. It was efficient, quick and as logical and unemotional as one would expect, but if something was not programmed into its sphere of operation, if there was a gap in his knowledge or experiences, then his brain could not simulate an appropriate response. He learned incredibly quickly, was shrewd, calculating and decisive, but the first time he encountered a situation, particularly one as unpredictable and emotional as Stuart Evans, he simply did not understand it and had no idea how to handle it. Jokey nicknames of 'robot' or 'calculator' had always dogged him, even amongst the select few he allowed near enough to him to entertain the idea of calling one another nicknames and Palmer being Palmer, he had felt little either way about the mockery. He knew on occasion how he *should* react, but had on more than one occasion simply misjudged the appropriate response and drawn even more attention to himself by *overreacting* to a situation than he previously had by having *no* reaction at all. Perhaps Stuart would be fine, although Palmer doubted it.

The heat of the morning was steadily increasing and the sun overhead promised nothing but a glorious, scorching day. Thankfully, here along the Tagus, the breeze across the shoreline was cooling to the point of actually being bracing and whilst Palmer appreciated its temperature lowering effect, it made walking hard going, particularly for a man with knackered legs. He had turned right upon reaching the simply impressive *Padrao dos Descobrimentos* and was walking past some exotic palms along the wide riverside road with its fast traffic and rather unusually, a railway line separating the opposite directions of traffic. Across the road, a series of white, flat roofed buildings evoked a sense of being in North Africa and Palmer remembered that the continent was literally just a boat ride away from here and its cultural effects keenly felt in the architecture around him. The buildings were another museum complex and Palmer wondered briefly what it must be like to simply visit this intriguing city without the perils and pitfalls of an active investigation. The general heat and clamminess had begun to sap his strength once more and Palmer was soon weary and thirsty. He noticed a strangely narrow red and white brick arch which was a footbridge of some sort over the busy lanes of traffic and was relieved to see a refreshment stand of some sort nestling by it. The red and white striped roof and what Palmer discovered must be the universal symbol for a well-known ice cream company at the centre of it suggested the perfect place for a rest, so he awkwardly negotiated a soft drink and a choc ice and found a nearby bench to slump on.

It had taken him twice as long as it should have to cover this relatively short distance and coupled with the rest break, he was now cutting it fine. If only he hadn't studied the pamphlet by the dim light of his bedside lamp with tired eyes and no thought for a hidden message. He was getting sloppy in his old age, he chastised himself. He thought that it would probably have even been possible to catch that Belem Yellow Bus they'd seen by the monastery and arrive here in good time, together as a team, not drenched with sweat and gasping in agony as he now was. The park area he was sitting on the edge of was sandy and the trees were arched, bare things launching up into the air at odd angles before exploding in huge green canopies of foliage and shade at their extremities and again Palmer thought of being somewhere far further south like a middle eastern olive grove or a desert oasis. Suitably refreshed although no less in agony (the medication seemed to be having no effect since he was putting so much strain on his joints) he crossed the park diagonally and found the milling crowds gravitating towards the river again. There was the tower at the end of the path, a strangely singular cathedral like thing, thrusting up against then blue sky as though it had fallen into the river itself. There too were the inevitable queues, seemingly not even inching forwards in their quest to gain access to the historic building and promising little in the way of Palmer making his deadline.

How flexible was such a timing anyway, he wondered? Whoever had slid the message under his door could just as surely have knocked on it and spoken to him there and then if they had an urgent message to impart, and if it was passed on by a third party, a courier of some kind, then the message could have been a little more precise in its details. It occurred to Palmer that the cryptic hiding of the true location amongst the words scrawled on the back was perhaps designed to hide the true meaning even from the person delivering it, or anyone else who intercepted it. Someone was going to extreme lengths to demand his presence here and if it was simply a trap, then Palmer had gone the extra mile (literally in this case) to fall into it.

The queue ended just as the wooden bridge reached the mainland and Palmer was surprised to see that he wasn't entirely wrong in his assessment that the tower was in the river as the bridge did indeed separate the tower from the land. The narrow bridge (just wide enough for a queue forming in one direction and the occasional couple of people milling in the opposite direction seeming to have left the tower) was the only way across and it made Palmer feel a little uneasy. This close to the tower, he could now appreciate its majesty even more. It was built out of dazzling pale yellow or white stone, it seemed, and each corner of it was adorned with a cylindrical shaped addition like a watchtower, with rectangular window and domed roof, like some exquisite jelly mould. Atop each dome was a regal-looking decoration, like a crown or fleur de lys. Between these corner domes, the walls were trimmed with great shields, carved from the same rock and emblazoned with crosses which reminded Palmer of the crusades. Judging from the height and the number of visible windows, Palmer estimated the building rose at least six or seven storeys, possibly more if the windows were purely for surveillance rather than light. He joined the back of the queue just behind some American tourists and appreciated their conversation about the lack of theme park style signs indicating the length of wait at this point.

It was impossible not to repeatedly crane one's neck and look up at the imposing structure whilst waiting in its environs and also to wonder at the spectacular view awaiting anyone arriving at the very top. From here, the river was already a beautiful sight, glittering like a carpet of blue and white jewels and to the left, Palmer marvelled again at the *25 de Abril* bridge. Had Celia really sailed down this wide river, posing beneath the bridge for a picture destined to be sent as a clue to bring him here to this mighty tower at the end of her journey. If so, where had she been hiding herself this whole time? Not in the tower, this hotbed of touristic attention, that was for sure. And had that actually been her he had seen on the bus tour, the ghostly sight which had sent him hurtling down the steps from the upper deck, like a madman chasing a figment of his imagination?

The queue shuffled forwards slightly and Palmer once more craned to stare up at the upper reaches of the tower. People were posing, rather daringly it seemed from down here, right on the upper crenelated levels, leaning over the edge with ridiculous selfie sticks and precariously clutched i-Pads too it seemed. Of course, people were waving down at those in the queue, perhaps mocking their interminable wait to gain access and celebrating their own forethought in getting there earlier, or simply waving with childish abandon at the boats and people below, but Palmer could see one figure more insistently waving, rather like a warning signal, with both arms fully extended. The figure was tiny but from the great distance between them, Palmer could see that they were making a nuisance of themselves, risking bashing their arms into those around in their exaggerated gesture. Others may have been directing less specific waves in different directions, but Palmer couldn't help but feel this was aimed at someone down here in particular. Perhaps a group had been separated. He couldn't help but watch as he shuffled forwards again, as the person stopped, throwing their arms down in frustration.

Spurred on by a strange impulse and totally ignoring the people around him who would ordinarily have prevented Palmer making such a spectacle, he suddenly decided to mimic the waver's actions in a two-armed gesture. To his surprise, the person atop the tower immediately responded and joined in the action, even more frantically than before, if that were possible. Could this be the person he was due to meet? It was impossible to see anything but a pink figure and Palmer cursed his lack of a decent camera phone which might have allowed him to zoom in on the figure. Their waving was becoming even more urgent and for some reason, Palmer felt like he was now being warned and glanced over his shoulder. The queue of people snaking behind him was even longer than when he had joined, but he could now see someone pushing their way along, shoving people who were waiting and even the odd few exiting, out of the way. As a gap presented itself in his line of sight, he suddenly realised who was approaching and knew for certain that they were approaching *him*. The man looked pathetic, like the true 'Brit abroad', lumbering through the crowd, oblivious to those around him, pink with sunburn like a lobster, almost operating on a different plane of existence. His eyes were white with terror and his lips were formed into a dramatic pout of concern. Palmer was alarmed; what on earth was Celia's ex-husband, Gerry Payne doing here in Lisbon looking for him?

33.

Stuart was more than familiar with rejection. He had been knocked back by girls, shunned by people he thought of as friends and actually, properly abandoned by his own family, but it never got any easier to stomach. Being ditched always stung but being ditched in a foreign country by someone he thought he'd recently had a breakthrough with was the worst. He plonked himself on the stone bollard and devoured the entire batch of custard tarts without even pausing for breath or thought. A family similarly perched on the next set of stones gave him an odd glance once he wiped the pastry crumbs from his face after the final tart, but by then he had given up caring what anyone else thought. Palmer was supposed to be his sidekick, his newfound friend even, but he had done a runner, hobbling away on his knackered legs whilst his back was turned. He momentarily entertained the idea that Palmer too had been taken away, just as Jon Scott Campbell had been, bundled into another mysterious car by unknown agents, but it seemed unlikely. *Why had he not insisted on exchanging phone numbers?!*

It wasn't as if he was relying on Palmer though, more the other way around. The strange, limping wannabe detective had definitely come to partly rely on him, if only for his unswerving sense of direction and potential in protecting him from assailants. Stuart had finally wormed his way into Palmer's life and it had felt good. But things never really lasted and his own friendships were often quite shallow. In his youth, he had been more open, more likely to lay his feelings on the line, but in the years since, he had retreated to a life of superficial acquaintance and online anonymity. Part of him that thought that Palmer was a kindred spirit, not just because they were both seemingly embroiled in a Portuguese mystery together, but because they were like-minded deep down. But Palmer vanishing like this just reinforced how foolish it was to form attachments so easily when you didn't really know the person at all. He dismissed the idea that Palmer might have betrayed him somehow and settled on the equally unpalatable idea that he had in fact, very simply, dumped him.

There was still a chunk of time before noon, before Palmer's supposed invitation said he should be here, possibly at the very tart emporium he'd just left, so Stuart held onto the tiniest possibility that his companion might reappear in the next couple of hours. It was a very slim hope. He was resisting the urge to check in online and investigate whether his entire life online had been a lie, whether most or indeed all of his internet forum friends were as false as the two he'd thought of as his closest allies. Given the sense of misery and self-loathing which was rising inside him, Stuart couldn't decide if it were better to know right now whilst he was already on a steep downward trajectory, or whether it would actually be all too much for him to handle. He was an emotional fool really, despite his acceptance of a lonely life.

To distract his wandering mind, he tried to focus on the mystery of Celia Payne. It was a case he had spent some time on, but since then, others had taken his attention and proven far more attractive and solvable. To Stuart, true crime was fascinating, but also had the potential to be entirely frustrating with either no obvious solution forthcoming, or else the law makers having plumped for one version of the truth which he himself could not agree with. Celia Payne's vanishing had been instantly fascinating, mainly because it was so strangely connected to an earlier case, that of the Rusholme attacks, but as with most things Stuart did, he had quickly gone off the boil, only pushed along by his online forum collaborators. The thought chilled him suddenly. He had many times given up on wanting to investigate the Payne case due to the lack of not only a body but also an actual prosecutable crime, but also the chilling thought of Jon Scott Campbell lurking at its periphery. The fact that he had been egged on to keep looking into the case by online friends – people who may actually have been Jon Scott Campbell himself – made him shudder. That strange, slippery, violent man had practically dragged Stuart back into the investigation and then suggested coming to Lisbon on a holiday in an unrelated conversation. Their paths had now crossed a number of times, but he had failed to capitalise on whatever his odd scheme was.

Palmer was definitely no longer a suspect in Stuart's eyes, despite his own air of mystery. The suggestion of Palmer as a killer in a crime of passion did not float with Stuart. The guy was practically lukewarm in any emotional capacity and had no hallmarks of a hot-blooded impulsive killer driven by lust or jealousy. The alternative involving him had been that he and Celia were eloping lovers, choosing the Iberian sun over the rainclouds of the north of

England for a new life together, but again, Palmer was just not that sort of man. Stuart could imagine him being calculating, possibly even manipulative as he had caught glimpses of such behaviour in their brief time together, but not as a man controlled by love or passion in any way whatsoever. He seemed too nervy, too paranoid about finding Celia to be simultaneously pretending to know nothing about her whereabouts or mortal status. And yet, there was still that odd connection between the two of them...

The ex-husband, Gerry Payne had also been ruled out, despite forum members (*Jon Scott Campbell again?!*) fancying him for the crime. He was emotional, reckless and at times, unstable, but he was a broken man, hiding in rehab and therapy according to those in the know. The end of his marriage had shattered him into unreconnectable pieces rather than galvanising him as a force of vengeance. His alibi was unimpeachable.

A random attack had been the police's first line of investigation and Celia's drunken state (celebrating the end of the school year), her potential lack of familiarity with her surroundings (being in a different city from usual) and her recent ill-health and absence from work (her mother dying so suddenly and awfully) all contributed to a theory that she had just been in the wrong place at the wrong time and in no state to defend herself. But this theory did nothing for Stuart.

The sun was rising in the sky and warming the breeze and Stuart felt himself sweating more than he cared for. The bollard he was sitting on was directly in the sun now and he felt the need to move. When he was troubled, he often walked, laps of the area he lived in, carefully avoiding the parks which so bothered him, and found his thoughts began to organise themselves, his fears to subside and clarity to seek him out. Sitting in the Portuguese sun with his brain effectively cooking in his stupid fat head was not conducive to his health or his crime-solving ability. He got up and walked towards the monastery but realised the crowds had nearly tripled since their first arrival there and a long, snaking queue made its way across the previously empty lawn area. Instead, he did a 180 and headed across a road to another park area, one with playful fountains and sculpted shrubs. Not as busy, but still offering him a degree of safety and solitude at once.

His thoughts drifted back to Palmer for some reason. The man's connection with Celia Payne was the one part he couldn't fathom. Celia was a teacher of mathematics at a bog-standard comprehensive school in Greater Manchester (that had unrealistic dreams of being Outstanding), with no direct link to Palmer. She was older than he, lived in a different suburb, moved in different friendship circles and Palmer's job had no chance of providing a random crossing of paths with her. And yet, somehow, four or five years ago, they had supposedly been good friends. Stuart couldn't work out how they'd met and had wanted to find out from the moment he'd clapped eyes on him in the airport. By all accounts, Celia was haughty, stubborn and unemotional, known as being a bit of a ballbreaker at work, a bitch by those considered former friends and a battle-axe by those patient enough to remain in her social circle. She was a complicated woman and one hard to like which had presented the press with a slight problem. She wasn't the vulnerable, hopeless missing girl who made good headlines when coupled with photos of the damsel in distress and soundbites about what a lovely girl she was. Celia was trouble, her colleagues and pupils and friends all agreed on that. She had driven a cheating husband supposedly to the brink of suicide, made rivals and then enemies of those in her department, and then suffered a breakdown of her own which had drawn little sympathy from those who knew her. Stuart couldn't agree with those who said she'd asked for what had happened to her – no woman ever did that – but he knew that her time off work before the summer had led some to speculate she was skiving, possibly on a term-time holiday and that this recent disappearance was purely for attention. They even suggested she had scoped out a location back in June when she'd been off, then simply upped and moved there come July.

Stuart was aware of how a person could hop countries without a passport, but it was difficult and costly and sometimes quite dangerous, and for Celia to have done so made little sense. Unless, you truly believed she was a drama queen who engineered her own disappearance merely to make people talk about her. Stuart was having none of it.

He couldn't imagine a woman like this having any interest in Palmer. He was too much of a weak man for someone like Celia. She seemed drawn to dangerous men, people like Gerry who had womanised and betrayed her, or like Jon Scott Campbell who had probably entered her life as an exciting younger man and had most likely seemed to be a real challenge to tame. Palmer equally would have had his work cut out to want to spend time with her. He seemed too fussy, too particular to deal with the random inexplicable whims of this whirlwind of a woman. Palmer liked order and familiarity, not impulsive jaunts to foreign countries or fiery relationships built on sparring and deception. The way Palmer and Celia's friendship had broken down was the only reason people seemed to think he could have had some involvement in her vanishing. For whatever reason, and again, Stuart could not fathom the circumstances, Celia had apparently mistaken Palmer's friendship for something more and despite her years of marriage, had made a move on him. His rejection of her had driven her wild, being already quite drunk, and in the middle of a classy bar on West Street in Sheffield, she had smashed a glass over his head in front of hundreds of witnesses. Thankfully, there was little other than superficial damage to Palmer's head and some denting of his pride it seemed, but he had refused to press charges. Some thought he had been biding his time, awaiting a more permanent revenge, but Stuart didn't think it added up at all. And yet, strangely, Celia had visited that same bar in Sheffield, just hours before her disappearance. Some thought that this was where she had arrived for her rematch with Palmer, but a lack of clear CCTV footage and Palmer claiming to be in town, but *not* at the bar, made people question the series of events.

Palmer had supposedly spent the day in Sheffield city centre alone, then been wandering in the woods near his mother's house on the outskirts, but no one had seen him and his own mother had been vague on the details. She was rather a formidable woman, Stuart recalled from one anecdote he had heard about her, the kind you would ordinarily expect to come out punching for her loved ones, and yet she had done little to help her only son. In fact, it was her lack of clarity over the timings of the day which had led some to believe Palmer could have been menacing Celia in the town centre, then duping his mother about the hours he had come and gone. Stuart had found the idea tempting, but not a great fit. Palmer's past, his impeccable record and his demeanour led most to laugh off the possibility, but not all. The further convenient arrival of a postcard from Celia at Palmer's Manchester address seemed contrived to prove she was alive and he had no involvement in her disappearance, but Stuart took it as what it was: an attempt from *somebody* to subvert the investigation and if not Palmer, then another interested party. Stuart was just considering who that might be, when he looked up from his trudging feet out across the park. Either a ghost, or a fevered hallucination, but surely not the actual real thing, there, bold as brass, defiant as ever, was Celia Payne.

34.

The anonymous voice threatening him and sending him to the park that morning had nothing to do with Marujo, Jon was certain. It was more than likely that he had been watched at his apartment earlier, then followed in his taxi to the park and intercepted by those goons. Whatever had happened to Matilde to make her father so aggressive, Jon had no idea. The stupid girl had probably wandered off with another man, as was her wont. If her father couldn't accept the idea his only daughter was a nymphomaniac slut, then it wasn't Jon's business to tell him.

Jon had assumed the summoning was connected with the repulsive Palmer, having run into him time after time now, but the voice had been distorted and menacing and laughed at the idea of being the insipid creep. Why was he perpetually surrounded by fools? His wife was a waste of skin, his family had been beyond pathetic and this once fulfilling city was slowly filling with idiots, incapable of even carrying out the simplest of tasks. To make matters worse, Jon knew he was starting to unravel a little himself. He had always known his keen mind and viciously competitive streak were a transitory thing, a passing phase that sometimes propelled him to success and other times left him sorely lacking in focus and identity. He could feel his once-firm grasp on reality beginning to slip again and had no way of regaining it at the moment. A run might help him settle his thoughts, but that awful teetering into what some 'experts' called a fugue state was the only thing he could now see ahead of him. It was like his mind was a completed jigsaw and someone was slowly prising out random pieces of it until the table top was empty again.

Sprinting now, he barged past the sheep-like tourists and idly strolling locals who had no sense of urgency or the importance of the next few hours of his life. Around him, women were leering and ogling him like the cheap tarts they inevitably were, and the men, the younger men, were staring with a penetrating jealousy which made his blood surge even faster within him. Jon hated the people around him, the meandering, directionless flocks who could never even begin to appreciate his strength or trajectory. More than once he shoved someone bodily to the ground and did not bother to turn and see what happened to them. They were disposable, collateral.

The thought of Julie momentarily flashed through his mind like a glancing blow and he wondered if she was okay. She had come close to being fit to swim in his wake but had soon also proven herself unworthy. His chastising of her, both verbal and physical, then through neglect rather than actual attention, had done nothing to shake her off. Perhaps his final dealing with her had finally sent her on her way for good. Matilde too he felt certain he would never see again. He pictured her supple body always nicely a few years younger than this, her inviting thighs, then saw a wave of blood crashing over her inert body like a hellish wiping clean of the slate. For some reason, he now thought of Celia Payne, brittle and yet broad and so difficult to break. Women were ridiculously fragile.

Celia had always been a walking contradiction. She was strong like a rod of iron, yet so pathetically bendable he had manipulated her from day one. She was so much older than him and yet so naïve with it. Her head had been turned by a handsome, muscular, younger man and Jon had had his fun. A mature woman was a real breath of fresh air after so many younger girls in his life. When Celia had disappeared, Jon had not been surprised. The woman courted trouble like no one else and most likely had it coming. He hadn't seen her since he had stopped working at the school where they had met, when he was a hungry NQT and she an aspiring member of the senior leadership team. She had jumped at the chance of staying behind after school to help Jon plan his bottom set Y9 Shakespeare lessons, enjoying the company and the power play and despite her being a maths teacher, she had a love of languages. For two years he had used her to try and get ahead in his career, flattering her and giving her pleasure in exchange (not that she quite appreciated the transactions) for her turning a blind eye to his occasional lapses in professionalism. Then, in 2013, he had resigned, fled the area with his latest girlfriend, later his wife, Julie, and eventually ended up in Portugal. He had barely given Celia a thought since.

And yet now here she was rampaging through his thoughts and making him even more confused and angry. And not just his thoughts. He saw her face everywhere he turned, even here in this sun-drenched exotic climate where her grey, sallow face had no right to exist. Being an English teacher and a writer,

Jon knew only too well the heavy metaphor which suddenly seeing a figure from one's past suggested: guilt. But Jon didn't *do* guilt. He never had. He had no feelings towards any of the many women he had wronged, he cared nothing for Julie's life and reputation left in tatters back in England and he most assuredly had no feelings of compunction about his mistreatment of Celia Payne. The very fact he was sure she had been killed so horribly by that misfit Edward Palmer could have aroused some sort of feeling in him, but Jon was gleefully happy it had happened and ecstatic that he felt nothing for the loss. He'd have done it himself, given the opportunity.

The mists were descending now and Jon knew he had moments of clarity left before he was plunged into the murky depth of this ridiculous sludge of amnesia which he now more often found himself paddling at the fringes of. When he had first awoken a number of years ago, with no memory of the night before, he had attributed the loss of recollection to the heavy drinking and huge doses of recreational drugs he had consumed. It was normal. Typical. He had deserved the stinking headache and loss of a day of study time. But he had found himself experiencing these losses more and more throughout the months and years that followed and actually found himself hungering to recreate the experience. To wake up with a brain like a wiped Etch-a-Sketch was refreshingly empowering. He enjoyed the heavy nights more and more, knowing there was a small chance he would remember nothing of it the next day and it gave him a rush of power to be able to act exactly how he desired deep down. A doctor had failed to find anything in his explanations and thankfully (for Jon), had probed no further. He was just a fantasist in the eyes of that time-strapped G.P. and Jon's closest family had to give up on their theory he was mentally unbalanced, at least, for the time being.

A successful stint at university, then teacher training, then a few years as an aspiring teacher had been in no way impaired by his lapses in memory or focus and he found that as he threw himself into new avenues of pleasure, he relied less and less on the memory gaps and actually experienced them less and less, perhaps as a result. It felt like he could even *create* the perfect situations in which to trigger amnesia if he so chose, he was so in control. Megalomaniac that he was, Jon felt he no longer needed the release. But then, out of the blue earlier in the year, he had disappeared for an entire weekend. A *lost weekend*, Julie had joked, not referencing the classic 1945 Billy Wilder movie but more likely something she had read about one of her trashy reality TV star icons in one of her dross-filled magazines. Jon had made up that he had gone for a few drinks with the boys and Julie had accepted it and moved on, no alarm bells triggered and stupid enough to overlook the fact that Jon *never* went anywhere with 'the boys', whoever they even were. Jon had no memory at all about his movements across those days but had changed clothes, was drenched in sweat and had blood under his fingernails when he slid back into the real world that roasting summer morning, slumped in the bushes near the *Parque das Nacoes* area where his publisher had offices. He was clutching a woman's bag filled with clothes and behind him on the bejewelled grass at dawn, he found the bloodied knife he had since rid himself of in the Tagus.

He had clearly done something terrible he had no memory of, but with no crime reported and no body found or evidence trail to follow, he had simply stowed the items in his apartment closet, away from Julie's prying eyes. Panic had set in at first, but a quick call to his closest friend had assuaged his fears. After that, the exhilaration had washed over him and the way he felt that morning was like nothing he'd felt in years; he was keen to feel it again, whatever had triggered it. So he fell back into his old ways, driving his body to extremes both through exercise and through drink and drugs, each time hoping the veil of confusion would drift over him following a bout of extreme or violent activity. But it didn't. And he remembered every sickening moment. For months, his body and mind refused to cooperate and he would return with his bloodied knife recalling each and every misdeed, whether it was butchering animals in the remote woodlands, mugging gullible tourists lost in the mazes of streets in the less-trodden districts, or the few times he allowed himself to recreate past pleasures and actually plunged the blade deep into human flesh. The trophies he kept were the one thing which would bring about his downfall, and just a week earlier, he had experienced a genuine bout of overwhelming emotion and a loss of time and place. He found himself weeping uncontrollably in the shower of the apartment, bloodied and with no idea what had happened and realised that he needed closure on the earlier chapters of his life.

Months of stalking and monitoring the Celia Payne case and those involved in it had led him to realise he needed to find out the truth for himself. It was too much of a coincidence that she had been linked to the very city he was now living in and had disappeared around the time of his summer memory lapse. It took very little to bring his chief accuser to the decision to fly over there on an impromptu holiday and Jon was relishing coming face to face with the idiot Stuart Evans after all these years. But he still had need of ridding himself of the clues which would surely damn him, and so he had spent the previous days scattering bits of evidence to the four corners of the city, some in a freshly excavated building site, some in the Tagus and some burned in an oil drum on a nearby patch of wasteland. With Stuart incoming and the question mark over Celia's death still burning into Jon's mind, there was just final piece of the puzzle he needed to confront.

As Jon staggered to a halt and clung to the nearby wall having almost run himself into the ground through his insane bout of sprinting, he looked wildly around him, desperate to latch onto his location as he lapsed into nothingness. He had hurtled headlong across the busy lanes of traffic and was now in the shadow of the gleaming white building draped with a red banner advertising a new exhibition. It was the *Fundacao Oriente* museum, somewhere on the banks of the Tagus and he could feel his heart shaking as if to loose itself from his chest. In his last moments of clarity, he realised it was his phone ringing and he took it out of his jacket pocket and saw the caller was the one person he'd been thinking of. His one-time friend and respected associate, despite the many, many layers of complication between them, who was here in the city and had met with him a number of times in the last few days.

'JEEP CALLING' said the phone and Jon dismissed the hazy memory that he wasn't even supposed to have his phone with him. He accepted the call before plunging into oblivion.

35.

The view from the top of the tower was spectacular and well worth the slightly odd way of ascending which involved a narrow spiral stone staircase and a strange traffic light and timer system which only gave permission to traffic to move in one direction for a limited time. Palmer couldn't fathom how such a system could work in the event of an emergency, but it now went a long way to explaining the barely moving queue he had seen and then become part of and a further sign added details about the limited number of visitors allowed in the tower at any one time. Everything within the tower was arched and of polished marble, making the place slightly slippery underfoot and creating the illusion of height within even the lowest-roofed levels. Palmer had struggled quite a lot to climb the first series of steps up to a flat open roof which was dazzlingly white in the glare of the sun. He had wanted to rest there and possibly even call this the extent of his exploration of the place, but Gerry had other ideas.

Whilst the two men hadn't exactly had a warm reunion, Palmer found it strangely reassuring to see someone he knew from England, from his own past, here in this confusing exotic heat. Gerry was as awkward as Palmer knew himself to be. Whilst Palmer knew himself to be an uncomfortable presence in anyone's company these days, Gerry Payne was the sorest thumb he had ever met. He was red-faced even away from the Mediterranean heat, blustery and prone to filling silences with long-winded rambling nonsense. It was no wonder he had done so well as a lecturer over the years – he could stretch any topic to an hour and beyond, whether it was called for or even invited. He had a strange sense of superiority too, which he exuded in good measure and Palmer knew him to be quite a petty, small-minded man, despite

171

his education and continued immersion in the field. Many a university student had complained about his unfair or dismissive treatment of them, particular the female or foreign students and his whole Little England mentality made it all the more hilarious that he taught European history. Perhaps it was his very knowledge of it which made him so insufferably racist at times. Palmer could see why Celia had so often turned to others for comfort.

Gerry had merely greeted him with a stiff but sweaty handshake and he had taken the chance to pull what Palmer could only describe as a 'Trump move', using the handshake to assert his assumed superiority and only releasing it when *he* felt it was right. His wild eyes spoke of some other preoccupation and Palmer could tell that his fiery cheeks were from blood raging to his head, either out of embarrassment or fury. If he had been the one to summon him here, why did he seem so damned angry about it? And who was the figure atop the tower, waving so energetically? Palmer had tried to ask more, but Gerry had shook his jowly head and held up a finger to silence him, a move he often pulled in his professional capacity which had led him to acquire the unfortunate nickname amongst undergraduates of '*The Finger*'. He also stank of alcohol, a particular fragrance which Palmer thought was Portuguese rosé. It was still barely noon and he reeked of the stuff, a further reason for his ruddy face.

"But Gerry," Palmer had protested. "What the *hell* are you doing here?"

Gerry simply wobbled his head, either from his arrogant know-it-all nature or reeling from the amount of drink he must have consumed. He pursed his lips again in a grotesque parody of a pout and Palmer had to look away. The man was physically as grotesque as was his behaviour. He now turned the pointing finger to aim it upwards at the tower and shoved his way into the queue alongside Palmer, much to the disgruntlement of those who had been patiently queuing behind. Palmer shook his head, not concealing his disdain and looked out at the view along the river. If Gerry was here, then was he too looking for Celia, or covering his tracks? Why had he not got in touch properly with him, if this was part of his engineering? Gerry was known for his obscure teaching methods and inclusion of some frankly baffling minutiae in his lectures but had he really stooped to sending threatening messages, unsolvable riddles and vague invitations? Palmer recalled that he had only just finally eliminated the man from his suspicions of having done something to Celia, based on the alibi confirmed by his old school pal George. Avondale Row was a hospital of sorts in a pleasant enough suburb of Sheffield, close enough to where Gerry now lived, following his bitter split with Celia. He had somehow managed to get himself another plum role lecturing at one of Sheffield's universities and Palmer thought it was the former polytechnic Hallam rather than the main, sometimes more prestigious university. At least, he imagined it was anyway, baffled at the idea that people would continue to employ this strange, dinosaur of a man in any kind of decent job. Gerry had obviously been mortified at suffering such an emotional and psychological break and had kept all detail of it quite, quite secret. Palmer toyed with the idea of simply coming out and asking him about it, just to see if he blew his top. He knew Gerry wanted no further discussion until they had reached wherever he was vaguely indicating, but Palmer couldn't help himself.

"I'm not sure I can make it all the way up there, Gerry, old boy," said Palmer, using the sort of language he knew the old git dealt in. He pointed to his legs. "Copped a bit of grief back in Blighty."

Gerry simply raised one hilariously bushy eyebrow as if in disgust at this show of weakness and then rolled his eyes. Palmer was certain he even harrumphed, though he felt he had only ever *read* such a move coming from a fictional old colonel or two in the works of Christie or Wodehouse. Gerry really was ridiculous.

And so they had queued and entered and paid and begun their ascent. Gerry was practically glowing as they reached that first-floor terrace of sorts.

"Here?" Palmer had gasped as Gerry leant against a low wall with his mighty bulk, his chest rising and falling so heavily in a parody of breathing.

Gerry shook his head again and this time Palmer couldn't be sure if he was still doing his whole secrecy thing, or was just out of breath. The man was the wrong side of fifty, but his body, through a combination of indulgences of food and drink, little to no exercise to speak of and a fairly sedentary existence, might as well have been in its late sixties. As he scrunched up his face, blinking as if to clear his tiredness through wishful thinking, Palmer couldn't help but look at all the broken capillaries on his ridiculous gammon face. The man was a waddling advert for gout. His hindered mobility made Palmer feel slightly less self-conscious about his own. He imagined what a pair they looked to anyone paying attention.

"Up again?" Palmer tried to confirm, but this time, Gerry simply waved his arms lazily, as if ushering him on past.

He seemed tired but also determined to reach the top; the wildness in his eyes was *not* fear as Palmer had initially read it, but a singlemindedness, bordering on obsession. Palmer squinted up at the top of the tower, a pure white headache now in the glare of the midday sun. He couldn't see the waving figure anymore, but given it was a pink speck minutes earlier and now he was nearer, could be any one of several milling visitors just above, he wasn't sure of what exactly he had even seen.

"Are you meeting someone else here?" Palmer chanced, as he took the lead towards the stairwell.

The traffic light sign was indicating that the stairs were now only for going down, but not from this floor, from above. The screen became a countdown, then changed to green for go, but still only in a downward motion. The change to allow them to go up would take further waiting.

Gerry gave him a filthy side eye and scowled, making his red craggy face even more like corrugated bacon. Palmer figured that if the man wasn't even going to reply to him with a grunt or a simple non-verbal response, he would keep asking him question after question until he blew his stack. He knew that Gerry had no great love of him and as Palmer's path had crossed with Celia all those years ago, things had become even more complicated. Palmer had already known Gerry from a few years earlier, but hadn't realised the woman the man was bemoaning and blaming all his problems on was the same woman he personally was currently trying to assist. A strange, brief period (and now oddly calm, looking back) followed, where the three of them had acknowledged their connections and even managed to keep things civil and professional at a few public events. But it was short-lived and it was evident to Gerry that Celia had cited him as the cause of a lot of her problems. Then came Celia's bizarrely miscalculated pass at him and Palmer had severed all ties. Palmer wondered just what role Gerry believed he had played in the breakdown of his marriage. It was hard to tell, as Gerry was so aloof to everyone around him, it was just taken for granted that he had a low opinion of you.

It was also clear that he was becoming more smug and even more insufferable as they ascended, as if he knew exactly what was awaiting them both and was dying to tell. His reticence in answering any of Palmer's questions was not from fear or breathlessness, Palmer now decided, but out of some strange thrill, like a child with a terribly exciting secret.

"Was *this* from you?" demanded Palmer, waving the Belem leaflet right under Gerry's nose now.

He was hot and weary and the last leg of the ascent had wiped him out completely. Whatever Gerry was planning on doing or showing him at the very top, Palmer had little energy to be upbeat about. It was just as likely a ruse to wear him out, a shrewd move in eliminating an unwanted presence, were it not for Gerry's own knackered heft.

Gerry snatched the leaflet and his eyes bulged. He looked furious as he turned the leaflet over and saw the handwritten message Palmer had finally decoded. His screwed up little piggy eyes scanned the black and red script until he too reached the same realisation. He looked around, the breeze cooling, but whipping flags above them atop the tower. Other tourists were strolling around, enjoying themselves, snapping photos and enjoying the view. The low crenelated wall around the top of the tower suddenly seemed mightily low and Palmer's head began to swim. He should have known his fear of heights would kick in around now. It could be sometimes controlled, behind high fences and walls, but not here in this vast open space with only a thin iron railing and an inadequately low wall beyond which there was a fearfully vertiginous drop. No one was near enough to see as he stumbled suddenly, caught in that terrible compulsion he always had which saw him practically *lurching* towards the drop and no one was near enough to overhear their conversation, something Gerry had seemed to bank on.

"So *that's* why you're here," he said, scathingly. "I did wonder why you left the monastery lawn in such a hurry."

Palmer was agog, but crippled by nauseating visions of plummeting over the side of the tower. Gerry stepped right in beside him, into his personal space which made him sicken further. He could smell the sweat and awful musky aftershave and see the grim smile on the lecturer's face.

"You…you were the one who sent me this?" Palmer managed to blurt out, putting out a hand to steady himself but finding nothing to connect with other than Gerry's fat arm.

"No, not *this*," said Gerry, flipping the leaflet over in annoyance. "Not *here.* I'll admit I've been monitoring your movements, as they say, hoping you'd show me what you know. I've tried to be subtle, but enough is enough. It seems dear Celia had a plan for you which didn't include me."

36.

Stuart knew once again why he hated parks so much. They were full of ghosts. He had frozen upon seeing the apparition that was Celia. His urge would have been to shout out to her, to stop her, detain her, interrogate her and find an answer to her disappearance, but even if she *had* been real, someone yelling her name across a foreign park, miles from home, might only have spooked her. Seeing Stuart, a stranger who seemed to know her too well, looking shocked, angry and sweaty, aside from the fact he looked physically formidable too, might all be too much for her and she would surely have bolted. But she was a ghost. So it didn't matter. Stuart kept repeating this idea to himself. The first time he had seen a ghost in a park that too had been a woman, a desperately missed one from his life, and that time it *had* to have been a ghost as the woman was definitely, definitively dead. Perhaps it had been unresolved grief, or a mental break, or the drink or the drugs that time, but Stuart knew he had been seeing things.

Of course, Celia could have been real. It could actually have been her. But she was dressed in a floaty white outfit, maybe befitting the weather or local styles, but strangely ethereal. There was a pink scarf wrapped around her shoulders, a thin floaty material not designed for warmth, but for style, and it trailed after her as she vanished out of sight behind the bushes. Why would the ghost of Celia Payne be haunting *him*? And why here? Stuart snapped out of his pitiful trance and actually gave himself a full-on physical slap across the face. It made such a sound that a mother pushing a pram on the other side of the fountains stopped, stared at him for a moment and then swiftly turned around and headed away. He was being stupid and he knew it.

He wished Palmer hadn't scarpered like he had as this vision (surely, actually now he wandered back from insanity, the real woman herself) was for his eyes

176

and peace of mind. He checked his watch; Palmer had only been out of his company for less than twenty minutes. Perhaps if Stuart pursued the woman, he could detain her, or at least try and persuade her to come with him and find Palmer. Then again, the woman had been effectively on the run, hiding from sight, for the last three months. What made him think he could change that? Regardless, he set off at a steady jog through the park until he reached the point at which the woman had vanished. To his annoyance, he saw a taxi which had pulled up just beyond the point he'd lost sight of Celia. It was a white Mercedes of some kind and it hared off at an alarming speed along the road to the right, a direction of which Stuart had no memory. Across four lanes of traffic was a pair of railway lines, then seemingly more road beyond it, then a petrol station and the glittering expanse of the Tagus just peeking out behind that. The dark mountainous skyline of whatever was on the other side of the river ran beyond that and as Stuart turned back to see what lay in the direction the car had gone, he saw, towering over a mass of boat masts, the strange monument to exploration the bus tour had introduced to him a day ago. *Had it really only been a day since?*

Traffic was whizzing along at a steady rate, but Stuart could see nothing resembling a taxi, so he began to jog along the side of the road, passing a palatial white building set back from the road with a line of flapping flags in front, and more distressingly, several street adverts for McDonalds which made his stomach gurgle again. As he reached a major crossing and what appeared to be some gleaming white military complex which was probably only a museum, he noticed a young lad on a scooter struggling with a delivery box. He was one of those Uber Eats delivery guys presumably on his way to take someone's takeaway before it got cold or fell off the back of his wobbling vehicle. Stuart ran up to him so abruptly that the young man nearly leapt out of the way. Whilst his Portuguese wasn't amazing (and nor was the boy's English much better), he somehow managed to speak the international language of pointing and waving which was sealed when he produced a handful of twenty Euro notes. Stuart had wondered if he could simply rent or borrow the scooter, but the guy wasn't getting off it, so he hopped onto the back after helping him re-secure the delivery box and off they lurched into the busy flow of cars.

Stuart found himself clutching onto his chauffeur far more than he would have cared for and the young tanned man didn't seem to flinch as he held on for dear life, gripping his midriff and feeling the bones beneath his brightly coloured polo shirt. It was freezing on the scooter too, and Stuart wondered how the lad managed to fly around at such speeds without his coat. He was starting to sound like an old woman, doing his best mother hen as always. They had put the strange white complex behind them and passed other intriguing museum like buildings on the other side of the railway line including what appeared to be a large marina. He was wondering if they'd ever catch sight of the white Mercedes again, when suddenly, there it was, on the other side of the train tracks, pulled up and with a passenger getting out, the ghostly woman. There were no crossing points by road for the railway line and Stuart urgently squeezed his driver's body, hoping he would notice the pressure and react. Thankfully, the lad swung his head around a little, taking his eyes off the road, but seeing where Stuart was nodding his head to the car which was now pulling away again and leaving the woman in white to walk away into another park area. If the delivery boy pulled up now, Stuart noticed a pedestrian footbridge he could try and race across, but the boy showed no signs of slowing. In fact, he began to accelerate dangerously, slaloming between the much slower cars on the road and Stuart's grip on him tightened further.

Finally, they reached an impossible manoeuvre as Stuart worked out what the lad's plan was. To their left, a ramp took the other carriageway's traffic up and over the railway line, bringing it back down to merge with the flow, not far away from where the Mercedes had stopped. To reach the ramp, they would have to leave their lane, cross two lanes of traffic roaring towards them in the opposite direction, then merge into the two other lanes of traffic which continued up the ramp and over the bridge. It was insane. Stuart could feel his back drench with sweat in a moment and his bowels clench. He tried to shake the boy to stop him, but he merely whipped his head back to give him a determined, but thoroughly insane smile. He barely slowed, but as a gap presented itself in the traffic, he screeched the scooter across the road making an awful noise and an even worse smell, nearly collided with a small van which had slowed to see what was going on, then managed to right the vehicle before it slid away beneath them both and continue in an upright fashion onto the ramp. All around the honking of car horns seemed to celebrate their stunt rather than bemoan it. Stuart had seen plenty of manoeuvres like that in movies, but had never thought he would become part of one. He wasn't even wearing a helmet!

"Aguente firme!" or something which sounded like that came too late from the lad's lips to Stuart's ears and he could only assume it was some helpful advice about not letting go.

The bridge crossed and the ramp back down to the road successfully traversed with no further incident, the scooter pulled up practically where the Mercedes had been only minutes earlier. Stuart could see the park was much bigger than he had thought, with stalls and information plaques, but no sign of the woman. His eyes were swimming and sweat drenched his face. He staggered off the vehicle and almost crashed to the dusty ground. A few tourists were milling about by the street edge and took a vague interest in this unlikely passenger route. The delivery boy, hopped off the scooter himself and grabbed Stuart's hand, righting him before further mishap could occur. His face was a mixture of exhilaration and cheeky guilt at having been the source of it. But mainly, his face spoke of pride and having got Stuart where he had seemed to have wanted to have ended up.

"You ok?" he asked, falteringly, looking Stuart up and down and presumably seeing how awful Stuart imagined he now looked.

Stuart nodded, catching his breath and thanked the boy, handing him more of the money. The money was refused and instead the lad fished in his pocket and pulled out a business card. Stuart was confused. Was he being given some sort of discount on a takeaway delivery order? The boy beamed and seemed to blush a little now. Before any more could be said, he pressed the card into Stuart's hand and got back onto his scooter. Stuart was still far too dazed to fathom what was going on but looked down at the card as the boy prepared to set off again. It was an Uber Eats card with the website on one side and what must have been the lad's number on the other side.

"You call me?!" the boy cried hopefully, sheepishly, before merging back into the traffic and vanishing.

Stuart may have blagged himself a ride, but it seemed he had also landed himself much much more. Shaking his head in disbelief at the whole randomness of what had just happened, he felt a frisson of excitement as he saw the white figure at the far side of the park, amongst the more colourful hordes of people, heading to what seemed to be the Tower of Belem. He checked his watch. It was just after 11am. *Where the hell was Palmer?!* He stalked across the park, keeping the woman in sight until she paused behind a grove of trees. She was looking around and as he drew nearer, he could see worry etched into her stern face. It was Celia Payne alright, not quite as ghostly, with her three-month tan, but still strangely draped in the white robe-like outfit. Stuart circled around the outside edge of the trees, hoping to get in front of her and try and pre-empt her next move, but when he reached waterfront and turned back around, he saw no sign of her. He broke into a sprint and looped along the paved riverbank in the shadow of the strangely detached tower, eyes keenly searching for where she had gone. It was impossible that she had got far in the few seconds he had taken his eyes off her. As he reached the grove where she had previously been standing, he noticed an odd white block or cylinder of some sort between the trees, possibly left over from some sort of construction or environmental protection project. It was the only place she could be hiding. It was fifty-fifty as to which way to go around it, but for some reason he chose left, expecting to find the woman hiding behind it. As he reached the back and realised she wasn't there at all, he felt a hand on his shoulder which made him gasp with shock. She *had* been behind the block but had circled around the *other* way.

"What the hell do you want of me?" she demanded, haughtily.

It was Celia Payne alright.

37.

Jon had no idea where he was when he came to, suddenly, as if snapped out of a nightmare, except that whatever slumber he had been caught up in, it was a dreamless one and the horror before his eyes was as bad as any bad dream he'd experienced. The entirety of what he could see was a glassy eyed woman's face, right before him, her nose only inches from his nose and the same start he awoke with propelled him closer, before he caught himself and tried to leap up and away. His head collided with hard metal as did his legs and he realised he couldn't move his arms as they were bound tightly behind his back. He wriggled a few inches away from the woman's face and collided again with another barrier. It was dark and stuffy and hot wherever he was trapped and the woman in front of him seemed to be dead. Her face was spattered with blood and it was dried, so not a recent spraying, and encrusted in her dark hair which was so thickly coated that Jon couldn't tell if the source of the blood was a head wound or not. She was pretty and probably in her twenties, not much older than Matilde, wherever *she* was. It was only when he tried to call out to the woman that he realised his mouth was gagged too and no amount of biting or gurning could shift or loosen it.

His muffled calls unheeded by the woman or anyone outside of this tight prison, he tried again to squirm and rock his way back and found that the space was no bigger than the size of a small sofa and no higher either. He could smell petrol or diesel and as he tried to grow accustomed to the dark, he realised the uncomfortable floor he was moving around on was made uneven by the shape of a wheel slightly embossed into the dark carpeted floor. It was certainly a car boot he was trapped in, there was no doubt of that. But why? And whose? *Surely not Marujo's?*

181

He strained his ears to listen to any noise he could hear outside the vehicle, but either the car was somewhere so quiet that there wasn't any particular nearby noise, or else the boot had some sort of sound-proofing, but he couldn't hear anything other than the steady, distant sound of traffic.

Turning his attention back to the woman, he made himself rock close enough to her to see her again, as aside from a tiny shaft or two of light coming from either a keyhole or badly joining seam somewhere, it was pitch black and by moving just a few inches away from her, he could no longer see her. She wasn't moving at all. Her chest didn't seem to be rising or falling and there was no glow or heat apparent from her body. She too was bound, most likely in the same fashion, although she was not gagged. Her mouth was parted in a slightly sad gasp, her lips full and inviting, despite her state.

Jon had no memory of meeting her and she was not at all familiar to him. Then again, were these women ever truly known to him? They were brazen, most of them. Wanton. They prowled around in their states of undress demanding male attention, and then when they received it, they toyed with their pursuers, emasculating and humiliating them. Women like this got what they deserved. But Jon never remembered it.

Her eyes were open which suggested death, but Jon had seen women incapacitated, catatonic through some fix or other, still seemingly bolt wide awake, their eyes wide and doll-like and dead, despite the life persisting within. *The lights are on but no one's home.* A man could do whatever he wanted with a woman like that. But not like *this*, he suddenly thought, grimacing at the amount of blood. He had never been keen on the substance, either inside or outside the human body. Outside, it was messy, sticky, tacky to the touch and then dried and crumbly and forever reappearing despite hours of hand rinsing. Inside, it was the source of childhood embarrassment, his already reddy complexion made ruddy through quick flowing liquid shame. Jon found himself retching now and was thankful for the gag which prevented him tasting the smell he thought was in the air and in his nostrils already.

Whoever this woman was, Jon had *not* done this to her. He couldn't have. The fact he was bound and gagged himself and locked in the same space as her was surely proof. Times had gone by where Jon had had to admit to a fit of rage or blind, mad jealousy which had blanked out his thoughts, pre-fugue diagnosis, and often the evidence was there for him to see: a broken glass crushed in his own torn hand, a terrified looking former rival lying whimpering on the dirty floor of a pub toilet, or the worst, a beaten, bruised, bloodied young woman shrieking in the bushes nearby, clearly his victim, clearly trying to escape or summon help. He had manned up and taken responsibility for his actions in a fair number of those cases, either tidying up his mess where possible, or what tended to most shock his victims, helping them back up and apologising. Each time, his help was refused angrily, bitterly, confusedly, and he simply slipped away into the night. Boy could he run when he had to.

Usually he needed to calm himself, as his pulse would be rocketing and his body full of adrenaline he had little need for in the aftermath of such attacks. Perversely, running away was one way of coping, the other was the steady, grounding influence of his long-standing friend from university, Jeep. Just chatting with him was enough to bring Jon back down, like a drug addict coming back from the ecstasy of a fix and whilst Jon never went into the specifics, he knew his friend must have had more than an inkling that all was not well with him over the years. That friend was sorely needed here, right now. If Jon could only reach his phone, he might be able to kill two birds with one stone and also secure an escape. He had a vague sense that Jeep had been calling him recently, but without reaching his phone, he couldn't be certain. He couldn't even be certain he *had* his phone.

Nothing like this had ever happened before, in quite a lifetime of strange and awful experiences and even now, Jon could muster little sympathy for the anonymous girl alongside him. This was all about self-preservation, as it had always been. Preservation from the law and potential prosecution and preservation of his mind in keeping himself from entirely cracking up. Jeep understood all that and despite how complicated things had got between them over the thirteen or so years they had known each other, the man knew what made Jon tick and was always there for him.

A quick journey through the potential guilty parties at work here did not serve to calm him at all; if anything, he became more agitated when the answers floated through his head. That pig Marujo was the most obvious candidate and Jon had to admit to himself that it might have been fitting or poetic or downright karmic for that inert brown-skinned beauty to have been Matilde and him being thrown into a car boot with her was some sort of awful retribution from the disgusting criminal. But Marujo loved his daughter too much (a little too much in the wrong kind of ways, Jon knew) to do something so callous with her body, and so it was a riddle as to why he would throw this girl in with him, having presumably tracked him from Rato down to the riverfront.

In second place, though it was a photo finish, was the nameless aggressor, hiding behind a random phone number and some cheap voice-altering software. Threats had been made against him, but they were more than likely in the 'crank' category. Someone who thought they smelled money via blackmail but ended up getting more than they bargained for. Jon had written several tawdry thrillers about such characters, inspired by his favourite Patricia Highsmith novels. Men who sniffed guilt in others rarely went to the authorities. Instead they favoured personal gain and they always ended up dead. Always.

The third most likely candidate was Palmer. The man was a maniac. Jon had heard that during some kind of rejected advance towards Celia, he had attempted to glass the woman, in plain sight of a hundred witnesses in some tawdry Sheffield bar. He was sexually violent, Jon assumed. Any man so obviously alone and unattached couldn't be anything other than a massive sex pest. Where else was he getting his kicks? Or perhaps, that stupid oaf, Evans was the cause of this. Given a fair match, Jon knew he could take the guy. He might layer his muscles in rolls of fat, but he had muscles all the same and he looked pretty handy on a construction site. But he was also lazy and hilariously insecure and gullible. If that idiot had got the better of him now, Jon would find it hard to forgive himself.

Jon drifted off into his memories, in lieu of any idea of how to get out. He remembered the first time he had met Jeep. It had been in the dense bushes on the outskirts of the parkland near The Whitworth off Oxford Road, Manchester. A statue of King Edward VII stood proudly, bizarrely right in Jon's line of sight and he found himself half-undressed in a thorny hedgerow in the dark of a typically cold and wet Mancunian evening in December. Perhaps he had blacked out following a session in the nearby union, or hammered it too hard at the gym before that, but he had no idea how he had wound up scratched and bleeding in the bushes with his shirt off and nowhere to be found. He felt angry, terribly, monstrously angry, but didn't know why. It wasn't a reaction to finding himself like this; it was an earlier, latent feeling which surged to the surface now. He had got up, shivering, looking around to find no one he knew, none of his drinking friends from earlier were anywhere in sight and his glow in the dark watch told him it was the early hours of the morning. He was about to give up trying to figure out his situation and find a way home, when he practically tripped over the body behind him. A young woman, unconscious and soaked from the wet grass. Her clothes were a little torn and her breathing was shallow, but she was okay. Jon almost reached out to shake her awake when the realisation hit him that he might have been connected with her state. In a blind panic now, he sprinted deeper into the park, veering right towards the art gallery which was smack bang next to some of his favourite drinking establishments. He didn't see the man he collided with until it was too late. But it was how he had met Jeep and how the strange, older man had become his friend.

He had only just been sixteen at the time and too young to be legally drinking and cavorting in such a fashion, but Jeep had understood and helped him out.

He'd been helping him out ever since. Jon never knew what happened to the girl, if Jeep had simply left her there, or had gone to tend to her and silence her with words, or threats or money, but he'd been mopping up his messes for close to half his entire life now.

Jon was rudely thrown out of his reverie by the most unexpected thing. The girl, who he had now concluded was dead, suddenly lurched back into life, banging her head on the ceiling and screaming in agony. She lashed out, trying to kick and scream but finding that screaming was her only option. Jon winced, wishing he could escape her mindless attack, but they were at close quarters in this air-starved boot. *She's alive.* For some reason he was disappointed. Before he could fully adjust to this latest development, a further one presented itself. The dark roof was suddenly wrenched open and glaring light and heat flooded in. Someone had opened the car boot, possibly in answer to the screaming. Jon screwed up his eyes at the sudden blinding light but when he opened them again he was appalled to see none other than Stuart Evans leering over him, his stupid, fat face full of shock and disgust.

38.

Salvador Marujo was a man used to getting his own way. People respected him. And if they didn't, then they paid. This disrespectful British *ruivo* had dared to show open, defiant disrespect to him and worse than that, he had defiled his precious Matilde. Marujo took pride in all his various businesses and enterprises, even the mostly illegal ones (especially those some days) but above all of that, he prized his precious daughter. He knew she would never understand if she learned the truth of her father's wealth and power, but he still did all he could to protect her, giving her whatever she wanted, keeping his trusted friends around to keep an eye on her when he was away on business as he often was. Now she was missing and he was worried that no good had come to her. The British spineless *cretino* was surely responsible for whatever had happened to her, Marujo had no doubt.

Marujo also prided himself on his genial manner and business-like approach, despite the murderous rages which consumed him and allowed him to exact quite hideous revenge upon certain enemies from time to time. People thought of him as being a gentleman. A vicious, dangerous gentleman, but always fair. If someone stole from him, he took a hand – not removing it, that was for those barbarous Africans who flooded across the Mediterranean – and if someone wounded him, he maimed them in equal measure with no prejudice. He had lost track of the number of business associates who had been on the receiving end of his most violent outbursts who had barely been able to drag themselves out of his cellar offices to find a nearby hospital. The many many suitors who had tried their luck at winning Matilde's hand had also suffered badly. She never knew why these men vanished from her life, but she herself was so flighty, like a butterfly he often commented, his little *borboleta*, she

186

rarely dwelt on their absence. As they were often hot-blooded locals, full of the flame of passion, Marujo's method of dissuasion involved fire. Only a month or so ago, he had lit the brazier in the car bay and plunged the latest idiot who had broken his daughter's heart, headfirst into it. They always lived. He wasn't a *murderer*, despite the rages. But they rarely walked away intact. How the boy had screamed as the flesh on his face began to bubble and melt. It had set Marujo on for his afternoon game of golf and he had thrashed his rivals in that field too.

Monitoring Matilde's actions was the responsibility of Marujo's staff – he had no time for such observations himself – but he relied upon their notifications to exact his fatherly duties. No man would ever defile his beautiful rose, not in the way they brutishly wanted. She was still young, still in need of her father and the love *he* could show her. But he had taken his eye off the ball, allowed his staff too much free rein and she had not only met a new man, but taken him to her bed. The thought of her perfect, unblemished flesh being pawed at by that dirty red-headed Englishman made him feel sick and furious. When he had discovered this, he had insisted on being driven around the city on the lookout for this man. He knew nothing of his name or background especially, other than his nationality and the fact he lived somewhere in the east of the city and after a fruitless day of cruising around in search of him, he had finally spotted the man. *Nojento!*

Taking him in the park was the suggestion of his bodyguard, Francisco, who also loathed loose ends and took it personally that the men in his employ had let his boss down. Broad daylight was brazen, but Marujo had never once met a policeman who had managed to make charges stick against him and certainly found that more of them were open to the level of bribery and corruption which law breakers surrounded themselves in. Marujo wasn't the biggest mogul in town, nor the richest or even the most dangerous, but he was high enough up on each of those indexes to finish up on top overall. He ran a string of bars and restaurants throughout the city and neighbouring areas, and had a huge chunk of the sex industry in his pocket. But business was going badly, hence the reason for his distraction.

Someone, and he now felt certain he knew who, had been harming his girls. He didn't think of them affectionately, they were business units, stock, cattle, but he still felt protective of his assets. The women who plied their trade in the red-light areas gave their share to the pimps who managed them, who were in turn managed by Marujo in his role as all-round business investor and racketeer. Recently, girls had been failing to turn up for their routine shifts in their regular spots, some complaining of illness or accidental injury, but upon further investigation by Francisco, it had come to light that the girls were too scared to do their job. Marujo couldn't understand why a woman who saw no problem in selling herself like that could suddenly have a problem with it, until he met some of them and saw the fear in their eyes. Apparently, some months back a high-class escort girl named Beatriz had met a client at his place, but on her way back, she had been viciously attacked and left in a gutter. She hadn't dared to report the crime or even get herself medical help, but had instead locked herself away in her home and told her friends about the terrible experience. A second assault, more random in nature this time, had followed on the streets of *Baixa* and the girls had fled. Fear might have been good for *doing* business with others, but it was bad for running one's own.

Marujo now felt certain, having clapped eyes on the man, that this *Scott Campbell* man was both the one to have stolen his Matilde's innocence, but also most likely attacked his call girls. Francisco had deduced that his was the credit card which had paid for Beatriz's time. Marujo had wanted to wade straight in and hurt the bastard, but Francisco had advised caution, especially when it was discovered that Matilde had not returned home the previous night. A bout of interrogation and torture was planned, but the little *diabo* had got the better of them all and escaped, humiliating him in the process. He now feared the man was lost to the maze-like streets of Lisbon and short of blocking the airport, Marujo wasn't sure how to catch him. He knew he would get him eventually, but he was more angry with himself for having let him slip out of his grasp so foolishly. He also feared that without catching the man again, he would not find out for certain what had happened to Matilde. He hoped she was well, staying with a friend and not at all involved in the horrors, but he couldn't shake the feeling that Scott Campbell had done something to her. He imagined her trussed up naked at the man's whim and grew angrier still.

He was now sitting in the back of his BMW whilst Francisco and Afonso drove him around the area searching for the rat whilst other teams looked into Matilde's last movements and visited her usual haunts. He was sweating, despite the air conditioning, and felt like he needed a change of clothing. The tinted windows didn't allow him much of a view outside anyway, but his mind wasn't on what was going on outside. He was lost in his thoughts of Matilde and her mother and how similar the two of them were in every conceivable way. When the mother had died, the daughter had taken her place in his affections and the idea that both of them were gone – to have lost love twice over – was too much to bear. This Scott Campbell would lose more than his looks, Marujo decided.

"Boss," came Francisco's gravelly voice from the front of the car.

He repeated it a few times, respectfully as ever, before his words broke through Marujo's daydreaming.

"What is it?" asked Marujo snappily.

"I've just had a text from Tomas down by the waterfront," continued the security chief. "And the hospital has called back."

"And?!" demanded Marujo, losing his patience entirely now.

"Tomas says they've spotted him, *chefe*. They've found the man we are after."

Marujo leapt forward in his seat until he was gripping the back of Francisco's.

"What? Where? Tell me!" he demanded.

"Well…" Francisco hesitated. It was unheard of. The man was beyond confident and nothing ever spooked him. "Someone else has grabbed him."

Marujo couldn't even begin to process how odd that sounded. He was more preoccupied by Francisco's annoying slow drip of information.

"And the hospital?!" he snarled, having waited long enough for Francisco to continue.

More hesitation. Despite his loyalty, Marujo made a note to review Francisco's contract of employment.

"They've found Matilde, *chefe*," said Francisco at last.

Dead or alive. Dead or alive. Marujo's mind was racing now. Francisco was almost *teasing* him with the news now. But Marujo already knew the answer in his heart of hearts. He didn't even *listen* to Francisco's answer. He slumped back into the sumptuous leather of the car seat which didn't even feel sticky anymore, despite his perspiration. His was face was a mask.
*Someone…anyone…*would pay for this.

39.

As soon as the masking tape was torn from his face and the gag lifted, Jon hissed as menacingly as he could: "*Evans!*"

The fool standing over him instantly gave away that he hadn't been expecting to see any of what lay before him – the dead/dying girl, his nemesis gift wrapped for him – and so at least one theory was eliminated from Jon's troubled hypotheses.

"You again!" blurted Evans.

He looked sweaty and out of breath and close to throwing up, but he looked past Jon to the writhing woman who was hysterical by now. Using the frozen moment to his advantage, Jon heaved with all his might and threw himself up and out of the boot onto the dusty ground outside where a sandy cloud rose up. The additional space provided by his escape made the woman thrash around even more and Jon was thankful she was gagged as her movements were noisy enough. Outside of the boot, the world expanded around him again with dizzying clarity. They were on a deserted road, one that seemed abandoned right by the Tagus, with warehouses and docks either side, but nothing remarkable nearby. The busy traffic he had heard was the main road, some distance away and now noise from the river mixed in too. He squinted painfully in the bright afternoon sun and could make out the dark silhouette of the *25 de Abril* bridge far away in the distance. He had been intent on continuing his worm-like method of motion to escape or possibly even *attack* Evans but before he could do anything at all, he felt large firm hands on his shoulders, slipping under his armpits and he was hoisted up entirely off the

190

ground. It was such a shock to him – the builder looked strong, but his chunkiness disguised his powers entirely – that he went limp and allowed himself to be hurled anew to the ground, landing painfully on some rocks.

The fall was awkward and Jon felt something twinge and worse, heard something crack or snap in a way it shouldn't have. Broken bones, particularly in the foot, were the enemy of runners like Jon. He had nursed many an injury from the most pathetic of misstep and knew that Evans had deliberately or blunderingly accidentally and luckily for him, incapacitated him. He sagged to the ground and took a moment to watch the man he had so carefully lured to the city deal with this situation that neither of them had expected. Momentarily stunned, he found Evans replacing the gag even more tightly around his face.

Evans then crept slowly to the car boot, glancing occasionally back to where Jon now lay and he gingerly reached out to touch the girl, who thrashed so much that he withdrew his hand and attempted to calm her with some clumsy Spanish/Portuguese hybrid. In the end, he gave up and spoke to the woman in English. His voice was even thicker than he looked, sounding hoarse and nasal all at once, with h's and g's dropped left, right and centre.

"Shush love," he said, pathetically. "'ang on and I'll find somethin' to help you out with."

He looked around somewhat helplessly and shot daggers at Jon.

"This is all *you*, I'm bettin'," he cursed and Jon tried to muster up a sneer in response, knowing how wrong he was.

"Calma, calma!" cried Evans, having now tried the car doors and found them locked and with nothing nearby to help him out. "I'm gonna 'ave to come up close to you and 'elp you."

He reached in and whether it was something in his face or eyes which spoke to her or she had simply tired of resisting, she allowed him to ungag her and loosen the bonds around her hands and feet. He then offered her a hand and she warily swung her legs out of the boot, wobbling and sagging to the dirt. Evans was looking at the wound on her head all the while and spat a curse at Jon, obviously blaming him again.

Untie me, you idiot! Ungag me at the least! Jon didn't care what Evans thought of him, but he wanted to at least deny any involvement in this particular crime. *Did the idiot think he had attacked the girl, then promptly tied himself up and locked himself in the same bloody car boot?*

"Are you alright, love?" asked Evans, bending to speak to the girl.

As he got close enough to dare to reach out and touch the girl, he triggered something in the deranged girl and she lashed out with a quivering hand, dealing him a slap to the face which echoed with a sound suggesting more force than it was possible to have contained. Evans stepped back, shocked, though why he expected the terrified, injured girl to react in any other way, Jon didn't know. Her head wound must have looked worse than it was, for she leapt to her feet in the aftermath of the slap and ran a sort of zig-zag disorientated path along the road, perpetually leaning one way or the other as if ready to collapse. Evans could easily have caught her, even with his extra weight, but he just stood and gaped at the woman, maybe reeling from the blow, or else just glad to see the back of her. She was certainly an additional problem Jon wouldn't have wanted to have to deal with at the moment. She had seen both their faces though. Loose ends and all that.

Whilst Evans was lollygagging around, Jon tried to get up, but his ankle buckled underneath him and a bolt of white pain shot through his brain and blinded him. The oaf *had* hurt him, on purpose or otherwise. Before Jon could make a second attempt, Evans had turned back to face him.

"Did you 'urt 'er?" he demanded.

Jon shook his head in despair. *How was he expecting a response when he was still bound and gagged?!* The idiot lumbered towards him, muscles or else just moobs rippling beneath his too tight shirt and Jon wanted to sprint away. Scurrying would have been nice as an option right now. Evans had loathing all over his face, but Jon knew his own expression was more than matching the sentiment.

"I've waited a *long* time to catch you red 'anded like his, *Jon*," said Evans and Jon shuddered at the familiarity of his first name.

Evans knew *nothing* of him. But it hadn't stopped him meddling over the years, spreading his crackpot theories across the internet. Well, Jon had more than shut that all down, by first infiltrating the idiot's forums, then flooding the net with even more crazy theories to make Evans' ideas look just as unbelievable. Replacing every genuine member of his forum with fakes was Jon's crowning achievement. Sure, it took ages to set up and the hours spent pretending to be different characters taking part in the idiot's theories was time he'd never get back, but it had been worth it when Evans had announced he was off on holiday to Portugal and then again, when they'd clapped eyes on each other at the airport. Shocking as it all was, that the plan had worked. Jon had to admit he'd been waiting a long time for this himself.

"All them poor lasses in Rusholme, you sick fuck," Evans hadn't stopped his tirade of abuse. "'ow many girls did you 'urt?"

He had edged closer to him now and if Jon hadn't been restrained *and* injured, he would have lashed out already. He knew that the knife he'd taken with him that morning had *not* been removed by Marujo's incompetent men and he wondered if it was still in his pocket. Grabbing it and swinging it right at the lumbering fool would definitely give him the rush he was craving. Even though he was never keen on the blood, it was satisfying to see and feel the metal slicing through soft, stupid flesh. He could have messed up Evans' daft face good and proper. In the flesh, he was far less gross looking than Jon had assumed over the internet. He had to admit he was actually not unattractive when he wasn't trying too hard to look like a tough guy.

"I'm gonna take you back to England and make you pay for everyone one of them lasses," Evans spat, but Jon was losing interest.

He was thinking how if he moved just another step closer, he could try and propel himself bodily at his legs and knock him down. He wasn't sure what to do then, but he felt certain that once Evans was down, he could keep him down, even if it meant straddling him, headbutting him and somehow getting access to his knife. Just one step closer…

"I know Wrigley'll be chuffed to bits to 'ave you 'anded to 'im on a plate, even if e's no longer investigatin'."

Would his insufferable rambling ever finish?! So what about all those girls, he wondered? They were asking for it, the lot of them. Jeep had helped him to understand the way the world worked today. How impressed he would be too when Jon told him how Evans had blundered right into his trap and he had bested him. Just one more step!

Evans had stopped suddenly, infuriatingly and was rummaging in his pocket.

"Bloody phone!" he cried, looking at the device in disgust.

Jon couldn't see what his issue was, but he was fuming about something, shaking the handset as if it would respond to his actions. Jon couldn't wait any longer. As Evans turned to look back down the road behind him, Jon was like a coiled spring, despite his injury, despite the distance, despite the disparity in their size and strength. He collided with Evans' solid legs painfully, jarringly but ultimately triumphantly. Evans toppled to the ground, raising a cloud of dust and Jon was on top of him in seconds.

40.

The harder Jon struggled to remember anything which had happened during his 'absence', the more it seemed to slip away from him. The car, the girl, whoever had placed them both in there against their will were nothing but elusive fragments: a jigsaw he could never solve without seeing the full picture on the box. He was stalking along the riverside now, with what in England he would have assumed to be a series of red rust-coloured bus shelters on his right. A tall red brick building like a Victorian textile mill or factory of some other description loomed ahead on the left. It was most likely a museum, Jon concluded, having already painfully jogged past three or four along this stretch of the Tagus. He was certain Evans had to have come this way as he hadn't had much of a head start and however badly *he* was limping, Evans too couldn't do much better.

The wrestling match in the dust of the dockyard which Jon now realised had been in a deserted area just beyond the *Torre de Belem* had not last more than a few moments, despite the titanic nature of the struggle in Jon's mind. He had retained the upper hand for a few brief seconds, trying to use his thighs to apply pressure around the thick neck of his adversary and aiming a solid head butt right on his temple, before Evans had thrown him off like a bucking bronco. Being bound and gagged and potentially in possession of a fractured ankle had left Jon badly outgunned. Evans was yelling at him for being a "Cheeky fuck" or something and had grabbed him roughly around the waist, aiming it seemed to hurl him once more to the ground and incapacitate him. Jon shivered at the rough hands clutching at his shirt and under at his bare toned flesh as Evans clumsily seized at him. Jon could do little to resist and found blinding stars showering before his eyes as the Mancunian returned the

194

favour with a brutal head butt which seemed to split his entire skull open.

For all Jon knew, the next part had been yet another of his absences, but in reality he suspected he was just knocked out for a few minutes and when he came to, he found his gag removed and his hands untied. His legs were still bound, but he looked down to find himself sitting cross-legged and barefoot. Evans had positioned him so and was standing over him, holding his boots and socks in one hand, looking smugly victorious. Confused, Jon glanced around and found they were still right by the car he had found himself in only now the rear windscreen was missing, smashed to pieces which were scattered all around him. Evans seemed to think a bit of broken glass was going to stop him moving, but he was sadly wrong.

"Welcome back," said Evans. "Don't even think about runnin' off."

He waved his mobile phone in his other hand. Jon rubbed his sore head and felt his wrists which were slightly chafed from the bonds. Reaching slyly behind his back in a fake yawn, he found no knife in his pocket. He struggled to remember if he even *had* a knife at all now. His head was still throbbing and he bet good money that the lunk had either broken his nose or at the very least given him a pair of black eyes.

"What's the plan, Evans?" he demanded bitterly. "You must know I had nothing to do with this girl."

"*This* girl," said Evans cockily, relishing the moment a little too much. "But all the others? Get talkin', fast. I want a recorded confession and then, maybe then, I'll 'and you over to the police. If not, I'll 'ave another go at crackin' your bloody 'ead open."

Jon almost laughed out loud at how deadly serious Evans was about it all. Evans detected the smirk on his lips it seemed and stepped towards him, scowling.

"Summat funny?" he growled.

"Oh no, no," said Jon, still not entirely sure any of this was actually happening for real and not some awful dream filling in the black blank between lucid thoughts. "It's just so strange to actually properly *see* you and *talk* to you, that's all."

Evans stepped back again, thrown by the strangeness of Jon's words. He took a deep breath, as if reframing what he had been previously about to do or say.

195

"Right then," he began. "Firstly, I want to know-"

"No, no, no," interrupted Jon. "Not like this."

He wagged a finger at Evans and shook his head, disappointedly.

"Our little showdown isn't meant to be like…" He looked around disgustedly at the dusty wasteground, the broken car window and its glass around him and his bound, bare feet. "*This*. You got *some* of my lures, but not all of them, it seems. Tell me, how did you find me?"

Evans looked even more weirded out. He was *not* good at this.

"I didn't *find* you," he admitted. "I mean, I wasn't exactly *lookin'* for you any of the times I found you. Not at the station, or at the bus stop or anywhere. When I 'eard a noise from the car boot, I didn't know it was *you* in there. I was actually lookin' for…"

He trailed off, suddenly aware of his oversharing.

"*Looking for…?*" Jon echoed, mockingly, knowing it would work.

"Palmer," finished Evans.

"*Palmer?!*" spat Jon, actually spitting in the dirt. "That fucking psychopath?"

Evans raised an eyebrow and frowned.

"Palmer's not a psycho," he retorted. "You're the fuckin' psycho mate. Palmer might be many things, but he'd never 'urt anyone like you 'ave."

"Such faith," hissed Jon. "Perhaps you should explain what a gentleman Palmer is to the poor lamented *Celia Payne?*"

"Celia fuckin' Payne?!" roared Evans now, turning bright red. "Celia fuckin' Payne is anything *but* poor or lamented. She's *alive*, dickhead!"

Before the weight of Evans' words could properly hit Jon, before he could deal with what was most obviously a fiction born out of intense denial or devotion to his murdering friend, Jon felt his phone begin to vibrate and then to ring loudly from his pocket. Whoever had taken him, had failed to remove his phone and he reached it and connected the call in a split second before Evans could decide what to do.

"I know where you are. I'm coming," was all that Jon heard.

It was Jeep and a momentary flash of answering the phone to him earlier but not knowing anything more of the conversation suddenly hit Jon. This call was over and his phone hurled away before Evans had settled on trying to swipe at him from across the broken glass barrier.

"Who was it?" demanded Evans, glaring at Jon and across to where his phone had skittered into some weeds bursting up through the dry, cracked ground. It was as if he didn't dare retrieve the phone for fear of Jon doing something out of sight behind him.

"Jeep," said Jon, smiling slyly now.

"Who or what the fuck is *Jeep?*" demanded Evans.

"My good friend and mentor," said Jon. "He understands what I am. He's very sympathetic." He could see Evans struggling to understand. "He thinks *you're* a dick by the way," Jon added.

"*Jeep?*" repeated Evans. "Like the vehicle? Army type?"

Jon began to chuckle.

"No, you oaf," he snarled. "Jeep, *G.P.* As in-"

"Gerry Payne?" blurted Evans, the colour draining from his face. "*You* know Gerry Payne?"

He tossed Jon's boots and socks into the dust and frantically tapped at his own mobile phone. Jon couldn't help but laugh at his idiocy.

"FUCK!" he roared and to Jon's surprise, he turned and ran hell for leather along the road, in the direction of the river, before veering to the left, disappearing through some bushes.

It had taken Jon only a few moments to decide to pursue, leaping agilely over the broken glass with barely a scratch. He took a further painful minute or so to untie the bonds around his ankles before stooping to snatch up his boots and carefully slipping them back on. After retrieving his phone, he quickly inspected the car for anything of use and was amazed to find that his knife was lying on the passenger seat. *The knife he'd thrown in the Tagus or a different one?* The car appeared to be a hire car, from documentation sticking out of the glove box, but he didn't stick around to remove it or read it. He set off in the direction Evans had gone, knowing that even with his lame hobbling, he would be able to see him and track him while ever he stayed on the riverside. He didn't know where Jeep was coming from, where he intended to meet him, but he knew he was a resourceful chap and would soon work out what was happening. There was no response when he dialled his number, as often was the case.

Jon realised he must have missed Evans somewhere along the way. Perhaps he had ducked into one of the museums, or headed off the river front and back to the main road, perhaps even back into the heart of Belem. He needed to find him and silence him, stop him from alerting the authorities to whatever he thought Jon had done. His only solace was that despite Evans' pretence, Jon had recognised that his mobile phone had clearly run out of battery power and despite him waving it threateningly his way, he had no method of calling the police as he stood over him. Ahead, Jon could see the *25 de Abril* bridge and behind, the *Padrao dos Descobrimentos*, which he had already hobbled in the shade of to reach this point. Something told him that Evans had doubled back on himself and he was already heading back towards the monument when his phone buzzed with a series of texts as if it had suddenly been awakened or hit a pocket of strong signal. Nothing from Julie or Matilde, but a series of texts, all from Jeep. If he hadn't trusted the man with his life, he might have found his constant vague summons to be rather tiresome. The messages read:

"Padrao des Descobrimentos."

"Roof."

"Now."

41.

The view from the top of the *Padrao des Descobrimentos* was really rather stunning. Jon had lived and breathed the city of Lisbon for so long now that perhaps he had taken it for granted, feeling less like a visiting tourist and more like a local himself. The hills and higgledy piggledy streets of the city had become second nature to him and whilst he had visited many of the famous attractions the city had to offer, he had not risen to the top of the 50m monument before or taken in its staggering views across the Tagus. If anything, he had marvelled at the sight from outside and below but never considered the possibility or indeed the need to enter it or ascend to its viewing platform at the very top. The monument resembled a gigantic cruciform or sword, with arc like struts rising up to meet the horizontal bars of the cross, at the foot of which were rising steps with some of Portugal's most noted explorers queuing up, jostling almost as if to achieve supremacy on the higher steps. Jon imagined they were queuing to hurl themselves or each other into the river itself.

It was typical of Jeep to want to be looking out over the world from somewhere like this, Jon thought. He liked high places and casting his wise gaze down over the world. He had been looking over Jon for years now of course, even if Jon found it a little odd at times. Mind you, Jon's entire life was rather odd when one stepped back to take a look at it. Such a mess of violence and random life choices. And now Evans himself had blundered right in, second guessing his moves and claiming *ridiculously* that Celia was alive. Somehow he also had an intense fear of Gerry Payne but Jon couldn't imagine why.

There was a small charge to enter the monument and a wait for the lift. Jon was disappointed that the building was actually much smaller on the inside, like a reverse TARDIS, with just a lift ride up to the viewing platform and some sort of small exhibit he had no interest in. It was hardly the Empire State Building, he scoffed. But if Jeep had chosen this place to meet, it must have some significance or else he simply found it a quiet meeting point maybe, away from the bustle of the rest of Belem and less glamorous, historic or appetising. The wind had been gusting quite fiercely as Jon had entered the monument, but upon stepping out onto the roof platform, he found it strangely calm.

He could see exactly why Jeep would choose a place like this. The observation deck was high-walled, which may have held the gusts back and narrow, with little room for swarms of gormless tourists. The view though was stunning. The Tagus was always worth a gawp from any angle or altitude, but it was the view back over the city which proved most fascinating. Of course Jon had appreciated many of the patterned tiled areas around the city, one couldn't move from a street to a square without noticing an intriguing geometric pattern mosaiced onto the floor, but it was the stunning centre piece of the wave-like pattern in the shadow of the monument which caught Jon's attention. A huge circular compass design with points like the thrusting petals of an opening flower lay beneath him, also bearing a resemblance to the ever-present dazzling sun. On either side of the design were marinas, and further into Belem, splendid white buildings of palaces, museums and galleries. Tiny people crossed the design, miniscule, worthless, making Jon realise just how high up they actually were. He felt quite giddy.

Fewer than a dozen people were crammed into the narrow viewing area and Jon quickly spotted Jeep at the far end, gazing out at the river. He assumed he hadn't been seen, but as he drew close behind his friend and mentor, he began to speak, clearly having known he'd arrived all along.

"Jon, Jon, Jon," he said slowly and evenly, not turning around or tearing his eyes away from the glittering river. "Why can't you ever just slow down and *enjoy life* for once? Me, for instance, I could *live* out there on the river, y'know. It's beautiful. I felt certain I saw you out there on your boat, y'know?"

"Jeep," said Jon; he never called him anything else, despite appreciating what an odd name it sounded to those in earshot. "I think I'm in-"

"Trouble?" said Jeep, a little more tersely, still with his back to Jon. "I suppose you may well be. But when are you not, my boy?"

200

Jon didn't know what to say. He always felt a little chastised in the older man's company. Forever the student before his wiser mentor.

"I suppose I'm to clean up your mess again, am I?" asked Jeep.

Jon wanted to respond but knew that he would stutter as he did so, so remained silent.

"Who and where?" Jeep asked, taking out a small notepad.

It was the same notepad he always had, A6 Jon thought the size was, like a detective or something and Jon felt the suggestion was always that it was filled with problems *he* had caused. He flipped through page after page somewhat theatrically, as if Jon had caused him endless problems, until he found a blank page.

Jon knew he ought to hate a man who could be so aloof, so condescending, but their history made him rely entirely upon his help and his discretion. He felt his heart pounding and knew his cheeks were flushed. He wondered how awful he looked following his fighting and escape attempts and realised he hadn't even thought to check, Had the employee on the desk downstairs looked at him strangely, or was that just his imagination now he thought about his appearance?

"Evans *is* here, like I told you," Jon mustered up the nerve to get out without faltering.

He was hiding his anxiety behind a layer of aggression now. It was always easier to be angry than to be scared, he found.

Jeep actually laughed, somewhat jovially, Jon thought at the mention of the name.

"I wouldn't worry about *him*," he said, still gazing out at the view. "He's nothing but a grade A dick."

"I told him you said that," muttered Jon.

At this, Jon noticed Jeep tense slightly. His hands, resting casually on the ledge, suddenly gripped it. Still, he didn't turn.

"You told him *I* said that about him?" he asked, his teeth almost gritted.

Jon nodded although Jeep must have already known the answer as he didn't turn to see.

"So he knows *I'm* here?" he continued. "That I *exist*?"

Jon wondered which was worse. It was odd the way Jeep had phrased it. Surely it was worse to know someone *existed* rather than their general location?

"No, not really," Jon said, feeling his neck growing even hotter. "He's an idiot. A dick, like you said. He actually thinks you're-"

Jeep interrupted once more, still quietly cool with a hint of menace:

"Jon, it's becoming increasingly difficult to look after you when you're so *reckless*. A few drunken slappers in studentville is one thing. Whores in the *Baixa* is another. You mess with someone who might actually get noticed, someone who might actually be *believed*, then we have trouble. You should never have begun something you couldn't stop like this."

There was a long silence and Jon heard laughing from a pair of young girls trying to get a good photo from just behind them. The entire world seemed to cease to exist when Jeep was talking to him.

"Who's this Marujo guy?" asked Jeep. "Some sort of dago Kray by all accounts, I'm guessing?"

Jon bristled slightly at the name and the casual racism. Marujo was a lot less easily dismissed he found, despite his own low opinion of him. Jeep was crafty, an ideas man, not a fighter. He wondered what the two men would make of each other.

"His daughter went missing," said Jon. "I was...*seeing* her."

A loud sigh came from Jeep and his shoulders rose and fell dramatically, like a huffy teenager. A decade or so ago, he might have dared lay a hand on those shoulders, to calm him in exchange for the calm *he* brought about in Jon. But things had changed. Jon knew that.

"More mess," sighed Jeep, now shaking his head pitifully. "You must *control your urges*."

Jon's eyes were boring into the back of Jeep's pink neck now. The years of gratitude were so easily hurled aside when he was so scathing to him. He imagined his hands around that neck now.

"If any of this was to get out, Jon…" said Jeep, warningly. "…I'm not sure I could protect you. That *anyone* could."

All these years Jon had known him, Jeep had never openly threatened him like this. They'd often spoken in plain terms about what might befall him were he arrested or actually properly investigated as a suspect outside of the deluded forums people like Evans chatted nonsense on, but this was the first time Jeep was suggesting he might give him up. Something had definitely changed. Despite the man's education, he was a brute, Jon suddenly thought. He had taken the high ground, patronisingly guiding Jon through his episodes, rehabilitating him with a lecture or a place to hide out, but he too had broken the law. Whether he had actually literally, physically tidied up after Jon, or whether it was just a euphemism he used for the general aftercare he provided, it made Jeep an accessory too. Jon had never aimed his rage at Jeep directly, but he could see how easy it would be to do so right now.

A young girl was waving her phone at Jon and he realised she wanted him to take a photo of her and her friend. Having ignored her for a few seconds he finally gave in and turned, his snarling face instantly becoming a smile as he took the phone and allowed the girls a moment to pose before taking their photo. He wasn't sure what language they were speaking (some odd Asian dialect), but their English was good enough to request the picture, then to his horror, to offer to return the favour. Jon shook his head sternly. He had no desire to be snapped up here and Jeep would certainly not be up for it. Did anyone even *know* he was in Portugal, Jon wondered. Then, suddenly, impulsively, mischievously, he sensed an opportunity. He dug his phone out and offered it to the girl who was about to give in and follow her friend to the opposite end of the platform. He quickly showed her which button to press, but figured her youth probably offered her a technological advantage over him anyway (if not her race also) and stood back to smile for the photo. The girl was waving her free hand to indicate that Jon should get his friend to pose properly, and so Jon tapped him squarely on the back. Jeep turned around, disgruntled and was captured in the photograph.

Before Jeep could respond, Jon took back his phone and escorted the girl along the rooftop as he uploaded the photo to his cloud storage. No amount of deleting from the phone itself could remove it now. He had a timestamped, geolocated photo of himself and Jeep now and if the onetime mentor and helper was going to try and manipulate or threaten him, then he had proof of their connection. The girl was giggling away now as Jon walked with her and as she rejoined her friend, he nodded thanks to them both and gave them a gentle nudge towards the way back down. As he turned back to face Jeep, he found the man right behind him, scowling murderously.

"Look at the state of you, Jon," he said, eyeing him from top to bottom.

He had a point. Jon's normally impeccable attire was scuffed, torn, bloody and stained. There were welts around his wrists and lower calves, his right ankle was purple and grossly swollen and goodness only knew what his face looked like, but he imagined the swelling which came with such a violent head butt or two. Jon felt belittled again and wondered what it always was that made him feel this way when Jeep shifted from avuncular to patriarchal. His own hopeless parents had never had this power over him. It couldn't be the age gap as despite his wisdom, Jeep was barely ten years his senior and no amount of degrees or educating or hanging around with troubled young minds could make Jon so subservient to his supposed authority. It all came down to that first meeting, when Jon as he was today was effectively born. Jeep had been the first person he'd seen and had helped him. Whether that had been the right thing to do or not, Jon now questioned. A spell of rehabilitation or some restorative justice might have cured him of his ways, might have sent him down a different path, with no Celia, no Julie, no other women harmed in his wake.

For all that Jeep had done for him, Jon knew it must now all come to an end.

42.

Persuading Jeep to go along with him had been easier than he'd imagined. Getting him alone would be trickier, if not impossible. He now sensed an irreversible barrier had sprung up between them, watered by years of poorly hidden distrust and given momentum by this awkward sense of mutually assured destruction which Jon's photo had confirmed. He now realised that he could no longer rely on the man to keep his secrets and worse, he now suspected that if Jeep wasn't the strange threatening aggressor, then perhaps he knew who it was. They had been surprisingly quiet since the morning and he felt it had been entirely conjured up to cause a collision between himself, Evans and Palmer, like throwing three fireworks into an enclosed space for maximum destruction. Well, two could play at that game.

From the top of the *Padrao dos Descobrimentos*, Jon had felt certain he could see Evans, limping away back towards the city, continuing the direction he must initially have set out on after their confrontation, and whilst he knew it could just as easily have been his imagination, he didn't doubt that Evans' move would be to return to his hotel, or to try and regroup with Palmer, wherever he was. Jon knew perfectly well where they were staying, having been standing outside the place 36 hours earlier, when Jeep had first indicated the possibilities to him. They had been working on different, overlapping ideas back then, but knew that everything would come together nicely in the end, thanks to the dear, departed Celia Payne. Jon would simply leave a message at their hotel to meet him to end all of this. The same message would be relayed to Marujo and his heavies and finally, to Jeep. Jon would light the blue touch paper and stand well back, having hopefully stirred up enough resentment between the parties to ensure violence. He had already prepared

205

that today might be his last day on earth, but now he was feeling a little more hopeful. He didn't *have* to get caught in the crossfire. He could stand well back and enjoy the show.

Jeep had descended with him in the lift and they'd parted on decent enough terms, following their hostile exchange on the roof. Jon had assured him that he would deal with Marujo himself and that he should return to his hotel, which Jon also knew to be just a few minutes from his planned showdown spot. It seemed there was a Sana hotel in every district in Lisbon. In a few hours, he would call him there and summon him for one last chat, and the location would be irresistible to Jeep – another high place for him to look down on the world. *The ego on that man!* Marujo would be harder to persuade to venture out in broad daylight again, but if he offered himself up on a plate, alongside a pledge to reveal Matilde's whereabouts, then what psychotic mafioso daddy could resist? Besides, the once sunny skies were beginning to darken and rainclouds were glowering overhead. Once the heavens opened, the streets would thin out a little and Jon's choice of location would become deserted, possibly even closed, he worried.

He checked his online accounts, ready to book himself a ticket out of the city immediately after the showdown. He didn't imagine that flying would be an option, not if police got involved and his name became known to them. He had already been freaked out seeing his face on a British newspaper but they had nothing to pin on him in that respect. No, he would take a boat, possibly even charter one across the Tagus, maybe even further on to North Africa. He had time enough to plan his escape in small steps and money, well his bank balance was flush with the proceeds of his penny dreadful empire. It took him six attempts logging into his business account on his phone before he gave up and tried his current account, which was linked. The stupid app sometimes failed to grant him access and he was forced to turn to the good old-fashioned website on a laptop, but he sensed something different here and now as he stalked along the curving *Rua da Boavista,* following the tramlines rather than any sense of actual direction. His personal account was empty. His business account showed as closed and also empty. He couldn't view the transactions in the latter, but knew there had been close to 50,000 Euros in there, money made from JSC publishing and his little goldmine of cheap, tawdry e-books. Someone had cleared him out. Perhaps a fourth invitation to the showdown was now necessary as Jon realised that only two people could have possibly done this to him (outside of a random hacker or scammer, which he doubted severely) – one was his errant wife, Julie, the other, his rather faceless investor and business partner, Kulani.

It had been a rushed job, moving overseas so quickly, uprooting himself from his little measured world and ending up in Lisbon's seductive clutches and

Julie had been next to useless, but his little anonymous writing blog had grabbed the attention of some online publishers and before he knew it, his stories were being published and money was trickling in. The fact that people were actually interested in reading his dark little fantasies (mostly made up, but generally based on crimes he'd seen, heard and in a few cases, *done*) amazed him and the offer of investment in getting his own publishing company up and running had been unbelievable. This exotic Kulani woman even had an apartment in Lisbon she offered at mates' rates and Jon had imagined her probably as some dowdy, middle aged, bored woman with a pedestrian bog-standard name living out a dream as a purveyor of cheap, cheesy chick-lit. He had tried to joke with Julie that her name was more likely to be Kelly than Kulani, a name which suggested Hawaiian exoticism, but Julie showed little interest in his incomings, being more happy to contribute to the outgoings. Jon should have found it odd that he'd never met Kulani in person, but she painted herself as a worldwise woman, a constant globe trotter who was forever in demand at book launches and business meetings around the world. She had written a few of the books herself, but relied on other authors like Jon and he was content that her grainy, black and white, bespectacled photo in her writer's profile was innocent enough. For an entrepreneur who mostly hawked her wares online, she was strangely unaccounted for on the internet, which made Jon think she was a more mature woman, caught up in the spicy anonymity of writing and selling racy reads to equally mature audiences.

Once or twice Jon had found it odd that she'd pulled out of a meeting at the last minute, but knew how older women could be so moody and self-conscious and if she looked half as awful as her photo, he didn't question her shyness. She'd snapped up everything he'd ever written for publishing, not even questioning the more lurid, grounded stuff he'd sent over, the tales ripped straight from his own fragmented history rather than his imagination and had seemed keen to publish his latest manuscript in progress provisionally titled *How Not to Murder Your Wife.* Jon's research to date had been purely theoretical, acting out the processes, but he knew how easy it would be to plot the thing for real and was waiting for Kulani's feedback on his recent revisions. Now he came to think of it, he hadn't heard from her in days. Weeks even. *Could she really have taken him for a ride and cleared out the business account?!*

Perhaps she had learned some of the truth about the handsome young British writer and former teacher she had leapt into bed with, metaphorically speaking. The gossip and innuendos were all out there, if you knew where to look. The girlfriend who cried foul, the rumoured workplace affairs, the accusations of improper conduct and the mental health issues, but Jon on paper was nothing compared to Jon in the flesh, a swaggering powerhouse of good looks, intelligence and bravado. Whatever Kulani might have read about him, he felt sure he could charm his way out of it. If that *was* what had happened. And it still didn't explain the missing money. He tried phoning Julie first of all, but it just rang and rang. Then, he dug out Kulani's contact details, a local number in the *Parque das Nacoes* area of town, only a few blocks from where his own apartment was. So strange she was never in town. The number went straight to voicemail, a robotic voice which asked him to leave his details but gave no clue as to who he was leaving them for. Jon felt himself getting clammier as he continued walking, trying to keep the pressure off his badly swollen ankle but still make good progress towards his destination. The neighbourhood he was passing through was not the most inviting, with dirty brickwork, graffiti everywhere and cheap-looking shopfronts. He knew that if he just kept following the tramlines, he would soon be back to where he was more familiar.

Jeep would have been his next call in any other situation. Whether it had been in Manchester, London or on the continent as now, the man was always reachable and always managed to talk him down in those initial panicked moments. Jon knew his blood ran too hot, that he was too impulsive, too prone to rash action but after his latest meeting, he now knew what he had feared for some time. Jeep was no better. He had seemed initially to thrive on the chaos Jon brought to his door, to get a power trip from temporarily seizing control of Jon's mad life and restoring it back to order, but over time, he seemed to have grown bored of it, to have started looking at Jon as if he were some mad dog turning up on his doorstep that ought to know better. He had never stopped helping, but he had stopped looking like it suited him to do so. When Jon had called him after his desperate, bloody blackout, Jeep had seemed uninterested, as if bored by Jon's antics, or worse, as if these matters were no longer a surprise or a draw for him. At the mention of Celia Payne's name, Jeep had gone quiet, as if in disgust and only after prompting, had he resumed the conversation, giving Jon some instruction as to what to do about his fears.

Jon passed through several arched bridgeways and took the *Calcada Ferragial* which took him steeply up and away from the tram route, curving towards streets on the edge of the *Baixa-Chiado* district he recognised from visiting Matilde on previous evenings. The undulation of the city, meant he was soon heading down a steeper winding street the yellow trams routinely clattered along down and as the road levelled out once more, he knew instantly where he was. Practically a block from where he had been just a day ago, enjoying a drink in view of the Yellow Bus tour stand, waiting for Jeep to show up. It had been far from the happy reunion he'd been expecting after their less friendly meeting the night before, lasting barely a minute, with the supposed mentor offering him a few terse words of advice, slipping him his hotel details and then heading off into the crowd. Jon had put it down to travel tiredness, having recently flown a couple of hours purely to help him out, but couldn't help noticing in the daylight now how alert and tanned Jeep already was. Life was treating him well in England, he had thought. The brief advice had given Jon the reassurance to act as normal and so he had set about charming the girl at the ticket stand, almost winning her phone number before Evans had blundered along and accosted him. It was alarming to think how, despite his unsettledness yesterday, that feeling was now a million times better than the panic rising in his gut.

He practically jogged up the *Rua Aurea* which he knew like the back of his hand, headed for the destination he found bizarrely could not be seen until one was right beneath it. As he reached a pedestrian intersection, he looked up to his left to see the towering metal construction of the *Elevador de Santa Justa*. The sky had darkened ominously above it and rain began to pelt viciously down on the streets. It was as good a place as any for a showdown, he mused.

43.

Waiting was agony, but there was little point in attempting to go up the lift just yet, particularly when he was certain the staff wrangling the queues and operating the aged machinery looked set to close up shop for the duration of the storm. He had seen the disappointed faces of tourists before as he wandered this area, the first to complain should they be drenched or slip on a metal ramp in the downpour but equally prone to huff and puff when their desired attraction closed for a few hours for safety reasons. Now was one of those moments, at barely half past two in the afternoon, the staff at the *Elevador de Santa Justa* were weighing up the likelihood of turning away the huge queue already snaking around the foot of the tower and bringing those atop the place safely back down. It wasn't just the rain which tipped the argument in this case though, as the muggy weather across the afternoon had suddenly broken and thunder was rumbling away in the filthy grey sky, the occasional fork of lightning lancing across the sky in sympathy with it. Jon didn't know if the tower acted like a lightning conductor but he bet it was a pretty spectacular sight from up there, either way.

He was lurking at a restaurant at the foot of the tower, chairs and tables spread out across the pedestrianised road, seeming at first to belong to none of the shops on the street which were clothes shops, gift shops and a jeweller's, but here any open space was game for outdoor seating and Jon soon found the eye of a waiter who it turned out had to dart around the corner to where the indoor part of the business was. Tucking into a tuna fish toasted sandwich of sorts, Jon satisfied at least part of his stomach gurgling issues. He had forgotten how late in the day it was and despite the nerves over his money issues, he needed to take time out to feed. He had placed several calls to the bank whilst awaiting his order, all fruitless, but had definitely learned that app glitches aside, he was penniless and actually had been for a couple of days now. He started to track back the last time he'd actually communicated with either Kulani or Julie, the latter causing him to strain his memory thinking back to when they'd last interacted in person rather than sniping passive aggressively via texts. Straining to recall caused his head to pound and he feared triggering another blackout at this crucial stage, so he simply sat and watched the world go by in the tremendous downpour.

A message had been left at the Sana Reno where he knew Evans and Palmer were staying, requesting their presence at the top of the *elevador* at three thirty precisely. He figured that Evans would have retreated immediately back to the hotel and wherever Palmer was, they were undoubtedly in touch somehow, despite the depleted phone battery. He had left the same message at the Sana Lisboa, where Jeep had said he was staying, somewhere near the *Pombal* roundabout and not too far from Palmer and Evans' place of choice either. It felt odd to use Jeep's real name when he left the message as he so rarely referred to him as anything other than his nickname. He had tried contacting him by phone, but as was often the case, he didn't pick up and showed no sign of reading the text message Jon sent. His final invitation was to Marujo and he knew exactly where to reach him, calling the restaurant Matilde worked in and demanding to be put through to the *chefe*. Matilde never really seemed to twig that her father owned the place in which she worked, which was why she got away with murder when it came to punctuality or professionalism and if anyone was missing her there, the staff member Jon spoke briefly to didn't show it. Marujo himself was as impotently vicious as ever, describing how he was going to slice Jon into little pieces and throw his remains into the Tagus. *You'll have to catch me first*! Jon told him that whilst he didn't have Matilde himself, he knew she had passed into the hands of an English gang of *vilões* who wanted to discuss terms with him. He made sure to describe Palmer, Evans and Jeep in as much detail as he could muster in Portuguese, then hung up, leaving Marujo to no doubt froth at his henchmen.

Jon knew the best bet was to scarper. To forget the money, forget any belongings he might treasure, to give up on either Julie or Kulani for the moment and just get away, but he couldn't. His vicious streak, his insatiable thirst for witnessing or inciting violence just wouldn't let him. He wanted to get up the *elevador* as soon as it reopened, then witness the mayhem that ensued when the various people who had pissed him off, all came face to face. He knew for a fact there wasn't even really anywhere to hide up there, perhaps behind the ornate metal struts of a spiral staircase or viewing from a distance might have worked, but he wanted to see this up close.

He doubted that Marujo would actually wait for the time he had suggested and

211

sure enough, a black BMW was prowling along in the rain, its headlights on full and despite the tinted windows, Jon thought he could see the ugly face of the criminal boss pressed up against the glass. Jon was sitting at the furthest table from the road, sideways on, hidden by the number of umbrellas above the tables, barely keeping anything dry in the deluge, but he knew it was Marujo. The car passed up and down a few times before Jon noticed it pulling up and the same two goons who had manhandled him away in the park leapt out with umbrellas before opening the back door to let their boss out. A flash of light, either in the sky or a passing car, lit up Marujo's face. He looked beyond livid. Jon finished his tuna toastie and dabbed at his mouth with a paper napkin. This wasn't going to be easy at all. He could see the henchmen struggle to keep Marujo sheltered as they crossed over to and ascended the steps which led up to the *elevador* and found it closed. He was too far away to hear any of the conversation which ensued, but after a few minutes, the two overlapping umbrellas scuttled back down the steps and fed their sheltered contents back into the car. One goon got back in, the other seemingly having drawn the short straw stood out in the rain, keeping a lookout.

Jon checked the time. It was 15:10 and the rain was showing no signs of slowing or stopping. As the waitress came to clear his plate, he glanced up at her pretty, inviting face. The urges he felt were almost uncontrollable and it took every fibre of his being to stop himself grabbing her slender wrist as she collected his unused cutlery. Had he always been this way, he mused? Was that first rush of unknowable pleasure always intended as the first step on the path he had chosen? Or was it the careful manoeuvring of one who he had assumed was helping him, that had led him where he was today with holes in his memory and a larger one in his finances now? *There's a hole in my bucket, dear Liza, dear Liza.* He felt the dripping of rain on his nose and saw that the umbrella above was no match for the amount of water cascading down it. He took out a bank card, realised it would probably be declined, then found a few notes instead which he tossed down onto the table. It was probably safer that he didn't wait for the waitress to return with the bill. He figured that if he headed along the pedestrianised street away from the *elevador*, then did a complete lap of the block to his left, he could pitch up on the far side of the construction, the lesser accessed side which spilled out onto a wide commercial street.

He was thoroughly drenched by the time he wound up on the steep *Rua do Carmo* passing a bookshop on the corner and finding himself facing the rear view of the *elevador*. He had already passed under the high connecting bridge which he knew led from just below the upper viewing platform of the lift across to the *Largo do Carmo* where cheapskates with decent fitness levels could admire the view without paying for the lift up and down. Jon suddenly realised the flaw in his plan and whilst Marujo, the lazy fuck, would wait for the lift to open again, or else use his heavies to grant him access, that anyone else could simply have traversed the steep hill and steps to the upper level without waiting for the storm to end. He knew the uppermost platform would be closed – it had strict health and safety regulations about capacity, let alone being accessible in a storm – didn't know whether the way up to that point was similarly restricted. Gazing at the water gushing down from the wrought iron gantry above, he guessed it was probably restricted by tourist enthusiasm, if anything. The streets had soon emptied as the downpour started. He was about to thank the stars he was wrong about the other access route, when he realised there *were* people crossing the elevated walkway. He jogged far enough away from the underside of the bridge to be able to see and was thoroughly irritated to see Evans stomping his way across with not only Palmer in tow, but a woman who looked for all the world like Celia Payne.

44.

Blood gushed from the terrible wound and was further dispersed by the heavy rain which was still pounding down on the city. There was a definite reason why this upper level was closed off in the rain and Marujo's men forcing their way in had learned the hard way. Their boss stood frozen, machete which had once been in his flailing wild hand, now embedded in his own neck. He had lunged out with the deadly weapon, slipped on the wet floor and thrown his entire body weight onto the blade. It was perhaps only his additional weight which had saved him as the blade would surely have decapitated a thinner man, but instead Marujo lay there gurgling pathetically as twin rivers of red emerged from his mouth and the neck wound. Lightning flared dramatically above and the wind which had calmed earlier in the day, whipped ferociously around them on the exposed tier of the tower. Cries from below still persisted, in response to their hostile trespassing rather than the injury of which they could have no knowledge.

Jon smirked in delight. The flow of blood both excited and reviled him but it was satisfying seeing the red wash away in the endless rain only to be renewed by Marujo's racing heartbeat. The heavy holding onto him finally let go in order to check on his boss and Jon took the opportunity to scarper. He knew that he had been right to insist on being here to witness this. None of it would quite have played out the way it did if he hadn't been here, but now was his time to go before the police or emergency services were called in. The chaos would soon expand, rippling through the rest of the assembled crowd and Jon, whilst still badly needing answers, had to go. He skidded along the wet platform, barely the size of a small classroom and headed down the spiral staircase at one end, not looking back at all and barrelling through the security

214

guard who had been poised at the bottom of the steps, unsure whether to disregard the threat and investigate. Thankfully, miraculously, the awful weather meant that there were only one or two people even close to the walkway as Jon legged it across and swiftly descended to street level.

Jeep hadn't shown up, but Evans and Palmer had almost got caught up in the carnage and Jon was sure that if they didn't make their own escape soon enough, the authorities would detain them for long enough for him to stop worrying about them. Celia being there was a turn up for the books, one Jon's wavering mind couldn't quite rationalise. She had looked thoroughly miserable, even discounting the rain, seemingly in a foul mood, and Jon wondered if it was because her secrets had been uncovered. She must surely have faked her own disappearance and then laid the blame at every man with a pulse with any connection to her whilst sunning herself here in Lisbon. That explained Evans' garbled claims of her being alive, but not Jon's own, strange feelings on the matter. He reached the steep street beneath the *elevador* walkway and looked up to see if there was any commotion. It looked like the two henchmen were carrying Marujo across the gantry but there was no sign of the others, or the staff of the lift itself.

When Jon had reached the top, not some ten minutes ago, he had found the way up to the observation deck closed off as the spiral stairs leading there were within the structure of the lift's tower which had its outer doors closed. A sole female employee was standing watch having just sent a couple of eager tourists back the way they had come when they had asked about reaching the top. She wasn't bargaining on anyone forcing their way inside. Jon had almost missed Evans and Palmer in his rush to reach the kiosk, now noticing them lurking behind him, standing either protectively or menacingly either side of the stern-looking woman between them. *What a reunion this was!*

"Celia!" Jon cried out, unable to help himself. "I see you've partnered up with my two favourite Brits abroad. Sucker #1 and sucker #2. What's going on?"

He saw Evans tense and push the woman further behind him. He made a fist with his other hand and held it up as if Jon ought to be awed by its potential. It merely made him smirk. Palmer's face was harder to read. He looked genuinely unsettled by events and who could blame him, when the woman even Jon thought he had done in was standing right next to him? Celia, for her own part, gave nothing at all away. She narrowed her eyes when she saw Jon and bit her lip, which could have meant a number of things.

"Get away, you maniac!" cried Evans, but Celia touched his shoulder and there followed a heated exchange of whispers between the three of them.

215

Finally, Celia, stepped from between her hapless bodyguards and Jon took a step himself, closing the distance between them which he now felt crackled with strange electricity.

"Looking very alive for a dead woman," he said neutrally, genuinely unsure how to process whatever feelings he was meant to be experiencing.

"Jon Scott Campbell," said Celia, as if chewing on something unpleasant. "I've thought about this moment for a long time." She looked around at the dark slanting rain and the broiling sky. "I didn't quite imagine it like this," she continued.

"Did you know I was here when you came here?" Jon demanded.

He had to know whether she had always planned to throw his name into the mix as a suspect, or whether the choice of both their flights to a new life had been merely coincidental.

"Of course, Jon," said Celia. "We all followed your *progress* with interest."

She was practically purring now. So much for the tortured victim fleeing for her life.

"I might have helped cover up your sordid little fling," she said bitterly now. "But I never expected you to be so fucking consumed with lust to take the dozy tart with you!"

Jon shuddered at the slight. Celia had been more appalled at the rejection he offered her rather than the relationship he'd been in with a student. In some ways, when she found out about the latter, it had made her feel like she might have stood a chance, had his interests not lain elsewhere. Jon knew she had planned to pin everything on the girl and try and win him over for her efforts. When he quit and ran off with the student, it had no doubt enraged her even more.

"How is young *Julie* these days?" she sneered. "I hear you married the little trollop."

She didn't know the half of it, Jon mused. He could see Evans and Palmer bristling to do something behind Celia, shifting from one foot to the other in the dismal rain. He wondered how much of all this they knew. *What did it even matter?*

"How insane are you, Celia?" Jon asked. "Insane enough to follow me around? Insane enough to get my phone number and harass me? Insane enough to use a *voice changer?"*

It had suddenly dawned on Jon that Celia was the only viable candidate for the threatening calls he had been receiving. She hadn't even been a contender, given he'd assumed she was dead in a ditch somewhere, but Evans' earlier mention of her being alive, then seeing her in the flesh had made it all come crashing into focus. Would those two idiots dawdling behind her be so quick to defend her when they realised she was playing the lot of them?

Before he could delve any further, the lift mechanism behind them ground suddenly into motion, much to their surprise and that of the female employee. The rain had got worse, if anything and she wasn't expecting the attraction to reopen just yet. She went in and Jon took the opportunity to dart past her inside, then up one of the spiral staircases which led to the uppermost level. He knew exactly why the lift was moving again. Either money or threats had been exchanged downstairs, and Marujo was on his way up. All he needed was for Jeep to arrive and this showdown would be complete.

As he splashed across the tiny rooftop to the furthest edge, he took in the glistening red rooftops and the bizarre roofless arches of the Carmo convent nestled amongst them. Whirling at the sound of the clanging of the metal steps, he took in the distant Tagus and high amongst greenery on the horizon, Lisbon's very own castle, the *Castelo de Sao Jorge*. He hadn't expected Marujo's men to be so quickly behind him, but he instead realised it was Evans and Palmer standing atop the roof with Celia lurking behind them, scowling in the incessant rain. Both staircases were at that end so there was no easy way down now, but he hoped it would be far simpler getting down once he'd set the various factions against one another.

"Where are you runnin' to, Jon?" yelled Stuart, as thunder rumbled overhead.

"Yes, Jonny, where are you going?" gasped Celia, theatrically, in a gross, breathy parody of Marilyn Monroe.

He had backed right up against the lowish decorated railings and felt the cold wet metal against his back. Below he heard the machinery stop again and the sound of angry yelling.

"It's the end of the road for all of us, I think!" cried Jon, running his hand through his sodden hair, wiping the water from his eyes.

Evans and Palmer looked puzzled but Celia was giving nothing away. Behind them suddenly, from the other staircase, loomed the two bodyguards Marujo

217

took with him at all times. Their umbrellas forgotten, they stood glaring in the rain. By default, the three in the middle moved to the left-hand side of the deck as Marujo joined his two heavies who were sizing up the situation. They moved instinctively towards Jon but he held up a hand and yelled:

"*Pare!*"

He explained quickly in Portuguese that the two men and the woman were part of the gang he had mentioned who had Matilde (he planned to land Jeep in the mix at a later point, if he ever showed up) but as he explained, he saw Marujo shaking his head.

"*Ela está morta!*" howled Marujo.

Jon realised he had either missed something in translation or events had unfolded he wasn't yet privy to. *Matilde was dead*?! There wasn't time to properly process any of this, but Jon knew what he had to say next.

"*Eles a mataram!*" he howled, summoning up some primal angst from somewhere, genuinely spitting out the words as if he believed them to be true and had been robbed of his love.

It was enough to make Marujo at least leave him alone for the moment. He held out his hand and one of the heavies handed him a gleaming machete. Jon couldn't believe his eyes. Marujo rarely dirtied his hands himself in public, but when it came to his precious Matilde, he seemed prepared to make an exception. Palmer and Evans gawped in horror and Celia threw Jon a look which said he had gone too far.

And so Marujo had fallen on his own sword, so to speak, and taken himself out of the equation. One down, four to go, Jon mused. And Matilde was dead? *Bonus!* Jon shook his head at his own sudden, unexpected callousness. Jeep definitely had a lot to answer for. *Where the hell was he?* Then he remembered Jeep waxing lyrical about the river and knew exactly where to find him.

45.

The rain was starting to ease off but the sky was still black and bleak as Jon dragged himself along unfamiliar streets. His sense of direction was still sound and he knew that sooner or later he would be presented with a clear view of the Tagus as long as he kept going, regardless of the up and down and left and right folds in the street network. He crossed over an intersecting tramline which confused him as he generally knew their layout; he feared being caught up in the tangle of streets which sometimes confounded the tourists trying to dart between city districts off the beaten path, so was relieved when he saw a sign for *Rua do Arsenal* which signified he was close to the water. Grand white stately government buildings and echoes of historic revolutionary meetings surrounded him and as there was no easy way through, he turned and followed the tramlines this time until he was able to veer off to the left again and head directly for the river. The whole city suddenly fell away and aside from a strangely modern building lined with odd U-shaped trees in front of it on his right, there was simply a wide-open space of tarmacked road and verdant lawns. The sky ahead of him was dazzlingly light as the storm clouds hung over the city centre but left the river clear and ethereally bright.

It would be quite a trek along the riverside to reach his destination, the *25 de Abril* bridge, where he felt certain Jeep had retreated to. He knew his mentor had waxed lyrical about the river, but to be *permanently* on the river meant a bridge in Jon's mind. The half-forgotten mention of thinking he'd *seen* Jon on the boat, made Jon certain he'd been on the *25 de Abril* bridge that afternoon, watching as the Yellow Bus boat tour chugged along below. Jon remembered hiding in the freezing cold, waiting to dump the wretched bag of trophies and

219

ill-thought-out clothing he'd intended to act out Julie's murder with. Had Jeep really been watching down, once more from on high, as that all took place? That first night he'd met him, Jeep had taken him for a stroll up Oxford Road in Manchester where they'd sat under the railway bridge which connected Manchester's Piccadilly with the less frequented Oxford Road station. He'd spoken about connections between things, some high and visible like the bridge rattling above their heads, and some invisible and delicate, like the bond he felt between the two of them. He should have known he was barking mad back then, but who was Jon to talk? He'd just confessed to a complete stranger that he thought he'd attacked a girl, then left that stranger to deal with the mess, before spending the rest of the night walking around talking philosophically together. Jon had been half-cut and the next day he'd nursed a foul hangover, questioning whether any of the night's events had taken place. He wouldn't have believed it all if it hadn't been for the SMS he'd received which read:

'Building bridges together. Call me whenever you need me. Jeep.'

He had struggled to even remember the precise events of the night, let alone who this mysterious man was and part of him was disappointed to imagine that he might well have wandered over a few streets and ended up in Manchester's gay village and offered himself up to a predatory homosexual or two. He'd been barely 16 and he knew from shows like *Queer As Folk* that lads like him were catnip to the older gays. Thankfully, after responding to the message, more of the evening came flooding back: the long walk 'til daybreak bonding with his newfound mentor, the potentially savage assault he had perpetrated and the way it had left him feeling, and finally, most lucidly, the reason for his new advisor's odd nickname.

Evans had been so wide of the mark when he butted in with the idea that 'Jeep' was a shortening of G.P. as in Gerry Payne. The letters were correct, but their meaning was far more pedestrian and guessable. G.P. stood for general practitioner, as in an ordinary doctor. Jeep had introduced himself as a newly qualified doctor when they first met, specialising or aiming to specialise more in mental health, and intrigued by Jon's strange break with reality. Jon had refused to give him his full name, so had been called 'J.C.' all evening, whilst Jeep for his part, offered his full name, but Jon settled for calling him 'Doc' and then finally 'G.P.' The name had stuck over the thirteen years despite Jeep not actually being anything *like* a G.P. in his career. Jon had almost become his personal project and he dreaded to think what else was contained in that little notebook of his. Whatever happened today, he would confront him, lay the accusations at his door, then take that notebook and destroy it.

As he rounded the edge of the strangely modern building, he caught sight of the hobbling duo of Evans and Palmer way back in the distance. Himself slowed down by his swollen ankle, the knackered pair had managed to keep up with him, despite his slightly random method of reaching the river. He had to lose them, regardless of the pain, so he sped up. Celia was nowhere to be seen and Jon couldn't quite convince himself that he hadn't imagined seeing her all along. Beyond the curve, the riverfront zone opened up into the more touristic appealing areas Jon was accustomed to. Strange, multicoloured seats lay around a wide parking area and former warehouses or fish processing buildings buzzed with new life as bars and restaurants. The road took him past the port and some industrial buildings still clinging onto the old way of life, before the waterfront buildings gave way to an amazing panoramic vista of the river, with the bridge dominating the view. It was still at least a half hour's walk away, despite the misleading proximity it suggested. He tried phoning Jeep's number again but it rang without evening going to voicemail. He kept trying for the entire length of his journey along the riverfront.

He was about to replace the phone in his pocket when suddenly it began to ring. Unknown number. He answered hesitantly and was surprised to hear Celia's voice, undoctored and undistorted.

"Jon?"

"So, it *was* you," he said. "How brave of you to drop the vocoder efforts after I outed you."

"About that…" Celia sounded almost…*embarrassed*. How odd.

"What, Celia? Not like you to be lost for words."

Jon was trying not to let the conversation slow him down and even though he was maintaining the faster pace, it made him huff and puff slightly as he spoke.

"I haven't told Edward everything about what happened," she said somewhat enigmatically.

Jon wasn't sure he understood even a *fraction* of what had happened to her, but she was here discussing things with him as if he ought to. Even cowed and coy she still sounded haughty.

"I noticed you weren't with them just now, following me," Jon observed.

"No," she replied. "I promised I would wait for them."

Jon couldn't help but laugh loudly and raucously.

"And they *trusted* you?!" he cried.

This was a woman who had fled the country without a passport, faked her own disappearance, allowed people to be investigated for it, then menaced and harassed him for some past indiscretion or outright jealousy.

"Don't laugh, Jonny," she chastised, using the name he hadn't been called in years. "If you must know, they've said they've called the authorities on me. There's nowhere for me to run. I've been stuck here for far too long and I was trying to get my passport back so that I could legitimately, properly move on, but it's all gone wrong."

"Why are you telling me all this?" Jon demanded, somewhat angry at her nerve.

Sure, they had once had this sort of relationship, but that had been five years ago and the little matter of her threatening and manipulating him over the last few days had sort of got in the way.

"Because, Jonny, I'm sorry to have to tell you that I'm going to make sure I take you down with me," she said bluntly.

Jon had to stop himself from freezing in his steps, such was the shock. Instead he channelled his surprise into quickening his pace.

"What do you mean?" he asked, fairly certain that Celia was bluffing.

She might have been stalking him, monitoring him, but he had done nothing she could prove. Not recently anyway.

"I mean that I recently learned about your fucking psychotic spree in Rusholme, Jonny," she said triumphantly. "And that's why I've taken all your money. I mean, I was *always* going to take it, if I'm honest, Jonny."

What was she raving on about now? How could Celia access his business account? Unless...

"You're Kulani?" he whispered.

He ought to have known it. Should have figured it out. There would have been clues. Celia was just like that, prone to giving clues, then basking in the smug feeling as she watched people fail to solve them. She might have been a terrible writer, but she had been an *appalling* Maths teacher.

"Who else?" she said and Jon knew she was smirking. "I started using the alias to write my little fictions years ago, but it came in quite handy here in Portugal. I was always a writer Jonny. Even before *we* met. But not before you met my darling husband…"

Jon frowned and looked over his shoulder. If Palmer and Evans were still following him, they ought to have been visible by now, across the long open stretch of riverside, but they were nowhere to be seen. Perhaps they had given up, their collective injuries getting the better of them.

"What the fuck are you raving about, woman?" he snapped.

"You and Gerry," she explained. "Working together, being fucking psychos together. I never realised I had such a clear type."

Now Jon did halt in his tracks, mainly because he had finally reached his destination. He was at the foot of the broad white stanchions holding up the gigantic bridge. The building on his right, across the lanes of traffic had the *Ponte 25 de Abril* sign on it and he recalled this contained a lift and viewing platform. Aside from crossing half the city to where the actual bridge met the street level roads, this was his only way up. Jeep had to be there.

"I've never met your fucking husband," Jon replied, and despite the years of working alongside Celia, it was the truth. Jon had never once met Gerry Payne.

46.

Jon didn't want to fall. His suicide was not intended to include a hair-raising tombstone drop from the upper stanchions of the bridge, but once he had set himself on fire, he had little control over events.

The weather and time of year had meant that the place itself, the *Experience Pilar 7* attraction, had been virtually empty and as Jon had paid his dues and gone up in the lift, he was disappointed to find no sign of Jeep at all once he reached the top. There was a glass platform to test your nerve or faith in Portuguese engineering and a dizzying view of everything around, from the bridge itself, to the river far below and the city rising up away behind them. The glass enclosure was fairly claustrophobic, despite being see through in every direction and aside from a nervous young couple who seemed unable to move either onto the glass platform section or away back into the lift, it was deserted. The strange, alien rushing sound of traffic over the bridge drowned everything else out and Jon immediately regretted going up there. Jeep wouldn't be here, in this fish tank, he would be out *there* on the bridge itself, but Jon could see no pedestrian traffic on the bridge. In addition to that, there was no obvious way from the viewing deck to the bridge, although Jon could see that there *must* be a way that wasn't accessible to the public, given how joined together it all was.

The lift returned after a few minutes during which Jon awkwardly ignored the nervy couple and gazed out at the Tagus. Thankfully they gave up and edged back into the lift, leaving Jon alone. He took out his phone, having ended Celia's call shortly after their disagreement about his link to her husband. Sure, Jon knew *of* Gerry, most of the school knew about him. Their marriage

224

was a joke, hence why he had found her so easy to flatter and use to make his time there easier. Of course, he had read about their eventual divorce and his breakdown, but never bringing partners along to staff dos meant that their paths had never crossed. Gerry was a lecturer of some sort at the university and whilst Jon had spent plenty of time hanging around the campus, before and after actually studying there, he had never, to his knowledge, met the man. The initials 'G.P.' seemed to be the source of the mistake and Jon smirked at Evans' stupid assumption.

As if sensing he was ready to use it again, the phone rang the second he got it out. Unknown number, quelle surprise!

"Hello Celia," he said, wearily.

"Not Celia, pal," came the nasal reply.

It was bloody Evans.

"How did you get this number?" he demanded.

"Celia gave it us," replied Evans breathily.

He was clearly still on the move and a whining noise made it difficult to hear him properly.

"We 'ad 'er over a barrel to be 'onest," continued Evans. "All the trouble she'd caused, we called the old bill on 'er. But you my friend, well you're a different matter."

"Just fuck off," said Jon, unable to do witty or eloquent in his current state of agitation.

He was unconsciously tapping on the glass railing now, scanning the horizon.

"We're on our way," said Evans. "We reckoned you were 'eadin' for the bridge, that right?"

Jon cursed silently. His confrontation with Jeep didn't need those two mugs ruining things. It was private.

"Gonna chuck yerself off, pal?" asked Evans. "Do us all a favour?"

Jon hung up and threw his phone to the ground where it skittered along the glass section of the floor. Good thing he wasn't squeamish about stepping across it to retrieve it. Before he did so, he suddenly spotted Jeep. He was standing on the far side of the bridge, leaning over the edge, with vehicles honking at him as they passed in the opposite direction. If he'd been there the whole time, Jon ought to have seen him from the ground as he approached the bridge. Was he there then, Jon wondered? Was he even there now? His mind was fragmenting again, he knew. Jeep had been there at the start, when his mind had begun to crack and instead of piecing it back together as he had assumed over the years, Jeep had driven a huge wedge into it, forcing it so far open through his unique forms of therapy, that it had never been able to fully heal. Jon might have been a psychopath, but Jeep had firmly pushed him in that direction, he now realised. Not once had he ever offered him any actual medication or useful therapy, and there he was, just a hop, skip and a jump away. There didn't seem to be a realistic way of getting out of the glass booth other than to go back into the lift, but Jon knew he had to act quickly. When the lift returned, he dashed in, scaring the attendant somewhat.

"Someone's dropped their phone out there," he told the attendant in Portuguese and when the man went out to investigate, he grabbed the lift controls and took himself away.

By using the override key, he took the lift down just a level, rather than all the way to the ground where he ought to have returned. A maintenance area lined with tools and oil cans of some sort awaited him. Beyond that, he found himself bracing against the rushing wind, at the same level as the railway line which ran directly beneath the road bridge. Gantries and staircases offered a crisscrossing way from his side of the bridge to the other, and up to the top where he had seen Jeep. He was thankful he wasn't particularly put off by heights as being out of the protective enclosure of the lift or the viewing deck was fairly daunting. Seeing no trains approaching, which might have knocked his confidence, he danced nimbly across the gantries until he reached the steps leading up on the opposite side. The wind became more insistent as he hauled himself up to the very top of the bridge and the deafening traffic noise and eerier sound of the bridge responding to the traffic made it impossible to concentrate.

"Jeep, you bastard!" he yelled, hoping his voice wasn't lost to the wind.

The older man looked as if he had been expecting him but unlike at their previous elevated rendezvous, he immediately turned and made eye contact. He had a weaselly face, Jon decided. He should never have trusted him. How was this guy a healthcare professional? So many people had been in his care – damaged, vulnerable people too.

"Well well, Jon," he replied. "Upset I blew off your little meeting?"

226

They were both having to yell to be heard above the wind and traffic and intermittent beeping of horns. Jon held on tightly to the railing on the narrow strip of paving which wasn't road. He could see that a huge section of the floor of the bridge was actually a gigantic grille which accounted for the awful whistling sound as traffic rumbled over it.

"Not really," yelled Jon. "I never expected you. I had a reunion with Evans and Palmer without you. And Celia too, funnily enough." There was no reaction from Jeep. "Marujo's probably dead by the way," he added. "So I *can* on occasion tidy up my own shit."

Jeep nodded slowly. He was wearing a dark grey longcoat which was perfectly suited to the freezing gale blowing up here. He was a strange, thin man when Jon looked at him properly. In his late 30s, but looked easily a decade older. His hair was greying at the temples and his face drawn and weathered. He had never looked young, Jon decided, which was probably why he had assumed a position of knowing authority.

"If only you'd done it that first night," roared Jeep. "You'd probably never have done it again, y'know?"

"What do you mean?" demanded Jon, moving as close to Jeep as he dared. Any closer and he might throttle him.

"Well," began Jeep and Jon could see a change in the man. Gone was the sly, manipulative air hidden vaguely behind a kindly smile and suddenly there stood a raging megalomaniac, proud of his interference. "You were never a violent thug. You were just a stupid teenage drunk prone to blackouts."

Jon struggled to fit Jeep's version of events alongside the version he believed to be true. The version he had been *told* was true.

"You never touched that girl," Jeep continued. "In fact, the ultimate irony was, you ran into *me* on *my way* from attacking her. You were so *earnest*. It was *perfect.*"

Jon felt the ground tumbling away below him. Years of strangely aligning himself with psychopaths and violent criminals, of trying to fathom out his dangerous mind and its irresistible urges, of desperately hoping to understand his memory lapses and that feeling he had experienced which even though it was triggered by something awful, had been the only time he'd felt alive. And it had all been a lie.

"*You* hurt those girls?" Jon asked, now leaping ahead in Jeep's narrative,

227

knowing where it was heading.

"You gave me free rein," said Jeep, simply. "Whilst ever you kept losing track of what you were up to, it made it like *child's play* to do as I wished. I just had to make sure I matched my attacks to your pathetic episodes. And I'm fairly certain half of it is psychosomatic, y'know."

Jon knew what he meant, but still he elaborated.

"You just *think* you're losing your memory, losing your mind, and so you do," concluded Jeep.

Jon wanted to rip his head off.

"You…encouraged all this?" he said meekly, not voicing his inner rage.

"But you made it so easy," said Jeep. "And I moved on to bigger and better things, but you never did, Jon. So sad."

Jeep turned and looked at him, with almost a genuinely sad expression on his face, but Jon was trusting none of it. He knew what Jeep was alluding to – his work in a psychiatric hospital probably gave him access to all sorts of impressionable, malleable cases to continue his wicked manipulation.

"Why are you telling me all this now?" Jon demanded.

Jeep shrugged.

"Why not?" he said callously. "It was all getting rather tedious. Plus, the net was closing in somewhat thanks to that blundering fool you lured here."

Rather than rush him as his instincts told him, Jon found himself backing away, slowly, deliberately heading for the steps he had just climbed. As much as he despised Jeep, he hated himself for being so weak and foolish to allow any of this to happen. He felt the floor disappear behind him and knew he had reached the steps. Before he could back down them, he had one last query.

"Julie?" he asked. "Did I…? Did *you*..?"

Jeep smirked.

"Call her collateral damage," he said wickedly. "She's been gone weeks, Jon. You should've seen the blood! But you barely even noticed. I think on some level you knew deep down, but were just sort of…*glad.* All I had to do was send you the odd text and you actually *invented* that she was still in the flat with you. Remarkable!"

"And Matilde?"

Jon wasn't sure *what* if anything he had felt for her truly, but he knew that he stood accused of harming her and Marujo had been broken by her death.

"Call *her* a...bonus," Jeep said, grinning.

Jon hurried down the steps as quickly as he could until he was in the howling shelter of the lower railway bridge. He felt his blood boiling within him like hot lava struggling to burst free through his rocky exterior. No, not lava or magma, but pure, combustible, toxic fuel. He knew what he had to do. Why his skin always felt like it was burning from inside. He had doused himself in the contents of one of the oil cans without even thinking and despite the breeze, had managed to strike up a lighter. He was startled by how quickly he caught fire.

47.

Good God Celia Payne was hard work. No wonder someone murdered her!

Stuart had to chuckle to himself at this unpleasant thought and realised that despite all his research into the woman, knowing her reputation and her particular movements before and on that fateful evening, he had never considered that he might actually really, properly, painfully *despise* her.

Not only did Stuart have a mother hen streak, but he also had something of a white knight complex, imagining himself riding in to save the day, to sweep helpless damsels and whatever the male equivalent of a damsel was off their feet. He wasn't especially heroic generally, but his investigations gave him an enormous sense of what was right and just and what *ought to be* even if it never was.

"You're dead!" was all he could say to her and the look she shot back could have curdled milk.

It was clear that she had some huge superiority complex and thought it hilarious that she had got one over on the man tracking her and surprised him as she just had, leaping out from behind the odd white box in the grounds of the *Torre de Belem*. It was hard to remember she had only been a teacher, and yes, a middle leader too, but hardly a superhead or the secretary of state for education! The way she spoke and the filthy looks she gave Stuart made him feel like he was an inconsistent teenager again, railing against the system and coming up hard against the immovable object that was Celia Payne.

"No fucking shit Sherlock," was her response.

For a middle-aged woman (Stuart thought of her as such, even though he knew she was 42, or had been when she vanished. He couldn't remember if another birthday had passed since then) she had a bad attitude and a foul mouth. How had this woman got by day to day dealing with the scrotey teenage types she must surely have pissed off on a daily basis? Perhaps she hadn't, hence her breakdown and flight.

Stuart had planned all kinds of scenarios out in his mind. He was methodical like that and always had been, long before the construction industry took over his daylight thoughts. The scenarios were as follows:

1) Celia Payne was dead and always had been. She was killed near to where she vanished but her body was yet to be found. The killer was someone she knew;
2) As above, but it was a random attack. Less likely to be tracked down;
3) Celia Payne had been attacked but had fled. In her panic, she had left the country by some off-the-books means and started a new life in anonymity;
4) Celia Payne had faked the whole thing as a way of either getting revenge on the men in her life (4.1), as a tax or insurance scam of some sort (4.2) or just for the sheer cruel fun of it all (4.3);
5) A variation of 3 or 4 but she had subsequently been killed here in Portugal.

Stuart had narrowed everything that was possible down to these main scenarios, dismissing other crackpot theories and using all available evidence, such as the postcard Palmer received and the other links to Lisbon. What he hadn't really bargained for was that Celia was brazenly stomping around the city, not as a wounded bird or damaged soul, but as a bitchy, downright unpleasant force of nature. Even when he considered she might have been out to get the men who wronged her, he imagined her as a feminist hero bending and breaking the rules, but with good reason, possibly driven half-insane by their mistreatment of her and still able to ultimately heal. The Celia he found was not like that at all.

"Which one are you, then?" she asked snidely.

Stuart had no idea what she was talking about. They had no connection in the real world. She was an online true crime fantasy for him to solve. A proper genuine field case for once. They had not, to his knowledge, a single connection in reality. Apart from Palmer now, he supposed.

"Which one what?" he blurted artlessly.

She laughed, a braying, unkind sound which made her look even less like a kind soul in need of a friendly deed.

"Wait," she said, walking right up to him and then around him, checking him out in a manner Stuart couldn't help but feel was borderline lascivious. "I've seen you. You and he have been riding around together, haven't you? Bus buddies?!"

She fell about laughing so cruelly now that Stuart flushed. This was the woman he was here to save, not to be bullied by.

"Er, yeah, we- we were on that Yellow Bus Tour thing looking for you," he stammered. "'arry thought he'd seen you."

"'arry?" she repeated, mockingly dropping the 'h'. "Who the fuck is 'arry when 'e's at 'ome?"

Celia was a northern girl too, but she had rid herself of any broad traces of accent and Stuart was bemused by her mockery of his. His cheeks were burning redder than ever. He didn't like this. He was about to suggest he call Palmer, when he realised – again – that he didn't have his number. He was glad he'd stopped himself before launching into the idea, as he wasn't sure how much more of Celia's mocking he could take.

"Edward," Stuart corrected. "*Palmer*. 'e felt sure 'e'd seen you, but we both thought 'e must 'ave imagined it."

He looked up from the ground where he'd naturally averted his gaze following her unpleasant tone and words and found her holding his gaze for close to a minute.

"You *are* a funny fellow, aren't you?" she hooted. "Chasing around after Eddy like, well, like a lost lamb. Or a big *docile* bull or something! Where *did* he find you?!"

Stuart couldn't help but feel that whilst she was being terribly unfair, judging him on his voice and his appearance, he felt reassured that she seemed to have no idea who he actually was. Whatever strangeness had been going on online amongst his forums, she either had nothing to do with it, or hadn't yet linked him to the name Stuart Evans. He would keep anonymous for as long as he was able to.

"People think you're dead, Celia," he said, knowing it was stating the obvious, but that it needed saying.

He wondered if she felt *anything* about the mess she had left behind.

232

"It's hardly a fucking walk in the park for me here, you know," she said, waving her arms around her. "No pun intended," she added, glancing around what was effectively a park they had been walking in. "I *had* to come here. To get away from them all. Then I found out he'd followed me. He wouldn't let me go." Her voice quietened and quickened. "He's not *normal* like other men. He's absolutely insane. Jealous and insane!"

Her eyes were wide now, almost as if she was on something, Stuart noted. The brashness *was* an act, he suspected. It was easier for her to be rude to people than to show her own weaknesses. He'd met people like that before. Certainly a teacher or two back in the day too.

"Who, Celia?" he asked gently.

She seemed like a wild horse, eyes white and full of fear, almost ready to rear up or bolt at the wrong word or touch. She opened her mouth to speak, then stopped. After a moment she laughed her awful grating laugh and Stuart now knew it was entirely fake. There was no humour to be had from any of this. She used it to move away from the truth, away from her real feelings.

"But I don't even know who you are, you strange man," she said, almost flirtatiously now. "I just spotted you coming towards me in the park and grabbed the first taxi I could hail. I thought perhaps you were working for…*with*…*him.* But now I see you up close, I realise of course you're not. You're with Eddy, aren't you? Here to clear his name, no doubt? Or were there clues? He loves a good clue! Who doesn't?!"

She was rambling now and Stuart was tiring of her constant rollercoastering. She dropped in so many unspecific 'he's' that it made her exposition almost unfathomable. He sensed he needed to get her away from here, as she was agitated and still glancing around expecting trouble. She was still awful, there was no getting away from that, but most of it was a front. If he could just break through to her, get her somewhere safe, he could find out what had actually happened. Which 'he' had hurt or wronged or chased her and try and offer her his protection. And most of all, get her in the hands of the authorities who could then reveal her continued existence to the world and end the unclosed case.

"Celia," said Stuart, a little more firmly and loudly than he ordinarily might have. "You need to come with me. I'll take you somewhere safe."

"But where is safe?" she asked dreamily, rolling her eyes up as if imagining heaven.

233

"My 'otel," he replied. "The Sana. We'll get a cab or somethin'."

At the mention of the hotel, Celia seemed to lose it again and waved her arms warily between them,

"Oh no no no," she said, backing away. "No you don't! Not there! That's where *he* had me. He came all this way for me and I was supposed to be flattered?!" Her voice began to rise as she continued now and people were starting to look over at them. "I just wanted my fucking passport back! Do you realise how hard it is to leave the country without your passport?! I spent three fucking days hiding in a lorry!"

At the last word, and Stuart's attempts to approach and pacify her, she lashed out, slapping his face, as if *he* were the one to place her in such discomfort. Stuart stepped back in surprise and then shame as he saw people definitely watching now. It wouldn't be long before someone either came to intervene or called someone else to do so. He took a chance and instantly regretted it.

"Your passport?" he asked. "I've got that!"

It was a lie, he *had* had it, but now someone else did. Someone who had deliberately broken into his room, no less.

"You have my passport?!" she shrieked.

She glared at him in silence for another few moments and as Stuart dared to sneak a look around, he saw people moving on with their lives now, with just one or two people still watching in concern. He didn't know what to say to her that wouldn't cause her to blow up again. She was definitely unhinged.

"Who sent you?" she demanded now.

"No one," he said quickly. "No one sent me, Celia. Well, no one who wants to *hurt* you, anyway."

He hoped he wasn't speaking out of turn. Palmer hadn't sent him, but they were on the same page he thought. Palmer surely didn't want her to come to any harm, did he? He wanted her found and returned to England to stop the rumours and insinuations. Maybe he was feeling charitable enough to be worried about her mental health and wellbeing too?

"You and Palmer then?" she asked, suddenly less frantic and more lewd.

She winked suggestively and licked her lips.

"Is he a good fuck? I never got to find out. Explains a lot though. Pretty bit of rough like you would be *right* up his alley!"

Stuart had seen this sort of behaviour before. The swing from the hysterical, the paranoid, the violent aggression to the coquettish, suggestive and downright inappropriate. If he had to put money on it, he'd bet Celia was battling some sort of bipolar disorder and probably not well, if she was in a foreign country, dodging someone pursuing her, probably with no medication or support of any kind.

"No, Celia, not like that," said Stuart, trying to smile kindly, despite his urge to just grab her and drag her off.

It all felt like a dance he wasn't suitably kitted out for; a negotiation he wasn't ever going to win.

"Oh, shame," she said, sadly, almost sulkily. "I always felt it was such a shame poor Eddy never got any. His head was too full of other things." She was gazing off into the sky now, wistfully. "Too full of death," she added dramatically, bitterly. "That's why I tried to crack it open that time. To *help* him!"

Stuart hoped that he, or someone soon could help Celia. She was so out of it now, that it was like that old image of trying to catch a butterfly in a net. If he wasn't careful, she would flutter away and he'd have lost her.

"'e'll be pleased to see you," Stuart said, possibly believing it to be true. White lies wouldn't hurt right now. "Come with me, Celia."

He offered his hand out and like a nervous dog, she shuffled forward a little, then edged back, clearly *wanting* to approach, but backing off at the last minute. Stuart's phone suddenly went off, making the most awful shrill, squawking noise he had ever heard. It was loud in his pocket and deafening as he fumbled it out to silence it. As he pulled it out, the corkscrew, still glinting with a little of his own blood, tumbled onto the grass. It triggered something in Celia and she screamed and ran off. Stuart dropped his phone in surprise and it clattered nastily onto a rockier part of the earth. He stooped to retrieve both items, saw his phone protesting crazily about something on the screen and by the time he had managed to turn off the noise, Celia was nowhere in sight.

48.

It was too hot for all this hurtling around. Stuart was drenched and the cool breeze gusting over the Tagus along the riverfront did nothing to cool him. He had felt certain that Celia must have run across the park and out of the other side, somewhere in the direction the insane scooter ride had taken him. The only other option was that she had joined the ridiculous queue for entrance to the tower itself, and that seemed unlikely for someone so wired and intent on escaping to have suddenly calmed their anxiety enough to have faced standing around for goodness only knew how long to enter what seemed to be an actual dead end in terms of an escape route. So Stuart continued past, hoping to see a glimpse of her strange floaty white outfit somewhere on the outskirts of the park.

He had barely paused to inspect his damaged phone but was furious with himself for having dropped it. The screen was a third black now, as if an inky substance had crept in behind the shiny surface and was slowly growing, taking over the device. He couldn't access his message properly, but could see that he had received an alert from his supposedly closed down forums. That meant two things which he wasn't entirely happy about. It meant that someone had sent him an urgently-tagged direct message from the forums, but it also meant that someone, somehow had *reactivated* the forums to begin with. Someone with administrator privileges and he was the only person who had those. Well, there was no point dwelling on it. It was obvious that someone had hacked him, played him for a fool, taken over his online life as he knew it. That person was surely Jon Scott Campbell, although he hadn't figured a former English teacher with a violent history for someone with the prowess to pull off such a feat.

Who was the 'he' that Celia continually rambled on about? It couldn't be Jon Scott Campbell, surely? He had already proven that he had been closely watching Stuart's actions just by the amount of times they had crossed paths which was beyond mere coincidence. If Celia really was on the run from some vindictive figure, Jon didn't fit that profile either. He wouldn't have let her go unscathed, and if he was playing cat and mouse, well, he wouldn't have let her run so far from the mousehole, so to speak. So that left few other suspects, especially the way Celia spoke about her *him* as if it should be someone Stuart knew or knew of. Her husband? Gerry Payne was an oddball, a Brexiteering port-swigging snob of a man, but politics aside, did that make him a suspect? If Stuart suspected everyone with a different viewpoint of being a nutjob, then half the country would be lumped together in the spotlight. Gerry was at least more fitting in terms of his profile. They had played a terrible game of passive aggressive tennis their entire marriage as far as even a distant outsider like Stuart could tell. Gerry *would* chase her across the continent and make life difficult for her. She had supposedly given him a nervous breakdown. Perhaps their tit for tat knew no common decency at all.

It appalled Stuart that people could treat one another this way, so apathetic about the value of human life, so unfeeling about basic human emotion. Of course, he knew that without this unpleasant side to life, he would have no true crime to pursue, no purpose to his solitary twilight hours, but he also knew that were it not for one particular random act of violence and sadism, he would not be the person he was today. *Bloody parks.*

He was glad to reach the edge of the grassy area and what appeared to be some sort of military museum, complete with medal motif signage and cannons by the entrance. Celia was nowhere to be seen. The entire area was dazzlingly bright and such a wide-open paved area that he realised she could have gone anywhere. The museum looked like an old fortress given a modern revamp, with flags flying proudly above and a strange triangular monument in front it like something from a sci fi movie. Celia didn't look as if she could have covered such a distance in the short time it took Stuart to give chase, but he regretted letting her go in the first place. As a detective, he had done the hardest bit of the job, finding his target (even if it was more by chance than good policing) but had now let her slip through his fingers. He doubted he'd get such an easy second chance.

There was no point continuing his pursuit in a random direction and he simply couldn't imagine that Celia had willingly entered either of the two attractions he had passed. He took a moment to catch his breath, wipe the back of his head which was teeming with sweat and simultaneously glowing with sunburn and try to access his phone again. The dark matter surging over his home screen had continued its relentless advance and worse than that, the damage seemed to have triggered several of his apps making the phone hot, not with the Iberian heat as he had assumed, but with painful heat of an overworking device sapping itself of battery life. The tiny icon showed he had less than 50% battery left, despite having fully charged it overnight. Something was causing the phone to run hot, something he couldn't seem to cancel or power down and he was worried that if he rebooted the device, he might not be able to get it back on again. In frustration, he tapped at the shortcut to his online forums and was surprised to see it not only load up, but display his private messages at the top, as the phone's orientation had now jammed into landscape mode. Ordinarily, the message feature was at the left-hand side of the screen but with the phone deciding it was on its side, everything had rotated accordingly. He could access and read the latest message and decided he had better take advantage of this quirk before it righted itself and the screen was lost to the invading darkness.

A user – though how was this possible?! – had left him a message which read:

'*CAR BOOT SALE. FABULOUS BARGAINS! DOCA PEDROUÇOS NOW!*'

While he still had any functionality left in his phone, he exited to the homepage using the central button on his phone and tapped where he knew the map button would have been, had he been able to see it. He pinched and massaged the part of the screen he could see until he had manoeuvred the map to centre on his current location, then zoomed out along the waterfront. He knew very little Portuguese but he knew that 'doca' was surely *dock* and that whoever had sent him this message had intended him to be able to reach the destination quickly, given the wording. He could now see the *Doca Pedrouços* was not far away at all, in the direction he was already heading, beyond the military museum. He took note that it was the new username *GepettoPsych* again and wondered why the use of the Disney character's name. Most of the users on his forums had quite macabre names, ripped from the annals of crime, either lurid takes on serial killer nicknames or those of the poor victims themselves. Of course, some merely had takes on their own names or online personas, but he'd never encountered one as odd as this. A fairytale character and an eminent psychologist had little in common.

Whoever was sending him these messages clearly either wanted to be caught themselves, or was trying to stitch up or implicate another party. Stuart couldn't help wondering if he would find Palmer himself at the end of this particular breadcrumb trail, trussed up and waiting for the authorities with some fabricated evidence and a deranged Celia Payne ready to testify as to his guilt. And obviously, this could all just be a trap for *him*, Stuart thought. Those were *his* forums that had been repeatedly hacked and he had been manipulated from day one by Jon Scott Campbell or someone in his employ.

As he tried to pick up the pace along the riverfront, he could only once more regret having no means of communicating with Palmer. He wasn't sure if his newfound colleague would have been keen on the idea, he seemed not at all keen on any sort of basic human contact, but he would have insisted on it, in order to successfully continue their investigations. As he came within sight of a dusty open expanse of land right on the riverfront, possibly used for storage, certainly within spitting distance of dock-like buildings and warehouses, his phone made the same awful alert noise and he nearly dropped it.

To his surprise, it was another new forum member. This time the username was far less enigmatic. One *EdwardPalmer* had just signed up for the forums and was requesting authorisation. This had to be the real deal as otherwise the user would have been instantly cleared by whoever was assuming control. Had Palmer really been so resourceful as to find some wi-fi or else activate his roaming internet allowance, track down Stuart's forums (he had never really referred to them by name), and then try to join, purely to get in touch? Perhaps he had him wrong all along. A man who he didn't dare to ask to swap phone numbers with in case he took it badly had somehow beaten the technological odds and a whole heap of social issues and was trying to reach out to him. Stuart only hoped he could still grant Palmer access and then they would be able to direct message each other at least.

Before he could work out how to do so, there was a ping which told him a new member had been authorised. Someone else, whoever was running the show, had actually okayed this. Perhaps it *was* part of the game after all, Stuart thought, despondently. But then, almost immediately, his inbox chimed and he opened the message from *EdwardPalmer*.

'It's really me. I know you stole my biscuit on the plane. This is my number. Please call me.'

Underneath was a mobile number which Stuart was just about able to copy and paste but he was alarmed to see that his battery was down to 25% now. He tried to call the number, but his phone simply rejected the process, as if there was no signal or his phone had lost the ability to dial. Then when he tried again, it went straight to voicemail. Palmer had an odd message, but it was clearly his voice. Finally, Stuart decided to access text messaging, barely visible behind the dark curtain rising across the display. He quickly typed and sent a message:

'PALMER. IT'S STUART. CELIA'S ALIVE! PHONE'S FUCKED. AT DOCA PEDROUÇOS. I NEED A VACATION! WHERE R U?'

He suspected Palmer would hate the text speak at the end, but he was running out of time and battery life. He couldn't wait for a response, but he knew from the messaging on the forums that Palmer must be able to respond.

The view ahead was stunning, brilliant white land and azure skies above, with a strange, almost boat-shaped building to his right which was surely yet another museum. He crossed the open ground ahead and finally saw a desolate area with a few cars randomly parked on what seemed to be an abandoned stretch of road. '*CAR BOOT SALE*' the message had said. He sprinted over to the first car, but then an idea hit him. What if Palmer was messaging on the forums because he didn't have his phone. It was easy to forget in the modern age that people previously used PCs or laptops and even internet cafes to communicate when phones had not yet advanced to conquer the online world. Perhaps he ought to have messaged Palmer back via the forums first.

Just then he heard a strange noise coming from the next car along. A wild, panicked screaming as if someone were being murdered was coming from the boot. '*FABULOUS BARGAINS*' the message had said. It really didn't sound like it. Taking a deep breath he tried the boot of what was a battered old Mazda. To his surprise it opened. A fabulous bargain it was, after all. A terrified shrieking woman, yes, but also, seemingly gift-wrapped, was the source of her suffering, Jon Scott Campbell.

49.

Stuart didn't know why he had trusted the message to come here, he didn't know why he had opened the boot so casually and he didn't know why he had torn the masking tape from Jon's face, but as soon as his enemy hissed at him, he knew what regret was.

"You again!" he said, somewhat pointlessly.

Stuart was caught off-guard by everything thus far, and could only watch in shock as Jon hurled himself out of the car boot, despite being tied up and practically lying next to the shrieking blood-soaked woman. He hit the dirt, sending up a cloud of dust so Stuart acted quickly and grabbed him, finding him surprisingly light and easy to manoeuvre, despite his hostility. He threw him aside like a rag doll, hoping the fall would knock the wind out of him. It gave him the chance to reattach Jon's gag properly whilst he was reeling in the dirt. He then set about tending to the poor girl, remembering all the terrible reports of those assaulted in Manchester over a decade ago, and that was only the poor few who had come forwards.

The reason Stuart had even linked Jon to any of these crimes was the odd fact that the first girl set about by a random attack in the park had been one Sally Shaw, 17, romantically linked to Jon Scott Campbell, despite the age gap, and despite her turning up for college masking her bruises with extra foundation and eye shadow, it didn't take long for her to crack and confess that she'd been badly beaten up on her way home from an evening shift at the 24 hour Spar on Oxford Road in Manchester. She claimed it was a random attack, that she had never seen the guilty party, that her on-off boyfriend had been nothing but supportive when she'd told him, but Stuart didn't buy it. Sally had been thinking about leaving Jon due to his erratic, overly emotional outbursts and inability to stay faithful, according to her statement to the police at the time, but despite him being grilled by the authorities, Jon had dodged further suspicion. Now here he was, caught like a fish in a barrel with one of his victims. Perhaps apprehended by a vigilante of some sort?

"Shush love," Stuart said, tenderly appealing to the desperate woman who apparently did *not* recognise him as a friend rather than a foe. "'ang on and I'll find somethin' to help you out with."

There wasn't anything at all to help with and after casting the finger of suspicion and blame firmly in Jon's direction, he attempted to help the woman out with his bare hands. This did not go well, and despite her allowing him to assist her out of the boot, as he approached her again on the ground, she slapped him, then legged it, running like a drunken gazelle across the wasteland.

His instinct was to pursue. He couldn't let another damaged woman give him the slip, but he noticed Jon attempting to get back up and had to deal with him first. The woman clearly wasn't badly injured enough that a mad sprint in the noon sun was too much for her, and Stuart had begun to reassess what had been laid out before him. Clearly Jon hadn't locked *himself* in the boot, certainly not managing to bind and gag himself in the process.

"Did you 'urt 'er?" he demanded.

Jon merely looked disgusted in return at him as if he had asked a stupid question.

"I've waited a *long* time to catch you red 'anded like his, Jon," said Stuart, now definitely thinking the psycho had been set up and trapped and left for him or someone else to find. "All them poor lasses in Rusholme, you sick fuck. 'ow many girls did you 'urt?"

He wanted to specifically mention Sally, but he wanted to be able to judge the reaction a little better, to have Jon properly disabled and at his mercy. Preferably filmed or recorded in some way too, but his phone wasn't up to that. Instead he told Jon how he would enjoy taking him back to England to face justice for his attacks, but the man in the dirt merely scowled even more disgustedly. Jon was thinking now of poor Inspector Wrigley, the shadow of his former self, unable to ever pin any of that string of violent assaults on *anyone*, let alone one single-minded serial attacker. He found himself stepping closer to Jon, wanting to properly study his face now that he was tied up and cowed. He was within striking distance – not that he would have approved of simply kicking the shit out of the maniac – when his phone suddenly vibrated hot in his pocket again. He rummaged to find it.

 "Bloody phone!" he cried, seeing a message from Palmer flash up before the battery seemed to die entirely.

He shook the phone angrily but to no avail. It was dead. The last message from Palmer said:

'SHE'S DEFINITELY ALIVE?! I'M WITH GERRY PAYNE OF ALL PEOPLE, AT THE TOWER. HE'S LYING ABOUT SOMETHING. WHERE SHALL WE RENDEZVOUS?'

Stuart barely had time to take in Palmer's message, when he was knocked to the ground by Jon who must have seized the moment of distraction to launch himself bodily at him. The tussle didn't last long, as whilst Stuart could feel powerful muscles in Jon's taut body, Stuart had bigger muscles and about five stones of extra weight on him. He straddled the angular red head very easily, his thighs pressing down on him, despite his wriggling legs and the urge to simply press his hands about his pink throat and squeeze him into submission almost too strong to resist.

"Cheeky fuck!" he yelled at him, channelling his rage into words rather than murderous actions.

He grappled with the thinner man, trying to get a hold on him, deciding he would rather hurl him around a little and knock the life out of him than simply smother him. Finally, realising Jon was more slippery than an eel, he aimed a solid head butt at him and knocked him out cold for a few minutes. He was slightly concerned about his breathing, what with the gag and everything, so he removed it, hauled his enemy across the dirt to a suitable distance that he could both keep an eye on his movements but also put him out of temptation's way. The urge to simply brain him was too too strong. To stop him going anywhere, he quickly removed Jon's boots and socks and took them with him as he investigated the car. He could see no link to Jon himself and thought that this was simply a place to trap and detain the man, not his own vehicle. It seemed to be a hire car, but the name on the documentation Stuart dug out meant nothing to him. Looking around and seeing no one on land who could identify him, he smashed the rear windscreen of the car and carefully collected as much of the glass as he could in a blanket which he found in the car boot. It was probably a forensic dream in there, but Stuart needed to try and slow down any escape attempt Jon made whilst he thought what to do next. He scattered the broken glass all around his unconscious foe, ensuring he placed some of the more jagged shards right by his bare feet. He was surprised that what he supposed ought to have been safety glass produced such hazardous results.

Jon came to much quicker than he expected and Stuart was glad he hadn't taken off to find Palmer as he'd initially planned. He'd thought of sticking Jon back in the boot and going for help, but didn't know how long it would take to find his colleague, particularly if he had to queue to get into the tower to find him. He welcomed Jon back to consciousness and allowed him to take in his rather simplistic deterrent to run. Of course, Jon could still ignore the danger and leg it, but Stuart hoped he could at least get some answers first.

Despite Stuart having the upper hand, he still felt like Jon was acting as if *he* did and it unsettled him to trade barbs with the trussed-up psychopath who spoke like he had an ace up his sleeve that Stuart hadn't bargained for. Tiring of the enigmatic nonsense, he took a deep breath and began his interrogation as planned.

"Right then," he said. "Firstly, I want to know-"

"No, no, no," interrupted Jon. "Not like this."

Stuart gaped as he wagged his finger and sighed at him like a scolding teacher. The poor kids at that school who might have had both Celia and Jon as their teachers back in the day!

"Our little showdown isn't meant to be like…" Jon said, looking around disgustedly. "*This*. You got *some* of my lures, but not all of them, it seems. Tell me, how did you find me?"

"I didn't *find* you," Stuart admitted. "I mean, I wasn't exactly *lookin'* for you any of the times I found you. Not at the station, or at the bus stop or anywhere. When I 'eard a noise from the car boot, I didn't know it was *you* in there. I was actually lookin' for…"

He trailed off, realising he didn't want to tell him about the compromised forums, as he still suspected Jon had been his initial tormentor there, but that someone else, perhaps whoever had stuffed him in that boot, had taken on the task.

"*Looking for…?*" Jon echoed, mockingly, really getting Stuart's goat.

"Palmer," said Stuart, knowing there was enough truth in it for him to sell the lie.

"*Palmer?!*" spat Jon, coughing up some blood onto the ground. "That fucking psychopath?"

"'arry's not a psycho," snapped Stuart, tired of the hypocrisy. "You're the fuckin' psycho mate. He might be many things, but he'd never 'urt anyone like you 'ave."

"Such faith," hissed Jon, and as he began to talk about Celia, Stuart realised there was something he didn't know.

"Celia fuckin' Payne?!" cried Stuart triumphantly. "Celia fuckin' Payne is *alive*, dickhead!"

Stuart waited and watched Jon to see how he took this news. Of course, he might not even believe him, but Stuart needed to know if this was news to Jon. Before Jon had a proper chance to process the information, he was rummaging in his pocket for his phone and Stuart cursed his incompetence at leaving him with the device. Before he could do anything about it, Jon had taken the call.

"Who was it?" Stuart demanded, failing to knock the phone out of Jon's hand, but watching the psycho instead hurl it himself across the wasteland.

"Jeep," said Jon, smiling slyly now.

"Who or what the fuck is *Jeep?*" demanded Stuart.

Was that even a word? A name? A place?

"My good friend and mentor," said Jon, raving now. "He understands what I am. He's very sympathetic. He thinks *you're* a dick by the way."

"*Jeep?*" repeated Stuart, determined to get at least one proper answer from him. "Like the vehicle? Army type?"

Jon began to chuckle and it made Stuart's blood boil. He would approach him now and slap the truth from him, despite his noble intentions.

"No, you oaf," snarled Jon. "Jeep, *G.P.* As in-"

"Gerry Payne?" cried Stuart, blanching. "*You* know Gerry Payne?"

He was suddenly very aware that he was still holding on to Jon's boots and socks and hurled them to the ground as he tried to jab his phone back into life. If Jon was working with Gerry Payne and Gerry Payne was here in Lisbon, somewhere with Palmer, then it stood to reason that Palmer was in a great deal of trouble. He had to be the 'he' that Celia was driven insane by. Who else, but her awful husband? And if Gerry had Palmer at the tower, then he was sure to be in trouble. Also, G.P. = *GepettoPsych*!

"FUCK!" he roared, calculating the distance back along the riverfront to the tower.

Perhaps Celia was there too? He ran at full pace along the dusty road, back in the direction he had come knowing that he was abandoning his chances of hauling Jon Scott Campbell to justice, but that he was doing something far more important – saving a friend.

50.

"Pics or didn't 'appen!" said Stuart, not ordinarily prone to saying that turn of phrase outside of his macho posturing at the builders' yard, pretending to be a well-adjusted straightforward guy.

Palmer merely looked at him as if every word he had just said was in some exotic alien language. To be fair, Stuart's response was directly proportionate to the tale Palmer had just told him and he knew it. Who was he to judge?

"I thought it was only the youth of today who spoke in such *soundbites*!" said Palmer, scowling but with a glint in his eye.

Stuart was starting to severely doubt Palmer's robotic lack of humanity. He wasn't dead inside, just dormant. Stuart felt certain he could be the one to kindle that flame. Then he heard himself think those words in his head and laughed. He was bloody potty sometimes. And a little bit gay.

They were on the Yellow Bus heading back into the city centre and Palmer was certain if they rode the right route round, it would drop them off mere minutes of hobbling and stumbling from the Sana Reno hotel, saving them valuable hours. Palmer was quite calm, considering his troubling experience and whilst he seemed slightly positive about his reunion with Stuart, Stuart for his own part still felt hurt that he had abandoned him and confused about their next move.

"And so, since you're ever reliant on telephone communication, I've now got your number in my phone," said Palmer. "I trust you'll do the same?"

"If I ever get it recharged again," Stuart replied glumly, and then presenting the damaged screen to Palmer, he wondered if it could be fixed or would need replacing entirely.

He knew of somewhere cheap in the market back at home where he could get a reasonable quote, no questions asked. Palmer merely looked a little disappointed as if Stuart had let him down again. He seemed to genuinely have no idea how his supposed sidekick was feeling and Stuart was in no rush to set him straight.

"So," said Palmer, unexpectedly, looking like he had rehearsed his next words to the point of pain. "Cards on the table, Stuart, cards on the table."

"Meanin'?" asked Stuart.

Palmer turned and eyed him suspiciously.

"You don't know the meaning of the expression?" he asked, cocking an eyebrow.

"No mate, I meant I don't know what *you* mean by usin' it," Stuart replied. "I did well enough in my education thank you very much."

"Uni?" Palmer asked.

"Not for me."

"A-levels?"

"Started 'em, got booted out in the end," said Stuart, not ordinarily embarrassed by the fact, but feeling shamed under Palmer's intense spotlight.

"Further education's not for everyone," said Palmer, perhaps aiming for generous but coming across as patronising to Stuart.

"With teachers like bloody Jon Scott Campbell and Celia chuffin' Payne out there, it's a wonder any kid gets through their education," said Stuart sardonically.

He was tired now. Tired of running around, tired of fighting, tired of hiding or exposing secrets. He knew what Palmer meant by 'cards on the table'. He meant he was expecting Stuart to share everything he knew and had learned, whilst most probably *he* would continue withholding vital points of interest as he had done over the last two or three days in each other's company. Stuart

248

decided there was nothing to lose now.

"Jon Scott Campbell attacked a load of girls back in the mid noughties in Manchester," said Stuart, plunging straight into a breathless explanation of events, forgetting which things he'd already shared. "I followed the case as a lad myself, then got into it big style on the forums."

"Handy those," observed Palmer with what seemed like another hint of a smile.

Had he been practising? Obviously it had occurred to him to access Stuart's forums to get in touch with him after he had mentioned them before, but was there another reason for the smile? Was he mocking the very idea of the forums?

"I always figured 'e'd resurface one day and slip up, but would never 'ave tied 'im to the Celia thing," Stuart continued. "Anyway, 'e's infiltrated those forums, basically steered me into comin' 'ere so 'e can fuck about and either drive me crazy or set me up or do me in somehow."

Stuart realised how vague and paranoid he was sounding and hoped he didn't catch the look in Palmer's eye he had noticed in Belem.

"I'm not mad, I swear, pal," he added quickly.

"I believe you," said Palmer, surprisingly. "I'll admit, what you said at the monastery freaked me out a little bit. The whole online world and the ideas of conspiracy nuts and so on are definitely outside my knowledge *and* interest. But I think apart from being a tad too obsessive about a few things, and a *terrible* liar, you seem like a decent enough chap."

Stuart smiled. Acceptance. It was all he ever craved really. Palmer was a strangely old-fashioned guy for someone still years away from his forties who did work which *surely* required him to be a little more tech savvy and web-conversant than he seemed to be. Stuart took the compliment as a cue to continue.

"Weird thing is, Jon was surprised that Celia was alive. 'e seemed to reckon *you'd* done 'er in, 'arry."

"Charming," said Palmer. "Celia is many things: a victim, a nightmare, a hypocrite…" He trailed off as if thinking about her had triggered an unwanted feeling or memory. "…But she never really deserved what you've described. Basically, she's just fallen apart by the sound of it?"

Stuart nodded. He had already described at length to Palmer his sighting of her, the ridiculous scooter chase (omitting the brief moment of sexual confusion) and their subsequent strange conversation in the park near the tower, which he had latterly realised was only minutes before Palmer himself had hobbled into the park. Palmer's excuse about dashing off was fair enough, and made him realise that they had at least both been on the same page when it came to their need to be able to communicate more easily.

"I honestly thought *you* were working with Scott Campbell," admitted Palmer. "I saw the two of you together, then when I thought I saw Celia just after, well, it all seemed like someone was contriving to frame me."

"I reckon you're right, mate," agreed Stuart. "But I still think there's two different things goin' on 'ere. Maybe at cross-purposes too. Jonny boy seemed to 'ave fancied 'imself quite the mastermind, gettin' me 'ere to fuck about, but I reckon Gerry Payne's the real villain in all this."

Palmer looked doubtful.

"Gerry's a dickhead," he began and Stuart wondered if his own vernacular was rubbing off on his new friend. "Had no love for me, or Celia for that matter, truth be told. But a criminal mastermind? He can barely organise his own breakfast into his own fat mouth without spilling it down his tweed jacket."

Stuart chuckled throatily. Casual Palmer was a lot more fun company than uptight stressed Palmer. Perhaps it was the lifted burden of knowing Celia's fate, or the rest from putting weight on his knackered legs or that something had changed during his own meeting with Gerry, but he seemed a different man.

"You're sure 'e's not violent then?" asked Stuart.

He had been certain Gerry was dangerous, abandoning Jon to hurtle to Palmer's defence, now a totally ridiculous move in hindsight. Hearing that Jon was working with this 'Jeep' character had made perfect sense at the time, that separately they were tangling with he and Palmer, and that whilst he had bested Jon, Palmer was unlikely to be a match for Celia's dodgy ex. It had seemed a logical move to rush to his wounded friend's aid. He knew Palmer *ought* to be able to handle himself, but he had seen little to suggest he was anything other than a doddery chap, soft and weak long before his time.

"To be honest, I think Gerry does have a violent streak in him," Palmer said at last. "The way he confronted me in the tower, the haughty nature he has where he thinks people are beneath him and therefore *disposable*, is all a little worrying. I actually thought for a moment he was going to shove me over the edge at the top of the tower…"

Palmer trailed off and Stuart could practically see the cogs whirring around in his mind.

"The woman on the roof," he said quietly.

"Who, mate?" asked Stuart, noting a detail Palmer hadn't mentioned before.

"I think maybe when you lost Celia, she *did* run to the tower and somehow got herself up to the top. A woman was waving like mad down at someone. Maybe me, maybe Gerry. Maybe warning *me* about *Gerry*. She was dressed in white you say?"

Stuart nodded.

"Pink cravat thing. I think it's a cravat any rate," he said.

"Shit," said Palmer.

He was definitely more comfortable with swearing now it seemed.

"You just missed 'er too?" Stuart asked.

Palmer nodded now and suddenly looked decisive. He glanced out of the bus windows. They were downstairs this time, no need for panoramic sightseeing. Suddenly he jumped up in his seat as the bus slowed down to reach a stop on a busy road. Stuart was confused. They weren't yet near their hotel.

"What's the plan, 'arry?" he asked, getting up too and following Palmer's lead.

As they stepped off the bus, Stuart recognised the road they were on. It was somewhere near the *Avenida da Liberdade* he thought. Near that funny roundabout. In fact…

He turned to see where Palmer was now dramatically pointing. The Sana Lisboa hotel loomed over the street, a shiny construction of light stone, steel and glass, more impressive and business like than their own Sana branch.

"We're gonna try that room card," said Palmer. "As I probably should have done from the start. If my hunch is right, then this is where either one or both of the Paynes have been hiding out."

251

51.

"I need a vacation," said Stuart, slumped in a sumptuous chair in the foyer of the Sana Lisboa hotel.

"You keep saying that," observed Palmer. "Am I meant to get the reference?"

"Arnie," said Stuart, guessing that wouldn't be enough for Palmer's sparse cultural databank. "Terminator 2," he added.

Palmer nodded unconvincingly.

"Ah, a *film*," he said, then with his eye firmly on the front desk, he whispered to Stuart. "You keep an eye on that desk and I'll go and try the key."

The lobby was a touch more stylish, a little more business-like than their own still-welcoming hotel nearby and Stuart guessed that this branch's location made it a busier choice, bustling on the edge of the city's heart. Odd little yellow armchairs faced each other at angles around the vast lobby whilst stairs and a bank of lifts offered a way up into the towering building's upper reaches. There was nothing stopping either of them from ascending, it wasn't that sort of hotel, but Palmer had suggested he go alone whilst Stuart hung out down here, watching for Celia or Gerry arriving or departing, since they truly couldn't be sure of their movements. A smiling dark-haired woman with bright red lipstick and tired eyes was just one of the staff manning the reception area and Stuart decided to sidle over to her and see what his rusty charms could deliver in case the room key was another dead end.

She was in conversation with another member of staff, clearly a subordinate, who was being firmly guided in some duty and whilst Stuart struggled to pick up much meaning from their words, he could tell from her tone that she was

252

business-like but approachable. She smiled as she saw him getting closer and opted for English as a greeting, something he wondered whether was standard or if she could just tell from looking at him. He knew he did not look his best, but had brushed off the dust of his scuffle and any bruising or swelling to his head had not yet manifested.

"Hello, sir," she said. "How can I assist you today?"

"'ello love," said Stuart, grinning like an idiot. She was really rather beautiful. "I was wonderin' if you could 'elp me."

"Of course, sir," she replied. He noted that her name badge said 'Sylvia' and her English was flawless. "What is it regarding?"

"I need to leave a message for my mate...*friend* who I *think* is stayin' 'ere," he began, then pre-empting any professional interjections about confidentiality and so on, he added, "I know you can't tell me their room number and I'm an idiot for forgettin' it, but if you could just *confirm* they're definitely in *this* Sana, it'd be amazin' please, love."

He smiled winningly and the woman took a deep breath before nodding, then extending a single long-nailed finger in his direction, the universal gesture of 'wait a moment'. She turned to her computer desk and moved the finger to her lips in a symbol of maintaining secrecy. Clearly, his charms had partially worked as she tapped away at the computer.

"Name, please?" she asked.

"Stuart," he said, grinning broadly, enjoying the moment. "Stuart Evans."

He had seen this done to a tee by flirtatious women, playing up their own foolishness to win over a man charmed by their naivety. He saw her own grin widening and a slightly disapproving glint in her eyes.

"Oh, my *friend's* name!" Stuart continued, tapping his head to chastise his silliness. "Payne. P-A-Y-N-E. A couple really, so could be under either Gerry or Celia."

He wasn't sure if either of them would have checked in using their real name, but with the way bookings were made and payments taken, it seemed harder to go incognito than in the dark ages. The woman was still smiling, clearly aware of the charm offensive, but not minding it too much and had resumed her tapping.

253

"Yes," she said after a moment. "Both here…" She stopped a moment and checked something, checked it again and then frowned slightly. "A couple you say?"

Stuart nodded.

"Well, ex-couple really, *Sylvia*," he said, using her name to hammer home the charm.

"Ah," she said, her face relaxing again. "That explains the two rooms then. Different rooms, different floors…" She hesitated. "Obviously I *can't* give you the details, but if you wish to leave a message for both…*either*?"

Stuart hadn't quite counted on this option. Clearly his charms were stronger than he had thought! What would Palmer do in this situation, he wondered. But he couldn't imagine Palmer managing to connect with Sylvia like this, the idea of him flirting was inherently bizarre. He was genuinely unsure what to do and thought he had better wait for Palmer.

"I'll just think what I might leave as a message, if that's okay?" he asked, indicating back to the seating he had just risen from.

Sylvia smiled and nodded.

"Make yourself at home," she said warmly. "Do you have a pen and paper?"

"I do, thanks," said Stuart, thinking that even if he didn't, he knew that Palmer did. Something occurred to him and he asked, reaching the cheekiest level he'd ever managed, "You don't 'appen to 'ave a charger for a Samsung do you?"

The woman laughed loudly and openly now and after a few moments, she produced a cable which she plugged in behind the desk and allowed Stuart to connect his phone to. It meant he didn't get to sit back down on the comfy chair, but he had spied that Palmer had left his own shoulder bag next to where they'd first made base. He knew he didn't know Palmer terrifically well, but something like this seemed very uncharacteristic. As he was standing watching his half-dead phone very slowly sputter back into life, he took the opportunity to have a quick nose through the bag, now keeping his eyes in three separate directions: at the entrance for Celia or Gerry arriving, at the stairs and lift for those two or Palmer descending, and on Sylvia, who was going about other duties behind the reception desk and would occasionally look up and smile his way. Palmer had little of immediate interest in his bag – no murder gloves or bloody knives or anything – but the journal or notebook he had in there was clearly a prized possession. Stuart delicately took it out and hesitated before inspecting it. There was no going back from an intrusion like this, he thought. The book was old, years old and the pages were curling at the edges from use, water exposure, possibly even sun damage. This must be Palmer's place for collecting evidence, theories, clues and suppositions. Stuart wondered what he might find in there. Even about himself.

Before he could take the plunge, the phone behind reception rang. This was no oddity, a phone somewhere had been constantly in a state of ringing, being answered and put down almost since they'd arrived, but this time the call was straight to Sylvia's desk. She answered it, in English again, Stuart noted, and although she was being very quiet and professionally discreet, he could tell what the topic of the conversation was. Someone else was leaving a message for someone in the hotel. Nothing out of the realms of possibility, Stuart thought. People must leave messages all the time. It was the details of the message as Sylvia read them back which caught Stuart's attention. He turned fully away from her now, scanning the lobby so as not to draw attention to his eavesdropping.

"The *Elevador de Santa Justa*, yes sir," she repeated back. "At 3.30pm today...from Mr. Scott Campbell...of course sir. I'll see the message is passed on. Is there anything else I can help you with today?...Then enjoy the rest of your day, sir. Goodbye."

Stuart couldn't believe his luck. A message from Jon to one of their targets here in the hotel, right within his earshot?! He didn't expect Sylvia to comment on the coincidence or let on that she suspected him of eavesdropping, so he didn't turn back to face her even though he felt certain she was watching him closely from behind. He turned instead to look at the entrance way. The sky outside had darkened and seemed to threaten rain, and Stuart knew from his English studying days that *pathetic fallacy* was the technique at hand. The weather reflecting the mood. How fitting a storm was coming. He checked the time. It was after 2. If Palmer hurried, they could be back into town and at the *elevador* in less than half an hour. Why did Jon want a meeting in such a busy, public spot, he wondered? For safety, perhaps? Gerry or Celia could both be unhinged and potentially dangerous, it seemed.

Seeing his phone slowly charging back up, he chanced accessing the forums to see if there was any new activity, but all he found was that *EdwardPalmer*'s membership had been instantly revoked and he was now on a banned list which Stuart had been forced to impose upon a few of the loonier elements at the fringes of his discussion groups. *GepettoPsych* had started a new thread now, not content with the appalling lies in the other thread about his past. Stuart wondered for a moment if Palmer had simply accessed the forums to get a message to him or if he'd been tempted to read more, particularly the thread about him supposedly getting away with murder. It was all very unpleasant. The new thread was entitled: *'ENDGAME'*.

He clicked onto the thread but was irritated to find he could only read half of the post, whichever way he tilted the screen made no difference. It said:

'Stuart Evans, mild-mannered builder or -

care homes, foster parents and halfway h-

drink, drugs and who knows what else? A-

feelings. Never truly recovering from the-

matricide. It all ends here today.'

There was enough for Stuart to piece together the gist of what *GepettoPsych* was getting at. His childhood was a troubled one, one which sounded infinitely worse when the facts were printed without any of the surrounding story to explain them. What Stuart couldn't fathom was why this new poster was revealing these things to such a small, focused audience, one which Stuart couldn't even be sure was made of genuine real people any more. How many of these posters were actually aliases of Jon Campbell Scott's, and was this *GepettoPsych* also actually another fake alias, or Gerry Payne, joining in the character assassination? The reference to it all ending here today was more sinister, as if something decisive was planned. The meeting at the *elevador* perhaps? Stuart contemplated sending Palmer a direct message again, telling him about the 3.30 rendezvous, but he doubted Palmer would be using his internet access again, being so odd about using his phone at all. He would just have to wait for him to return.

Eventually, at close to 2.45pm, Palmer slunk out of the lift looking very sheepish. He darted into the foyer as quickly as a man who could barely walk properly could manage, then after looking around and spotting Stuart, beckoned him over. He himself had gone back into the lift and was clearly holding the doors until Stuart arrived. As Stuart reached the lift, he saw why Palmer was acting so mysteriously. Cowering in the corner of the lift, stubbornly refusing to leave, was Celia Payne. She had the pink cravat wrapped around her face like a highway man's mask, or a paranoid Asian tourist and her eyes were furious.

"C'mon Celia," said Palmer. "We need to sort all of this out, like I told you upstairs. Please step out of the lift."

She shook her head furiously and when she clapped eyes on Stuart, her eyes widened and she began to frantically press buttons on the lift panel. Palmer wasn't moving from keeping the doors open, so the lift was going nowhere but it was clear Celia had not got this far by her own volition.

"You found 'er!" cried Stuart in admiration.

He wondered what the odds had been in a hotel this size with however many floors. Now wasn't the time to find out though, he had to help Palmer and also let him know about the imminent meeting.

"It's me again, Celia," he continued. "Sorry I scared you earlier."

The woman looked alarmed, but not because she particularly remembered what had happened, more because she probably didn't like the look of him and was already agitated by whatever Palmer had done to get her down this far.

"C'mon Celia," Palmer repeated, holding out a hand now for her to take.

His shoulder was firmly against the begrudging lift doors but the outstretched hand seemed tempting to her now.

"We'll go for a stroll, talk about old times. It'll be lovely," Palmer sounded strained and not at all convincing in his persuasion, but it was doing the trick on Celia with her fractured mind.

She reached out and took the hand gingerly and then threw herself against him, clinging wildly, as far away from Stuart as she could get. Palmer gave Stuart a strange look which seemed to question why she was behaving this way in his company and Stuart remembered he hadn't mentioned the bloody corkscrew which had sent her fleeing.

"That's a good girl," Palmer said, leading her out into the foyer, still attached to him like a frightened child.

Stuart looked around, wondering what anyone would think, seeing this oddly tactile display, but saw Sylvia from reception walking directly towards him. She looked a little bit confused and Stuart struggled to conjure up an excuse for their extraction of this frightened woman. As she got nearer, he was relieved to see her holding out his phone, which he had left charging when he dashed to the lifts.

"Your phone, Mr. Evans," she said, placing it in his hand delicately, so that

257

their palms brushed against each other for just a second longer than the handover took.

You've still got it, pal!

He quickly walked towards the foyer with her, asking her about the weather outside, which had turned violently stormy in the last few minutes, but ultimately turning her back on Palmer and Celia as they edged out of the lobby and onto the rainy street. He nodded his thanks once more to the pretty receptionist and smiled, thinking how odd it was that he had seemingly pulled twice today after months, no *years* of nothing, but that he would likely see neither person ever again anyway. Holiday romances were for the young. Or the rich.

He rejoined Palmer under the spacious front canopy of the hotel and was pleased to see a regular stream of taxis pulling up and departing their passengers at the different hotels and buildings along this street. He noted that Palmer had reclaimed his shoulder bag. *Did he think Stuart had sneaked a look?*

"We need to get to that *elevador* down in town," he quickly explained. "I overheard a message from Jon Scott Campbell inviting *someone* there from this hotel. Do you think it was…?" He nodded at Celia who was gazing around at the busy street as if she found it mesmerising but also terribly offensive.

"She's in no state for messages I'd say," said Palmer. "She has lucid moments, but she needs help. I say we take her with us, purely to keep an eye on her, but I'm not sure she's up to a confrontation like that."

Stuart found Palmer's worrying about Celia after everything she had put them through to be strangely admirable. Palmer didn't seem to know much about what to say or do with people in real life, face to face, but he had a strong sense of loyalty. He hoped it would now extend to him also. As a taxi pulled up and the driver looked hopefully through the wound-down window, Stuart stepped into the heavy rain and barked their next, perhaps final destination.

52.

Celia had become incredibly lucid during the taxi ride and despite Stuart having to ride in the front seat so as not to upset her, she kept tapping on the back of his seat to get his attention until finally he turned around sharply and stared at her.

"What?" he asked, trying not to lose his temper, but equally not up for further harassing from the damaged woman.

"I know you," she said. "You're that Evans boy."

She didn't sound impressed, but merely waved at Palmer who was sitting in the back beside her.

"Do something about him, Eddy," she commanded.

"Like what, Celia?" asked Palmer quietly, who had suggested they keep her onside by humouring her.

"I think he wants me, Eddy," Celia said breathily. "All the boys used to want me. I remember you in sixth form! You were in Bill Jacobs' form, weren't you?"

Stuart looked passed the gog-eyed woman to judge Palmer's reaction to all this. Did humouring her include pretending to be someone he wasn't? She was confusing recent history with fantasy and it put Stuart on edge. Palmer gestured that he had no idea how he should play it and Stuart cursed inwardly. The man could be socially useless sometimes.

"That's me," said Stuart, half-heartedly. "Old Jacobs was my form tutor!"

"Jacobs was younger than me!" Celia snapped haughtily.

She leaned forward to properly eyeball Stuart now.

"I'm not sure I care for your attitude at all!"

With a grunt of annoyance, she sat back in her seat and said nothing more for the remaining minutes of the journey. Stuart was glad for the quiet, although the heavy pounding of rain on the taxi windshield and the repeated whirring and sloshing of the wipers kept him from relaxing at all. He couldn't imagine anyone meeting atop the *elevador* in this foul weather, but if Jon had arranged it, he must have a plan. He had been living in Lisbon long enough to know the weather and how it affected a major attraction like the lift, Stuart assumed.

The cab pulled up on a street behind the *elevador* as Palmer had suggested, rather than right outside it. There was apparently a different way to reach the highest point without queuing for the lift itself. As much as Stuart fancied the novelty of the jerky old machinery of an ancient elevator, he didn't fancy it in this storm and didn't imagine it to be much of a draw, even if it were open. They paid the driver and hurried out through the filthy weather up a steeper street, then some steps, and more steps until they reached a high terrace with a stunning view over the red tiled roofs of the city. Stuart could see a number of places from his earlier adventures but couldn't appreciate the view due to the heavy rain which blinded his view. Celia was complaining about the rain and had wrapped her scarf up over her head like a classic Hollywood movie star. She might well have been almost as glamorous were she not also ranting and raving like a lunatic. Stuart was glad there were few people around to observe her or apologise to.

"That husband of mine will have a *lot* to answer for!" she cried for what Stuart felt must have been the tenth or eleventh time.

It was all she said when anyone tried to ask her about Gerry or who else might have been after her in the city. Stuart was still banking on her spilling the beans on who the 'he' was she had been going on about at the tower, but as she flitted in and out of reality, the odds were slipping. They hurried over the walkway which crossed the street they had driven up earlier and reached the upper entrance to the *elevador* which was firmly closed, with an apologetic member of staff explaining it would reopen when the weather lifted.

"What now?" Stuart asked of Palmer.

"We wait I suppose," he said, looking around nervously. "For whoever arranged all this. If it's Jon Scott Campbell, or Gerry Payne or someone else, then we wait."

He looked serious and grim again and Stuart knew it was from the renewed pain of walking up here and having to face whatever might be coming next. He definitely preferred him when he was less troubled. They didn't have long to wait, as the slinking shape of Jon Scott Campbell moved quickly past them, so quickly that it made Stuart jump when he noticed him and as the red head reached the closed kiosk entrance, he suddenly turned back and spotted the unlikely trio.

Stuart automatically braced himself for trouble, ready for another round against the wiry man, possibly to get another bash on the head for his efforts. Jon merely howled out for Celia, then insulted him and Palmer, dismissively calling them both a pair of suckers. Instead of deteriorating in his presence, Stuart was amazed to see Celia suddenly quite steady and steely-eyed. This man might have caused her harm, but she looked like she was ready to right the balance. As Stuart tried to warn him off, Celia instead brushed him aside slightly and Palmer held her back whilst they hurriedly exchanged ideas.

"Celia, you don't have to do this," hissed Palmer, urgently.

"That *bastard* has a lot to answer for," Celia replied, looking as lucid as Stuart had ever seen her.

He wondered what she was referring to, if it was simply Jon's using of her to further his career as had been often suggested, or if something more sinister was implied.

"Let 'er do this, 'arry mate," said Stuart.

It wasn't that he didn't relish the idea of knocking another chunk off Jon, but more that perhaps Celia had a different approach, a rapport with the psycho that might save time. Palmer nodded his agreement but didn't look happy at all and so Celia adjusted her headscarf and stepped out from their little huddle.

"Keep a close eye," Palmer hissed, grimacing at his own inability to do much, Stuart thought.

"Looking very alive for a dead woman," called Jon through the rain.

All subtle tone in his voice was lost as he howled over the noise of the wind and rain. It was hard to tell if he was angry, surprised or irritated at her

261

continued existence.

"Jon Scott Campbell, I've thought about this moment for a long time," Celia replied, glancing around at the drenched terrace. "I didn't quite imagine it like this."

They both lowered their voices and despite only being a few paces away, Stuart strained to hear their voices above the heavy pounding of the rain and growling storm clouds above. Jon seemed to be asking something and Celia's response was very scathing, like she had been with Stuart when they met in the park. There was a quiet menace in her voice, a cruelness which Stuart really didn't care for. If it really was part of her mental health issue, then he'd be glad to see her robbed of the power by some serious therapy or medication. There was a mention of a "Julie" now which confused Stuart. The name clearly meant something to both of them, but Jon looked furious. Stuart looked to Palmer, who was watching intently, but he couldn't imagine he could hear much either.

"What do we do, 'arry?" hissed Stuart.

Palmer shrugged, and cocked his head, not as if trying to hear the words of those just ahead of them, but as if he had heard something else close by which intrigued him. Sure enough, Stuart realised what he had detected – the sound of the lift groaning into life below them.

"Who's comin'?" Stuart whispered, shivering with anticipation.

Suddenly, Jon dashed into the kiosk, following the employee who had gone to where the lift was due to arrive and they could see the flash of his brightly coloured clothing as it showed through the ironwork of the spiral staircase up to the observation deck above them. He wasn't trying to escape it seemed, but he was definitely keen to drag things out. Maybe he knew who was coming?

"Let's follow," said Palmer, gesturing for Stuart to go first.

As they guided Celia inside, the female employee was standing by the lift, trying to use her walkie talkie to speak to her colleagues below. She turned to chastise the latest trespassers, but Stuart had already thought of what to say to her.

"Interpol, love," he said, not even sure if Interpol was even a thing any more, but hoping the word carried enough weight, or at the very least, surprise factor, to get them past her without interference.

The woman looked confused, but made no effort to stop this strange trio of people from proceeding up the spiral staircase, Stuart first, then Palmer who clung onto the railing, wincing at every step, then finally Celia, grumpy to have to bring up the rear and constantly moaning at Palmer to speed up. On the observation deck, Jon was drenched, staring out at the view down over the city towards the Tagus.

"Where are you runnin' to, Jon?" Stuart yelled as the storm intensified above.

He hoped that they'd be safe up here. The whole thing was metal which potentially meant electrocution as far as Stuart knew. Celia had stepped forward again, now touching herself suggestively as she looked at Jon. The woman was unstoppable.

"Yes, Jonny, where are you going?" she asked.

He didn't seem overly interested in talking to Celia any more, and was glancing at the stairs behind them, presumably knowing or sensing that someone's arrival was imminent. It had obviously spooked him.

"It's the end of the road for all of us, I think!" he said, slicking his hair back with rainwater and grinning like death.

He had obviously now seen something and as Stuart turned around, he saw the two eerie men in dark suits who had appeared in the park and taken Jon away what seemed like a lifetime ago, but had in fact only been about six hours previously. They looked for all the world like government agents in some conspiracy thriller, but Stuart knew he was just being foolish in his fantasies. A smaller man was behind them, protected, then as they parted, stepping forward to show he was in charge. These men were some sort of organised criminals, Stuart realised. He was trembling involuntarily, somehow shaken by the sight of these phantom heavies, but shook himself when he realised Jon had been expecting them. He turned back as Jon yelled at them in what must have been Portuguese. His words were loud, desperate and quick and Stuart thought it sounded like he was bargaining.

It didn't seem to be working, because the boss man looked furious, stricken with some awful anguish and howled at the very heavens something about someone being dead. Jon hurriedly yelled something back which sounded like he was blaming the three of them standing there, the unlikely trio who had first given him chase. The next few minutes passed by in an awful blur which even afterwards Stuart struggled to process. One minute he was exchanging glances with Palmer about whether they needed to get the hell out of there somehow, the next he saw a flash of something and had assumed it was lightning, but it was in fact a large knife like a machete. It looked too big for the man, too silly a weapon, like something a pirate, or an explorer or a terrorist would have, not a dumpy Latin-looking man with a deep tan and thinning hair. It was definitely too much for him, as before he could even advance upon them, he had slipped and fallen on the blade.

Stuart had almost expected to see the man's head tumbling from his body, such were his experiences of machete crimes, so was surprised to see the jerking, shuddering form in the rain, almost trying to rid itself of the blade now embedded in its neck. Blood cascaded out from the wound, over the ground, lost in the rain. An awful gurgle came from his mouth and as if to make up for the odd silence upstairs, angry shouts came from below. Palmer looked sickened and Celia was staring transfixed as if loving the show. As the two heavies rushed to their boss's side, Jon skipped past them all and down the staircase. Stuart yelled after him, but his words were lost in the storm.

"We have to go," said Palmer, suddenly very calm and collected. "Celia, my dear, we have to go," he added, tugging on her arm.

She had one hand outstretched as if she was swirling it around in the blood coming from the mafia boss's wound and was enjoying it. She was an odd odd woman. Palmer pulled harder at her arm and she moved along with him, still keeping her gaze fixed on the body until she had to descend and could no longer see it. Stuart brought up the rear, expecting trouble from the two men, but finding them more concerned with keeping their employer alive it seemed. They didn't even notice that they had set down their bags in the rain, unattended. Downstairs, the *elevador* staff had congregated on this level, confused and concerned about what had happened.

"Interpol!" yelled Stuart again, not caring if any of this words were understood, but wanting to get out without any questions being made about their own movements. "A man – a *bad* man – has tried to kill himself up there. We need to catch his accomplice. Where did he go?"

It seemed enough of his words were clear to the staff, despite the strangeness of his hurriedly improvised story. He hadn't wanted to say that anyone else had *attacked* the man, as that patently hadn't happened, but he also wanted to make it plain that *they* were no danger, but that Jon Scott Campbell may well have been. They indicated that he had gone the way they had all come up and so together they pursued. The woman they'd first met up here shouted something about calling the police, or an ambulance, but Stuart just waved dismissively as they left, hoping everything might be stalled long enough for them to be far away.

Was that strange man, the vengeful man, really Jon's 'Jeep' character? There was some odd subtext to their conversation, but Stuart couldn't see how this unknown player could be such an important part of the mystery. Besides, he had barely acknowledged them and 'Jeep' was surely watching them, manipulating them, and ultimately, probably quite keen on rubbing their noses in it.

The rain was easing off now – *pathetic fallacy for sure!* – but despite the shock and Palmer's injury, heading downhill was easier and Jon couldn't move very quickly. Perhaps their earlier scuffle really had done him some damage. As Stuart tightly gripped the mafioso bag he had just snatched up on the way off the observation deck, he realised with excitement that they would catch Jon within minutes.

53.

"In case anything happens…" Palmer began, but then stopped awkwardly and his eyes drifted to the ground. Rainwater was collecting on his nose like a big dewdrop and Stuart had to catch himself from laughing.

"Normally I'd be expectin' a confession of feelin's or summat," said Stuart, far too jovially for the mood. "I've seen too many films, 'arry pal. Don't be shy, spit it out."

Palmer looked up nervously, clearly missing the joke. He reached into his jacket pocket and pulled out his phone.

"We should properly check we've got each other's numbers," he said, and Stuart realised this was a huge deal for him. As big as a confession of love to a romantic movie hero.

Stuart got out his phone too, clinging onto life at 11% following its brief recharge. Palmer was trusting him to check *his* phone as well as his own and so Stuart accessed the contacts list. He made sure his own number was saved and chuckled as he did so.

"What's funny?" asked Palmer nervously, watching him closely.

"Check what I've saved my number in your phone as," said Stuart, handing the handset back.

"Sucker #2?" Palmer read. "I don't follow."

"What that nutter called us," explained Stuart. "Seemed fittin'. 'ere, you do mine."

Stuart handed his damaged device over and after looking at him in disbelief at the state of his phone, he struggled to match the action. Finally, he handed it back.

"Sucker #1 I am then," Palmer said and Stuart grinned insanely.

This was definitely acceptance. Today was a strange day and getting stranger. The low growl of a scooter sounded behind them and Stuart looked over his shoulder to see Hugo, the Uber Eats delivery boy skid around the corner of the deserted street. The rain had stopped and the sun was coming out, especially over the river, but this part of the riverfront had no passing trams or buses or taxis to hail. Palmer's legs were giving up and Jon had begun to extend his lead, disappearing out of view. Digging out the business card, Stuart had expected to have to explain how he acquired it a little more than Palmer had made him, and whilst he had told him of the hairy scooter ride, he hadn't told him of the young man's interests in him. When he called the number, the answer was at first in Portuguese, then in English but still business-like until he reminded him who he was and the lad, who he discovered was called Hugo, suddenly sounded incredibly excited. He explained he could take a short break, but his shift didn't end for some time. Palmer had suggested a better idea which was that they would simply book his services for the afternoon, to ferry *them* rather than food.

Celia had been left behind at the *elevador*, a taxi quickly hailed whilst there was still the chance, and despite all their misgivings, she was bundled back to her hotel with a hefty tip for the driver. Stuart once again had used his charms and phoned the Sana Lisboa hoping it would be Sylvia he got through to. He was thrilled that it was and he left her with an instruction to look after Celia who was feeling unwell and see that she didn't wander off please. Celia for her own part, had promised to stay there, but what good was the promise of a woman who had fled the country and lied about her whereabouts? Stuart knew that Palmer was wary of the plan, but he had been convinced that there was no way they could look after her or keep her out of danger if she took flight in the middle of the coming confrontation.

Hugo had the scooter balanced beneath him as he took off his helmet and held it under his arm, smiling broadly at Stuart. He looked thoroughly thrilled to see Stuart again and Stuart could see that Palmer was thrown by the weird energy suddenly manifesting itself on that strangely deserted street corner.

"Hey English," said Hugo. "You ride?"

He patted the back seat and Stuart had to laugh at his brazenness. He was too young for him, even if he were that way inclined, probably by about a decade, Stuart guessed, but he had a winning smile and there was something he found magnetic about him. Had a crazy scooter ride of less than a quarter of an hour really bonded the two of them to closely? There was definitely something odd about this Iberian heat, Stuart noted.

"Not me yet, fella," Stuart replied. "I need you to take my mate first please."

He could see Hugo's face fall as he looked at Palmer, then back at Stuart, doing some serious mental gymnastics and extrapolating about their relationship. He raised an eyebrow as he looked Palmer up and down and then threw such a look at Stuart that suggested he couldn't believe his taste included this man.

"No, no, Hugo," Stuart said quickly. "Friends. Just friends!"

He wanted to also extend this to *their* burgeoning relationship, but didn't want to jeopardise their chance of a ride on this deserted stretch of road. Stuart had decided that today, he could flirt with anyone and as long as no one got hurt, he would get what he needed!

Begrudgingly, Hugo allowed Palmer onto his scooter and even more begrudgingly, Palmer got on. He looked so stiff and uncomfortable that Stuart feared he would fall off the moment the vehicle set off and if Hugo rode like he did earlier, he doubted both of them would get there intact. As he stood by Palmer and patted him on the shoulder, he noted that his new friend didn't shudder at the contact as he clearly had earlier. Perhaps he was just distracted by the terror ride ahead. He regretted ramping up quite how crazy the ride had been now.

"You and me, later?" asked Hugo, hopefully and Stuart could see not just the desire in his young eyes, but also something hopeful, something actually rather pure and sweet.

A shame he was barking up the wrong tree entirely, but he would make sure the lad was compensated for his time and potential heartbreak.

"Sure mate," he replied. "Now take my friend down this road, you're lookin' for a ginger bloke with an 'orrible face."

He pulled a grimace as he described Jon and knew most of his words were lost on young Hugo, but hoped their earlier conversation had given him instruction enough. Their target should be easily visible once they got up to speed and

Stuart couldn't imagine him getting that far away. Palmer had theorised that he was heading for the river, then for somewhere high up along the way. He hoped his theories were right. He gave Hugo an encouraging squeeze of his shoulder and felt a very firm bicep as he moved his hand away. Nope, not going there, Stuart told himself as the scooter whined away. He sensed that Palmer would turn and give him a worried look if he was truly unhappy being on the scooter, but as he didn't, Stuart simply chose to believe that everything was going well. He waited until the scooter had disappeared around the bend and then set off after it. They had agreed that Hugo would bring the scooter back around once he had found somewhere to drop Palmer off, but until then, Stuart would race along after it as best he could.

Stuart tired much more quickly than he had hoped and it felt like he had spent most of his time in the city running to or from someone or something. He kept imagining that he could see or even hear the scooter buzzing along ahead of him, but each time he squinted to make out the shape of Hugo's vehicle, he was rewarded with either nothing, or a car or bicycle rattling along the riverfront. The roads got busier, with tourists and traffic and docks looming on the waterfront, but it was the huge, ominous bridge, the *25 de Abril* which dominated the horizon. Stuart had a bad feeling about it, as if this iconic construction had been the centre of their investigations all along, that they'd merely been circling it constantly for days, only to finally land at the centre now as everything came to a head.

Pausing momentarily for breath, he decided to try the number he had prised out of Celia. She had been babbling about calling Jon; it wasn't clear if she had held onto his number over the years and he had never changed it or if she had newly acquired it for some reason, so Stuart had taken the number whilst Palmer was sorting out the cab for her. He hadn't wanted Palmer to know as whatever was going on with Celia and Gerry and whoever Jeep actually was, he felt like the Jon Scott Campbell angle was entirely personal to him. He dialled the number, knowing Palmer wouldn't approve if he knew about it, but given Hugo hadn't yet returned, he might catch Jon off-guard. A brief, hostile call followed before Jon hung up. The call might not have been particularly illuminating in terms of the conversation, but Stuart had clearly heard the busy road traffic and odd howling noise of the bridge in the background, pinpointing Jon's location.

He was practically in the shadow of its colossus as he finally spied Hugo hurtling along towards him. The road was wider now with multiple lanes and a railway line down the middle and Stuart wondered how far they were from the stretch of road he and Hugo had first sped along together. The scooter skidded to a halt and Hugo leapt off, rushing to embrace him, which was quite a surprise. The lad was shaking.

"What's wrong, mate?" he asked, returning the hug which was purely for comfort rather than anything more romantic.

"Your friend…" whimpered Hugo and he turned and pointed up at the bridge.

Stuart struggled to see anyone on the road at the top of the titanic bridge, but could see plenty of vehicles. Amidst the sound of roaring traffic from up there and down along the road they were at the side of, almost buried beneath a strange howling coming from the sound of the traffic traversing the bridge, he could hear honking of horns, like people responding to bad driving or someone jaywalking. Still he could see no one up there. Hugo let go of him with his other arm and followed Stuart's gaze. He took Stuart's hand and pointed it to where he had intended him to look, the lower level of the bridge, where the railway line thundered below the road.

Stuart could see suddenly a bright ball of fire, tiny and deadly between the latticework of the bridge, then a second shape engulfing the fireball. Both shapes fell out of sight, one falling from the bridge itself, the other disappearing from sight within the framework. As he watched the tiny smoking shape plummet from the bridge into the depths of the Tagus, Stuart knew that those two shapes could possibly be Jon Scott Campbell and Palmer. *But which was which?*

54.

It was stifling hot again in the staircase of the *Torre de Belem* after the mightily breezy and cool uppermost level. The traffic light system to get them up there had proved problematic, with many tourists simply not noticing the lights or the countdown to hurry them in or out and others choosing to deliberately ignore it. On the way back down, it was equally odd and the tight, steep spiral stairs did not favour the chaos that haphazard holidaymakers brought with them. The alarming noise which signalled it was time to get off the stairs and allow the next directional flow only added further panic. For his part, Palmer was keen on the order and control the system suggested but not the reality of it and with his slower pace and Gerry Payne literally breathing down his neck, he found the whole experience to be one he wasn't keen on repeating.

"So what did you mean, Gerry?" demanded Palmer, breathless and trying to ignore the searing white pain behind his eyes that his legs were sending upwards.

They had stepped off the stairs into a strangely peaceful room, like a chapel of some sort which clearly didn't have the same pull as the stunning view from the top. The noise had sounded indicating the flow on the stairs was about to change and rather than force their way awkwardly on past people trying to get up, Palmer had dodged off the steps. He could hear Gerry's disapproving chuntering behind him and he knew that Gerry would not have thought twice about barging people off the stairs in his singlemindedness. He was a pig. But was he a killer?

"You're talking about Celia as if she's still alive," Palmer continued, seeing the impassive red face glaring at him out of the corner of his eye as he scanned the small antechamber. "You know for certain?"

Gerry stood now, blocking the medieval archway entrance, which Palmer noted had a couple of anachronistic LCD screens above, indicating the flow of traffic and countdown to the next change. He smirked now, a look which looked awful on his jowly face.

"She's alive, Palmer, you dunce," he growled. "It takes a really bloody *awful* detective to miss out on the obvious facts in a case like this."

"I'm no detective," Palmer said, not rising to the insult.

He kept his eyes away from Gerry, knowing that one of the many power plays that the lecturer like to use was to unblinkingly eyeball his targets until they were forced to look away from his weird intensity.

"But you like to play one, don't you, Palmer?" Gerry continued. "Helping the weak and dispossessed."

Palmer frowned outwardly and inwardly. Was Gerry mixing him up with someone else? Palmer didn't care very much at all about the weak. They were generally an annoyance in his view. The dispossessed he might share some elements of personality with, but not to the point of sympathy and certainly not to the point of *empathy*. He didn't *do* empathy. A good sociopath rarely opened himself up to such frivolity. His so-called friend and brain expert George had teased him about this before.

"You make me sound like some sort of superhero crimefighter," said Palmer, wishing he could think of a good cultural reference to toss in. *Was Batman a good example?*

"That's what you see yourself as, isn't it?" Gerry said, scowling. "Instead of what you really are."

Palmer wondered now what Gerry thought he really was, but didn't want to interrupt the ranting.

"A bit of a sad loser, no friends, no family – apart from that sick mother of yours – and on indefinite leave from work. How long *has* it been since you were last in, Palmer?"

Palmer wondered if Gerry had been stalking him or something. His assessment of the *facts* was accurate enough, though if he had been banking on it causing him shock or pain, then he was wildly misguided in his evaluation of his *character*.

"Cut the crap," Palmer said, knowing Gerry would regard it as an angry response to his provocation, but in truth he was just tired of the waffle. "How do you know Celia's alive?"

Gerry rolled his eyes so dramatically that Palmer swore he could hear them swivelling in his fat head.

"I've *seen* her you fool," he retorted. "Here in Lisbon. She was spotted by a mutual acquaintance so I flew out to drag her sorry arse back to England."

"And you've been following *me*?" Palmer asked now, certain he had seen someone heading the wrong way down the stairs, barely a blur of white and pink but definitely defying the flow.

"I was surprised that you were here too," Gerry said, the heat and exertion making him look like his face was melting, despite the rest period. "I had to know if you were in on it."

"So you know nothing about this message?" Palmer asked, becoming annoyed now.

He'd got it straight in his head that Gerry had Celia locked away somewhere, possibly on a boat, but that she had managed to break free a number of times or had befriended a local in her captivity in order to send the strangely cryptic messages to him. It felt a good fit that the Belem leaflet under his door was a trap set by Gerry but that Celia had added her own hidden message somehow, to steer him to the right location. Given he'd actually met Gerry in the tower, it now felt more likely that he'd got everything completely the wrong way around.

"Not a clue," said Gerry smugly. "But that's our dear Celia's handwriting and as we both know, she loves a good puzzle." He dabbed at himself now with a handkerchief. "Have *you* seen her here?"

Palmer had been prepared to lie about anything Gerry asked him, but found he could be entirely honest now.

"I thought I had, then I convinced myself I hadn't and that I was seeing things, but now you've said all this, I'm as unsure as ever," he admitted.

273

To his surprise, Gerry merely laughed. A cruel, mocking laugh which broke into a hoarse cough born from too much tobacco and not enough exercise.

"I was an idiot to think you might actually be of some *use* in all this, Palmer," he said dismissively.

Any other time, he might have defended himself, but he had no desire or energy to draw out this confrontation with Gerry any further. The man was an imbecile. He had only one view of the world – his own – and nothing was going to alter that. It was easier for him to continue to think that Palmer was useless rather than have him trailing after him, getting in his way. But Palmer was now concerned for Celia. She might not have been in her right mind.

"I'll see you at the bottom," Gerry barked, not checking that the direction of flow had changed, but neatly coinciding his exit with the change to a green light. "You'll excuse me if I don't wait for you."

He huffed off through the arch, practically shoving a young woman out of his path who had dared to pause on the stairway and peer into the antechamber. He was an odious bully and a bore, but hardly a killer, Palmer concluded. But that didn't mean he still wasn't dangerous.

55.

Palmer knew he needed to communicate with Stuart. He was the only other person in the city who might be of use to him and he had dodged having to exchange contact details with him repeatedly. Perhaps the internet would help him out. It was worth activating his roaming for.

There were plenty of other Stuart Evanses online from all around the world, but he navigated back to the Facebook profile page of the one he knew for sure was *his* Stuart Evans. To message him on that platform, he would need to *join* and that was beyond the pale for Palmer. Then he remembered the forums his Mancunian would-be sidekick had mentioned. He racked his brains until he remembered their name. He *had* been listening vaguely when they were mentioned, interested in the implications of the story rather than the fine details. He knew Stuart had mentioned something about shutting them down, but perhaps he could find the contact details for one Stuart Evans online, maybe a forwarding email address or something. It worked and to his surprise, the forums were active and whilst there was no way to contact Stuart directly without being a member, he could quickly fill in his email and request to join. An online forum was different from a parasitic social media behemoth, he reasoned. He had no idea if Stuart would see this, but it was worth a try.

A few more lost-looking tourists wandered off the stairs into the nave-like room and Palmer moved to the window in order to let them have their space. Far below, though his dizziness prevented him looking for too long, he saw the same white and pink blur dashing away from the tower. Gerry would probably still be stuck on the staircase, he thought. He felt a buzz of an email asking him to confirm his membership request, then within seconds, a second

saying he had been approved. If Stuart was perhaps looking for him after his
sudden disappearance by the monastery, then for once, Palmer was glad of his
companion's obsessive nature. Palmer fired off a quick direct message to
Stuart, using a detail he felt certain would confirm he was who he said he was,
along with his mobile number and then waited.

He decided he might as well start to descend the rest of the tower as whatever
Gerry was up to, whoever that blur might be, he wanted to keep a close eye on
what happened. Stuart might have some better information on his movements.
He held his phone out in anticipation of a phone call from an unknown
number, but nothing came through. Perhaps the signal was poor in the
confines of the tower's staircase? A response finally arrived as he reached the
bottom, having missed the signal ushering him off the steps and keeping a
queue of people keen to ascend in suspense. It was an email saying he had a
direct message on the forums. Strange that Stuart hadn't called him. He
checked his inbox.

'*PALMER. IT'S STUART. CELIA'S ALIVE! PHONE'S FUCKED. AT DOCA
PEDROUÇOS. I NEED A VACATION! WHERE R U?*'

The text speak ought to have made him shudder, but he was too anxious to
care. So Stuart was somehow also convinced that Celia was in the land of the
living? Palmer crafted his response and sent it, waiting for more information.
He had no idea where Stuart was, but knew it ought to be easy enough to
locate online. He wrote and sent:

'*SHE'S DEFINITELY ALIVE?! I'M WITH GERRY PAYNE OF ALL PEOPLE,
AT THE TOWER. HE'S LYING ABOUT SOMETHING. WHERE SHALL WE
RENDEZVOUS?*'

There was no immediate response, so Palmer looked about for Gerry. He had
already left the tower and was shoving his way along the bridge back to solid
land. He had clearly dismissed Palmer as no longer worthy of his interest; he
really was a megalomaniac.

In lieu of a reply from Stuart, he hobbled after Gerry who was standing by a
tiny van the like of which Palmer had seen in the city centre back home all
opened up and transformed into a mobile coffee bar. This one, he was
intrigued to find, was a speciality wine stall. A few deck chairs with the van's
company livery on them were lined up by the riverfront with an awesome
view of the *Torre* to the right and up the Tagus to the left. Despite the
breeziness, a few takers were ordering their drinks and Palmer could see that
Gerry was tempted.

Palmer knew full well that the man was a sot. He was probably an alcoholic but one of those middle aged red nosed men who simply drank out of habit and would scoff at the idea of addiction. It was tempting to see what change would come in the man once a drink or two had loosened him up. Palmer suspected that despite his air of superiority, he was actually itching to show off what he knew, to boast about his knowledge of Celia.

"Stand you a drink, Gerry?" Palmer asked as he reached where he was lurking.

Gerry turned and almost involuntarily sneered like there was a bad smell in his nostrils. He really couldn't help himself. Palmer wondered about the poor students forced to endure his lectures and whether Gerry could hide his disdain for those he considered inferior (practically everyone, Palmer mused) for long enough to educate them.

"Or is it a little too early, old chap?" Palmer continued, again knowing the lingo to reach out to him.

Palmer knew it was definitely not too early for a drink, especially to a heavy boozer like Gerry, but that he himself would never normally partake at this hour. It wasn't that long after noon. He could still taste the toothpaste, for crying out loud!

Gerry barely even tried to raise an argument against a free drink and potentially an excuse to get squiffy and loose-lipped and so Palmer was allowed to buy him a large glass of Portuguese rosé. He himself (to keep up appearances) asked for a glass of the local liquor, the fiery cherry *ginjinha* and was given a huge measure for his troubles in the same size collectors' glass as Gerry. The concept of a nice glass of wine somewhere outdoors with a spectacular view was one that Palmer could appreciate the appeal of to others, even if he couldn't quite bring himself to be seduced by it. As Gerry plonked himself heavily down in the one remaining free deckchair, Palmer could tell his little gambit would work. He had no chair himself and the group using the other chairs showed no sign of rushing to finish their own drinks, so he stood looking out over the Tagus, again deliberately avoiding eye contact with the mesmeric lecturer.

"You never did like it that she turned to me for help, did you?" said Palmer, quietly and slyly.

He wasn't one for emotional manipulation as to be frank with himself, he barely understood the depth of feeling most other people experienced and found it to be a dangerous game to try and provoke it in others. With Gerry, he

277

would make a special effort.

"Ha!" cried Gerry and Palmer looked quickly over his shoulder to see that he had already quaffed half his glass of wine. "*Turned to you*?!" he continued, his voice thick with derision. "Celia would have turned to anyone with a cock if she thought there was something in it for her. In your case, it seems she was barking up the wrong tree."

Palmer frowned, trying to make sense of Gerry's words. He was already slurring and Palmer now realised this glass was most probably not the man's first of the day. He was either slighting Palmer's manhood or else hinting that he was uninterested in women. It didn't matter to him much, either way to be honest. He'd never been one for entering into pissing contests and he genuinely had little interest in any sort of sexual encounter with anyone. Celia ought to have realised that early on and not taken his attempts to counsel her as anything more romantic.

"Celia was just trying to get away from the awful men in her life," Palmer said, calculatingly. "All I ever did was listen to her and not treat her like rubbish, unlike you."

Palmer chanced another glance out of the corner of his eye but this time saw that he had been monitored by Gerry who clearly knew he was trying to provoke him. He downed his wine and was about to set down his glass when Palmer turned and offered him another. Gerry barely hesitated in his acceptance. Palmer hadn't even got going with his, having a tiny curious sip of the *ginjinha* which seemed strangely medicinal and warming. When he returned with Gerry's next glass, the man already looked watery eyed and barely focused on him. He didn't say thanks, which came as no surprise.

"You can see why people thought *you* might have done her in, can't you?" Palmer continued, perching on the low wall over the river.

He popped his glass down next to him and got comfy. He didn't know how long this might take, but he knew Gerry's temper was ridiculously short and his ego thinner than veneer.

"And it's even more obvious why she was always after young men, isn't it, Gerry?" he pressed on. "When someone's as temperamental and *in their cups* as you are, what is there for a woman like her?"

Palmer deliberately didn't look back at Gerry now. He saw a Yellow Bus tour boat ploughing through the water and could vaguely hear the tinny narration of the tour guide drifting through the air. To his left, by the wine van, was another stall selling delicate themed biscuits, gift wrapped and artistic with icons of Lisbon and Portugal adorning them. Palmer wondered idly if Stuart would care for some; his appetite was ridiculous.

"And if it's to be believed that you were practically *impotent* towards the end of your marriage, then no wonder she wandered about looking for a quick *screw*," said Palmer, becoming more vicious in his words if not his tone.

Curiosity was getting the better of him as he finished this latest dig and as he made to look back at the deckchairs, he realised a looming shape was upon him. Gerry had leapt furiously out of his chair, stumbled on the pavement in front of him and thrown his glass towards Palmer. He braced himself, but realised the sturdy glass was merely plastic and felt it bounce off his ribcage. He was more concerned about Gerry himself now, as he continued forwards like a juggernaut, flailing and roaring like a demented steam train. Even injured, Palmer was still quicker on his feet than the drunken mass and he rolled aside and watched transfixed as the red-faced buffoon's momentum saw his feet hit the low wall and then his entire body flip over it and out of sight. Palmer knew from the higher viewpoint of the tower that there was a narrow beach area before the inviting river and as he peered over the wall, he heard a satisfying wet splat and saw that Gerry had landed firmly in the boggy sand, half in the water, half up to his knees in the mire. Palmer was half-tempted to activate his phone camera to capture this marvellously silly moment, but instead took advantage of the break from Gerry's company to concentrate on finding Stuart and the reason he wasn't able to phone him.

56.

"That is funny as fuck," said Stuart, after Palmer had finished relaying his encounter with Gerry to him in the shade of a quirky lighthouse they had both seen previously from the bus tour. "But also, totally unbelievable at the same time. Pics or didn't 'appen, mate."

Palmer stared at him, wondering why a phrase he had heard from the laziest and least ambitious amongst the youth of today was now pouring from the lips of a man he'd almost begun to consider might actually be quite shrewd and useful. Still, Stuart *was* much closer to what Palmer considered youthful than he himself was, so perhaps he was too quick to judge.

"I thought it was only the youth of today who spoke in such *soundbites*!" he replied, aiming for what those same youths referred to as *banter*.

He shuddered inwardly at the word and his own rubbish attempts at channelling it. He could see Stuart gazing at him, studying his face like an animal hoping for a scrap of food or an encouraging word but he had neither to offer him. Stuart really was canine in his loyalty; the way he'd come barrelling down the riverfront seemingly to his rescue, had been both faintly touching and quite hilarious.

It seemed that Stuart had mistaken his message about being in Gerry's company as a cry for help and the lack of a clear line of communication between them had only worsened the misunderstanding. The aforementioned '*DOCA PEDROUÇOS*' must have been very close by given the short time which had passed between him first hearing of it and then seeing Stuart, drenched in sweat, wide eyed and full of determination hurtling towards him. He had barely walked a hundred yards along the riverfront away from the *torre* and the splashing noises now coming from below where he had last seen Gerry when Stuart caught up to him.

"Are you alright, mate?!" he yelled between gasps for air. "Where is 'e?"

"Keep walking," Palmer had instructed, noting the people watching them as they moved away from where a man had just thrown himself over the low wall.

Palmer had quickly and succinctly explained that his so-called friend was a bit of a drunken fool who had tried to push *him* in the river but had misjudged and dunked himself in the drink. It was hardly even a lie – perhaps the *friend* bit was the worst mistruth – but Palmer didn't want to hang around to see what happened when Gerry was extricated from the water. The man at the wine stand who had been first to leap up to help merely shook his head as if he knew all too well the power of drink in these hot climes. Insisting he finish his *ginjinha* for the shock of it all, the vendor handed Palmer his plastic souvenir glass and watched him down it before clambering over the wall to investigate Gerry's state. Palmer bid him goodbye and set off and had kept his head down and his eyes on the path in front of him until he'd heard Stuart's heavy footfall and puffing behind.

Stuart obediently dropped into line behind Palmer, almost resisting the urge to look around but not quite managing it and Palmer chuckled to himself at another demonstration of dog-like behaviour. The builder trotted along behind him and he seemed to be both contented to be back with his master but also in a state of heightened awareness (his ears might as well have been pricked up) at the danger which might yet have been awaiting them. Palmer waited until they had cleared the park and the tower was beginning to shrink in its majesty behind them and stopped to turn to his companion. For a moment he felt a little too much like Gerry Payne, swaggering along insisting on controlling the power of speech and silence, but he knew that he was nothing like that oddball. Palmer had his foibles but he didn't use them as an excuse to exact misery on others.

"We safe yet, 'arry mate?" Stuart asked quietly and seriously as they stopped at the side of the path which would continue to lead them towards the *25 de Abril* bridge should they take it.

"For now," Palmer said at last, glancing back towards the tower.

He wondered why he had ever considered Gerry a threat to safety to begin with, but the alcohol-fuelled charge at him could have ended very differently had he been less aware of the danger. The shot of liqueur he had drunk was burning in his throat and stomach in a way which was both alarming and pleasing and Palmer cursed his intolerance but was glad it was nowhere near as crippling as Gerry's dependency. Should the fool have done some real harm to himself, he wondered what the wine vendor would say, what would be made of the fact he had topped up his supposed friend's glass before he drunkenly hurled himself into the water. He decided instead to make sure he was nowhere near any sort of investigation and remembered the mantra he had once been told years ago: no guns, no police, no hospitals. Perhaps Stuart was similarly minded.

"The Yellow Bus goes along this way," he said, waving vaguely along the river front, behind the *Padrao dos Descobrimentos*. "I say we take it back to the hotel and think about bringing this whole thing to a conclusion."

He was already thinking of the need to leave the city before Gerry launched into a deeper vendetta against him, but also knew that he and Stuart needed to compare notes about Celia's whereabouts. As they waited by the river at a brightly coloured bus stop next to the red and white helter skelter patterned lighthouse, Palmer told Stuart all about Gerry's tumble into the Tagus. A bus pulled up almost immediately after he had finished and as they sat together on the lower deck, Stuart began to laugh at the ridiculous image. Gerry Payne was a laughable figure at the best of times, but a wet, drunken riverbound Gerry summoned up hilarity. Palmer was glad that Stuart was smiling as he'd rather imagined that there'd be an air of sulking after Palmer had hobbled off and left him by the monastery, but the topic hadn't even come up yet. Palmer wondered if Stuart was only laughing on the outside. He'd seen people do that all his life, those who could be bothered to put on a show at all. Palmer knew exactly what to do to lift his mood and no, it was *not* manipulation.

"And so, since you're ever reliant on telephone communication, I've now got your number in my phone," he began. "I trust you'll do the same?"

"If I ever get it recharged again," said Stuart and Palmer now realised the reason for his elusiveness.

Looking at the device in Stuart's hand, it looked like it needed more than a recharge. The case was all cracked and a fine spiderweb of tiny fracture lines was set into the bottom of the screen. Anyone normal would ask about the phone or offer their sympathies, but Palmer really didn't care for the details. Smalltalk was the ultimate waste of air. They needed to get down to business.

"So," he said carefully, "Cards on the table, Stuart, cards on the table."

"Meanin'?" asked his companion and Palmer genuinely didn't know if Stuart had never heard the phrase before.

"You don't know the meaning of the expression?" he asked quizzically.

"No mate, I meant I don't know what *you* mean by usin' it. I did well enough in my education thank you very much."

He sounded annoyed and probably insulted, Palmer thought. Stuart's skin was no thicker than Gerry Payne's, it seemed. People were foolish to be so easily wounded by words. Palmer distracted him by asking about his education. He assumed Stuart wasn't especially well educated, being merely a builder, but was surprised to learn some of the details. Stuart seemed touchy and a little aggressive.

"Further education's not for everyone," said Palmer magnanimously.

"With teachers like bloody Jon Scott Campbell and Celia chuffin' Payne out there, it's a wonder any kid gets through their education," came the retort.

Finally Palmer steered him back to the purpose he'd had in mind all along: the sharing of information. No more secrets. Well, no more secrets that involved the Celia Payne business. There were still plenty of secrets Palmer would go to his grave with and others which were merely none of Stuart's business. He listened as Stuart recapped the Jon Scott Campbell case, rambling on about how he first discovered the string of assaults in Manchester and took to the online forums. Occasionally, Palmer would chip in with a word or two of observation or encouragement, knowing that highly emotional people like Stuart liked and indeed relished the attention. Finally, after bringing Palmer entirely up to speed on how he ended up in Portugal, he tried to defend how his story would surely have sounded to someone outside the events themselves.

"I'm not mad, I swear, pal."

"I believe you," said Palmer, and again he took a few moments to offer a little bit of faint praise to his newfound companion which didn't exactly ramp up the levels of trust between them, but certainly didn't do any further damage to them.

It did the trick, because sociopath or not, Palmer could tell that Stuart was thrilled by what he had said. He had an odd look like an old man who has become lost in a beautiful wave of nostalgia, but then can't quite remember the actual memories, just how they made him feel then and now.

"Weird thing is," said Stuart. "Jon was surprised that Celia was alive. 'e seemed to reckon *you'd* done 'er in, 'arry."

"Charming," said Palmer. "Celia is many things: a victim, a nightmare, a hypocrite…" *A liar, a deceiver, an attention whore…* "…But she never really deserved what you've described. Basically, she's just fallen apart by the sound of it?"

Palmer had nodded as Stuart filled him in on Celia's odd shifts of mood during his encounter with her by the tower. None of it had sounded strange to him, as he'd already seen her like this, that night she attacked him with a pint glass in a Sheffield bar.

Changing the subject, Palmer said, "I honestly thought *you* were working with Scott Campbell. I saw the two of you together, then when I thought I saw Celia just after, well, it all seemed like someone was contriving to frame me."

"I reckon you're right, mate," agreed Stuart. "But I still think there's two different things goin' on 'ere. Maybe at cross-purposes too. Jonny boy seemed to have fancied 'imself quite the mastermind, getting' me 'ere to fuck about, but I reckon Gerry Payne's the real villain in all this."

Even after what I've just told you? Palmer doubted Stuart's detective skills after that comment.

"Gerry's a dickhead," said Palmer, using a word not ordinarily in his vocabulary, but hoping to ensure Stuart understood. "Had no love for me, or Celia for that matter, truth be told. But a criminal mastermind? He can barely organise his own breakfast into his own fat mouth without spilling it down his tweed jacket."

Palmer continued to elaborate on his ideas that Gerry Payne was simply not a man with the capacity for such organised villainy. He was basically a man who traded on his privilege and perceived ideas about his place in the world and trod anyone underfoot who didn't live up to his ideals, which was pretty much everyone he met. He was a sexist, a racist, a homophobe and a bully, despite his fine background and when he drank too much, he did terrible things, like cheat on his wife, make passes at undergraduates, get into physical fights he hadn't a hope of winning and make a fool of himself generally. The pathetic way he was stalking after Celia after all this time…for *what* exactly? It wasn't as if he was here to save her; he was no white knight.

The image of white suddenly made Palmer think of the person…no, *woman* he had seen at least twice at the tower, once as he looked up at her from the

284

ground, then secondly as he returned the favour. He knew who she was now.

"Who, mate?" asked Stuart.

"I think maybe when you lost Celia, she *did* run to the tower and somehow got herself up to the top. A woman was waving like mad down at someone. Maybe me, maybe Gerry. Maybe warning *me* about *Gerry*. She was dressed in white you say?"

Stuart nodded.

"Pink cravat thing. I think it's a cravat any rate," he said.

"Shit," said Palmer, uncharacteristically again.

"You just missed her too?" Stuart asked.

Palmer nodded. He knew why Celia was so erratic. Anyone in her condition off their meds was bound to be like that. Palmer had seen her off that medication the night she'd attacked him, but as he had indirectly caused her to not take the medicine, it was the least he could do to not press charges against her. Now she was roaming around Lisbon, similarly out of her mind and Palmer knew why. Whilst he had never stalked her round the streets of Sheffield, or assaulted her in an alleyway, he *had* seen her earlier that evening and he *had* potentially caused her some of the pain which had later ensued. Whilst she was drunk (ridiculously earlier, barely 4pm) and her attention distracted by a tight trousered barista (an attempt to sober up in a branch of Costa in the city centre), Palmer had delved into her handbag, tampered with her tablets and replaced some of them with a similar-looking placebo. He had only wanted Celia to make a spectacle of herself.

All of this was his fault.

57.

Palmer cursed himself that the very hotel he suspected Celia was now in, was the one closest to his own hotel. She had most likely been there the whole time he had been in Lisbon too, but he simply couldn't see how she could have been roaming around like she had been the last few days without someone seeing her. But then, was anyone *really* looking that hard for her? It wasn't that he doubted the Portuguese authorities, but a missing middle-aged woman with no family, no kids was hardly as glamorous or headline grabbing as a missing child or backpacker. She hadn't even gone missing *in* the country, and it wasn't 100% confirmed she had ever gone to Lisbon, so Palmer had to fathom the bizarre idea that she may well have been living in this hotel for the last few months. What she was doing for money was a mystery. Her accounts hadn't been touched since she'd drawn that last £30 out on the night she vanished, a sum just enough for a local taxi ride but not enough for escaping the country. If she had savings, they were well hidden. The hotel Palmer was staying in wasn't cheap (he *had* secured himself a good deal though) and that was further out of the centre, so potentially less pricey than the one he was currently standing in the foyer of.

Stuart was wittering on a little and Palmer found it disconcerting how quickly his opinion of the man swiftly dropped and became hostile or belittling. It was as if he was subconsciously starting to resent how easy it was to be in the man's company. Palmer didn't *do* company. He did solitude and alone time and chosen isolation. Never loneliness though. What was there to be lonely about? Stuart kept repeating something about needing a vacation which turned out to be a quote from a movie Palmer had heard of but not seen properly. That was one mystery cleared up at least. Palmer thought it best to keep Stuart

286

down here in the foyer on lookout whilst he limped his way around the hotel. He wasn't intent on searching every floor, not now he had been reminded of Gerry's condescension, but rather, he would start at the top and work his way down. The most obvious floor for both an aloof megalomaniac and a woman hiding out from the world was the top floor – the one fewest people would ever encounter. If the room belonged to Gerry or Celia or both of them, somehow working together in twisted harmony, Palmer would find it up there, he felt certain. The room key arriving in the strange birthday card was either a supremely cryptic clue, or the work of someone deranged. Either idea pointed toward Celia, but Palmer still couldn't get his head round the last pieces of this mystery.

He left Stuart on guard and went to the lift which was much more plush than that in his own hotel. No one else was using it, so he slumped slightly against the wall and jabbed the button for the highest level. The lift wouldn't take long he thought, but he took a moment to look at the object he was clutching in his hands – the birthday card sent to him with the room key. He had slipped it out of his bag as they had sat and waited in the foyer, not wanting to look silly by poring over it with Stuart breathing down his neck. He looked at the message inside again:

'Birthdays are a special time for sharing love and sharing life,

A father who's as great as you deserves the best, that much is true,

I hope you have a special day that's wonderful in every way!'

The light in the lift was harsh and revealing and Palmer suddenly noticed something he hadn't seen before. Someone had very lightly, but deliberately traced over some of the printed letters in faint reddish ink, just as with the Belem pamphlet. Holding the card up so that the bright light shone through the thin card, he could now see which letters were emphasised, almost embossed:

*'Birthdays are a special time for **sa**ring love a**n**d sh**a**ring **li**fe,*

*A father who**'s** as great as you deserves the **b**est, that much is true,*

*I hope you have a special day that's w**o**nderful in every w**a**y!'*

Clearly, emphatically singled out were the letters which spelled out *Sana Lisboa*, the same bloody hotel he had now decided to search after close to two days of timewasting. The key might not have specified which hotel, but the imprinted message certainly did.

As the lift arrived at the top floor, Palmer went to reach for his shoulder bag to put the card away and found it missing. He had left it in the foyer, totally unguarded, potentially prime for invasion by an enemy, or worse, an ally, like Stuart. He should go straight back down, but as he was about to step back into the lift and return, he heard a strange groaning sound from down the hall. He *had* to find out, as by the time he returned, the sound might be gone. It sounded feminine but old and weary and for all the world like the disapproving noise Celia Payne used to make when she received advice she didn't care for or didn't get her own way. He hobbled down the corridor after the source of the noise.

About halfway down the corridor before it branched off into three, a room door was propped open. It could have been a maid at work, but there was no cleaning cart anywhere in sight, and the noises were louder and slightly disturbing. Palmer cautiously stepped into the entrance and saw Celia Payne on her hands and knees at the side of the bed, wailing. He glanced back into the corridor and saw no one else approaching, so he moved into the room and let the door slowly close. He caught the edge to push it to with as little noise as possible. There was nowhere for her to run now. The room was a mess and Palmer couldn't work out who it even belonged to. There were men's clothes strewn across the bed, then on the floor by what must have been the bathroom entrance, female underwear, not especially Celia's style, but who knew?

Palmer was contemplating sneaking right up on her, but it was as if she sensed his approach and leapt up, emitting a single, piercing scream which Palmer hoped hadn't travelled very far. Her eyes were brimming with tears which spilled out now as she stood shaking, her hands balled up into impotent fists at her waist.

"You!" she screamed, less violently than the first noise.

"Yes Celia, it's me. Edward," he replied, quietly and calmly, hoping that his placid tone would rub off on her.

"All the fucking men in my life show up here to…do I *don't* know *what* with me!" she screeched and Palmer couldn't help but grimace.

She was manic, fearful and agitated but also seemingly erotically charged, as if she was actually aroused by the potential. She was half-dressed, the white floaty outfit from earlier half torn off and her bare shoulder visible. Her skin was pale beneath her clothing but the parts normally on display were brown and mottled, almost sun damaged. She had *not* been in hiding it seemed.

"You're still off your meds, I see," Palmer observed neutrally.

He knew he might have been to blame for this a few months ago, but surely she was onto a different supply of medicine by now? She had taken all sorts of pills for her various problems whilst he had known her: diazepam for anxiety, temazepam for insomnia, fluoxetine for depression and norethindrone for her hormonal issues. And those were just the ones he had been vaguely aware of before all this kicked off. He felt sure there had perhaps been mention of clozapine or olanzapine for what he suspected as a psychotic break. When Celia was fully loaded up on the right medication, she was almost her vicious, bitchy self. Off them, she was erratic and dangerous.

"And don't *you* know it!" she howled, charging at him, placing her hands on his shoulders.

Her flesh was spilling out of her dress and it wasn't pretty. Palmer tried to feel pity for her, but he couldn't.

"Which men, Celia?" he asked, hoping she was clear minded enough to give him something he could work with.

"Oh, *all the men*!" she said, suddenly flirty, pushing him aside and turning back to the bed where she plonked herself down.

"Like who?" Palmer pressed.

"Oh, Gerry, of course, he never got over me," she began, counting off on one hand.

Her eyes were glazed over as if she'd been drinking and there was drool at the corner of her mouth. Palmer found it hard to believe men were queuing up for anything other than to feel sorry for her.

"Then there's *you*," she said, pointing at him with an imaginary gun and pulling the trigger as she winked at him.

Palmer shuddered.

"And that Stuart bloke of yours," she added. "Oh Eddy!"

She slapped her thighs and then ran her hands right up to her crotch.

"I feel bad that I turned you, y'know," she went on. "That Stuart is *no good* for you! I forbid it!"

Palmer didn't have time to decipher her ramblings or put up with her

289

innuendos. He needed to act quickly and find out anything he could from her which might help him out. Perhaps Celia could be encouraged to cooperate if they made it a game.

"Right, Celia," he began, doubting success. "We're going to play a game."

"Ooh goody!" she said, clapping her hands together and leaping up again. "Postman's knock? Kiss chase?"

As she stepped forward, Palmer automatically backed away, right into the door.

"No, not those, Celia," Palmer said, trying not to upset her. "Not yet, anyway. First we play *find the tablets*. Do you know that one?"

Celia looked cross now.

"We can't play that, silly sausage!" she said huffily.

"Why not?" Palmer asked cautiously.

He knew she *had* to have meds. There was no way she could run around town like this without drawing attention to herself.

"Because that horrible man has hidden them!" she declared. "Thrown them in the river he reckoned." She looked glumly at the floor, then looked up at Palmer, a question mark etched across her entire face. "And I don't know why you think you can help me, Eddy," she continued. "You took my tablets that time in the cafe! I saw you!"

58.

Celia was easier to manipulate than he had thought she would be. All the while, the image of haughty Gerry Payne flashed through his mind and if he had been truly plagued by that human flaw, the conscience, he might have felt more guilty about his actions. She was completely unpredictable, cooperative one minute, screaming bloody murder the next, but he was at least able to lead her on what she thought was going to be some sort of pleasurable afternoon out with him. She clearly hung onto fragments of that woefully misplaced desire she had for him and whilst it helped him steer her his way, it made his flesh crawl. He had always thought of Celia as a particularly ugly example of the female condition. Not outwardly, he was barely aware of boring matters like lust or desire, but deep inside her. She was unpleasant even as he had been helping her, cruel as he tried to bring her some modicum of peace in her life and oh so bitter when he had rejected her clumsy advances. Now, it was far too easy to lie to her that he was taking her out for a romantic trip to finally confess his feelings for her. All she had to do was follow him to the letter, and not, under any circumstances, talk about what she *thought* she might have seen regarding him and her tablets, which was clearly just all in her fevered imagination!

A quick search of the room yielded no medication and Celia tired of that particular game very quickly. She kept laughing about how silly it was to try and *find* her medicine when he had been the one who took it. It worried him that she had suddenly revealed this little nugget amidst all the chaos as it meant she was perhaps likely to drop it into any future conversation with the authorities about her disappearance, either deliberately, mischievously, or accidentally and damagingly. It might not matter much in the long run, given she had suddenly resurfaced after three months on the missing persons list, but for Palmer to have been identified as meddling with her medication was not something he wanted to have to explain. And it contradicted his alibi, which then left him open to all sorts of other accusations. Celia might be seemingly intact, but who knew what a medical examination might throw up. If Gerry or someone else had been holding her here, abusing her in whatever way, then Palmer might stand accused of being a part of it. He bitterly regretted the rash action of the medicine tampering, but she had threatened him about the bar incident again, suggesting she could spin a pretty tale about how he had been hassling her and make her seem to be the innocent victim lashing out, unless he met her odd demands.

He knew that Celia was off on a mad night out with friends, that she would assume the illusion of drinking heavily, but in reality stick to non-alcoholic drinks and mocktails without letting on, such was her pride. She didn't want people to know what a mess she was, least of all her ageing party friends, but Palmer now suspected that once he had swiped her pills, she had perhaps lost some of her self-control and actually started drinking which might have muddied her memories somewhat. Finding her tablets or at least *something* which might restore some balance to her faculties would make life easier, but Palmer had to give up, noticing how long he had been up in the room with Stuart left downstairs.

Each time he tried to question her about her movements back in July or over the last few days, about the postcard, the room key, the messages and the pamphlet, she merely giggled at him and called him silly, as if he were making then whole thing up. It was only when he reached out to grab her wrist as she stumbled getting up from the bed (against his better judgement too – he never touched *anyone* if he could avoid it) that she gasped in shock and pain and Palmer noticed the bruising all along her arm.

"Who did this, Celia?" he asked to no avail.

She merely wittered on about *him* again and left Palmer uncertain as to who she meant and why she wouldn't speak. At the mention of Gerry's name, she shuddered, but with a look of exaggerated disgust rather than fear and she spat on the carpet upon hearing Jon Scott Campbell's name as if the very words were a curse to her. Palmer gently inspected her whilst she was calmer again and found evidence of her having been bound in some way, possibly rope or some sort of fibre.

"Were you kept here, Celia?" he asked.

She nodded with a terrified look in her eyes now and Palmer wondered how any of that had worked, with hotel guests either side and maids calling in on the room.

"Jeep's secret," she slurred, enigmatically.

"Jeep? Like G.P.?" Palmer asked. "Gerry, you mean?"

He had no idea if Celia had such a strange nickname for her own ex-husband, but he could imagine the power trip a man like Gerry would get from imprisoning his own ex-wife, the woman he blamed for his breakdown and fall from grace. And yet, it didn't seem to fit.

She shook her head and drifted off again and Palmer swore under his breath that her lucid moments were so few and far between.

He quickly combed the rest of the room and whilst there were plenty of men's items scattered around, there was nothing telling in any way. The clothes were smaller than Gerry's size and a little more stylish than his tweedy academic look. In the bathroom, Palmer found strands of the fibre which he thought had been used to tie Celia up and a red pen stuffed in the bin under the sink. Surely the pen which had amended the secret message to his earlier summons. He now felt certain that Celia had been kept here and messages had been sent by her captor, but that somehow she had still managed to sabotage their efforts by leaving her own messages and instructions for rescue. She was a formidable woman. But how had she managed any of this whilst in this state? He couldn't imagine Celia only 24 hours earlier having the wherewithal to layer a coded message into the Belem pamphlet ready for it to be slid under his door.

Palmer was about to admit temporary defeat in solving this particular mystery and guide Celia out on their afternoon of fun when he noticed that behind her feet, carefully stowed under the bed, was a small clutch bag. It was pink and white and matched the outfit she had on. He moved towards her, indicating at the bag and she looked alarmedly at him.

"No!" she cried and kicked the bag under the bed,

"Celia, *please*!" Palmer urged, and got down to look under the bed as she began gasping, threatening to hyperventilate.

Once he was on the floor, she leapt up and gave him a savage kick right in the already damaged knee ligament and for a few moments, Palmer knew he had blacked out from the pain. Everything went white, then black and when his eyes opened again, Celia was scrabbling on her hands and knees, retrieving

293

the bag and seeming ready to flee.

"Please," Palmer groaned.

Celia glanced down at him and it was as if she was seeing him for the first time all over again.

"Eddy?" she cried, moving to his side, the bag in her hand. "Who did this to you?"

Palmer groaned again and she laid a hand sadly on his face. This mixed up woman clung onto some genuine feelings of affection toward him. It was sickening, but he ought to have found it touching.

"I've got something in here to help you," she said, scrabbling inside the clutch bag and Palmer saw small plastic bags, like those used to send kids off to school with their sandwiches preserved in their packed lunch, except that these were brimming full of different shaped, sized and coloured tablets.

Probably every type of tablet she had ever taken and then some. Had whoever was keeping her here simply not noticed this small bag, secreted away under the bed, or was this another part of their game, playing a strange sort of Russian roulette with the tablets? Palmer didn't fancy anything she was about to offer him, but as she popped out two tablets and placed them in his slightly unwilling hand, he recognised them clearly as something analogous to paracetamol.

"Thank you Celia," he said, hauling himself up and onto the edge of the bed.

Celia sat next to him, then noticing him deliberating over the tablets, she dashed and fetched him a glass of water from the bathroom.

"Do you have something in there for *you* to take?" he asked, nodding at the clutch bag.

"Jeep says I mustn't," she whispered confidentially. "He mixed everything up to keep me confused, but I can still tell everything from the shape and size."

She sounded proud, and Palmer remembered the once-arrogant woman who had so very much suited Gerry in her own levels of confidence and superiority. She had been a whizz at problem solving, puzzles and memory games. And now she was a shadow of her former self, but still had glimpses of brilliance.

"Find some to calm yourself," Palmer instructed. "Just so that we can enjoy ourselves this afternoon," he added as she looked nervous.

"A date?" she asked suspiciously and Palmer doubted he could truly convince her of his supposed romantic intentions.

"More of a reckoning," he corrected. "Settling scores with those men who've wronged you."

Whoever they bloody are! He hoped she might finally reveal something useful. Palmer's plan was to take her down to the lobby, see what Stuart thought was best, and if no other plan presented itself, simply hand Celia over to the local authorities and leave it for them to pursue. Job done.

He took the tablets, knowing they were safe and watched as buoyed by his trust of her, she did the same, taking the glass from his hand and sipping it to swallow whatever pills she had. For all he knew, they were painkillers like his, given she kept them hidden from him, but he hoped they were something more sturdy. He knew the response wouldn't be instant, chemistry and biology were far more cautious, but there was a change in her as she turned to him, this time with a warm smile.

"Right, Eddy, you gorgeous thing, let's go paint the town red," she said.

59.

It was one thing getting Celia out of the room and into the lift; it was another thing getting her out of the lift into the lobby. Palmer tried not to lean too heavily on his newly awakened wound or to show that anything had happened to him in case anyone was watching. He had carefully closed the hotel room door and out of curiosity, tried the key card against the reader, totally not expecting anything to happen. The light stayed red on the reader and Palmer wondered whether the card itself was cancelled by now after weeks of being buffeted around in the post, through various scanners and so on, or if the card just wasn't for this door. He had helped Celia to cover up her modesty by adding a white jacket to the ensemble but as they stepped into the bright glare of the hallway, she had insisted on pulling the cravat up around her face, covering her mouth as if somehow she was only recognisable from the nose down. He hoped she obeyed his instructions and he hoped she didn't mention the medication.

"C'mon Celia," said Palmer, mainly for anyone listening rather than for her sake. "We need to sort all of this out, like I told you upstairs. Please step out of the lift."

Stuart had come up to investigate which Palmer had thought might happen, but he didn't know how Celia would respond to another set of eyes upon her. The minute she noticed him, she regressed noticeably and started trying to get the lift to go back up. It was all Palmer could do to blockade the lift doors.

"You found 'er!" cried Stuart, slightly sounding like he'd had no faith in Palmer at all. "It's me again, Celia. Sorry I scared you earlier."

296

Palmer wondered just how scared Celia had been, as nervous as she was and as ridiculously erratic and paranoid, it had to be said that Stuart could actually be quite intimidating, being burly and stern faced. The fact he could suddenly switch to a goofy grin and that beneath the muscle (and the fat) he was a big teddy bear might have been lost on someone who hadn't got to know him properly. Celia looked like she wasn't about to give him a chance.

"C'mon Celia," Palmer repeated, holding out a hand now for her to take.

He sensed that the initial boost had started to wane and the medicine had not yet kicked in (if it was every going to), so he tried to appeal to her in terms of them spending some time together again. She seemed very open to him flirting despite knowing somewhere in the back of her mind or the bits of her heart not completely dead, that it would go nowhere.

"We'll go for a stroll, talk about old times. It'll be lovely," Palmer added, and she eventually reached out to take his hand before hurling herself into his arms.

He loathed the feeling of her, sweaty and heaving and so so womanly against his chest that it made him feel queasy. Looking round at Stuart, hoping he would save him, but caught a strange look in his eye which resembled guilt. What had happened between the two of them near the tower, he wondered?

"That's a good girl," Palmer said, remembering how he'd seen a frightened horse led out on a leash amidst noisy protesters once in the city centre.

Celia clearly wasn't a horse, but she swiftly devolved to animal stature each time she faced a setback. Someone had made her like this, beyond switching medicine or belittling their spouse. It was bizarre.

Stuart broke his gaze and wandered off to the woman at reception and Palmer scowled. Was the man on the pull? The woman was looking like she was definitely up for some action with him and as he studied them, he could see they were building on earlier interactions whilst he had been upstairs trying to calm Celia down. They appeared to be chatting about a phone, Stuart's phone it seemed, which she handed to him. Perhaps he'd been charging it. Perhaps there was something more going on. Paranoia again.

"You ok, Celia?" Palmer whispered.

She gazed up at him, still in his arms and looked like she absolutely despised him. As if the façade of playing a deranged woman had momentarily slipped and she was now her true self again. She quickly looked away, as if she was aware her act was not convincing him any longer and Palmer had to check his rampant imagination again. Either she truly was fucked up by mental illness and a bad case of no/too much/the wrong medication, or she was the greatest actress of her generation.

"'Cos if you're messing me about, *again*, I'll bloody get you for this, y'know," he hissed under his breath, not sure if she was even capable of understanding his words right then.

The look had vanished from her face as soon as it had appeared and it was almost as if he had never been intended to see it, or that his ridiculously overactive imagination had conjured up the vision of a steely eyed manipulative Celia, so totally at odds with the wreck of a woman she currently was again.

He spotted his shoulder bag by the seats they had waited in and leaned to collect it, Celia's arms still about him. Had his companion left the bag and its contents be, or had he, as Palmer would have been, tempted to sneak a look? Palmer also wondered what Stuart had actually been up to the whole time and what he was now discussing with the receptionist. It made him feel awkward. Not jealous, just irritated. *Was Stuart taking any of this as seriously as he was?*

As he led Celia out into the fresh air and discovered the storm had intensified to the point of a heavy, humid deluge, finally Stuart joined them properly, idly watching the traffic driving by in the rain.

"We need to get to that *elevador* down in town," he explained at last. "I overheard a message from Jon Scott Campbell inviting *someone* there from this hotel. Do you think it was...?" He nodded at Celia, almost afraid to include her in their conversation.

Palmer had to wonder who might be leaving messages for Celia, given the state she was in. It seemed like a fruitless task and one not guarantee to reap results. If someone wanted her to meet them, it would have been easier to come and see her at the hotel which they clearly knew she was at, if the message was actually for her. Could Gerry or the mysterious 'Jeep' be also staying here, either in her room, or an adjoining one, perhaps. Those male clothes had to belong to *someone*. And how was Celia roaming around getting herself all tanned and such if she was actually tied up in her room?!

"She's in no state for messages I'd say," said Palmer, not lying again, but not 100% sure what he was saying so definitely was the truth. "She has lucid moments, but she needs help. I say we take her with us, purely to keep an eye on her, but I'm not sure she's up to a confrontation like that."

Palmer really couldn't make his mind up about the woman. Was she truly suffering, or just trying to make everyone else around her suffer? The way she had painted Gerry as a cunning abuser had been swiftly undermined by his first and latest encounter with the blundering buffoon and there was the way she had covered up various workplace indiscretions so brazenly. He hoped the truth was something in the middle: that she was a medicated mess, but that there was also something else going on behind the scenes. Whoever had summoned a resident of this hotel to the *elevador*, it seemed likely they meant business. Palmer hated heights, but if it meant an end to this particular conundrum, he'd be happy to scale them all.

60.

Palmer's hearing was the one faculty he thought would last the longest. His eyesight was already verging on appalling and only a pair of rarely worn spectacles with one incredibly strong lens in the right eye and a minimal prescription in the other saved him from not being able to drive safely. His knees were repeatedly knackered, particularly on this occasion and he cursed that his fitness levels were nowhere near those he had enjoyed in his youth. His memory, once sharp and close to photographic, now had big embarrassing holes in it, often presenting themselves mid-idea or worse, mid-sentence and he found himself relying more on more on his notebook or at a push, technology. But his hearing was fantastic. If he closed his eyes and shut out the mindless white noise and inane chatter around him, he could satisfactorily eavesdrop on people at the other side of a busy room. He could hear students whispering under their breath, smug in their undetected blasphemies whilst still keeping remote and right now, atop the nausea-inducing *elevador*, at the centre of a Lisboan maelstrom of wind and rain, he could hear Jon and Celia's conversation.

The taxi ride to the *elevador* had been a strange one, with the constant whirring of the wipers punctuating the odd silence and then almost forming a metronomic rhythm to Celia's strange outbursts. She had claimed to recognise Stuart by name now, which surprised Palmer, and demanded he be removed from her presence. It wasn't just that she was intimidated by him as before, it was that she was disgusted by him. But also thrilled. She seemed intent that Stuart wanted her and had plucked a bizarrely specific person from her remembrances that Stuart now seemed to be accused of denying being. Stuart looked to Palmer for help, him being in the front seat at Celia's insistence and

Palmer half-cuddling, half-restraining the woman in the back. Palmer shrugged. His instinct would have been to play along to see what, if any, value could come from the charade, but he didn't think Stuart that game.

She quickly gave up, sitting back in her seat in a huff and began to whisper to Palmer some obscenities about what she would like to do to him. He wasn't quick to embarrassment but he felt his neck reddening and his collar becoming tighter. Palmer didn't *do* sexual tension and he sure as hell was *not* comfortable with her sexually charged and in close proximity. She then began to describe in lurid detail an encounter they had supposedly shared and it was only as she concluded the erotic anecdote that Palmer noted a reference to his freckled back which he assumed was either Gerry or some other lover during her teaching days. Palmer had wanted to fully inspect the clutch bag she had, but she would not relinquish it. He wasn't sure how dangerous she could be, but he couldn't shake the idea that that petite purse could easily conceal a small gun or a knife, or less pessimistically, but still an issue, a phone or something to aid her escape should she suddenly bolt.

"That husband of mine will have a *lot* to answer for!" she snapped loudly now and Stuart turned and rolled his eyes at Palmer as if her behaviour was *his* fault.

"Are you expecting him?" Palmer had asked, not even expecting a sensible reply as this was the fourth or fifth time she had declared as such.

She fell silent again and the cab reached its destination. Noticing the rain for the first time, she complained loudly about this being her husband's fault again and made her cravat mask into a headscarf now. She looked like Marilyn Monroe, Palmer thought, right towards the miserable end.

"What now?" Stuart asked.

Palmer suggested they ascend as high as they could (thinking that each step would be a lightning bolt of pain through his skull) and wait for whoever had summoned whoever they had summoned. It wasn't the *best* plan, he had to admit, but if Jon Scott Campbell was summoning people here, it seemed an endgame was in sight. Loathing the authorities as much as he did, there was still a part of him which considered calling the police and watching from down here to see if the maniac could be apprehended. For what crimes, he was unsure, but Stuart seemed certain he was a serial assaulter of women, was linked to organised crime within the city and had been behind some of their problems in the last few days, perhaps the burglary or his own tumble down the metro steps. At the very least, even if Jon didn't show up, or eluded the police, they could hand Celia over to them and be done with her. At the

301

mention of Jon's name, he saw Celia flinch slightly. Her responses, or her *performances*, were inconsistent. Either the meds were working, or her façade was cracking. Stuart looked at him with what seemed like sadness in his eyes. The big, dumb animal.

At the top, they took what little shelter there was away from the closed main entrance to the upper platform (the weather had shut down the whole lift system for now) and it didn't take long before the slinking shape of Jon Scott Campbell moved past them. Palmer found it odd to deliberately see him now, not as a seemingly accidental crossing of paths or a manipulated manoeuvre, but intentionally, purposefully face to face with him. He looked much smaller than the bogeyman figure in his mind, perhaps set against the larger figures of Gerry and the masked burglar he actually *was* small, but he looked like a coiled spring, like a wild thing ready to run or to attack. His eyes were beady and narrowed and the rain had drenched him to the point of his clothes being plastered against his lean body. Honed musculature was visible and whereas before there was something vaguely rakish or handsome about him, he looked sinewy and haunted now. Deranged perhaps. He howled out at Celia, seeming to ignore the two of them standing in front of her.

Stuart noticeably tensed and began flexing his own muscles. Palmer really had had the measure of him wrong as he noticed the enormous bicep lurking beneath Stuart's sleeve. It did nothing to dent Scott Campbell's resolve as he simply hurled insults at them, calling them suckers, numbering them as if he had his own system of tracking the idiots in his life. Celia was not impressed by Stuart's standing in her defence and made to brush him aside. She was the only one here who actually knew the man, Palmer realised.

"Celia, you don't have to do this," he pointed out, wondering what exactly she hoped would come from the confrontation.

The man had most likely attacked dozens of women and the little issue of eyewitnesses didn't seem to be an issue to him in his current rage.

"That *bastard* has a lot to answer for," Celia replied, her voice sounding almost like her old self.

He had used her and abandoned her during their teaching careers, both now long out of the profession, but was there more to it? Had he claimed her as another of his assault victims and it had gone unreported? Caught between Gerry and Jon, no wonder the woman had lost it. Turning to Palmer for comfort was just another misstep and he had become another man in her life who had let her down.

302

"Let 'er do this, 'arry mate," said Stuart and Palmer wondered what *he* thought she was capable of.

Palmer reluctantly nodded his consent and Celia stepped from between them. He knew he would be useless should things turn physical but gave Stuart the order to be ready to spring into action.

"Looking very alive for a dead woman," howled Jon.

This was odd, as if this was the first time he had seen her in Portugal, as if he too believed her dead. Not what Palmer had expected at all.

"Jon Scott Campbell," Celia called back as she stepped through the puddles on the walkway. "I've thought about this moment for a long time but I didn't quite imagine it like this."

Palmer watched as they moved closer and began to almost circle one another like predators before a fight. They were speaking much more quietly now the distance had closed, too quietly to be properly heard above the storm. Knowing that Stuart had his eyes on the scene, Palmer dared to close his and narrow down his sensory experience to audio only. At first, just snatches of tone and emotion filtered through, but then as he lifted out layer after layer of interference and tuned himself in to their two quite different pitches, he found he could hear every word.

"Did you know I was here when you came here?" Jon was asking angrily.

"Of course, Jon," purred Celia. "We all followed your *progress* with interest."

"I might have helped cover up your sordid little fling," she said scathingly. "But I never expected you to be so fucking consumed with lust to take the dozy tart with you!"

Which dozy tart was this? Another of his victims?

"How is young *Julie* these days?" Celia sneered. "I hear you married the little trollop."

Jon was married?! Palmer couldn't imagine it. He might have been a catch physically speaking, but the man was a monster. Then again, monsters wore masks. He knew this only too well.

"How insane are you, Celia?" Jon asked. "Insane enough to follow me around? Insane enough to get my phone number and harass me? Insane enough to use a *voice changer?"*

So Celia was *more in control than they'd thought. Was she in turn menacing this maniac?* It was a dangerous game she was playing and Palmer struggled to hear now as another sound broke through his filtering, a sound of groaning machinery below.

"What do we do, 'arry?" hissed Stuart and Palmer fought the instinct to berate him, knowing he had heard nothing of the conversation and had probably assumed he too was ignorant.

Instead, he shrugged and tilted his head to indicate the new sound's direction. At once, they both realised it was the lift.

"Who's comin'?" Stuart whispered and Palmer thought he detected fear in his companion now.

Whoever was about to arrive had either been invited by Jon Scott Campbell or else they had simply tracked one or all of them and come to deliver some sort of reckoning. Palmer dealt mainly in anxiety and paranoia rather than fear, but he felt his innards clench as he prepared for whoever was now clanging up the spiral metal staircase.

61.

Minutes later they were on the roof, Palmer dizzy and losing his composure, threatened by the lurking mafioso types who had some issue with Scott Campbell, and then moments after that, the sickening and ridiculous sight of the head of this criminal faction impaling his own neck on the machete he had clumsily wielded. Palmer could barely keep himself from heaving now. But Scott Campbell fled into the night and Palmer knew he would not be able to maintain the pace to catch him. He hadn't told Stuart about his new injury but figured he must have noticed. Celia appeared mesmerised by the blood pooling around the fallen man. Whatever happened, they couldn't linger here any longer.

The sense of urgency meaning they needed to leave was matched in its intensity by the utter disappointment of these men being no one he recognised, other than from the park earlier that morning. No big reveal like at the end of a classy murder mystery or even an old *Scooby Doo*. Just a bunch of faceless thugs who couldn't even stage a hit properly.

"We have to go," said Palmer, urging the transfixed woman to move. "Celia, my dear, we have to go."

Pulling her practically all the way down the stairs, one painful step at a time, Palmer was glad to see Stuart keeping an eye on the men kneeling around their fallen boss. He was still in protection mode, but he had lingered a little longer than Palmer would have expected and when he caught up with them on the lower level, he seemed secretive. The *elevador* staff were standing around looking alarmed but Stuart yelled out that they were police agents and that

305

they were in pursuit of the culprit – Jon Scott Campbell. It was something Palmer himself might have done, so he was momentarily impressed at the improvisation. Reaching the street level, they could see Scott Campbell was only a few hundred metres ahead, himself in some degree of pain which had slowed his progress given the way he was awkwardly hurrying along. Stuart looked down at Palmer's legs and didn't even need to voice his concerns. They both knew he wasn't up to a long chase on any kind. Nor was Celia, now distractedly tugging at Palmer's sleeve to go in the opposite direction. They had to make a quick call.

"Stuart, would you please check on the rough direction he's going and we'll catch you up?" Palmer asked. "I think he'll be going down to the Tagus."

He nodded down the street and hoped Stuart would hurry to the end and at least see which way Scott Campbell had gone, whether it was down towards the river or back up into the city. Before he obliged, he nodded towards Celia with a raised eyebrow.

"I'll grab a cab," Palmer said.

The rain was lifting and he could see a couple of taxis just over the road waiting for business to pick up again. He would pay one handsomely to take Celia back and Stuart said he would phone the girl on the desk at the hotel to keep an eye out for her. He really was a charmer, it seemed.

Taking advantage of the moments alone with Celia, Palmer had made his mind up. Whatever problems she was going through, she was capable enough of running rings around her captor and tormentors and even now was presenting a false persona.

"The game's up, Celia, dear," he said. "Cut the crap."

She looked at him disgustedly now, the same face that her ex-husband Gerry wore so quickly and so often.

"I reckon you came here alone, sure of your little plans, to get away from the men in your life, but one of them caught up with you, tried to control you and you went along with it until you could get the upper hand, just like you always do," Palmer theorised. "You were always capable of putting up with a lot of *shit* if it meant you got to the rhubarb eventually."

He wasn't sure where the horticultural metaphor had come from, or what purpose it even signified here and now in this drizzly Iberian street a world away from an English allotment, but for a moment he thought of the overgrown rhubarb patch near his mother's house.

"You're going back to the hotel, and then back to England. You're going to tell everyone the truth about what happened to you and no playing the mental illness card. You *do* have problems, but some of them you've caused yourself and others you've outright *lied* about."

Palmer knew he sounded harsh now, but spitting these words through gritted teeth at Celia was actually helping distract from the pain of his knee. He realised Stuart was almost back now and walked Celia roughly across the road to the first taxi. Celia had said nothing in response to him now. She was either stunned or playing dumb. He didn't care which.

"'e's 'eadin' for the river as you thought, pal," said Stuart, panting and dripping with rainwater.

"Good," said Palmer. "Will you mind Celia a moment whilst I speak to this cab driver?"

He ordinarily loathed trying to speak to taxi drivers. They were bad enough in England, let alone the added language barrier, but he needed to make sure Celia got where she was supposed to be going. Money exchanged hands and the driver nodded. Stuart had made his phone call and was messing with the damaged handset as Palmer walked back over to escort Celia. He was certain they'd been talking, which he found odd as she had been so quiet a moment before.

"Off you go," said Palmer, manhandling her into the back seat.

As the taxi drove off, Celia seemed to blow a kiss at him and he flinched, but was distracted by Stuart enthusiastically waving to her. He was a strange man.

"Do we get the other taxi after Jon, mate?" he asked.

Palmer shook his head. The streets of Lisbon were well-known to Jon it seemed and a taxi might soon lose him down a side street. They would pursue him on foot and rely on Stuart's superior sense of direction. His knee pains had lessened a bit thanks to the tablets he had taken earlier and it was then that he realised Celia hadn't pursed her lips in a kiss at all. She had mouthed the word "pills".

62.

Palmer was glad they hadn't relied on a taxi to pursue Jon Scott Campbell as he zigzagged his way through the narrow and lesser known streets but still headed in the direction of the river. He was further relieved that they hadn't brought Celia along with them as her final mouthed word to him seemed to suggest she wasn't going to easily give up on the idea that he had done something to her tablets a few months ago. Compared to what the likes of Gerry and Jon and this elusive 'Jeep' had done, it was small fry, but still definitely rash and cruel and would not look good in the eyes of anyone who discovered the truth. The one thing Palmer was *not* glad about though was the fact that his leg pain was not fading away quickly enough for his liking. However long the painkillers he'd had took to work, it would not be fast enough to save him from the lumbering agony of trying to keep up. Occasionally Stuart would glance back at him and the wry grimaces he returned were not fooling him any longer. He must have known the time was almost up for Palmer's continued mobility.

"I've got an idea," he said, pausing on the corner by a large government-type building from where they could see the pink and ginger shape of Scott Campbell disappear into the distance.

He related his plan to summon his earlier saviour, the Uber Eats delivery boy, back into action, that despite the obvious relying on the young chap's hot blood and his highly dangerous riding style, it might be just what they needed to catch up with their prey. Palmer wasn't convinced it would work, so was amazed when Stuart got through to him very quickly and despite the language barrier, managed to negotiate his services. It seemed obvious to Palmer that

308

they could simply *pretend* they needed a delivery from somewhere and the lad could *pretend* to oblige, if he needed it all to be above board.

In the surprisingly short time between hanging up and this eager boy – Hugo, it transpired – turned up, the two men had chance to finally, properly ensure they had exchanged phone numbers. Given Scott Campbell had labelled them suckers, they entered their numbers as such and shared a brief moment of unity in both being foolishly lured to the city and manoeuvred around. Had they not been so easily dragged into affairs, they would never have met and Palmer had to admit, that even though this partnership was about to come to an end, his time in Lisbon wouldn't have been half as...well...*enjoyable*. Palmer had to admit that despite the fear and anxiety, the adrenaline rush of unravelling the mystery surrounding Celia, Gerry and Jon Scott Campbell had been addictive. He could tell that Stuart definitely felt the same way and then some. Palmer might have been inclined to say something complimentary to the man had they not been interrupted by the whine of a low horsepower engine.

Hugo the scooter driver was a handsome, brown skinned youth, probably barely twenty years of age, who was clearly not only motivated by business given the strange goofy look he had on his face as he took off his helmet and smiled at Stuart.

"Hey English," he said. "You ride?"

Palmer wondered what exactly had gone on with these two in his absence and whilst it wasn't quite jealousy he felt, there was definitely a sense of having missed out on something somewhere along the line. Hugo patted the back seat and Stuart laughed.

"Not me yet, fella," Stuart replied. "I need you to take my mate first please."

This was the part Palmer wasn't looking forward to. He hadn't been on a bike or a motorbike in years and didn't relish the freewheeling calamity which it brought with it. Hugo seemed to eye Palmer with suspicion now and for some reason Stuart felt he needed to point out they were only friends. Barely that really, Palmer thought.

He mounted the scooter stiffly and wondered what exactly he was supposed to hold onto. Surely not the lad himself? Stuart stood by him and patted his shoulder and whilst the intimacy was still uncalled for as far as he was concerned, he could see that it meant something to Stuart and so nodded in response. Hugo listened as Stuart gave him some half-understood instructions and a description of Scott Campbell, then arranged that he would be next to be picked up but that he would set off running behind them. With a jolt, the scooter pulled away like a rocket along the road. Palmer found his arms unwillingly around Hugo's midriff and winced at how damp his top was and how he could feel the muscles of his body heaving underneath it.

It didn't take them long to reach the *25 de Abril* bridge and they had already been able to see along the long straight highway, that Jon Scott Campbell had entered the base of one of the stanchions which was some sort of interactive exhibition it seemed. Hugo pulled up abruptly right outside the entrance and Palmer hobbled off. As he stepped up onto the pavement, he stumbled badly and Hugo insisted on dismounting himself and moving to help him up. Palmer felt woozy now, like he had missed a meal (which in truth he supposed, he had) and maybe shouldn't have had the tablets on an empty stomach. His legs didn't hurt quite so much he found, but that was mainly because he could barely feel them. He could barely feel anything at all.

"You two, you...*friends*?" Hugo asked, nodding back in the direction they had left Stuart.

He seemed a bright eyed honest young thing, perfectly matched with Stuart and Palmer realised that even if his companion was that way inclined, that they were due to leave the city behind soon enough and Hugo didn't seem to have a clue. It was easier to answer in the affirmative to the delivery boy rather than explain the rather complicated nature of their relationship and Hugo smiled at the response. Smitten, Palmer thought. Poor boy.

"You go back to him now," Palmer said, accidentally becoming like every Englishman overseas that he loathed, in speaking loudly in broken but accented English as if that magically made it understandable to non-native speakers.

"I go, sir," said Hugo loyally and he got back on the scooter but stayed and watched as Palmer entered the attraction before he walked the vehicle along and off in a different direction, presumably knowing of a shortcut to turn and get back to where he could intercept Stuart.

Palmer looked up just before he entered and he wished he hadn't. The bridge stanchion telescoped off above him like a dizzying jet of something fluid and intangible and the bridge itself then shot out in either direction threatening to come tumbling down upon him should he stay beneath it. He felt terribly terrible sick and had to lean against the counter as he reached it. The range of bad experiences up high combined with his injuries and the fact there was definitely something off about the painkiller he had taken made him feel weak and ready to collapse. He knew he had gone pale and felt sweat beading on his forehead. The nervous glance the woman at the desk gave him suggested he looked even worse than he felt and he doubted she would let him in even if he wanted to.

The woman was about to open her mouth, perhaps to ask if he was okay, when the lift doors across the room opened and another employee dashed out of it, walkie talkie in hand. Palmer couldn't quite make out what the issue was but the man seemed alarmed and was gesticulating up. Perhaps Jon Scott Campbell had already made a nuisance of himself here. Palmer doubted it would be so easy for him to gain access to wherever he had gone now. Maybe there was a different way up, via the bridge itself from wherever it connected with the land, which surely it had to?

Ignoring him now, the two staff members turned to study a bank of CCTV monitors and Palmer could just make out the grainy image of Jon Scott Campbell struggling against a strong breeze on an isolated gantry somewhere high up above the river. His hunch that this rendezvous would be somewhere up high had sadly been entirely correct.

"Eu acho que esse é o celular dele!" cried the employee, waving a phone in his hand.

It was certainly Scott Campbell's phone, from the way he was pointing at the screen and Palmer wondered how he had gained access to the upper reaches of the bridge but also lost his mobile in the process. Palmer had to act quickly.

"Excuse me," he said. "That's my friend. I need to get up and speak to him. I think he might do something silly."

He was as British and plummy accented as he could manage, using what he referred to disparagingly as the *Hugh Grant effect* whereby non-native English speakers could somehow understand an affected posh English voice like the movie actor better than any regional variation, but how also it disarmed and charmed them into cooperation.

"No, sir, no," said the man and the female employee looked horrified at the idea, presumably based on Palmer's whey faced expression on arrival.

"We call police," the woman added, reaching for a phone.

"Please," said Palmer, reaching over the desk and holding out a hand to try and block her use of the phone. *"Please.* Just give me ten minutes."

He mimed ten with both hands, then pointed at his watch. He didn't care if these staff members spoke perfect English, he wanted them to simply remember his silly British condescension and ignorance rather than anything specific about him. They would most likely still call the police or some sort of crack rescue team, especially if Scott Campbell was somewhere he wasn't supposed to be, but he needed to sound as inoffensive and unmemorable as he could for the moment. The image on the bank of screens switched to show a low angle of the upper road bridge with traffic rumbling silently over it, but Palmer could now see his quarry approaching another grey figure who could not be made out.

"Please," he said one last time and he could sense the man wavering.

He turned to the woman employee and they muttered. She wasn't happy but it seemed he had negotiated a stay of execution as she threw up her hands in frustration and backed away from the phone and turned to watch the screens. The man beckoned for Palmer to follow him to the lift and once inside, he turned a key in the control panel which allowed him to select a floor not ordinarily accessible by the experience it seemed. When the door opened on a howling, deafening gantry below the main road bridge, Palmer immediately regretted all this. He could simply *sense* how high they had climbed so quickly and it felt like they'd left the rational world behind.

"Be careful, sir," said the man, waving his hand out at the cluttered metal walkway.

"The phone?" Palmer asked, feeling there was nothing to lose in asking, and the man handed it to him.

He seemed as if he was going to wait for him there, but after he had lurched forward a few steps, the lift doors closed and the lift descended again. It felt as if the cold metal deck was rushing up towards him suddenly and Palmer realised he had tripped over something and fallen hard against the walkway. Everything was swaying violently and it wasn't clear what was real and what was simply imagined or feared. The phone had clattered to the ground out of his hand and unlocked right in front of his swimming eyes. An image, clearly the last one taken, appeared on the screen and Palmer wanted to be sick for a number of reasons. He realised that Celia mouthing "pills" was most likely because she had given him something far stronger than paracetamol, something which was making him feel even more sick and dizzy than the altitude, but also because he recognised the man in the photo on Jon Scott Campbell's phone. The image had been taken at the top of a high building somewhere, Palmer could see, and the subject of the photo seemed to have been caught off-guard, looking out of the corner of his eye with distrust. Palmer hadn't seen the man in the flesh in a good few months, but had been for a pint with him sometime back in late spring and had known him very well throughout their shared time at school together. As Palmer struggled to get back to his feet, all he could wonder was why did Jon Scott Campbell have a photo of his oldest friend, the psychiatric medical specialist George Davis?

63.

Aside from on television, an old terrifying news story about a monk making a protest in flickering monochrome, Palmer had never seen someone set themselves on fire before. The terrible smell which suggested not only the usual acrid smoke of accelerants burning, but of the fuel itself *cooking* – in this case, a person – was all-consuming. Even if it was that crazy bastard Jon Scott Campbell, Palmer couldn't tolerate it. It had to be brought to an end somehow, but there was nothing around of any remote usefulness and whilst time had slowed to a sickening crawl, valuable moments were still being lost if anything were to be done about this awful act of self-immolation.

The worst thing, Palmer decided, wasn't even the smell, or the sight itself, but the calmness with which Jon Scott Campbell had started the fire and the swiftness with which it had consumed his body as he staggered around the gantry ahead of him. He hadn't seen Palmer before his act of attempted suicide but Palmer didn't know if it would have made a difference anyway. There was something mesmerising about watching the way the flames danced about his body, rippling and billowing as if Jon was made of tasty tasty paper the fire was hungry to consume.

Palmer might have only been watching him for a second or two before he moved, but it felt like a lifetime and like he had already left it too late to make a difference. What difference *could* he make? This man was their enemy and he had almost certainly hurt people over the years, if not killed or abducted, then gravely assaulted. What did Palmer owe *him*?

He charged over to the stumbling figure who was close to toppling over the

314

railing of the gantry they were on. One side led to the railway track a bone-shattering fall beneath, the other to the river even further below. Palmer had whipped off his jacket in the three steps he took and had it in his outstretched arms ready to wrap around the blazing shape. It actually *helped* to shield him from the horror of what he would have otherwise seen. The jacket was nothing to the power of fire and Palmer felt the flames licking above and around the fabric, then catching hold of it too and his only instinct was to let go and back away. Instead, he fought that instinct, digging deep into reserves he didn't know or *want to know* that he had. He wrapped the jacket around the thrashing shape even more, closing his arms tightly despite the heat which was now radiating unpleasantly *through* the jacket itself. He hoped the enclosed fiery form would be starved of oxygen – just one part he knew of the triangle of fire from his training – although whether what was left beneath would be worth saving, he didn't know.

There was resistance and Palmer felt elbows and what might have been a fist in his midriff and the flames which had roared up and over the jacket were now scorching his own hands and face. It seemed like an utterly thankless task to try and save this ungrateful creature, but Palmer knew that he ought to. That there were answers he still needed from Jon Scott Campbell. A horrific thought of a melted face without lips and a burned-out larynx incapable of speech made him reel slightly and he knew that he ought to have been feeling more pain from the burning. Celia's pills had numbed him completely and whilst he hadn't passed out, he still felt like he was outside his body, floating just above his right shoulder, looking down, seeing Jon Scott Campbell wriggle so much that he shook the jacket and Palmer completely off him and tottered towards the railing. An inhuman noise roared as the form broke free and Palmer fell back, seeing a blackened, red and smoking shape tumble fully over the railing and vanish.

Palmer felt himself swooning and whilst he wasn't being pulled in the direction Scott Campbell had disappeared, he felt himself teetering backwards, hitting the railing hard against the lower part of his backside and then somehow tumbling over the railing on his side. He was so disorientated that he had no idea who had fallen which way and what lay beneath. The strange weightlessness of the fall took him over and for a split second it felt glorious, invigorating and free to have nothing beneath him, caught solely in the clutches of merciful gravity.

He could see water far below, dark and grey and rippling but couldn't tell if it was his own fate. It made him think of how even the tiniest amount of water could take the most innocent of lives. He could see the strange metallic intricacies of the bridge's structure, rivets and welding and faith, holding then whole thing together like the web of life itself. Stuart was now connected to

315

him and even if he never saw him again, he knew the man would feel the loss of that connection. Finally, he saw smoke and knew that Jon Scott Campbell was falling below him somewhere. He doubted he would survive the burns, let alone the fall, be it riverbound or onto what must have been an active railway line. In the howling, blurring, dizzying fall, Palmer knew that he had at least done the right thing. Not because trying to save Scott Campbell was a good thing – Palmer didn't *do* things because they were good, or right or wrong per se – but because he had realised that everything he did was being captured on that grainy CCTV footage and had he done nothing and just watched the burning man with a strange expression on his face, that someone might have zoomed in, cleared up the image, studied it and realised that there was something very very wrong with a man like Edward Palmer.

64.

Opening his eyes to find he wasn't dead or burned or drowned or worse, Palmer found that he was paralysed instead, rigidly spread-eagled on what felt like cold, jagged ground. His entire body was aflame, though thankfully, only with pain, rather than being on fire. It was difficult to tell if the irritation and soreness in his extremities was a relief or not as the major limbs of his body felt nothing. As if the very life had been dashed out of them by the fall. He had expected (if he had awakened at all) to see the bridge high above him like a distant humming stripe in the sky, perhaps slowly rippling out of view as he sank into the depths of the Tagus. But instead, he could see the dark, rusty, dripping underside of the bridge as his entire heaven; he could see and even *feel* the vibrating traffic rumbling overhead like a never-ending furious storm cloud. This gave him hope in two directions. Firstly, that he hadn't in fact fallen very far and was perhaps now just a few metres lower down, on the edge of the railway tracks. Secondly, that he wasn't a prisoner inside his own deadened body as he could still feel *something* in his shattered form.

Palmer only hoped that it was Celia's pills which had robbed him of full sensation but he dreaded how it might feel as the nerve endings returned to life throughout his body. His scorched hands felt tingly, and he found he could flex his fingers, but they looked pink and swollen as they hoved into his periphery. He felt that it would be good advice or even best practice, to stay still and await medical attention, but the more pressing issues if he wasn't in fact paralysed as he had initially thought, was to find out what had happened to Jon Scott Campbell, if he *had* been meeting someone here, then was it actually his supposed friend George Davis? There was also the further need to escape, dodge the potentially incoming authorities and reconvene with Stuart.

317

He could hear the faint scream of a siren somewhere and feared an approaching emergency services vehicle but as he groaned inwardly and tried to sit up, he saw the strobing of blue lights through the underside of the bridge and realised the vehicles were rushing *away* from the bridge. Perhaps he was overestimating the speed of Portuguese emergency services. Perhaps the staff at the pylon experience hadn't even got around to calling them yet anyway. He had wondered if his actions had been caught on CCTV and had overthought what they might see in those actions, but recalling the fuzzy images he'd caught on the ground floor he now realised that they would have been lucky to even make out the age or gender of someone via those cameras, let alone their sinister machinations. He had only recognised Jon Scott Campbell because he already knew him and the camera had been pointing only at the staircase, not the gantry where they'd grappled. Perhaps no one had seen the incident at all from the CCTV bank or from the busy bridge above. He figured the only way anyone would have seen their fall would have been from the river or its banks, if they were looking.

A clanging noise rattled through every fibre of his being and he feared that yet another catastrophe was looming: a train. The noise grew louder and closer and he realised that it was far too chaotic and irregular for a train, too quiet even as it approached for the sound of a locomotive. It was in fact footsteps down the metal stairs behind him and their reverberations shuddered through his body. For some reason he welcomed them, hoped they were coming for him; whether it was to aid him or take him away, he no longer cared. Sitting up had vaguely worked out and he could see the train lines just a few feet away beyond his immobile legs. A fence ran along the side of him and he used it to hoik himself up to a painful crouched position with his back to the oblivion below. He had fallen solidly a good few metres but given how limp and unfeeling his body had turned, it seemed that Celia's medicinal mix up had probably saved his life. That and him being lucky enough that the 50/50 odds of which way he would fall had sent him *inside* the bridge rather than out of it.

"'arry, mate!" roared Stuart and Palmer knew why those footsteps were pleasing to his sore ears.

Stuart was sopping wet and bright pink, having clearly sprinted his way to his rescue and Palmer even imagined his companion hurtling up some sort of staircase all the way up here rather than wait for the lift or argue with the staff below. The big sweaty mass of Stuart's torso filled Palmer's view as the builder hurled himself down to inspect his condition. Palmer dreamed now that Stuart had picked him up like a prince rescuing a damsel in distress and carried him in his strapping arms away from the danger. He floated away, relaxed and safe and the rushing of traffic and the coarse low voice of his friend all faded out of earshot as he closed his eyes, then disconnected his hearing, then lost consciousness.

When Palmer awoke, he found that yet again, within the space of what must have been no more than half an hour, he had passed out but that very little time had gone by without him. He realised it was the cliché of movies for someone to pass out and awaken the next morning, tucked up in bed somewhere strange yet safe and for the audience to breathe a sigh of relief, knowing their trials were over. Palmer had fallen off a gantry and knocked himself out, then passed out as his companion came to his assistance and now he was in the back of a car which was careening around the sunny streets of Lisbon. It felt like it ought to have been night time by now, or at the very least, the next day. But it wasn't. It was still that afternoon and Stuart was sitting beside him, with an arm around the back of his neck, gingerly making sure he didn't slide around too much in the car. Palmer appreciated the remoteness of his touch, but when he looked down at himself and saw the charred mess of his clothes and pink scarring of his outstretched hands he realised that Stuart was probably being delicate because of his injuries.

"Where are we going?" Palmer murmured, happy that he still had the power of speech.

"'ospital mate," said Stuart, flashing him a worried smile.

"No," Palmer groaned, becoming agitated.

Hadn't he learned the mantra? Stuart could be so obstinate. And forgetful. Then he realised he had never shared the motto with him.

"No guns, no police, no hospitals," he croaked and Stuart glared at him.

"Whaddaya mean, mate?" he asked.

Palmer tried to sit up properly and Stuart barely moved his arm, so that when he was in a proper seated position, Stuart's arm was still around his shoulders. It felt painful.

"No guns, no police, no hospitals," he repeated and shook his head.

That hurt too. He knew he wasn't *too* badly injured as he was conscious, his heart rate was elevated but not too abnormal given the circumstances and he could move his limbs around, however painful that might be as Celia's pills

319

wore off. He had been battered and bruised before he'd even arrived in this sunny city and he had only found himself all the more worse for wears over the last three days. He would survive this. Unlike Jon Scott Campbell.

"What about 'im, mate?" Stuart asked, eyes wide, and Palmer realised that he had been deliriously *saying aloud* everything he was thinking.

"He fell off the bridge," Palmer said.

It was true. There was no point lying about it.

"Dead?" asked Stuart.

Palmer was still very much aware that the car was roaring along, presumably towards the nearest hospital.

"Please stop," he groaned and knowing Stuart would be hard to persuade, he tried to lean forward to repeat it to the driver.

"'arry, take it easy mate," warned Stuart, using the arm around him to try and keep him back.

Sensing a fight on his hands, Stuart relented and as soon as Palmer was back sitting securely, he withdrew his arm and leant forwards to speak to the driver.

"Just pull up 'ere please, mate," he asked, his voice low and full of annoyance.

The driver skidded to a halt, mounting the kerb, as if himself irritated by the instruction. He was dressed in grey, like an old-fashioned chauffeur and Palmer wondered where Stuart had conjured him up from. *Weren't they on a scooter moments earlier?*

"Jon Scott Campbell," said Stuart, turning to him, his face earnest and urgent.

"Maybe dead," said Palmer. "He…" He couldn't think how to describe what he had seen, but he *must*. "He set fire to himself. I tried to stop him…but he fell…"

It hurt to relive these moments, physically rather than mentally and Palmer knew Stuart had a million and one questions on the topic. The driver made a strange noise as if trying to conceal a cough and Palmer frowned. Even frowning hurt.

"Jesus Christ, mate," said Stuart.

He looked him up and down now and Palmer felt helpless under his gaze. He supposed a builder knew a fair few things about injuries though whether that extended to burns, he had no clue, and the look Stuart was giving him was one of concern.

"How bad is it?" asked Palmer, nodding at himself.

Stuart grimaced.

"It's 'ard to say, mate," he said. "I reckon you need to get out of those clothes quick sharp. You've burned your 'ands, maybe your arms too."

"The hotel...please," Palmer said.

Stuart looked doubtful.

"It's gonna take more than some bloody germolene and plasters to sort this one out, mate," he said.

Palmer found himself giggling at the image now. He really was out of it still. He recalled seeing a video somewhere of a poor American kid who had been to the dentist and had strong medication, making them hilariously out of it, spouting random comments, dreamy non-sequiturs and all cruelly captured on film by the kid's mother who had shared it straight online. He thanked goodness that Stuart wasn't filming him right now. He randomly remembered that Stuart's phone probably *couldn't* film anyway. Then he remembered the phone he had acquired in the pylon foyer.

"I've got a phone," he murmured.

"What do you mean, mate?" Stuart asked and watched as Palmer patted his pockets.

He remembered that his jacket was gone, burned, flung over the edge no doubt. Was the phone in that pocket? But no, there were two different rectangular shapes in his trouser pockets and despite those too being blackened and damaged, he knew one of those shapes was Jon Scott Campbell's phone. Stuart had been watching the ritual and without even asking, reached into Palmer's pocket nearest to him and drew out the newer phone.

"Whose phone's this?" he asked.

Palmer noticed the driver nosily watching them in the rear-view mirror now.

Was this a taxi they had hired or a friend of that boy...*Hugo was it*?...that had helped them before? The driver's eyes looked stern and somehow familiar, against all odds.

"Jon's" Palmer said.

Stuart had been vaguely interested but upon hearing the name, he practically kicked into a higher gear and swiped the phone which was improbably still not locked. The photo still displayed was that of George Davis.

"Who's this, 'arry?" Stuart demanded.

He had been terribly worried for his health only moments ago but now his attention was 100% on the phone. The picture looked odd from the angle Palmer was slumped and he now realised the blue sky was surely here in Portugal. High up, like the *torre* or the *elevador* or the *Padrao dos Descobrimentos.*

"Jeep, I think," Palmer sighed.

The silly name which had conjured up images of an evil genius manipulating them all when Stuart mentioned it, of being linked to Gerry Payne by virtue of the sound of his initials, was now somehow just a stupid alias for a man he had thought he could trust: George Davis.

"Oh, you just couldn't let it alone, could you," came a low, dangerous voice from the front seat.

Palmer glanced blearily up at the rear-view mirror again and saw the eyes glaring back at him. No wonder they looked familiar. They were the same eyes in the photo.

"George?" Palmer croaked.

George Davis didn't turn around. He was wearing a long grey coat which looked for all the world like an old-fashioned driver's and Palmer could see from the back of his head, that his hair had greyed and thinned considerably since the last time he had seen him.

"You know this man?" Stuart asked, suddenly alert and holding up the phone, bobbing his head to try and see the driver.

George had already locked the car doors and turned around now at last to confront his passengers.

"He certainly does," said George slowly and malevolently.

Instinctively, Stuart reached for the car door handle and found it locked. In a flash, George had a long dangerous looking knife in his hand and he pointed it at the two men who were now his prisoners.

65.

"Who the fuck are you?" Stuart snapped.

"It's George," said Palmer wearily. "Hello George."

George narrowed his eyes and pointed the knife towards the two of them on the back seat.

"George Davis – *Jeep* to certain friends," he said.

"What the fuck?" cried Stuart.

He was still caught somewhere between wanting to shrink into a ball, hedgehog style and wanting to rise up against this ridiculous turn of events.

"You offered us a lift!" he complained. "You saw me 'elping Palmer down and said you'd *'elp!*"

"And help I have," said George, gurning like he wasn't quite altogether there.

He made a little slash in the air with the knife and gesticulated towards Palmer.

"What the fuck are you on about?" asked Stuart.

George rolled his eyes, clearly disappointed in the builder's reaction to events. He took a deep sigh, never moving the knife away from its potential trajectory, barely a foot from Palmer's face.

"I'm George Davis," he explained wearily. "Palmer and I were at school together. I'm a psychiatric medicine specialist."

Stuart waited a moment as George let that all hang in the air as if his words had great weight,

"AND?!" he exploded, furiously.

George could hardly help stifling his laugh and as Stuart lurched forward angrily in his seat, the knife didn't move towards *him* but instead towards the rather more inert Palmer who was struggling to take everything in.

"And, I'm holding this fucking knife," George stressed. "So just sit tight you ridiculous little man and listen to me. I'm *Jeep* to that psycho, Jon Scott Campbell. I understand he's gone?"

Palmer nodded slowly, as if his head were some gigantic weight which took every ounce of his strength to stir.

"Gone but not forgotten," he wheezed.

"Justice for all those girls at the very least," Stuart muttered.

"*I'm* the one who fucked up all those girls," George continued, almost glowing with pride. "But little Jonny boy was so easily manipulated thanks to his pathetic little ego and his handy memory problem. Oh sure, he might have shoved a few women around over the years – he just couldn't help doing that – but it was me…*ME*…who wreaked that path of bloody devastation across Manchester."

Palmer thought suddenly how odd all of this was. This was his *friend*. The one guy he *chose* to socialise with when he could stand socialising with anyone at all. His drinking buddy. They had discussed Celia and Gerry and ultimately it had been George who had assured him that Gerry's nervous breakdown and time spent in a mental health hospital had been his alibi for the Celia matter. But *he* was the one behind it all? Had he hurt Celia too?

"You 'urt those girls," Stuart said warningly. "But did you 'urt Celia too?"

It sounded odd Stuart speaking threateningly to Palmer's *friend* and asking about *Celia*, his old acquaintance. Their worlds had collided in the most bizarre fashion. George was laughing and Palmer noticed something dark behind him, a shadow outside the car. Was it his imagination?

325

"I hurt Celia on a daily basis," said George. "She was *pathetic*. Just like the rest of you. She fled here, I followed her, messed with her meds and kept her on a short leash whilst I figured out what to do about her. She might have tried her best to second guess me, faking her worst behaviour patterns and slipping away from me on occasion, but *I* sent those messages to you, Palmer."

He looked directly at Palmer now and Palmer was glad he was slipping further away from reality again. He didn't like this one bit.

"Oh Palmer," he continued disappointedly. "A shadow of your former self. Shadows can't survive in the sun, can they?"

All Palmer could see now was the looming shadow outside and he saw Stuart had noticed it too. He was grinning, the goofy bastard. Seconds later, the driver's window of the car was violently smashed and a large rock came through, glancing against the side of George's head. He dropped the knife somewhere between the front and back seats and slumped sideways across the passenger seat. The last thing Palmer saw before he passed out again was Stuart's broad grin and the equally idiotic face of the delivery boy – *he wanted to say 'Hugo'?* – leering in through the broken window.

When Palmer awoke again, he found the stench of antiseptic heavy in the air and that he was shirtless in what appeared to be his own hotel room. For a moment he thought he was alone, but then he heard the sound of the toilet flushing in the bathroom and Stuart came ambling back through, beaming at the sight of him awake again. Palmer's wounds were grim looking at first, but someone – he assumed Stuart – had carefully removed his clothes and tended to the burnt flesh. It wasn't severe enough to need reconstructive surgery thankfully and Palmer knew a thing or two about that, but it still smarted. He saw tablets on his bedside table along with a bottle of water which must have been chilled as it had beads of condensation on it. A magazine lay next to that and then Palmer's phone charging in the socket. Stuart had thought of everything.

Stuart's own little bag was on the floor next to that and Palmer noticed a faded photograph of a woman with the same sad puppy eyes as Stuart poking out of it. There was something infinitely tragic about the memento and Palmer wondered what Stuart's full backstory was. Noticing Palmer's gaze, Stuart pushed the photograph back in and moved the bag away without commenting on it.

He perched on Palmer's bed and patiently explained that during his time unconscious Hugo had helped them to incapacitate George further, delivering him on the doorstep of the nearest police station. Celia too had been deposited into the arms of the law, by the helpful Sylvia at the Sana Lisboa at Stuart's request; everything, or at least *most of everything,* had come out. Palmer was astonished by Celia's secret life as a writer and publisher. A thinly veiled version of her name Celia Payne was Kulani Kanaka'āina (roughly translating the underlying meaning heavenly countryman into Hawaiian) and had seemingly been a shell company for her to get her revenge on and begin to extort money from the men who had wronged her, beginning with Jon Scott Campbell. Palmer's head was aching, from too much information too quickly, from his many batterings over the last 72 hours and from dehydration too he suspected. He sat up and sipped the pleasingly chilled water Stuart had provided for him. He hesitated before taking more random tablets, but he trusted Stuart a hell of a lot more than he trusted that harpy, Celia. The idea of her being dragged off to explain herself, possibly back to England to answer charges of wasting police time, was eminently pleasing.

The burglary of Stuart's room must have been George too, looking for Celia's passport that Stuart had found and brought here, inadvertently saving her a huge leg in her quest to escape 'Jeep''s clutches. Palmer felt ridiculous, not helped by his weakened state, about the way they had been played – Jon Scott Campbell included. But he was missing presumed dead, not that anyone was looking for him. No one had seemingly come looking for them after either the *elevador* stabbing or the bridge fall. It made Palmer feel emboldened that their actions had either gone unnoticed, been hushed up, or had been judged unnecessary to be investigated or pursued.

Stuart seemed particularly embarrassed as he explained how he had become so suspicious after being lured into George's car (a second hire car in his name, it transpired) that he had not trusted anyone on their way back to the hotel. He went so far as to accidentally jab a homeless man near the park with his corkscrew who had only stepped forward to offer his help. He'd pacified the protesting tramp with a wad of cash he'd hastily thrown at him and with Hugo's help, got Palmer to safety.

Palmer felt like he should ask how Stuart was, after all, the hapless fool had also been ridiculously played and manipulated, had got into fist fights with his supposed nemesis and traipsed the length and breadth of the city on both their fools' errands. But the words died in his throat. Instead, almost needlingly, he asked about his delivery boy love interest,

"So, how *is* Hugo?"

Stuart chuckled his throaty laugh and wasn't at all rankled by the comment,

"'E's fine, bless 'im," said Stuart. "Totally lovestruck, the poor bastard."

He was both abashed and amused and Palmer liked him all the more for his response to his catty stirring. They both owed Hugo a *huge* debt of thanks. A five-star rating on the app was the least they could do and Palmer wondered if he could sort out some kind of cash reward before he left. After all, he still had hundreds of Euros left and wasn't planning on spending them anytime soon. It was still that same day, later that evening, no matter how many times he passed out and he knew that tomorrow would be his last day in the city.

"No reports about Jon Scott Campbell or that mafia guy – Marujo," said Stuart, suddenly a little more serious. "The big story – and I 'asten to add that this was just below a story about a rise in the inflation rate and the fact that no one's traded in their old pound coins yet – was about Celia suddenly showin' up again. Turnin' 'erself in, they're sayin'. Like we were never here!"

He waved his hand slightly theatrically as if magicking away their involvement in the whole affair and Palmer smiled wryly. Silence fell between them again and now that most of the mystery had been explored and unravelled, there seemed little to say now.

"You going 'ome tomorrow?" Stuart asked.

"Oh yes," said Palmer. "I'll book spare seats either side of me for the way home if I have to."

He waved his burned hands feebly and Stuart nodded but looked a little distant.

"I'd best be off 'ome too," he said quietly. "Business to run and that."

Palmer hated himself, but he responded before he could kill the instinct.

"I did fancy swinging by the tile museum early on tomorrow morning before my flight though…if you fancied it?" he said.

"Ha, yeah, good one," said Stuart, laughing, grabbing his bag and backing away towards the door. "I might see you for breakfast."

Palmer was confused. His invitation was genuine. The tile museum was supposed to be a marvellous attraction. But Stuart seemed to think he'd been joking. He left with a wink and Palmer knew that would be the last time he ever saw him.

EPILOGUE

Palmer rose early the next day and headed to the museum. He had enough painkillers to keep his burn injuries at bay but he found he couldn't enjoy the attraction. He still felt paranoid and suspicious of everyone around him and imagined Jon Scott Campbell as some sort of withered husk stalking him at every step. There was nothing in the morning's local news about their exploits other than a small paragraph about a missing girl called Matilde Marujo and appeals for news of her whereabouts.

It felt odd to be walking the sun-bleached streets of the city without the menace of the shadow of Celia Payne and the trail of chaos which followed her, or the reassuring presence of the bluff, plain-speaking Stuart Evans, but all that was behind him now. Life back home was calling him. A life he had done his best to avoid. His mother would be ready to nag him. His employers would want to know when he would be back to work. His dismal home would be airless and uninviting.

Palmer gazed out at the Tagus and wondered whether to take a trip to that dark and mysterious shoreline on the other side. Perhaps not today, he concluded. Perhaps not today.

THE END

COMING NOVEMBER 2019

ABOUT THE AUTHOR

Ben E. Lewis is a writer, teacher, husband and pedant from Sheffield, South Yorkshire.

When he's not planning needlessly elaborate psychological crime trails across Europe, he's planning the holidays which inspire them. Oh, and lessons too. He's always planning lessons of course.

Seek him out on Twitter or Instagram to nitpick things he loves or things he's written on @simfelemy.

Printed in Great Britain
by Amazon